No Life

Also by Anna Sheehan from Gollancz:

A Long, Long Sleep

No Life But This
Anna Sheehan

First published in Great Britain in 2014 by Gollancz
An imprint of the Orion Publishing Group
Orion House, 5 Upper St Martin's Lane,
London WC2H 9EA
An Hachette UK Company

A CIP catalogue record for this book
is available from the British Library.

ISBN 978 0 575 10477 8

1 3 5 7 9 10 8 6 4 2

Typeset by GroupFMG using BookCloud

Printed in Great Britain by Clays Ltd, St Ives plc

The Orion Publishing Group's policy is to use papers
that are natural, renewable and recyclable products and
made from wood grown in sustainable forests. The logging
and manufacturing processes are expected to conform to
the environmental regulations of the country of origin.

www.orionbooks.co.uk
www.gollancz.co.uk

This one has to be for Tom,
who kept telling me he missed the madness.

I have no life but this
To lead it here
Nor any death but lest
Dispelled from there

Nor tie to earths to come
Nor action new
Except through this extent;
The realm of you.

EMILY DICKINSON

prologue

When I was five years old I saw the planet of my origin for the first time.

Well, not a planet, really. Europa. Just a little chick of a moon, shadowing her hen, the great Jupiter itself. One of four tiny, helpless specks of light, circling round and round that swirling red-striped giant, so far away from this Earth upon which I had been born.

I remember squinting into the telescope as our kindergarten tutor told us old myths about gods and nymphs and bulls, but I wasn't really listening. I reached out with my tiny hand, already tinged with blue, as if I could grasp that tiny mote of light in my fingers, cradle it in my palm, listen to it sing. I thought it would hum in my mind, like electric equipment can. She was Europa, and I knew she was my mother. A cold and distant mother, heartless and unreachable, but my own. She had created life – strange, alien life, consisting of heat-fed algae and delicately boned fish and curious electro microbes like the ones used to create us. Even then, I knew that Earth was not my home. So I tried to reach out an impossible distance to a moon so far removed I couldn't even see it with my own eyes.

It was a gesture that did nothing more profound than knock the telescope, shocking Europa out of my view. I cried at the loss of her. The tutor recaptured Europa in the view-scope, and warned me not to reach for her again.

I never listened.

chapter 1

I woke with a bit of a headache that morning, but I dismissed it. I've always been prone to them. Having a genetically modified brain hypersensitive to electrical impulses did not make for an easy life in a technological world.

Around eleven o'clock my friend Rose's limoskiff arrived at the dorms. My roommate Jamal and I piled in quickly, thus managing to avoid the battle between my siblings Penny and Quin, as they fought over window seats. Eventually Quin won – as he always did. For all the argument was heated and forceful, it was silent and expressionless. Europa Project children were strange that way. Quin was the only one of us who could even talk – our vocal cords under developed and our soft palate still the same shape as an infant child. Also our faces naturally showed little to no expression. No one was certain if this was a genetic difference – akin to the neutral affect of some schizophrenics – or if it was simply a natural result of growing up apart from normal society in a laboratory. It didn't matter. What expression we did have was subtle. Most people said they couldn't read our expressions at all. I could. Of course, I'd grown up with it.

At her loss, Penny slumped glumly in next to me as my sister Tristan and her roommate Molly climbed in.

I envied Tristan her roommate. Molly was from the mining colony on Callisto, another of Jupiter's colonized moons.

Callisto had lost much of its economic viability during the colonial isolation of the Dark Times, so Molly had only managed to make it to UniPrep on a scholarship, just like the four of us EP kids. She studied hard to keep her grades up. By contrast stood my own roommate Jamal, whose family owned nearly a third of Europa. He had always been a bit of a spoiled princeling, and felt entitled to goof off continually. It was often hard to sleep with him in the same room, what with the girls he snuck in and the bizarre substances he managed to imbibe and the music he played at all hours. Even so, I was grateful to him. He was the only boarder in the entire school who had agreed to board with *me.* There was a lot of prejudice against us, ever since we were kids. Even the nurses who had cared for us as infants called us the 'Creepies'. It wasn't meant maliciously, but we heard it, and we knew.

The two other boarders who would have been members of our party were gone for the summer. Wilhelm had gone home to his parents in Germany, and Anastasia, who had come from New Russia on Titan, was spending the summer with her relatives in 'Old' Russia. The limoskiff twisted over on its cushion of magnetized air and left UniPrep's dorms for Unicorn Estates.

Penny looked purple, her blue skin flushed with renewed excitement at the thought of the upcoming party. My siblings and I all had blue skin, the reasons for which are complicated. Penny – her legal name was Pen Ultima, as her embryonic number had been 99 – was paler than most of us, and looked almost lavender when she blushed.

Penny was wildly excited. '*I've never been to Unicorn Estates before!*' she signed at me. '*Does it really have a ballroom? And a stables? Are there horses?*'

'*Calm down,*' I signed at her. '*You'll see soon enough.*'

Penny bounced up and down, unable to conceal her excitement. Whatever the genetic remodification had done to Penny's brain, she was emotionally much younger than she seemed. This wasn't strange for us. Many of us hadn't taken the genetic remodification well, and more than half of those who had survived gestation were severely cognitively disabled. Penny was actually one of the lucky ones. She wasn't damaged intellectually – as her math scores could attest – but when it came to her actions she seemed more eleven than seventeen. We all sort of babied her, which probably didn't help.

My brother Quin, as per usual, stared moodily out of the window. 'Hey, there,' Jamal said, kicking him in the shoe. 'Why so blue?'

Quin gave him a withering look. 'Aren't you sick of that joke by now?'

'Hey, stick with the classics.'

'If you have something to say to me, please raise your hand,' Quin said. 'Then place it over your mouth.' Quin was the only one of us left who was able to speak. Most people were of the opinion that it would have been better if he wasn't. He was often witty and cruel, and rarely said anything kind. He also did everything he could to make it seem like he hated absolutely everyone, and that included Jamal. I'd never bothered to find out why. That was just Quin.

I touched Jamal's wrist. *'Don't worry about Quin,'* I told him silently. *'He's always like this.'*

'I know,' Jamal thought back at me. *'I'm trying to make him laugh.'*

'Quin only laughs when someone is hurting somehow.'

Jamal thought about this, and then kicked me firmly in the shin. I squawked with pain and fell over onto Penny, who hadn't been able to follow our silent, telepathic exchange. *'What was that for?'* I signed.

'You said Quin only laughs when someone is hurting.'

As if to prove my point, Quin started to laugh. 'There you have it, brother,' he said. 'Don't make judgements.'

'Or state truths!' I signed.

'Boys,' Molly said with disgust. She looked over at Quin. 'Isn't Nabiki coming?'

Quin shrugged. 'Ask Otto. She's his bird.'

I glared at him. *'Couldn't we leave Nabiki out of this?'*

'I thought you broke up,' Molly said.

'We did!' I signed.

'Four months ago,' Jamal reminded her.

I sat back against the seat in Rose's limoskiff, fervently wishing that this conversation hadn't turned to myself and Nabiki. Mainly because it still hurt. I hadn't really wanted to break up with Nabiki, but I couldn't blame her. It wasn't even her doing. After all, I was desperately in love with someone else.

That someone else was the person whose birthday we were heading to right now. I didn't want to be in love with Rose. I couldn't help it. From the first moment I'd touched her, Rose had captured me. It wasn't merely that she was beautiful. Nothing so simple. It was her mind that held me in thrall. Rose was different. Like me. She was fully human, but she was loving, accepting, kindly and wildly talented. She was also a hundred years old.

Rose had been regularly locked in stasis by her parents, which retarded her growth, eventually culminating in a sixty-some-year sleep from which she had been awakened only six months previous. Those six months had been some of the worst of my life – and that was saying something. Since the first moment I touched Rose I suffered nightmares, long nights of tormented longing, and bouts of enraged self-loathing punctuated by moments of uncontrollable glee. I'd lost my girlfriend, alienated myself from my friend Bren, annoyed my siblings, disturbed my roommate, and probably tortured my therapist. I was even being haunted by ghosts of my own past. And all because I'd fallen helplessly, hopelessly in love.

Stupid, stupid, stupid.

Not only that, but Rose's subconscious was abnormally strong, due to a hundred years of dreaming. She kept picking things up from my mind – stray emotions and half-finished thoughts. I was terrified from the moment I touched her. Terrified and overjoyed and utterly overwhelmed. The day I met her I scheduled a special session with my therapist and mentally screamed at Dr Bija for an hour about how unfair everything was. I felt as if my life had been snatched by one of Rose's briars, and this sudden, overwhelming devotion was choking the life out of me. Eventually Dr Bija had managed to bring me back to centre, but it had been a tough session. Dr Mina Bija was, in my opinion, the greatest psychologist the world had ever known. She had been my saving grace for more than three years, helping me to sort out both my mind and my life, both of which were exceedingly complicated.

When we arrived at Unicorn Estates we were greeted by no less than an actual liveried footman. Unicorn Estates might have technically been a condominium, but for all it was separated into apartments and suites, it was the most affluent and exclusive living space in the whole of ComUnity – which was the most affluent and exclusive controlled community on the planet. As we filed out of Rose's limoskiff, another skiff slowly parked itself alongside. I knew this skiff. Sporty, bright yellow, tinted windows. Nabiki.

Nabiki lived with her parents in ComUnity, unlike us pitiful boarding students. After Rose and Bren, who both lived here at Unicorn, Nabiki was probably the wealthiest of us. Nabiki had changed a lot in the last four months. She had allowed her immaculately coiffed hair to grow out, and she'd added chameleon highlights, that changed depending on her outfit or the surroundings. Right now they were a piercing pink, echoing the shiny neon flight jacket she was wearing. She'd taken up some kind of high-risk air sport, sky-diving or atmosphere skimming or something. I wasn't sure what. She didn't talk to me much anymore.

She tossed back her highlit hair and ran up to hug Molly and Tristan. She gladly transferred her hug to Penny when Penny came bouncing up to her. Nabiki had become good friends with my sisters in the time we were together, and I was glad that relationship hadn't changed when we broke up.

She didn't look at me.

The footman bowed to us professionally and directed us behind the main mansion to the pool. Rose had decided on a pool party for her seventeenth birthday, mostly, I think, because she wanted to show off her new swimsuit, and her new body with it. The first few months after she'd come out of stasis, Rose's body was emaciated and frail, pale and sickly and skeletal. After last spring and through the summer she'd exercised and filled out quite a bit, and she was proud of her new, healthier form. She was still underweight, still had a long way to go, but she looked great. Her body had become something that made me drop a few IQ points the moment I turned the corner to the pool patio.

Rose's long gleaming golden hair captured the sunlight, set off by her pale white skin, shining with sunblock. Her swimsuit was a dusky red, almost exactly the same colour as her full lips. She wore a sarong around her hips with a green and red rose garden pattern. Rose wore no makeup, and didn't need it. Her skin was so translucent that her eyes were shadowed naturally by the veins in her eyelids, her cheeks rosy and her lips red with her own blood.

Rose looked up from the buffet and grinned when she saw us, her white teeth bright against her red mouth. I tried not to drool. It was pointless, anyway. There were far too many complications between us.

One of the larger complications was already on the patio helping to set out towels. Rose had fallen quite neatly in love with my friend Bren shortly after she'd come out of stasis. Considering he was the prince charming who had awakened her – and he was a gorgeous glimmering mahogany tennis athlete, who did not look unnaturally blue in the least – it wasn't very surprising. The other complication happened to be striding in through the other gate at that moment, leading Bren's sisters, Kayin and Hilary.

This was Xavier – Rose's old boyfriend from before she was stassed. Though he went by his middle name of Ron, she'd always called him by his first name. I'd taken to thinking of him by it as well, since I spent so much time with her. This man, for all intents and purposes an inter-planetary king, was now the president of UniCorp, Rose's guardian, and the love of her life. The fact that he was now in his seventies and their relationship could no longer be romantic meant very little when it came to Rose's emotional state. As of right now, she found it too hard to even think about being with anyone else. Which meant my pitiful infatuation had to be put on standby, most likely forever. So I kept my feelings secret, or tried to. Sometimes I thought she might have guessed, and then other times I was sure she was completely oblivious. I'd tried to bring the subject up a dozen times, but all I got from her mind in that direction was pain, and when I tried to talk about it with her over the net, she always changed the subject. I let her. It didn't keep us from flirting, though.

'They're here!' Bren's youngest sister Kayin jumped forward and grabbed Penny's hands. They had become fast friends in the last few months after Penny had been released from the laboratory.

'Hello, everyone,' Rose said formally. She caught sight of Nabiki. 'I'm so glad you made it!'

'Yes,' Nabiki said, striding forward to give Rose a birthday hug. I sighed wistfully. Rose was desperate to ensure that she and Nabiki stayed on good terms. Fortunately, Nabiki seemed determined not to blame Rose for my infatuation, even though part of her, I knew, really hated Rose.

I pinched the bridge of my nose. My headache was bothering me.

Quin glanced at me, and then, quite deliberately, caught Rose up in his arms. 'Happy birthday, princess!' He lifted her high above his head and grinned at her. He set her down, and I tried not to sigh. He touched her so easily. Quin couldn't read minds at all, so there were no nasty thorns tormenting his psyche as he touched her pale skin. The sight of Quin's blue skin against hers did strange things to my insides. 'It's so nice to see you finally admitting to your age,' Quin said. 'But I think you forgot to mention exactly how many years ago you reached it.'

Bren was the only one who chuckled. He took Rose's stass history in his stride. Rose had already learned that the best way to deal with Quin was with a series of impassive silences and occasionally rolled eyes. The eyes were important, otherwise he thought you hadn't heard him, and he'd keep saying whatever was rudest until he got some kind of reaction. She rolled her eyes and turned back to welcome the rest of us.

'What do you want to do?' she asked. 'Swim first, or eat?'

Penny clapped her hands and jumped up and down. '*Swim!*' she signed, waving her hands as if splashing through the water.

'I agree!' said Kayin, who loved swimming.

Tristan snapped her fingers and looked at Bren. With a look of challenge on her face she mimed playing tennis.

'Seriously?' Bren asked, his eyebrows raised.

Tristan nodded, grinning wickedly.

'Oh, you are *so* on,' Bren said, snatching up Tristan's hand and pulling her towards the tennis courts. 'I'll bring her pieces back in a bag for you, shall I?' he called over his shoulder.

I grinned. Bren was in for a surprise. True, Tristan wasn't a trophy-winning tennis player, but she was a highly accomplished athlete all around. She had cherished dreams of competing in the Olympics in track and field, until she was informed she didn't qualify. If enhancement drugs and bionic implants were banned from sporting events, genetic modification disqualified her also, even if that modification was not aimed at increasing her athletic abilities. There was also some question about what country she would have competed for. Technically, she wasn't a citizen of any country. She had human rights, but she wasn't actually human. She was number 32, Tristan Twice, an alien hybrid, and her DNA was still property of UniCorp. UniCorp was an international, even interplanetary, corporation. I remembered Tristan's fury when she realized her genetic status basically segregated her from normal society. We were probably the last humans on earth still discriminated against solely based on our 'race'. Still, Tristan didn't plan on giving up. She trained daily, hoping to compete in any sporting events that didn't disqualify her, and she hoped one day to be an Olympic coach. She would give Bren a run for his money on the tennis court.

Penny stripped down to her swimsuit – purple, to complement her skin – and dove deftly into the pool. She laughed, sounding infantile and odd. She couldn't control her voice as well as Tristan or I could. Kayin joined her with a splash.

I caught Quin watching furtively as Nabiki peeled off layers of clothes to a thin black bikini. I averted my eyes. I knew something about Quin that no one else did: he'd been in love with Nabiki almost since I started dating her. I think others suspected that he fancied her, but he was so cynical and hard to read that no one else had realized the depth of his feelings. I wasn't even sure he knew himself. But I couldn't tell anyone. Telling anyone what I saw in anyone else's mind was against my code of ethics. Even telling someone what I saw in their own mind was touchy. Much like a psychologist, if I told people truths they themselves denied, it usually went badly for me. Rose, for instance, had no idea exactly how lopsided her subconscious was compared to her consciousness, and I had no intention of telling her.

Nabiki stretched before she went to dive in, and Quin seized the opportunity to touch her. He tackled her violently and fell into the pool with her. Nabiki sputtered to the surface, furious. Her highlights had gone blue and wavery in the water. 'You sped!' she snapped, splashing him.

'Only on alternate Thursdays, bank holidays, and whenever I have a math test,' Quin retorted, splashing her back.

Nabiki went under the water and swam to the other side of the pool. I wished I could tell Quin this was the wrong way to handle Nabiki, but he would have hit me for it.

Jamal screamed 'Cannon ball!' and leaped from the diving board, half splashing Molly. 'Come on, Callisto, move your butt!' he called when he resurfaced. I shook my head. Europa had a very strange relationship with other colonies – particularly other Jovian colonies. Europa was the only place besides Earth on which indigenous life had been discovered. They also had ample water, so they were much wealthier than the other colonies. Even though Jamal didn't think of himself as prejudiced, he was rather scornful of Molly and even Anastasia, who was from the Saturn colonies and should have been beyond his arrogance.

Fortunately, Molly was used to other people's disdain. Scholarship students at UniPrep need to develop very thick skins – a fact I knew personally very well. 'Very funny!' Molly called out, and turned to remove her shirt. Molly was hesitant in removing her outer clothes. Her parents hadn't been able to afford gravity mats for their home on Callisto, and they certainly couldn't afford the full exo-surgery kit once she got to Earth, so her body had rebelled shortly after she'd arrived at school. She'd gained massive amounts of weight and her muscles had been forced to develop all at once, so she was an odd, squat shape. None of us really cared – after all, my siblings and I were blue, and Rose had been a skeleton until a few months ago – but Molly was self-conscious about it. Her swimsuit, when she finally revealed it, was almost a sundress. Everyone was careful not to stare at her, and she slipped into the water quickly after Hilary. Rose waited until everyone seemed settled before she pulled off her sarong – distracting me severely – and climbed down the ladder. Quin and Molly started a pool-volleyball game, and most of the others joined in.

Rose slipped under the water and then surfaced like a mermaid, the water turning her golden hair to bronze. It was some minutes before she realized I hadn't joined the others in the water. *'Coming in?'* she signed to me. She'd been studying sign for the last four months, mostly so we could share jokes across the room. She wasn't very skilled yet, but she was trying.

I shook my head, throwing her a careful smile.

'What's wrong?'

'I don't swim,' I signed slowly.

Rose looked horrified. *'I'm sorry! Come in, I'll teach you.'*

'No.'

She frowned. *'Why not?'*

I shook my head again, avoiding the answer. Rose looked concerned, but she had other guests to attend to, and Penny looked like she needed help on her team. I pulled out my notescreen and glanced at a book, but mostly I watched Rose in the water. I wished I *could* swim with her. I let myself daydream about floating in the clear blue water beside her, letting my hands touch her skin, caress the bronze wave of her hair.

Eventually, Bren and Tristan came back. Bren was scowling. 'You didn't tell me she was a ringer!' he told me angrily.

I chuckled at Tristan's broad grin. I touched Bren's arm. I rarely hesitated at touching Bren – his mind was so clear and concise, there were almost never any thoughts I didn't want to read. *'Did she win?'* I asked.

'No,' Bren said. 'But it was close.' He glared at her. 'Too close.' Tristan's face twitched in challenge. Bren stripped off his shirt and dove into the pool, shaking his head with relief at the cool water. Then he tackled Quin with a roar, at which Nabiki cheered.

Rose had frozen, and was staring at the rippling muscles under Bren's mahogany skin. Bren's body seemed to do much the same things to Rose that Rose's body did to me. I swallowed, but I couldn't turn my head away. Finally, she shook her head and turned back to Penny, who was trying to sign something at her. I finally pulled my gaze from her, to find Tristan staring at me. She reached out for my hand. *'I wish you'd just tell her.'*

Tristan was the only one of my surviving siblings with even a hint of my gift. Hers was limited. She could 'send', but she couldn't 'receive', so fortunately thunder storms and faulty wiring never caused her any discomfort, and she didn't have to worry about absorbing a thought or memory she didn't want to. Even so, she was the only person still living who had any idea what it was like to be me.

I shook my head. *'I can't.'*

'Why not?'

'It's complicated.'

'I don't think it's half as complicated as you make it out to be.'

I kept my thoughts still. Only Bren and myself knew about Rose's former relationship with Xavier, and Rose wanted it kept that way. Even the rest of Bren's family only knew that the two of them had been acquainted when Xavier was young – they had no idea how deep that relationship had gone.

Eventually, Xavier himself came down, and the swimmers climbed dripping out of the pool to eat. The food, of course, was fabulous, prepared by the gourmet chefs of Unicorn Estates, and served by liveried servitors. Nabiki and Bren, of course, knew how to handle it. My family and Molly were a bit more awkward with the fine dining, but no one seemed to notice. Finally, a birthday cake redolent with candied roses was presented.

Xavier opened a bottle of champagne and poured half a glass for everyone seventeen or older. This included everyone but Hilary and Kayin – except for Penny, who took one sip and put it down hastily. Then, holding up his own glass, Xavier sang a song to Rose in Swedish. Tears brimmed in Rose's eyes, and the hand holding the champagne glass trembled. 'Happy birthday, sweetheart,' Xavier said softly, and raised the glass. 'To Rose.'

'To Rose!' everyone who could speak called out.

Rose's trembling was harder to conceal, now. She looked over at Bren, who was still shirtless and gleaming. Clearly he was too daunting a figure in his current state of undress. Finally, she turned to me. I opened my arm to her gladly as she came over and rested her head on my shoulder.

'You okay?' I asked silently.

She was fine, it was only that Xavier and her old maid – really more a godmother – had sung that song for her at her last birthday, more than half a century before. *'I didn't realize he was going to do that.'*

'I'm sorry,' I whispered into her mind, and tried to smooth some of the sharper thorns from her emotional briars. She shuddered, but she let me. I try not to control people's thoughts or emotions, but Rose was one of the few people I would make an exception for. For one thing, I knew her subconscious was strong enough to erase anything if I made a mistake. For another, hers was the only mind outside of my sisters' I was willing to be responsible for.

Over Rose's shoulder I caught a glimpse of Nabiki. She stared at me, and then set down her plate of cake. Quietly, Nabiki went up to Tristan and gave her a hug. I frowned, but Rose was there in my mind, and I had to concentrate on throwing up shields. I didn't want Rose reading my confusion over Nabiki. Rose already – rightly – blamed herself for my breakup with Nabiki. She didn't need to know how torn I was over it.

One of Rose's birthday presents suddenly filed into the area around the pool. It was the band *Overwrought*, the members carrying their instruments and calling out a greeting. The band was a favourite of Hilary's, and she suddenly squealed. 'Oh my god, this is so sky!' She jumped up and hugged Mr Zellwegger. 'Thank you Granddad!'

'This is Rose's present, remember,' Mr Zellwegger said, laughing.

Rose pulled a little away from me, but I could still hear her thoughts from her hand on my arm. She was just as happy getting a present for Hilary, and the fact that Xavier knew that pleased her.

Personally I was a little shocked by *Overwrought*'s appearance. After all, they played to sold-out stadiums across the planet; there was no reason why they'd play a special set at a teenager's birthday party of no more than a dozen guests. But UniCorp had money, there was no denying that!

Overwrought greeted Rose, and then started by playing their hit song, *Dead To Me*. I thought it actually the best version of that song I'd ever heard. It wasn't blared loudly enough to shatter my eardrums, and it wasn't twisted through a thousand sound systems. I was enjoying it, but as soon as Rose headed out to dance I looked around after Nabiki. She was gone. I looked left and right, and noticed her bright pink jacket was gone, too. I slipped out the gate and away from the party.

Nabiki was there, heading for the driveway, already tapping her cell to call her skiff out of the garage. I whistled behind her. She hesitated, and then continued walking, even faster now. She had to know I was behind her. *'Nabiki, stop!'* I signed at her, but she wasn't looking at me.

I did something I don't like to do. I squawked. I sound like a dolphin when I speak, or a monstrous infant. It sounds so silly and freakish that I very rarely do it, and usually only in play. Nabiki knew this. She stopped and turned. 'What?' she asked. 'What do you want?'

'You're leaving?' I signed.

Nabiki shrugged. 'I told Tristan to say goodbye for me.'

'But … why go?'

'I'm just done.'

I wanted her to come back to the party with me, but I wasn't sure how to ask. It wasn't as if I could point out that Rose's embrace had more to do with the fact that she loved Xavier than it had to do with fondness for me. *'I don't want you to go,'* I signed to her.

Nabiki's face clouded. *'You don't care,'* she signed back at me.

'Look, I'm sorry,' I signed. *'What do you want me to do?'*

'Nothing. Don't you understand? It's already been done. There's nothing you can do to fix it, so you might as well go back to Rose.'

I was exasperated as I signed, *'I'm not* with *Rose!'*

Nabiki seemed to lose her temper then. 'Why not? She's not dating anyone. And you're single.'

'That was your idea,' I signed. *'You broke up with me, remember? I was trying to make it work. I knew I couldn't …'* I let my hands fall to my side. The idea that I couldn't do anything with Rose, and that therefore I was taking Nabiki as second best, wasn't accurate, but that's what it would have sounded like. That headache was still pulsing behind my temples. I rubbed them gently, trying to put my thoughts back together. *'I miss you, okay? I do.'*

'But you still love her, don't you.' It wasn't a question.

I shook my head. *'I can't help it. That doesn't mean I don't …'* I stopped. This kind of thing was always easier to convey with my mind, rather than my hands. The feeling I was looking for wasn't 'like,' or 'love,' or 'want,' or 'need.' It was an all encompassing 'wish-to-still-have-you-with-me-in-some-way-or-another-just-because-you're-Nabiki-and-I'm-used-to-having-you-around.' I clenched my fists, grunting with the frustration of having to find words for things I usually didn't have to try and find words for. I was brilliant at communicating, except when I so completely wasn't.

'Look, I can't help it, either,' Nabiki said. 'Did you think I could just sit there and watch? I'm not made of steel.'

'Watch what?' I asked. *'We weren't doing anything. We still aren't doing anything. We're friends, that's all. I don't see why you can't stay.'*

Nabiki's fists clenched, and her face scrunched up in anger. 'You don't *get* it, do you!' She hissed through her teeth. 'No. You never did.' She covered her face with her hands, and I realized she was brushing away the beginnings of tears. Nabiki never wanted to admit she could cry. Her hands snapped away, all trace of emotion scrubbed clear.

'I don't understand,' I signed at her.

'You don't want to,' Nabiki said quietly. 'You never wanted to see. Not really.' She leaned forward and kissed me, expertly.

The kiss was wonderful. Or it was at first. I'd really missed kissing her – kissing anybody. But she wasn't going to let my relief moderate this exchange. Nabiki and I had been kissing for more than a year. She knew how to do it. She knew how I liked it. She knew what my mind could do with it. And she used every nuance of it against me.

Her thoughts were sharp and almost poisoned with pain. First how she saw me; vulnerable, desperate, alone, and the need she had to wrap that frailty in her arms and keep it safe. There was so much fear, there; fear that I would be hurt, that I'd die, fear that she would do something wrong. And then an opening, like flowers, as every time I'd kissed her I traced her every desire, pulling out pleasures she hadn't even known she was searching for. The peace she had felt as she held me, knowing that I was safe with her. The self-awareness I brought which made her feel powerful and useful.

Then Rose. Not the beautiful briar roses I always thought of her as, but a white wolf, snapping at my heels and pulling me away from Nabiki's protective arms. Anger. Hurt. Fear. Then aloneness, sheer, horrific aloneness. She had cried for me. Cried and cried, even before we'd broken up.

And then the despair set in. After I was gone from her, as her magic faded and the world became grim and ordinary. As she searched for man after man. She'd hooked up with ten different guys in the months since we had broken up, and there wasn't a one who could compare. She expected more from them than she had any right to – every nuance of her thought, every hint of a desire was not fulfilled. And Quin's attentions were painful; he was too much like me, and not like me at all. She could find no one to take my place.

'You've ruined me!'

The clear thought came as she released me. I panted. I was shaking. 'You asked.'

I could barely move. So I did what I very rarely did, what even Nabiki had only heard me do a few times, in very intimate occasions. 'But I'm not with her,' I whispered. Of all the people living, Nabiki was the only one who had heard my whisper.

She stepped away. 'Your mind is. Your heart was breaking every moment for her. It would have hurt to watch even if you weren't supposed to love me. And I'm not Rose. You're fond of me, but I'm not what you want.' She shook her head. 'You would have come to hate me. You were already halfway there when I stepped out.'

I hung my head. I brought my fist to my heart, but the sign for *sorry* seemed so inadequate.

'I know,' she said. 'How you feel for her is beyond your control. Just like how I felt for you was beyond me. I didn't want to love you, either. You think it was easy? You're not even fully human, people called me a pervert. Well, I wasn't, but I am now. Because nothing feels right now. No one. No one human.' I wanted to reach out for her, but I didn't dare. 'My parents don't understand,' she went on. 'They're just glad you're gone, they think it was some stupid phase I was going through. I don't care about school anymore. I feel like I don't have any friends – they're all shallow and useless. I can't talk about this to anyone. No one could ever understand it but you. You've done things to my mind, you always have, and now …' She shook her head. 'I was always so scared I'd lose you … but I didn't think it would be like this. Just don't ask me to stay here any longer. I know it's not your fault. I know it's not even her fault, not really. I know for a fact that it isn't mine. So I'm going to go and make something out of my life, burn it, even if you have scrambled my brain. In the meantime, there's only just so much of watching you two that I can take, *okay*?'

I nodded.

'Okay.' She took another step away from me. 'Thanks,' she said quietly.

I wasn't quite sure what she was thanking me for, but I signed the word back to her anyway. I don't know if she saw it. When I opened my eyes she was gone.

I rubbed my forehead. What had I done to her? I should have stayed celibate as a monk. I already had the vow of silence down. What the hell was I? What had I done? I missed my sister 42, suddenly, with a pain that lanced me. She would have understood. The only person at all like me was Tristan, and she had never had my gift on the same level. Had I really scrambled Nabiki's brain? There was no way of knowing. In any case, I had skewed her view of love. There was nothing I could do to fix this. Dating me had been her idea. Breaking up with me had been her idea. My falling in love with Rose and her stunningly beautiful mind had definitely not been my idea.

I sighed. The sound of *Overwrought* echoed over the garden, having switched to some ballad I was unfamiliar with. The mournful romantic tune was annoyingly apropos. I wanted to turn it off, but it wasn't a netfeed one could switch off at will. I sighed. There was nothing to do, really, but go back to the party.

When I turned I nearly fell over my own feet. Standing by the box hedge, her face carefully constructed into a neutral expression, was, of all horrific things, Rose.

chapter 2

My jaw fell open in horror. *'What are you doing there?'*

I think Rose only understood the sign for *'what'* but she replied anyway. 'I was trying to be hostess. And show the guest who was leaving out.'

Rose and her old-fashioned customs! *'How long were you listening?'* I asked. I needed to know how much damage had been done.

Rose looked confused. 'Sorry?'

I slowed my gestures down. *'You heard?'* I asked instead.

She nodded.

'How much?'

She didn't quite succeed in suppressing a smile. 'Enough,' she said quietly.

'Coit!' I signed, which was a very rude gesture. *'I'm sorry.'*

'What for?'

I shook my head.

'Otto,' Rose said. She came towards me, and the look on her face was pure amused pity. Burn it, I did not want her pity! I stepped away, hoping to make an escape. We could talk it over tonight on the net – that's how Rose and I usually talked; in written words, kilometres apart from each other. It was easier that way. Easier when she wasn't right there with me, the sight of her doing uncontrollable things to my body. When the temptation to invade her mind was not tickling every thought in my head. When

I was able to decide what to say, and was still capable of telling a lie.

Then she opened her mouth. 'Did you think I didn't know?'

I froze. The idea was elating and horrifying in one. I shook my head, but I wasn't sure what I was negating. She reached for my hand and took it, and I was tangled again amongst the roses. I closed my eyes. Of course she knew. How, with her vast intuition and her immense subconscious, could Rose not realize that someone close to her was in love with her?

She reached up and kissed my forehead. It was not a romantic kiss, but she accepted my feelings and was neither frightened nor disgusted by them. This revelation was already going far and away better than I'd expected. Her pity was for my belief that I was hiding my feelings, not because of the feelings themselves, or even who and what I was. 'I'm sorry about Nabiki.'

'Me too.'

'I wish there was some way I could make it up to her.'

'Clone me,' I said. Then I realized what I'd just said, and who I'd said it to. Rose actually held the patent on my DNA – or would once she came of age. *'No, don't.'*

'I don't think it would help, either,' Rose said. 'A clone wouldn't be you. And if it was … it still wouldn't be what Nabiki wanted. Would it?'

'She wants me to feel differently,' I admitted.

Rose looked sad and pulled away, leaving me again alone in my thoughts. It was easier that way, but it also wasn't what I really wanted. Every moment with Rose was a war inside myself. 'What she wants is for me never to have existed.'

'She doesn't hate you.'

'No. But she doesn't like me, either.' Rose cringed. 'I guess she has reason.'

'Don't worry. I don't expect anything of you.'

Rose looked away from me. 'Otto, everything is just … confused, and …'

I squeezed her wrist, briefly, very gently. *'I know.'*

She frowned. 'Are you coming back to the party, or did you want to go home too?'

I shook my head. *'I don't know,'* I signed. *'I don't want to go.'*

'Come on back,' she said, taking my hand. 'Your brother is contemplating starting a food fight and I swear Hilary is about to swoon in the lap of the bass player. I need all the help I can get here.' She took my arm and led me back to the party. 'I'm sorry about the pool. I didn't realize you couldn't swim. Come over and I can teach you some time.'

I raised my hand, catching her attention. *'It's not that,'* I signed. *'I can* swim. *I just* don't *swim.'*

'Why not?'

'It's complicated.'

Rose held out her hand. 'Explain it to me.'

I reached out to her, and then pulled back. *'Later,'* I signed.

'Why later?'

It was really more difficult than I wanted to get into. *'Maybe I'll show you sometime,'* I signed instead. I had no intention of showing her what I meant in the middle of all these people.

Rose looked coy. 'I'll hold you to that,' she said with a mischievous grin. Then she grabbed my arm, and dragged me back to the party.

Overwrought finished their set and made a formal farewell to Rose. She came up and thanked them all individually, and then couldn't quite stop Hilary from coming up and begging their autographs. They were very patient with their fourteen-year-old groupie, and finally managed to extricate themselves and their instruments away from the pool.

Xavier came back to show them out. I watched him through the fence, formal and stiff and very gracious. I could see how he and Rose had once come from the same generation.

By now it was getting quite late in the afternoon. Penny suggested we go back in the pool, but Rose was uncomfortable about that idea now she'd realized I couldn't swim, so she cast about for something else for us to do. Quin made the suggestion that 'pool party' could mean billiards as well, and persuaded us to follow him to Unicorn Estates' billiard room. He and Jamal played a few times before Molly asked to play the winner – who was of course Quin. She flattened him, much to everyone's amusement.

By this time Penny had begged Kayin to show her the stables, and Hilary had gone with them. Bren and Tristan's ongoing competition had degenerated to table tennis, and the two of them were chasing ping-pong balls around the room. Quin lost his temper along with his third game to Molly and announced he was going for a walk, leaving Molly and Jamal playing contentedly, crowing the various virtues of their respective moons. There had always been quite a rivalry between them. Molly was an economist in the making. She kept trying to tell Jamal that Europa's trade policies were unconscionably steep, and therefore economically unstable, and Jamal basically didn't care. It made Jamal scathing of her, and Molly short with him. Only in UniPrep could those two have been part of the same clique.

Even though everyone seemed content enough, I knew Rose was bored. Her hands kept twitching as if aching to hold a paint brush. I could invite her to play a game of snooker – which she would have lost – or I could give her my present. I debated it for a bit. Before she had overheard me and Nabiki, I would have been more hesitant. Now, I wondered, what it could hurt. *'Hey,'* I signed to her. *'I have a present for you.'*

Rose looked chagrined. *'I said no gifts!'* she signed back.

'I didn't buy it with money,' I signed.

She sighed. 'Where is it?'

I pointed back towards the pool, and Rose frowned. 'Okay,' she said. She stopped and checked with Bren, making sure he'd play host while she was gone. He nodded at her before striking a ping-pong ball viciously at Tristan's head.

'Okay,' Rose said as we headed back out onto the patio. The servitors had already neatened up the buffet, and everything looked clean and expensive again. Everyone's towels were neatly hung or carefully folded, all the chairs were back in place. 'So what did you get me?'

I think I was blushing. *'I know you didn't want anything,'* I signed to her. I didn't think I could bear touching her just then. *'So I wrote something for you.'*

Rose looked embarrassed. 'Otto,' she chided me. 'You really didn't have to.'

'I wrote it for you months ago,' I told her. *'I just wasn't sure I'd ever give it to you.'*

'Oh,' Rose said. She swallowed.

'Don't worry,' I signed. *'It's not anything ...'* I couldn't find a word. *'It won't change anything.'*

Rose nodded. 'Okay,' she said.

I got my notescreen and pulled up the proper page. I handed it to her, and then I swallowed. I touched her hand and gave her the words as she read them. I had them memorized.

To Walk Alone.

I had determined many years ago
That destiny had scored my lonely path,
And I had been ordained as one so low
That I must walk through blood-soaked aftermath.
As death and solitude should scar my life

Then all that stood about me stood apart.
And I would walk alone along the knife,
And never more would any touch my heart.
But while I walked alone, my life deserted,
A briar rose was wakened with the spring,
And with her graceful pain was I enchanted,
I learn to love whatever she may bring.
Now when I think upon my life of rain
I think of Rose, and never feel the pain.

Yes. I had written her an Elizabethan sonnet. I was writing her poetry. BAD POETRY! This was the pitiful level I had been reduced to! But, against all sense, it actually seemed to work. 'Oh, Otto,' Rose whispered, and she stared at me. Suddenly she grinned. 'You've gone purple.'

My only consolation was that she was glowing red. The sunset fired the sky orange, and Rose was a flame. My eyes were drawn from her quite literally stunning body to the still, empty pool.

No. I couldn't. It was too early. I'd only just admitted how I felt – though granted, it appeared she had known for a while. Instead I just watched her. Her mouth opened slightly as she read the poem again. 'I …' She looked down. 'I wish I could show you what this means to me.'

I swallowed. *'You can,'* I signed. I couldn't believe what I was about to do. My mouth was dry and my hands trembled and my heart stuttered wildly. But I sidled up beside Rose and gently took hold of her hand. I tried to keep my mental shields up, but I don't know how much of my nervousness passed to her as I asked, *'You want to see why I don't swim?'*

Rose dropped the screen and turned to me, grinning. 'Yes!' she said with enthusiasm.

I nodded, releasing her. *'Okay,'* I signed. *'Stay there.'*

'Here?'

'Right there. I'll tell you when to come in.'

I took a deep breath as I stripped off my shirt. I wondered if I had hoped it would come to this; I'd unconsciously chosen shorts which could double as swim trunks. I took another deep breath as I poised at the edge of the deep end. Here I was. Not too late to back out, I reminded myself. But after what had happened this evening with Nabiki, I knew I wasn't going to. Something definitive had to happen with me and Rose, or I was likely to go insane, and drag others down with me.

I dove into the pool barely leaving a ripple, letting the water swirl over my body, carry me away. The temperature was perfect, of course, in carefully controlled Unicorn Estates – just cool enough to feel comfortable. I swam half the length of the pool, getting used to the sensations. I only swam late at night, or on days when there was no one else in the school pool. Which was something of a shame, because I actually loved swimming. I was extremely good at it, too. I loved the feeling of buoyancy in the water, the freedom of flight that it gave me.

I finally turned and looked at Rose, still fired in the sunset. She stared at me, confused. 'You swim better than I do.'

I nodded. *'Come in,'* I signed.

Rose moved for the ladder.

I clapped my hands at her. *'No,'* I signed. *'Jump.'*

'Why?'

I didn't reply, I just stared at her. My eyes can sometimes disturb people, the wide yellow gaze which doesn't seem quite human. Rose opened her mouth and then swallowed. 'Okay,' she said. 'But I can't dive.'

She paused at the edge of the pool and then jumped, far out into the centre. This could either go spectacularly well, or terribly badly. I tried to lock down my mind so that she wouldn't have too much of a shock.

Rose nearly sucked in a breath under water as she realized what was happening. I prepared myself to catch her and drag her back to the surface, but she controlled herself and made for the air. As her head broke out of the water her eyes were fixed on me. 'Otto!' she whispered.

But she didn't have to speak. I was already inside her mind, absorbing every nuance, swimming through her consciousness as much as I was through the water. Her thoughts were a ripple of stunned and almost frightened confusion. She hadn't imagined anything like this.

'I can hear everything in the water,' I told her. *'See everything. Touch everybody.'*

She could see why I never swam. I chuckled – Rose was one of the few people I ever let hear me laugh.

To be in a pool with someone was always very intimate for me. It felt like being two people at once – much more encompassing than just touching someone. When I touched someone, I knew I could let go, and it would all go away again. It's a bit like reading a book, and you know at any point you can put the book down and return to your own life. But in the water you can't escape. It's more of a surrender. Unless we climbed out of the pool, Rose couldn't escape my mind, and I most certainly couldn't begin to escape hers. And with Rose, the rapport was ten times as intense as it had been with anyone else, ever.

Swimming is not something I've done with many people. Some of my siblings – I used to swim quite a lot with 42 – and once with Nabiki, in a hot tub. We decided never to try that again after she'd fainted. I tried to keep that thought out of my mind, but failed. Rose picked up the thought and smiled sympathetically. She knew how hard it was being me.

As always when she sympathized I was struck with those pangs of memory she suffered from when she had allowed her consciousness to fade under the influence of the stasis tube her parents had kept locking her in.

I swam around Rose like an otter, trying not to let her overwhelm me, but I couldn't stop reaching for those beautiful wild patches of subconscious. For her part, she felt awed. I couldn't suppress a rush of pride at that; that I was something in fact awesome.

She wanted to know why I was showing her this.

Even the passing thought communicated itself to me. And of course the answer instantly sprang to mind – the mind I could not keep hidden from her here and now, no matter how much I might want to.

I loved her.

Of course, there were so many levels of love in that thought. The word itself is just a word, but for me, I was able to communicate the sympathy and similarity I felt with her, as we were both outcasts in a world that couldn't begin to understand us. Then the compassion I felt when I thought about how much pain she had gone through in her long/short life. The simply companionable friendship we shared, the way we wrote to each other in the evenings, how I could tell her things I could never tell anyone, ever. How wonderful it was that, my telepathy aside, she did not turn in disgust or horror at my blue skin or my strange, expressionless face. And there, through it all, a strong, purely physical current, her body, her eyes, the gold flow of her hair, poetry in human form; how much I longed to simply touch her – touch her anywhere, her wrist, the back of her neck, the tips of her fingers, any part of her that was *her*.

I was overwhelmed myself by the sensation of her absorbing this simple fact. The extent of my devotion hadn't really communicated itself to her before. This was how Nabiki had fallen in love with me – one instant of feeling how I saw her. It wasn't really fair to Rose.

I was instantly sorry, but Rose didn't want me to be sorry. Because she knew how it felt, to love someone, really love them for themselves. Suddenly I was inundated by what I'd never wanted to see; the pervasive, all encompassing relationship she had had sixty years ago with Xavier. The true understanding that had happened between them, the need, the desperation, the fear, and love above everything else.

But once she had thought of that the pain of losing him flashed through her mind too – how it felt to have had him ripped from her life, her life twisted until he was so far beyond her reach that even living in the same house he would barely touch her. I was torn open by the simple roar of *It's not fair!* It was a feeling she lived with every day. She was very used to it, she wasn't even dwelling on it – it was just a passing thought – but I was blasted by it. And the blast knocked me backwards until I nearly sank. My head ached with the pain.

'I'm sorry!' Rose swam for me and took hold of my arms, leading me to the side of the pool, trying very hard not to think about Xavier.

'My fault,' I tried to tell her. *'I knew … I knew about that.'* I tried not to think about 42. Rose knew about that, too, but there was no call to inundate her with my grief, or the memory of her death. I wondered if sharing our pain was really the best thing for either of us. I was about to suggest we call this off, but Rose touched my shoulder, drawing me to her in an embrace.

That threw 42 out of my head, sure enough. Rose's flesh was warm and soft beneath the water, and I could feel her bare skin against mine. My fingers gripped her, and I tried again to lock down my mind. I didn't want to think about what her touching me was doing to me, physically. I tried to think about what it meant to her.

I was disappointed. There was no physical rush, no sensual delight in touching my blue skin. It wasn't that she was repulsed by me, or didn't find me reasonably attractive, artistically. It was that every nuance of her physical desire had been locked behind an impenetrable wall when she'd discovered that her Xavier was alive, but in his seventies, and untouchable. He was off limits, so I was off limits and Bren was off limits and every other man and woman in the universe was sexually off limits until she could sort it all out.

But she did want to touch me. I let myself be content with that.

We were both beginning to get used to sharing mindspace. She grinned. 'Is that what you call it?'

I shrugged. It was as good a term as any. She was beginning to understand why words meant so much and so little to me. I had no words I could say, but words don't mean the same thing as thoughts. It was why I wrote poetry – or tried to. I saw words as a medium, like Rose saw her paintings. A tool, but not the thing itself. Because I could see the thing itself, and not only in my own mind.

She smiled at me as I took hold of the wall. 'This is strange.'

I'd known what she was going to say. I grinned at her. What about me wasn't strange? She chuckled. 'Does your head hurt?' she asked suddenly. 'That is you, isn't it?'

Now that she reminded me of it, my head did ache. I barely noticed anymore. I knew it would pass. I was pretty used to headaches, and I'd been under a lot of stress. I was sorry she was feeling it. She could get out if she wanted.

'No.' She didn't want to get out. This was a miracle to her, a gift, a strange journey. She wanted to know what all the colours were that she was feeling.

'Oh, hell.' The colours. She had to have seen the colours, the depth that I'd been trying so hard not to think about, so as not to shock her. But there it went. She brought it up, and there it went. My last lock. *'It's you,'* I thought. *'It's all you.'* And all the wild, tangled briars of her mind were completely visible to her, not hidden behind my veil of secrecy. Rose. Rose, as she was inside, a sea of vivid colour, the vast ocean of her subconscious. Rose stared at me, utterly stunned as the beauty of her mind became open to her, gorgeous mindscapes of colour.

She could see them, and they amazed her, and she carried me along. Suddenly she was amplified by her awareness, a mirror reflected upon itself, spinning off into infinity. I was overwhelmed. Completely. Suddenly there was nothing left of me but her. My own consciousness disappeared, buried under the avalanche of colour.

Then, without warning, my body melted into droplets of pain. The colours surged, a tsunami of subconscious time, and I was drowning under it.

The last thing I heard/felt before I was submerged in a hopeless agonizing vortex of everything at once was Rose screaming in sudden terror.

What I felt and saw and heard won't make much sense to anyone. Rose was so overwhelmed by being caught in the shock wave that she couldn't describe it any better than I could. When you ask Quin, all he does is look tragic and make jokes. The best way to describe what happened is to write out what was recorded on the security cameras. We start with a very pretty image of myself and Rose in the

Unicorn pool, both of us a little overawed by each other. Then a look crosses my face, something between pain and amazement. Suddenly, my body jerks, convulsively. I am caught in a sudden seizure. Blood begins to leak out of my nose and ears. I lose hold of the side of the pool. At first, Rose holds me, or tries to, but the moment she sees the blood she starts screaming. The crimson of my blood streaks her pretty white skin, matching her red swimsuit. She can't shake the seizure of my mind, and she's lucky she doesn't sink and drown. She isn't able to hold me any longer, and she isn't able to make it out of the pool. It is only her proximity to the wall that saves her, particularly as she's still so thin she doesn't float.

I, on the other hand, am seizing so violently I have lost all control. I sink beneath the blue water of the pool, blood clouding around my face. There are a tense thirty seconds while Rose is jerking, trying to close down her mind, and I am utterly helpless, sinking to the bottom.

Then, like some holovid superhero, a figure comes sauntering along the other side of the wrought-iron fence; blue skin, black hair, tall, arrogant. Quin listens to the sounds which come from the pool, which have degenerated from a scream to a thin, anxious whine, as Rose can't even maintain a scream any longer. He takes one look at the two of us in the pool, Rose in agony, me drowning in a cloud of my own blood. 'Holy coit!' Quin shouts, and without even stripping off his shirt, vaults himself over the fence and dives into the pool.

I, of course, am in the throes of a major biological crisis. My mind is going haywire, sending out waves of confused torment. Between my telepathy and Rose's overpowering subconscious, which was also caught by my telepathy, Quin's mind was likely reduced to marshmallows the moment he touched the water. Quin, however, reacts like a berserker under pressure. Roaring like a beast, his face twisted in agony, he drags my still convulsing body into the shallow end of the pool, and hoists me over the wall. My chin is banged against the tile and blood is still flowing from my face.

The moment I'm out of the water, Rose recovers. She holds on to the wall trembling in horror for a few more seconds until she realizes she's free of me.

Quin will deny it until the day he dies, but you can see it clearly on the vid. He is sobbing as he jumps out of the pool, and his face is purple with pain. He shouts at Rose to get a towel. Rose hurries to grab one, and rushes over to me to wrap me up. Quin swears at her. 'For coit's sake, don't *touch* him!' He pushes her roughly aside and wraps me tightly. He shouts at Rose to fetch Tristan and the others as he pounds the water out of my lungs. It's clear that I'm breathing, but I'm still jerking like I'm being shocked.

Rose is crying too. She stumbles as she runs to the wrought-iron gate. The screaming and the shouts have already drawn Bren and Tristan from the billiard room. Bren pulls his cell from around his neck and shouts for his grandfather.

Xavier comes down within seconds, and Penny comes with him. Penny starts to hyperventilate the moment she sees me, and Tristan has to comfort her. She takes Penny to the side where they converse in hurried, desperate sign. There are a few tense moments as Rose tries to explain what happened to me, but she's too shaken, and she's crying too hard. Bren finally goes up to her and wraps her in his arms. She sobs against him. I know Rose rather well, and when I watch this vid I know half of her sobs are because Xavier wasn't the one to come and hold her. Xavier is instead standing in the middle of all the chaos, efficiently trying to keep order. I think he's the one who celled the EMTs, but he might have been celling the lab. I never asked. Either he or Bren celled the EMTs in.

I spend all this time on the ground still jerking like a marionette in the hands of a demented puppeteer. Quin is just angry, and shouts at everyone. He stands over me like a guard dog, angrily barking at everyone who gets near me. He even threatens to hit Penny when she comes up to see how I am, holding his hand up in a powerful fist, and Tristan signs at him angrily. Finally, the seizures cease. Quin does a quick check to make sure I am breathing, which I am. But I do not wake up. Rose starts crying again, probably in relief, and Quin sinks onto his haunches, trembling. Tristan looks exhausted, her blue skin almost grey. She sinks onto the ground. Penny clambers over to her and climbs into her lap. They stay curled together, watching me, until the EMTs arrive.

When they do finally arrive, Quin is not helpful. He won't let them touch me for a full three minutes. He thinks my mind can't take it. Finally he allows it when they explain they'll be wearing gloves and won't touch my skin. Xavier goes with me as they carry me away, to be sure they take me to the UniCorp lab, rather than the regular hospital; no one else can handle my physiology.

Quin sits down on one of the deck chairs after I'm gone and stays there, trembling. Bren finally drags Rose inside, and Penny and Tristan sign to Quin that they're going to the lab to be there when I wake up.

For the next hour and a half my brother sits utterly still on the deck chair as the UniCorp servitors clear up the disastrous party behind him. I've never seen his dark, sardonic face look more empty. He almost looked dead.

chapter 3

I knew where I was before I opened my eyes. Even after three years at UniPrep, there was no way I could forget. There's nothing like the sound of the lab – the beeps of the monitors, the steady hum of the air conditioning, the professional office sound of the people in the corridors. When I opened my eyes my theory was confirmed. I'd been brought back to the lab, set into my familiar hospital bed, and a dozen different machines were monitoring every pulse, every breath, the firing of every synapse. I sat up and ripped the brain monitor off my scalp.

The machine started complaining at that, but I was finished having my every thought monitored by UniCorp. I'd escaped that three years ago, I was not going back now! Besides, it hurt – the same way the tape of a bandage starts to hurt your skin – a quiet, persistent annoyance, like a mosquito in my skull.

The disgruntled beeping of the monitor brought in Dr Svarog, my personal physician. Each of us had our own private doctor, all part of a team, but Dr Svarog headed that team. Our physicians were secondary under the geneticists and biologists who still ran the project. I rather liked Dr Svarog. He'd been hired when I was nine, and had monitored our growth ever since. Because he had come so late to the Project I couldn't fault him with anything. He was making do with the materials that had been handed him.

'Awake, I see,' Dr Svarog said. 'Feeling okay?'

Now that he asked me, I realized I felt wretched. My head throbbed, nausea lurked in the pit of my stomach, and my body ached all over. I signed something to that effect, but Dr Svarog wasn't particularly good at sign. He came up to me and held out his hand, asking my permission to touch me. I always liked that about him. I took hold of his hand and let him know *exactly* how I was feeling.

He reeled. 'Whoo!' he breathed. 'Not so great, then.' Dr Svarog's mind was always clinical, but there was a warmth behind it that made it okay. I was, to him, a person, and not just a collection of body parts and symptoms. Not every doctor was like that. He turned his attention to his notescreen and made a few ticks on my chart. 'Do you want to risk a painkiller for your head?'

Usually I was adamant about this. I got headaches so often, and the typical over-the-counter stuff did practically nothing. But if I kept myself on the heavier painkillers I was consistently useless and stupid, and likely to get addicted. The last thing my biology needed was an addiction, so usually I just endured my headaches and tried to ignore them. Today, I considered. My head hurt *a lot*. *'Something mild,'* I signed.

'We'll hope it works,' Dr Svarog said. 'I'll try and find something that will work as a muscle relaxant, too. I think you strained a few things.'

'What happened?' I signed.

'We're not entirely sure, yet,' Dr Svarog said. He leafed over some auxiliary pages on his notescreen. 'It is clear you had a blood pressure spike, and that resulted in a seizure, but we aren't entirely sure what caused it.'

My head throbbed. *'Yes we are.'*

Dr Svarog frowned at me. 'Don't leap to grim conclusions,' he said severely. 'There's no indicator that this is the same thing that happened to your siblings four years ago.'

'No? It sure feels like it.'

'That doesn't mean anything.'

I clapped my hands, '*Hey!*' Once I had his attention I added, '*I should know.*' Touching my head for the sign for 'know' made my headache spike. I winced, which didn't help, either. Suddenly my nausea surged. '*Sick!*' I signed desperately. Dr Svarog rushed to push a kidney bowl under my chin. Very little came up, and most of that liquid. I wondered how long I'd been unconscious.

Unfortunately, my retching made my headache that much worse, and I groaned – my whispery, dolphinish groan. I usually had more control over myself than that.

'I'll get you that painkiller,' Dr Svarog said gently. 'Don't work yourself up, Otto. There were all kinds of possibly mitigating circumstances which could have caused an unforeseen reaction in your biology. Unfamiliar food, harmonic resonances from the close proximity to music, various chemicals in the water of the pool. Not to mention your close contact with Miss Fitzroy.'

Oh, god, Rose! *'How is she?'*

'There seem to have been no lasting effects on Miss Fitzroy, though Mr Zellwegger did bring her here for a full evaluation.'

'Can I see her?'

'She's not here at the moment. Maybe when you're feeling a little better. Quin and your sisters would like to see you, but I think you'd do best to let your painkillers kick in a little. Shall I tell them forty minutes?'

I shook my fist in the sign for '*Yes,*' and closed my eyes as Dr Svarog injected me with something. I felt better within five minutes, but then I was drowsy. I drifted in and out of awareness, only half sensible of Dr Svarog recalibrating my monitors, or of 42 lurking in the corners of my consciousness.

I was asleep when Dr Svarog showed in Tristan and Penny. I opened my eyes to the sound of Penny bursting into tears. Tristan signed at her angrily to be quiet. Penny could only shake her head. I waved a greeting to them and Penny sobbed louder. Quin burst in behind them. 'Quit it!' he snapped at her, and slapped her arm. Penny cried out. Tristan clapped her hands at him angrily.

I covered my ears with my hands.

That made all three of them go instantly silent, though Penny still sniffed quietly. *'I'm sorry,'* Penny signed.

'I told her she couldn't come in unless she behaved herself,' Quin said, his voice still burred with annoyance.

The last thing I wanted to do was listen to Quin's ire at this point. I reached out for Penny, who grasped my hand fiercely. Her mind was such a roar of terror that I snatched my hand out of her grip, even though the movement made my head ache worse.

Tristan touched Penny's shoulder, probably saying something to her silently. Penny closed her eyes in the calming technique she'd been trying to develop since she turned fifteen. It was a little mantra she'd recite in her head, and she didn't open her eyes until she was finished. When she opened them she looked more in control. I reached out again, and found she had buried her terror behind the surface thoughts. I can read nothing but surface thoughts unless I concentrate, and I almost never try. It's against my personal code of ethics. There's a big part of me that feels a person's mind is their own, and I shouldn't meddle. It took some tough lessons to make me learn that.

'*Otto, are you going to be okay?*' Penny asked me.

'What does Dr Svarog say?' I asked her.

'*He says he doesn't know.*'

'I don't know any more than he does.'

Another tear snuck out of Penny's eye, and she sniffed and pulled away. Tristan took my hand then. *'Hey, 86,'* she said. '*You're not going to 86 on us, are you?'*

My eyes crinkled in our tiny version of a smile, but I didn't have an answer for her. Penny added her hand to Tristan's, and the two of them sent me fervent Get Well wishes. Penny had made me a card, but she'd forgotten it in her room and – I stopped her and told her to give it to me tomorrow.

Quin did not touch me. He stood brooding at the foot of my bed. Finally he looked at the girls and jerked his head towards the door. Penny and Tristan let go of me and looked worried. 'I'm not going to eat him!' Quin snapped. 'Now get!'

They left, Tristan biting her lip and looking meaningfully at the camera in the corner. You couldn't even see the minuscule thing, but we all knew it was there. 'Oh, give me a break,' Quin said to her retreating back. 'You think I'd drag him out of that pool just to beat him up?'

The set of Tristan's shoulders led one to believe she did not think such a thing impossible. I didn't either, really. I knew Quin of old. But I didn't think he was angry at me just now.

I was wrong. 'She's right, though,' Quin snapped the moment the door was closed, his fist closed. 'If you weren't sick, I'd hit you. What the coit did you think you were doing!' I closed my eyes and sighed. I really had nothing to say.

'Swimming. Swimming in an unknown pool, with Rosalinda Fitzroy? Have you a death wish, or something?'

'No,' I signed. *'Rather a life wish.'*

'What are you on about?'

'*I'm not going to live in fear!'*

'If you persist in this infatuation, you're not going to live at all!'

I shook my aching head and looked out of the window. It was getting on towards evening. The light was fading to blue outside, and the birds had hushed. Finally, Quin came closer to the head of the bed, standing between me and the window. 'What happened?' he asked. 'Was it like last time?'

'Ask Tristan,' I signed.

'She doesn't know. She can't receive, remember? She was just helping Una and the others. Besides, that was after the fact. You're the only one who knows what it feels like *before* the end.'

I looked away from him. I could hear 42 laughing in my head.

'Otto!' Quin snapped. 'Answer me!'

I heard something in his tone. He was shaking. I could have assumed it was with anger, but Quin's anger tends to be cool, if explosive. *'You scared?'* I signed.

Quin clenched his fists, but all he did was breathe heavily through his nose. 'This has to stop,' Quin said. 'I've been watching you moon yourself sick over that stuck-up princess for months! It's not as if they'd ever let you do anything with her. She'll probably marry Bren Sabah or Hank Guillory or the CEO of MonaCo in the most expensive corporate merger in history. You are an alien freak, or have you forgotten? You're a propertyless publicity nightmare. Do you think Mr Zellwegger or UniCorp's board would *ever* let you keep her? You'd be assassinated before they let that happen. Or maybe just declare you inhuman and strip *all* of us of our rights.' Quin was always afraid they were going to do that. 'Out of all of us, I never thought you'd grow up to be the ladies' man. Nabiki was next to impossible as it was, but Rose? It can only end in blood.'

Trying hard to keep my temper I signed, once again, *'She's just a friend.'*

'Oh, burn it, like I believe that.'

I clenched my jaw.

Quin wasn't finished. 'Then, suddenly you get into a pool with her – water, Otto! You get into the water with a hundred-year-old freak of science where you can't get away! – and of course you go into meltdown!'

'Rose didn't do this.'

'Oh, no? You didn't see the brain scans they did on her after you were dragged in here bleeding like a slaughtered pig. Do you know her brain is abnormal?'

I looked away.

'They can't even identify how!' Quin cried. 'Something to do with the stasis, they think, but they're not sure what it is, since her mental faculties seem, and I quote, Unaffected. But they aren't, are they. This is you, I know you. This is something you had to know. Is this what's been making you go all calf-eyed over that skinny bitch?'

'Watch it,' I signed.

'No,' Quin said. 'What are you going to do, bleed on me? Vomit on me? You're lying there half dead because of some anorexic bleach blonde with a broken brain, and I'm not about to sit here and let that happen!'

'You insult Rose again and I will break you!' I signed. *'You want to know how this feels? All I have to do is get my hands on you. You want last spring's broken arm? You want Nabiki's breakup? Do you really want to know how I feel for Rose? Do you? How about all of them at once?'*

'I'm trying to save the life of my stupid brother!' Quin snapped. 'Who can't keep himself safe from some broken-brained bitch. I don't care how you feel about her, she's dangerous! And if you won't listen, I'll bet she would.'

'You dare!'

'I would.'

'Rose didn't cause this, okay?'

'How do you know? Even Dr Svarog thinks it might have been contact with that UniCorp whore.'

'Call her that again!' I signed, sitting upright in the bed, headache or no. *'Just try it! I dare you!'*

'How do you *know*!' Quin challenged me again.

'Because I've been ignoring this for weeks!'

Nausea struck me again and I had to lie back down. I leaned over the side of the bed and dry heaved, but there was nothing left in my stomach. I couldn't even see, my head ached so violently. Finally, I just hung there, too dizzy to pull myself back into the bed.

Suddenly I felt a hand on my back. Very gently, Quin lifted me upright and set me back on the bed. There was a slight hesitation as he propped me up that was uncharacteristically warm. If I didn't know Quin better, I would have thought he was giving me a hug. But he would deny any such impulse if you asked him. He walked away from the bed and paced slowly at the far side of the room as I recovered. One hand was against his forehead as if trying to squeeze emotion out of his brain. 'How many weeks?' he asked quietly when my breathing had stabilized.

'Eight, maybe ten,' I signed. *'Since before normal school let out.'*

Quin's face twisted. 'And you didn't tell us?'

I pinched my fingers lightly together. *'No.'*

'Otto,' he sighed. Then he looked at me closely. 'What is it? Just the headaches?'

'Night sweats. Bad dreams. Dizzy spells.' I hesitated, and then figured, what the hell. I was telling him everything else. *'Disorientation. I've had moments where I thought I was somewhere else, or went looking for Una or 42 before I remembered they were*

gone.' I didn't mention that I kept hearing 42's voice. I wasn't sure that had anything to do with this.

'Coit,' Quin breathed, and he sank heavily into a chair. He seemed to be having a hard time catching his breath. 'What are you … what do we do?'

I looked up at the ceiling. Finally, I touched my forehead and signed, *'I don't know.'*

'How could you just ignore this?' Quin said. The anger was back, but it simmered now under every word.

I couldn't hold it back anymore, as much as I wanted to. Tears burned up my face until a few leaked from my eyes. I tried to blink them away. *'I didn't want it to be true,'* I signed, my gestures small and inhibited.

With a sound of annoyance, Quin took my hand and held the backs of my fingers to his forehead. I so rarely touched him that his mind was a bit of a shock. Usually his mind was nothing but scornful contempt, and I never wanted to spend much time there. Indeed, his surface thoughts at this moment were the words, *'You burning sped,'* but it was venomless. His anger was broken now, an armour that had been breached. His skin felt hot, and beneath his hopeless words his mind was one long, slow death knell of *'No!'*

It was worse than Penny's panic. And much deeper. Quin gripped my fingers so hard they hurt. I hadn't realized until this moment how much of Quin's identity was based around us. He was always so cruel and violent it was hard to remember he loved us. He loved us with a passion as violent as the rest of his nature, and the idea that I was dying was a stake through his heart. I tried to comfort him, but it was too deep a pain to be reached, let alone soothed. Maybe if I was more used to his mindscape I could have found my way to do it, but he had always made it such an unfriendly atmosphere. Quin was alone in this. Finally, he let me go.

'*Don't tell the girls,*' I signed to him.

'I wouldn't,' Quin said. He looked at me. 'You need to tell Dr Svarog.'

'*I know.*'

He nodded his head and left. He paused in the doorway. 'Get some rest, brother,' he said gently.

With one hand I flashed him the sign for *I love you*. He said nothing, but he did wave it back.

Quin had never done such a thing before.

chapter 4

They kept me in bed for two days. At first they wouldn't even let me have my notescreen. I lay battling headaches and boredom and bouts of nausea as my muscles ached – and my heart ached, too.

I wanted to talk to Rose. She hadn't come to visit me, and I wondered if I'd scared her off. When Tristan finally brought me my screen I was so glad I could have jumped up and hugged her, except that my head hurt so badly I could barely move it.

I hooked on a link to Rose immediately, but it was far too early. Her name just blinked unanswered on my screen. I assumed she was in her studio. She never brought her screen or her cell into her studio when she was painting seriously. I'd only been in Rose's studio a few times, but every time I had I just wanted to sit there for hours. On the wall at the foot of my bed at UniPrep I had one of Rose's landscapes. A large blue-black icescape which Rose always said was meant to be Europa. She'd seen some photographs of the glaciers, but this was her own composition. It was stunningly beautiful, the lights and shadows drawing your eye from one portion of the canvas to another. Most people thought it was abstract, but I could see the intricate accuracy she had painted into the shadows. I could stare at that painting for hours. Staring at the blank wall at the lab, I wished someone had brought me Rose's painting.

She had given it to me last spring, as I was getting over my broken arm. I'd sustained that broken arm trying to protect her from the Plastine assassin her parents had set after her. I probably shouldn't have put myself in the way of an undead plasticized robotic corpse, but I was in love – I wasn't thinking very clearly. I couldn't take much in the way of painkillers, and the electricity-based bone structure accelerators made my head short out, so I had to just wait until my body adapted and healed. I couldn't do much. Rose had brought me the blue ice world of Europa as a thank you.

Last spring, everything had seemed so easy. I had felt so sure of myself, so secure of my place with Rose. Like a fool, I had thought that once we cleared the Plastine out of the way, and I'd helped Rose find her strength, we'd fall in naturally. Like I had with Nabiki. I had been far too confident in my abilities. It hadn't happened that way. Once she had moved in with Xavier she'd actually distanced herself from me. It made sense, in a way. In her old life, it was Xavier she had shared things with. When she thought he was gone, she had desperately reached out for that kind of connection with someone – anyone – else. Now that reaching tendril of her emotional briars was anchored again, and it wasn't connected to me. Instead of things getting easier, they got harder and even more confused.

And I had no Nabiki to discuss it with. I couldn't talk about it to Bren or to Rose, since they were both principal players. That left Dr Bija, and my crush seemed so petty and juvenile compared to what I'd gone through with the dying times and my adjustment to the world outside the lab that I felt silly trying to sort it out with her.

I lightly touched Rose's name on my screen. As if I could caress her that way.

(You're being very stupid about her, you know.)

I closed my eyes. *'Stop it.'*

(Why should I? You dance back and forth about her, moaning in your sleep, no less, and I have to listen to it.)

'Shut up!'

(It doesn't matter anyway. You'll be like me soon enough.)

'And what will happen to you then?' I asked angrily. As usual, 42 didn't have an answer for that one.

I had to wait quite a bit before Rose noticed I'd linked up. I updated my journal as I waited, and tried to work on some poetry, but my head wasn't in it. It ached too much.

My screen dinged and I turned back to the netfeed page.

Otto! Are you still there? Are you okay?

I ache a bit. Are you all right?

Your doctors say so. But I'm worried. They got really quiet at one point and wanted to talk to Xavier privately.

Don't worry about it. It's just the stass reaction stuff I noticed the first time I touched you.

Briars and bright spots.

Yeah. I'll bet it's the same stuff they see in the brain scans of frequent interplanetary travellers, just more advanced.

I hope so. Otto, what happened? I was really scared.

No one's sure, I wrote. This was true. No one was sure what had caused the dying time, either. **I'll be okay.** That was a blatant lie. I couldn't help it. I wanted to protect her. **Are you?**

I think so.

I felt ill even thinking about it, but I needed to ask her. **Did I hurt you?**

I'm okay.

I stared at that. **That's not answering my question.**

And I said I'm okay.

She still wasn't answering my question. **I take it I don't want to know the answer?**

She didn't reply.

I'm sorry.

It's not your fault.

Yes it is. It was reckless, and I shouldn't have done it.

Done what? Gone for a swim?

With you.

There was a long pause before Rose wrote, Quin said much the same. He said it was my fault.

I tried really hard not to throw the screen across the room in frustration. Quin doesn't know coit all about it. And after I kill him, I'll tell him that.

Quin was just trying to protect you.

Quin's protection in the past has resulted in weeks in the lab infirmary, I wrote. His idea of what's best for me is usually loud insults, cruel pranks, or his fist in my face.

I've never seen him hit you.

Well, I conceded. He has grown up some in the last few years. And he's worried he'll get sent back to the lab if he's as violent as he usually wants to be. That doesn't mean he knows what's best for me. I'm the only one who gets to decide that.

Rose didn't respond for a long time. I'm not used to thinking that way, she admitted.

I suddenly felt like a sped. I was saying that to a victim of emotional abuse. I know. I'm sorry, I didn't mean to bring stuff up.

That's okay. It's my own can of worms.

We have plenty of those to share between us.

We do, don't we. She paused. I miss you.

That surprised me. Then come see me.

They won't let me.

What? Who won't?

I'm not sure.

I sighed. Sometimes Rose became so biddable and passive it was exasperating. It was a habit she would fall back to, like nicohol or nail-biting. It had once been a survival mechanism

– the only method she had to keep her parents from stassing her – but it was only detrimental now. She didn't have to be like that. **Is it Xavier or the lab?** I asked, trying to point out the obvious. This question was basically a wash, because if the lab said no, Mr Zellwegger could have made them change their minds.

I'm not sure if it's your doctors or your brother.

I heard laughter in my mind that wasn't mine. Cruel laughter. *'Shut up!'* I told 42 fiercely. **I think you can be reasonably assured that it's Quin,** I wrote. **He's decided not to like you.**

What a shock, Rose wrote, with her occasional wry sense of humour. I chuckled. You mean I haven't won him over with my charming personality?

It would take a lump hammer to charm Quin.

I'll go buy one.

Get the super family pack, I wrote. **You'll likely need more than one.**

I will. But your doctors agree with Quin, and I think Xavier agrees with them. He kept making them take neuroscans on me. At first Xavier thought you were the one messing ME up. He was really angry. Well, no, he was all stiff and dark sounding, but that's how he gets angry, now he's older. Quin thinks it's the other way around, that I'm the one who hurt you. Are you sure Quin's not right? I mean ... my brain is weird. You said so yourself. If I wasn't all stass twisted, would you be hospitalized at the lab right now?

Rose, you are who you are. There's no 'if' about it. You can have no one's life but yours.

But my life just sent you into convulsions.

I closed my eyes. **Whatever it was,** I wrote carefully, **it wasn't you.**

She didn't answer.

So what are you dreaming that's making you feel guilty? I frequently asked her about her dreams. I'd realized several months ago that Rose's dreams usually spoke more for Rose's world as it really was than her conscious mind.

You're turning inside out. I'm in the pool and I've reached inside your head and turned you inside out. There was a long pause before she added, There was a lot of blood. They had to drain the pool.

That probably had more to do with clearing my DNA out of the filters. I told you. I don't own my own blood. UniCorp does. Anywhere any of us get hurt they bleach out immediately, and we're not allowed to throw away any of our clothes or sheets. We have to incinerate any hair we comb out.

There was a hesitation before she wrote, There was a lot of blood.

I realized something. **You've never seen anything like that, have you.**

Not in person, no. Not with anyone I cared about.

She'd missed the Dark Times. She hadn't grown up with the memory of all that death in the social consciousness. **I'm sorry.**

It's okay.

You'd be saying that even if it wasn't.

Probably. Oh, honestly, Otto, am I supposed to get mad at you for nearly dying at my birthday party? It's not as if you did it on purpose.

No.

You sure it wasn't me?

Yes.

Otto?

Yes?

Is this likely to happen again?

(*Of course it is! Again and again until it finally wins ... and you become just like me.)*

I closed my eyes to block the laughter out of my head. *'I got rid of you two years ago,'* I told 42. *'Shoo.'*

(You never got rid of me. You just stopped paying attention.)

Rose was still linked up. You're not answering my question. I take it I won't like the answer?

I hedged. What did Xavier and my doctor say?

Nothing about you. Only that you were getting the best care possible.

So, then.

Otto, are you dying?

I blinked at the screen. Wow. She just came right out and said it. I could just picture her face as she wrote it, too. Hard and pale, as it always got when she asked tough questions of people.

(Tell her the truth.)

'I don't want to.'

Talk to me, Rose begged.

What do you want me to say?

The truth.

I couldn't answer. I didn't want to lie to her.

She realized that. Oh, hell. If everything was fine, you'd have said so.

She was right. She wasn't stupid, Rose. I'm scared, I finally wrote. I didn't think I'd be so scared.

There was nothing on the other line for a long, long time. I was afraid of what was happening, what I couldn't see on the other side of the screen. Finally my screen dinged. I don't know what I'd do without you.

Carry on, my love.

What?

Read it again. The words are still on the screen.

That's all you can say? Just go on?

Yes. Go on. There are no other choices. That's what I did. It's what we all do when we lose people. Keep living.

That's not fair.

Life isn't fair. I thought you'd figured that out a while ago.

Shut up!

Easy enough, I wrote dryly.

I can't believe you're just accepting this.

(Are you?)

What am I supposed to do? I wrote.

Fight!

Who?! I pounded out on my screen. What? I would give anything for the ability to even know what this was. But it isn't anything. It's just an end.

(And you've been living on borrowed time as it is,) 42 whispered.

I don't believe that. We could find something. Look for new doctors. Maybe we could, I don't know … buy you some time.

I blinked at the screen. You mean stasis, don't you.

It couldn't hurt. You'd be safe.

Anyone else would have been shocked that she'd even suggested it. Of all people in the world, Rose had to know the harm that prolonged stasis could cause. But I knew how Rose thought. She had grown up thinking the abuse normal. Though she was now of the opinion that the forcible stasis against her will was indeed a terrible thing, she still couldn't see the horror that was continued suspended animation, as the world carried on without you, and you were held back and back and back. It seemed a tool to her, sinister only in certain applications. Of course, despots think of torture as a tool, also.

I tried to be gentle. Rose. I love you. I do. But I'd rather die.

Don't say that!

Rose.

Now you read these words. I'm not going to let you just die!

Rose, do you think you have any choice? You can't control whether people live or die.

She didn't answer.

Rose?

There was no response. None at all. After a few minutes the link cut out automatically. She'd turned off her screen.

Hurriedly, I scrabbled on my bedside table for my cell. I rarely used the thing, considering I couldn't talk, but it had its uses. It was preprogrammed to respond to some of the noises I could make. I summoned Rose's cell number with a low whistle, but she didn't answer. Coit, I had to make this better! I brought up Bren with a different tune. Bren answered a second later. A hologramatic image of his head looked surprised as I held it in my hand. 'Otto, what's up?'

I brushed the sign of an 'R' by my cheek, which was the abbreviation for Rose's name. 'You need Rose?'

I nodded. His image shifted as he started walking. 'What's wrong? Her screen not working?' I shook my head, but I couldn't get much more detailed than that. Finally, I heard the sound of a knock as Bren arrived at Rose's condo.

After a minute Bren's face disappeared as he slid the cell into his hand to talk to his grandfather. 'Can I see Rose?'

I could hear the old man's voice distantly over the tiny speaker. 'I'm afraid Rose is a bit ill right now, Bren.'

After a pause Bren asked, 'Can I help?'

'In this case, I think not,' Xavier said. His voice was grim. 'But I'll tell her you came by.'

Bren hesitated, then said, 'Yeah. Thanks, Granddad.'

The door closed, and Bren's image returned in my hand. 'Okay, what's wrong?'

All I could do was look helpless.

'Rose was crying,' Bren said. 'I could hear her. She was nearly screaming.'

Oh, coit! My hands clenched and my eyes closed.

'Was she angry, or hurt?' Bren asked.

I shook my head.

'Screen, two minutes,' Bren insisted, and the cell blinked off. I felt ill myself. I couldn't explain this to Bren. Everything felt wrong, suddenly, as if the world was collapsing around me. Despite the fact that my entire body ached and I felt sick to my core, I threw my screen across the room and clambered out of bed.

I was dizzy for a moment, but I wasn't about to just sit here feeling like this. I could feel 42 in my mind, burning against my consciousness. Pushing me. Bren's chime dinged on my screen. I ignored it.

I'm not sure what manias overtook me, but I was suddenly very clear as I stood up out of that wretched bed. I felt dizzy, but there was no pain. I yanked monitors from my arms and chest and pulled plugs from walls so the machines wouldn't announce the disconnection. If I was lucky, I'd have about ten minutes before the nurse on duty noticed I was no longer on her monitor screen. I threw on clothes without checking to see if they were clean.

I opened the door and peeped out into the hallway. Everyone had moved back into the lab while I was sick. Quin's room was right across from me. He'd left his door open and the holovision on. Quin was asleep, but some actor was loudly and casually killing another actor about halfway up his wall. I was glad. The noise would cover my departure.

I'd done this before. Snuck out of the lab or the dorm at night, crept away from the safe place I was supposed to be. Sometimes I would go swimming, floating in the otherwise empty water in the pool at UniPrep, or even, if it was warm enough, at the manmade lake to the north of ComUnity, flickering through the instinctive minds of the fishes. Often I would flee up to the roof, try to find Jupiter in the stars. Europa was too far away to see without a telescope, but Jupiter was usually pretty easy to spot. But I wasn't well enough to swim, and I didn't want the solitude stargazing lent me. I knew I wouldn't be alone no matter what I did.

42 was whispering in the corner of my mind. Maybe she was the one driving me. I don't know.

She used to do this, years ago. 42 would frequently sneak out the window alone, or with 11, or with me. We'd flee down the street and across the park and under the hoverline past the bus depot, downtown. She'd even run away the night she died – it was mere chance they had dragged her back before it took her.

There was a club about twelve blocks away called the u*Night*ed. I walked alone in the moonlight, Rose's image burning in my mind. Rose was crying. And I couldn't comfort her ... because I was the one who was hurting her. I was dying.

There wasn't much vice in the controlled, gated ComUnity, but they were careful to keep enough avenues for trouble open to keep the 'inmates' happy. The u*Night*ed pulsed loudly by itself in the night, amidst shops and boutiques that closed carefully by sundown. It was late enough there was no line outside the club. The club mostly catered to the college age interns who worked for UniCorp, but the youth from all corners came and went, entering and exiting as if the club breathed them like oxygen. The music pulsed like a heartbeat, shaking the ground, humming through my back. The club a single animal, a growling beast, the only thing alive in the night.

There was a man checking ID at the door. This was no problem. 42 had pulled this off even when she was thirteen. She took hold of his hand and told him it would be okay. I didn't have a voice, but I knew how to do it. It was a different doorman, of course, than the one three years ago. He didn't recognize me, and started when he saw my skin in the harsh light by the door, but I grabbed him and stared into his mind.

'It's all okay. Let me in.'

He was tired, and not exactly sober, and the bass dazed his internal equilibrium. It was not at all hard to push his mind. He let me pass.

Six months ago, I'd have felt guilty about this. I would never have pushed another person's mind or read anything they didn't want me to see. I would never have told anyone what I saw there. Since I'd known Rose, my sense of ethics had become a little skewed. What I wanted and what Rose needed seemed so much more important than clearly defined rules of ethics and morality. 42 had never had such compunction – she was angry, like Quin, and willing to use any advantage her biology gave her. I hadn't made any decisions about what was or wasn't right until after she had died. I hadn't had to – she took care of all that for me. Once she was gone, I needed to figure a lot of things out. I had created a persona with a deep code of ethics and a strong sense of self – and all of that was slowly eroding, breaking away like the shoreline.

I dove into the sea of people, the music rattling my swollen brain, rolling through my exhausted body. The lights were dim and twisted with colour, strobing and dancing with the music. No one could make out faces, let alone complexion. Those around me were intoxicated with alcohol and nicohol and the sexual excitement of each other. The music drowned out all sound but itself, so there was no speech. No one would notice I could not talk. I went from an Eepie to a nobody the moment I walked through the door. No wonder 42 had been drawn here. You couldn't feel your impending death when you were a part of all this life. I closed my eyes and plunged on to the dance floor. I held my hands out. Bodies danced against me, and minds flowed through my head – drunken minds, empty minds, excited minds, frightened minds, hungry minds. All of them charged and activated by the music and the lights and the pushing crowd of people.

I knew why 42 had come here the night she died. The knowledge was too much, the terror. I needed to be part of everyone else, to leave my body and my thoughts behind, to become one with the whole. I let the music take me. My body pulsed with it, pounding, raging, tearing my way through the music as if I could break it apart. My eyes were closed, and amidst the muddled sea of people I could feel 42, almost feel her hands on my back, or dragging me through the crowd by my forearm. Her mind hummed inside mine, activated by the addled minds of everyone around me. I could barely hear the music anymore. Just the bass, pounding again and again inside me. The decibels in the club were stronger than were safe, anyway. Eepies tended to be hypersensitive – when I was younger and 42 had snuck me in here I'd worn earplugs. If I didn't have any, I'd make them out of damp napkins. I didn't care tonight. I wanted to go deaf. I wanted to go blind. All my senses, taken away. If I were to die, I could be washed away in this throng, swallowed by the beast, fade into a hundred intoxicated lives.

Rose was still there, though. Pure and perfect, her white rose petal skin, her sunshine hair, those dark, fathomless eyes, her burning, thorny, spiralling mind. Crying, because she was about to lose me. Like she had lost everything else. Her time, her whole world.

'I'm dying!' I told everyone around me. *'I'm dying!'*

Some of the throng dissipated, frightened by the disconnected thought that I had pushed through the sea of people. But many more danced more wildly, crying out in the night, dragging themselves into life, pulling me with them. People who had never met before clutched each other on the dance floor. Couples kissed. Some did more than kiss. I wasn't paying attention. My time was ticking away. Rose was beyond reach – even if I could have won her, I wouldn't have time. I wasn't going to have the time. And 42 breathed down my neck, dancing in the throng, as real and present a creature as all these bodies around me. She ate up all the life that they were shedding like old skin. The ghost of her made herself into a real person again, just so long as they surrounded me.

Then I saw her. Not in a fever dream behind my eyes, or an imagined glimpse behind everyone else's writhing bodies. There she was, her blue skin dark in the strobing lights, her hair a midnight cloud. For two seconds I was scared, until I realized I'd called her. This was it. I was never going to have the time to win Rose, and I had gone here to find 42. She would take me with her. Take me back down into death. I held my hands out to her, and she grabbed them, pulling me from the throng of people. She pulled me out of the sea of minds and into the corridor. Once I was free of everyone, I sagged against her, drained.

The mind holding me wasn't 42. It was Tristan.

I pulled away, but she held me fast. *'No you don't!'* She told me, and took me by the wrist. I was too exhausted to fight her. My mind was still a whirling pulse of sound. I had no idea how she'd managed to follow me in.

The answer to that mystery stood by the door, the doorman's throat held in his grip like a slaughtered chicken. I don't know what Quin was muttering at the poor man, but I could tell he thought Quin was the devil. Quin's angry face relaxed when he saw me with Tristan, and he let go of the doorman. 'Thank you for your cooperation,' he said with feigned politeness.

'Burn it, noid!' the doorman said. 'What planet did you spring from?'

'This one,' Quin snapped, 'but we haven't been sprung yet. Is he okay?' he asked Tristan.

Tristan nodded. *'He's dazed,'* she signed. *'Let's get him in the skiff.'*

I was dragged, unprotesting, to a hoverboat on the road. I tripped on the red and yellow curb and fell through the open door. I hadn't touched a drop of alcohol, but the minds of everyone around me had left me easily as intoxicated. Suddenly the darkness in my mind was broken by space and light and the scent of tea rose. I opened my eyes. Rose leaned over me like the vision of an angel. I wanted to kiss her. She read the impulse, either in my mind or in my eyes, and she pulled away, biting her lips. I sighed, and curled up on the floor of her limoskiff, hugging myself. Quin and Tristan clambered in behind me and folded themselves into the seats. 'Let's get him back,' Quin said.

I wanted to shake my head. I wanted them to take me back to the club, where I could let everyone else drag me away – even into death, I didn't care. Suddenly I felt Rose's arms around me again. She kissed my forehead. 'Don't,' she whispered. How she saw me pulsed in my head, painful and twisted by Rose's briar vision. I was hollow eyed and grey and sweating. My control was gone. I had been moaning quietly. 42 was laughing at me. I wasn't sure what I was going to do, and I didn't trust myself. I looked at Rose. *'I think you'd better let me go,'* I thought, very distinctly.

She blinked, but pulled away. She turned to Quin and Tristan. 'I need you to drop me off first. Can you get him home on your own? I have to get back to Unicorn before Xavier knows I've gone.'

'Yeah,' Quin said. 'Thanks for lending us the skiff. We'll send it back to you when we're done.'

'No trouble.' She looked down at me. 'Is he going to be all right?'

Tristan nodded. *'He's scared,'* she signed.

Rose looked worried. 'I am, too,' she said. She crept down onto the floor with me and looked into my eyes. 'I'm sorry,' she whispered. 'I …' Tears leaked from her eyes. 'I don't see stasis the same way everyone else does. I never did. It was always how I dealt with problems, I didn't mean for you to—'

I had to shut her up. I leaned my head forward and kissed her on the mouth. It was innocent, just a peck, but it shocked her from her self torment. Her lips were very soft. Her forest pool eyes poured over me. She swallowed, and leaned in close to my ear. 'I'm not going to let you die. Do you hear me? It's not going to happen!'

I closed my eyes. With the heat of her breath on the side of my neck, I didn't care if I died. 42 had been chased away by Rose's kiss, and I was again alone in my mind. I grabbed Rose tightly, and she gasped. I don't know what I was thinking. I think I wasn't. I was just open, and what she saw was *me*. All of me. She started trembling. After a second or a century, Quin pushed us apart. 'We're here. Now leave!' he snapped at her.

Rose did, without another word.

The door slid closed, and Quin glared at me. 'Lie down!' he barked. 'And stay there!' He pushed me onto the floor of the skiff and held me there, his blood boiling. I tried to get up. He held me down with his knee. 'Lab!' he snapped at the skiff. It beeped 'uncertain destination.' 'E.P. Laboratories!'

The skiff hummed and skimmed off. My eyes were closed, so I missed most of the silent scuffle that followed as Tristan and Quin argued. I could only hear Quin's replies. 'I'm busy just now. Can I ignore you later?' 'I'm not going to break him, I'm just going to bend him a little.' 'What do you expect me to do? Let him kill himself? That's my job!' Finally, Tristan dragged him off me, and I curled back up into my ball. 'Fine,' Quin snarled. 'Let him die. I hate him anyway.' This was followed by only a grunt, as he dismissed whatever it was Tristan signed in reply to this.

chapter 5

Fortunately, I didn't have to deal with the repercussions of my escape. There's a certain advantage to dying – no one thinks it's fair to punish you. Dr Svarog, however, seemed disapproving as he looked me over. I ignored him, staring into the ceiling as if I could see through it to the stars above. Ultimately he sedated me.

As the sedative worked its way through my system, I kept thinking of that kiss I had dropped on Rose. I had been very out of it. I would never have done such a thing otherwise. Not that I hadn't thought of it. I thought about it every night when I went to bed. Every evening was an exercise in self-restraint as I imagined touching Rose's white throat, kissing her soft red lips, feeling her fingertips against my skin. She helped me sleep.

But lately, it had been frustrating to 42, who surged up out of my subconscious before the sedative took hold. She hovered there, in my mind, exuding disapproval. I didn't want her there. I loved her, but I could never fully forgive her for dying on me.

'*You burning sped,*' she told me before I passed out.

'You burning sped,' Rose said as I opened my eyes.

That seemed to be the consensus. Quin, 42, now Rose. I blinked at her. She was sitting by my bed in the light from the window, working on her sketchbook. I sat up a bit. My head pounded, but not too badly. She set her sketchbook down on the chair and went to me. I glanced at the book – she was sketching my sleeping form.

She knelt by my bedside and took hold of my hand. *'You scared me to death!'* she told me silently. It was a very spiky thought, but I let her pierce me. I deserved it.

'Sorry.'

'Quin tells me this has been building for weeks.'

I was more surprised that Quin was willing to talk to her at all than that he had told her that, specifically.

'Probably years,' I pointed out. *'I've been living on borrowed time since the eighth grade.'*

She frowned. She was unconvinced. 'Your doctors thought that you had already gone through it,' she said. 'And came out unscathed.'

I shook my head. *'That wasn't me. That was 42. I just went with her.'*

'Then why did it take so long for you to react, if all the others died that year? And why is Tristan okay?'

I didn't know. I sent her one huge, long uncertainty attached to half a dozen theories and a dozen possibilities branching off each one, finally ending in a baffling and unanswerable *?????????*

She sighed and let go of me. 'Xavier and I spent all of yesterday looking for a solution.'

I frowned. All of yesterday? *'How long have I been out?'* I signed.

'The sedatives wore off yesterday afternoon, but you've been sleeping since then.' She glanced up at the monitor above my head. I felt the wires on my scalp and I knew it was monitoring my brain waves. These had let her know I wasn't dying, so she let me sleep. With a resigned tug I pulled the wires from my head. The machine beeped angrily, and finally went silent.

'Sorry about those,' Rose said. 'I didn't feel like stopping them.'

I nodded that I didn't blame her.

'I'm sorry about the stasis thing,' Rose said.

'I understand,' I signed to her.

'I just thought … it would buy you time to find a cure. I didn't think …'

I gently took her hand. *'I do understand,'* I told her. *'That wasn't the problem. Please try to understand about this. I'd be in there forever. There is no cure for "There shouldn't be anything wrong."'*

Her next thoughts surprised me no end. *'There might be.'*

I let go of her hand, blinking. She grinned at me. 'There's nothing Xavier can't solve. He's brilliant, and so are his kids. You know Bren's mom is head designer in the graphics department. Well, his Uncle Ted is actually a scientist, and he went up to Europa a few years ago to study the signalling … thing … that the M9 microbes do. And how to keep them alive. Xavier's been in contact with him since I told him you were sick.'

'Why?' I signed.

'Because I wanted you better.'

I knew for a fact that communications to Europa were usually sent on a weekly feed, rather than a continuous stream. The only continuous messaging system to Europa was the emergency feed. Jamal always had to wait to hear about anything from his family, except for the time he'd disappeared and they had to inform Captain Jagan that his son might be dead. Jamal had only skipped out to the beach with some college friends without telling anyone, but that was the only time I had ever heard of a communication outside of the weekly package. Xavier Zellwegger was pulling some serious strings even talking to his son.

'What's he say?'

'Well, he studies the microbe itself. He's been trying to keep it alive, so they can study it on Earth. You know they won't survive in a tank. Well, apparently, he's managed to extend their life spans with low level electro impulses, echoing the currents in the natural ocean. They *think* that your problem might be a flaw in your cellular communication. Like you're not getting the right signals or something.'

I nodded and took her hand. '*They've always thought that. It hasn't done them any good. They can't turn Earth into Europa.*'

'Which is why Ted wants you up there,' Rose said. 'He thinks the team on the *Minos* might be able to figure out something. They're the ones who created you, really. It's a risk, and Dr Svarog thinks we're nuts. But it's a chance, right? So ... do you think you want to go?'

I blinked. Wait a minute. Send me to Europa? Were they really thinking it? I didn't think they could cure me, not really. But to escape Earth, to travel to Jupiter, to see the moon of my origin ...! My heart beat a little faster in my chest, and I hoped it didn't mean I was going to be dead in a minute. My hands were shaking as I signed, *'You mean it?'*

Rose only looked confused, so I grabbed both her hands with me. *'Are you serious?'*

Rose closed her eyes as the immense joy I felt poured into her head. It was almost painful to her. I pulled away.

'Sorry,' I signed.

'It's okay, I know,' Rose said, though her voice was a little shaky. Then she looked up at me and laughed. 'I have *never* seen you look this happy.'

I realized I was smiling – really smiling, my expressionless face twisted of its own accord into a sunny grin.

'I take it this means you want to go?'

I lay back down on the bed, wordless with excitement.

'You realize this is experimental, right?' she said. 'We have no idea if this trick of Ted's will even work, and—'

I stopped her with a hand on her arm. *'Rose. It's Europa. Procedures or not, I don't care. There could be nothing there but ice and an oxygen unit, I'd still want to go.'*

Rose grinned. 'I guess I'll tell Xavier to make the arrangements.' She stood up. 'There's a colony transport leaving from Luna Base at the end of the week. I think we can go through the preliminary quarantine in that time.'

'*We?*' I signed.

'Of course. I'm going with you.'

I think a beam of sunlight might have passed through me at that point I was so happy. 'Xavier's been postponing a UniCorp visit to Europa, anyway. He was going to wait and send a delegation in another year or so, but he can do it himself.'

Even the knowledge that Xavier was coming with us did not dampen my spirits. '*You and me. At Europa.*'

'Mm-hm.' She kissed my forehead as she lay me back down. 'You get some rest and we'll start the legislation. I'll tell Dr Svarog to start your quarantine regime. He won't be happy about it.'

'*Why not?*' I signed.

Rose shook her head. 'He thinks stass might not be good for you, but I'll tell him not to worry. After all, it never killed me.'

chapter 6

'Be sure your head and genital shields are adjusted correctly,' said the disembodied mechanical voice. I checked my lead-lined shorts one more time, blindly. I couldn't see anything. My entire head was encased in an opaque helmet, and I was deeply glad of it. I had no desire to arrive on Europa bald, or sans eyelashes. Then I took the spread-eagle position the helmet directed me to take.

There was a hum and a blast of air. The helmet flashed a sign telling me to lift first my left and then my right foot. Finally, the disembodied voice politely told me that the irradiation process was complete, and asked me to step out of the irradiation chamber to the next stage in the systematic disinfection process.

So far in the last hour I'd been scrubbed, spritzed, sprayed, flayed and even had my eyelashes combed. Apparently they were removing from my body every single microscopic bacteria they could. My body must have been a site of micro-carnage. My eyelash mites had been eradicated and the bacteria on my elbows had been the victims of genocide. They had disinfected parts of my body that I couldn't even reach. The disinfection process required to board the moonliner to Europa was the crowning culmination of the flurry of activity I'd had to suffer through the last week.

I had spent a great deal of the last week just trying to hold my head together – literally. First they'd started me on an intense antibiotic and inoculation regime, to ensure that I wouldn't carry any undesirable diseases up to Luna. The medicines made me ill. (Of course they would have to, with my luck.) I had an allergic reaction to the first set, and they had to change the formula to work with my weird biology. The inoculations made my headaches worse – I think. My headaches were worse, anyway, and growing worse by the day. It might have been the stress. I underwent a lot of stress.

Bren came to see me the day after the trip was confirmed. 'I hear you're going to see my Uncle Ted,' he said. 'Congratulations, Otto. I know you've always wanted to go.' He reached forward and took my hand. He was optimistic, but worried.

Rose came in behind him then – they'd come to see me together. 'The paperwork came through, we're on. We'll give Ted your love, Bren,' she said.

Bren, who was still touching me, was suddenly horrified. 'We?' he asked. 'You're not seriously telling me you're going too.'

Rose looked taken aback. 'Of course, we,' she said. 'You didn't think I was going to send Otto halfway across the solar system on his own, did you?'

Bren let go of me abruptly, so I couldn't read his thoughts as he said, 'I didn't think you were going. Whose idea was that?'

'Mine,' Rose said indignantly. 'It's my company, my moon-liner, my patent – sorry Otto – and frankly Europa is pretty much my colony. It's high time I started exploring the different aspects of UniCorp, if only so I can know who to delegate to.' She smiled. 'Xavier agreed. He said since he had to go, it was only right that I get to come, too.'

'Has to go?' I signed.

Rose glanced back at me. 'What was that?'

'Why does Granddad have to go?' Bren asked for me.

'Colony protocol,' Rose said. 'Otto's under eighteen, he needs a legal guardian with him on Europa. That means someone from UniCorp, and ultimately it means me. And Xavier's *my* guardian, so that means both of us.'

Bren stared at her. 'You're going willingly back into stasis. Again.'

I looked down. This was something I'd been worrying about too. Rose shook her head at him. 'Xavier and I are both going,' she said. 'It's not stasis, it's interplanet travel.'

'But all interplanet travel has to be done in stass,' Bren said. 'You know that, right?'

Rose sighed, annoyed. 'Of course I know that,' she said. 'The shipping weights would be impractical otherwise. Food, oxygen—'

'But you're going back into stasis,' Bren said. 'Can your body take it?'

That thought hadn't occurred to me, though it should have. I'd been worried about the psychological implications, and I had decided that since Xavier and I were both going it wouldn't be such a strain on her. But physically, Rose had only barely recovered from the worst of her stass fatigue.

'Of course it can,' Rose snapped. 'They wake the passengers up every month to prevent stass fatigue.'

'But compounded with your history—'

'Shut up!' Rose said. 'Can't you see you're ruining this? Otto finally gets to go to Europa, and he gets to take a friend with him. Isn't that what's important here?'

She was talking over me, of course, but I'm used to that. I kept my hands still. I didn't want to get in the middle of this conversation. Bren was right, but then, so was Rose.

'It's going to be great,' Rose reassured both Bren and me. 'Otto will get to see Europa, Xavier will get to see your Uncle Ted and his kids, and I'll get to see how the colonies operate. It's a win-win-win.'

Bren was looking at her strangely.

'What?' Rose finally asked.

'You realize I'll be older than you when you get back, right?'

Rose kept her expression neutral, but her face went white.

'The world will have kept on turning without you,' Bren pressed. 'Me, Mom, Kayin and Hilary, the school year, your counsellor, Otto's sisters, Quin. We'll just keep going on without you. You're okay with that.'

I reached over and took Bren's arm. *'Enough,'* I told him. *'Stop torturing her. She doesn't let herself think that way.'*

'She's an idiot!' Bren thought at me, and snatched his arm away. 'She *needs* to think that way.'

'Look at her!' I signed.

Rose was crying.

Bren immediately looked chagrined. 'Oh, coit, I'm sorry.' He went up to her and hugged her. 'Hey. Don't cry, I'm sorry.'

'The travel time is only five months,' Rose said against his shoulder. 'The rest of the time I'll be awake on Europa. It's not the same!'

'No,' Bren said gently. 'I guess it's not.'

She pulled away from him. 'I don't understand you. You want to send Otto out there alone?'

Bren looked at me. 'No,' he said quietly.

Rose held her head for a moment, then brushed her tears away brusquely. 'I'm going to tell Quin and the others,' she said. 'The good news.'

Bren nodded as she went.

I shook my head at Bren in disapproval.

'What?' he asked.

I raised an eyebrow.

'Oh, come on. You know she won't stand up for herself. Someone has to think about what's best for her. She sure as squitch won't.'

I looked away, down at the corner. Bren touched my arm. *'That's how her parents used to think,'* I told him.

'That's not fair,' Bren said. 'I'm actually worried about *her*, not her standing or her appearance. She never thinks about herself.'

'I always liked how Rose thinks about others first,' I told him.

'That's 'cause you're crazy about her.'

I rolled my eyes. Noid, did everyone know?

'Yes,' Bren said.

I covered my purple blush with my hand. Bren quietly sent me another thought. *'Bit late now, isn't it?'*

He didn't think I was going to make it.

'No. I don't,' he said quietly. He pulled his hand away and looked down at the floor. 'I think it's worth the shot, though. For you. But I'm not sure this is what's best for her. It might be what she thinks she wants, but Granddad … I mean, he'll give her anything. He won't argue with her. It's a good thing she's obedient and docile, 'cause she could be throwing wild parties every night and maxing out half of UniCorp's credits if she wanted. He wouldn't stop her.'

'You don't approve,' I signed.

'Granddad hasn't been himself since she came,' Bren said. 'He's moody. Mom worries about him.'

'Rose isn't a problem, is she?'

'No, she's sweet. Everyone loves her. Mom, Hilary, everyone.' He looked down and rubbed his temples. 'But she causes problems. Without ever meaning to. Legal problems, social problems. If she wasn't going to be the most powerful woman in the world in about four years it wouldn't be such a trouble, but it is. It's hard being her friend.' He looked at me. 'I don't know how you can stand it. Looking every day at all that pain she won't let herself see. It's exhausting.'

'Only if you care,' I signed.

'I do care. I wish I didn't. It's like she *made* me care about her, without ever saying a word.' I looked confused, and Bren shook his head. 'You weren't there. You have no idea how she looked coming out of stasis.'

I knew how it had felt. Rose had shown me. I squeezed Bren's hand. *'Show me.'*

Bren blinked, and then let himself remember. The dim, abandoned smell of the sub-basement he had found her stass tube in; the horror as he discovered there was a body in the tube; the fear that he'd done something wrong and killed the occupant. Then Rose – impossibly thin, inhuman, almost insectoid, her skin pale as a grub, her hair brittle as spun glass, her eyes darting around, unable to focus. Her skull, so clear beneath the fleshless skin, her eyes bulging from sunken sockets. Then the weak, pitiful sound of her scream after Bren had told her how long she'd been asleep. The horror of her collapse, as he again thought he'd killed her. The moment of indecision, which was no choice in the end, as he picked her up in his arms to take her away from that dank hole. The thick chemical floral scent of her, her hair, her clothes, saturated with the dizzying perfume of stasis. The bone-thin weight of her as he carried her unconscious body up to his mother. At the time he had done it all with detached efficiency, no conscious emotion, but Rose's skeletal form still haunted his dreams sometimes. He pulled his hand away – he hadn't meant to tell me that.

'I should have left her there and gone to get help,' he said instead. 'The doctors should have been the ones to get her out of the tube. She was so frail I might have hurt her, carrying her. But I couldn't. She was so small and so alone, all alone in the dark … I couldn't leave her alone again. I just couldn't.' His eyes were unfocused, deep inside the memory.

I stared at Bren. This was something I hadn't really taken into account. He truly had rescued her that day, more than anyone could ever know but him and Rose. He might not admit it, but her very existence had changed his life, his whole view of himself and the world in which he lived. I wasn't at all surprised she had fallen in love with him.

'It was awful,' Bren said unnecessarily. 'And to top it all off, she won't blame them. Her ... *parents.*' I could tell he thought using that word for them was insulting to parenthood. 'I mean, I hate them, and I never even met them. Anyone who would do that to their daughter ... All three of their kids. Did you know, she thinks there's two more Fitzroy kids out there, slowly dying in stass tubes?' I did know this. 'But she won't let anyone say anything bad about them. It doesn't matter that they neglected her and kept her ignorant and sentenced her to a slow death by stass fatigue and sent a Plastine to assassinate her. She keeps coming up with reasons why they might have done all that. She insists they weren't malicious.'

'I know,' I signed. It was quite a trying trait of hers. She'd written me long treatises on how nice her mom really was, and that her dad wasn't that bad, really, and how they probably meant to let her out of stasis, they just ... That was where her rationalizations always fell down. It was easier in person. I could move her rationalizations out of the way and remind her how she really thought of them in a way she couldn't deny. But Bren didn't have that outlet, so he had to hear it all and just keep his mouth shut.

'Granddad says you have to just let her do it. It's what abuse victims do. They waver back and forth between love and hate like tennis balls, long after you think they should know better. He says she loved them, and she misses them. Then his face twists, and he says he knows how hard it is, and you *know* he does. You can just see that he grew up with it. It's like she's torturing him. And she's not doing anything wrong, she just *is*.' He shook his head. 'And then she looks at me, with those old eyes of hers, and it feels so weird ...'

'She loves you.'

'Yeah, how?' Bren asked, annoyed.

'She doesn't know.'

He held up a hand, exasperated. 'I know. And I *don't* love her, not like you do. But she needs looking after. And I don't know if she'll get it on Europa, not with you sick and Granddad like he is.'

I reached out and took Bren's arm. *'She's stronger than she looks,'* I told him. *'Have faith in her.'*

'I do,' Bren said. 'That's what worries me.'

And the history of UniCorp came pouring through his head, a thousand callous takeovers and economic assassinations and corporate slaughters and everything that had made UniCorp the most powerful, and most dangerous, corporation in history. 'Her father did all that. I've seen the holovids. And there are times she's just like him. I don't know if you've seen it, 'cause she tends to be gentle around you. If there's something she doesn't like, something she thinks needs to be set right, her eyes get hard and she'll say something – something so cold. She lived through everything they did to her, and she denies it. If she can deny that, what else could she be deluded over?' He stared at me. 'She was actually considering stassing you without your permission. Did you know that?'

'Yeah, I guessed. She doesn't see it the same way we do.'

'Well, that's her all over. If she doesn't want to see something, she won't let herself. In five years ... she has the power to do anything. And she could. She could be the best thing that ever happened to this world. Or she could be corrupted and become a total despot.'

'I wouldn't worry about her.'

Bren shook his head. 'You're as much an innocent as she is. It's a whole different *world*, Otto, literally. You say you only like people who are willing to expand their minds, well expand this. The colonies ... are not nice places. I know you've been dreaming about going to Europa forever, but I also know you don't know what that means. No one down here ever looks at it, but it's all still pre-Dark-Time mentality out there. Major class segregation, absolute dictatorship, utterly unregulated scientific experimentation, oxygen taxes and Plastines and genetic manipulation and terrorists and ... all those things no one likes to talk about.' His eyes were dark. Clearly he thought about it a lot, whether he spoke about it or no.

'That was why my uncle went there,' Bren said. 'Because things there were so chaotic, the reports from the scientific community were being corrupted. He went up there to stop that. And to get away from his ex-wife, but that's not the point. Rose is ... fragile. Seeing all of that could do things to her,' he finished. 'I don't think she should go.'

'She knows things she doesn't realize she knows,' I told him. *'You should have faith in her. She doesn't say everything she thinks.'*

'Then what kind of a leader could she possibly be?'

'You can't separate Rose from her position,' I realized. *'I see the person. You see the princess.'*

'I was raised at the epicentre of UniCorp politics,' Bren pointed out. And I had been raised isolated in a lab, he didn't say. But it was there. 'I have to see the princess. And that's just the thing. Everyone else will, too. Once it gets out that "The Fitzroy" herself is on her way to Europa, all hell is going to break loose up there. The Fitzroys founded the place! It's like getting a visit from Caesar. And you know what happened to him.'

'You make it sound like the whole moon is about to explode,' I told him silently. *'There comes a point where the chaos becomes the status quo. I know Europa isn't perfect; I live with Jamal, remember? But I also know that it's perfectly safe if you know where you're going.'*

'Nothing is perfectly safe,' Bren said. 'Not even here. If a Plastine assassin can go after Rose here, in ComUnity, how much danger do you think she'll be in if she goes off to the colonies?'

I frowned. *'Wait a minute. Are you worried* for *her, or worried* about *her? Make up your mind.'*

'Can't I worry about everything?'

I was incredulous. *'Since when do you worry about anything at all?'* I asked. *'Nothing's ever mattered to you but tennis.'*

'No,' Bren said, and he sounded annoyed. 'Everything matters. It would *all* matter too much to me if I let it. I'd go crazy. It shouldn't be my job to save the world.'

'It's not your job to save Rose either,' I said. *'Look, what's going to happen is going to happen. She learned how to make her own decisions, and this is one.'*

Bren's mind darkened. He hadn't realized when she learned to become a whole person that his influence with her would fade. He couldn't decide if he was glad or not.

'Don't let it end like this. Take her down for a game or to the art gallery. Don't let her go with you two at odds.'

'I know, O Wonderful Counsellor,' Bren said. 'I'll make it up to her.' He took a deep breath. 'Still don't think she should go.'

'You could come, too.'

'Mom wouldn't let me. She misses Uncle Ted something awful, and Granddad raised her with a dim view towards stasis. She wouldn't let her only son have bits of his childhood snatched like that. That's how she'd see it.'

I wasn't surprised.

Bren looked down at me. 'I'm gonna miss you,' he said earnestly. 'Both of you. Coit, I hope this works, and you'll come back better. Take care of her, okay?'

'I thought I was the sick one.'

'I'm going to tell her the same thing,' Bren said standing up. 'Hopefully you can take care of each other without my help.'

'Prince Charming,' I signed at him.

'Oh, shut up,' Bren snapped, but he was grinning as he left.

Dr Bija came to see me for one final session before I left. We both knew it would probably be the last time I saw her. I had plenty to tell her. The day before I had had my Bon Voyage party, and it hadn't been pretty. I'd managed to get myself dressed and upright, managed to look happy and excited about my trip. Everyone was there – school was about to start and Wil and Anastasia had come back from their vacations. But we had to have the party at the lab. Then Nabiki guessed almost instantly that I was not well.

'What happened?' Dr Bija asked.

She freaked, I wrote to her. Dr Bija couldn't understand much sign, and she didn't want to do all of our sessions in my head – she said it wasn't clear enough – so I wrote out my responses on my notescreen. Usually I won't do this for people. If they're too unpleasant for me to touch, and too ignorant or stubborn to learn sign language, I'd rather not talk to them at all. But I'd started showing Dr Bija some of my journal entries, and it became very natural to write her letters. **I suppose I should have guessed she'd know. She's known for so long.**

'Yes. Nabiki has been a very important part of your life, and you of hers. What do you mean by "freaked"?'

She started screaming at me, I wrote. She said she hated me, and she called Rose a bitch, and threw a chair. I tried to get up to stop her, but I was dizzy, and I staggered when I stood up, and she kind of ... sobbed. I've never seen Nabiki look like that. All that was strong in her was just gone. She ran out, and Quin followed her. To my horror. I mean, of all things to throw at her right then, Quin! No one deserves that.

'He's your brother.'

So I should know! I wrote, and Dr Bija chuckled. I tried to stop him, but I was too dizzy. I fell on the stairs, and Bren and Tristan had to help me back to bed. When I woke up it was too late. Quin was back. With a broken nose, I might add. At least he got what was coming to him. Too bad they fixed it. It's straighter than it was, his profile keeps surprising me. Poor Nabiki.

'Do you think she's going to be all right?'

I shook my head. I wrote her a letter. She hasn't responded, but I guess she doesn't have to. It was kind of a goodbye letter.

Dr Bija nodded. 'How did Rose respond to Nabiki?'

She cried. She was sorry. She's Rose.

'Will she be all right?'

I laughed fondly at the thought. She's Rose, I wrote again. Rose knows, I added. How I feel about her. She says she's always known.

Dr Bija smiled, and I knew she'd had known this all along, too. It's strange with the two of us having the same counsellor – she must find listening to us all quite the holonovella. 'Does that change things between you?'

A little, I admitted. Not enough.

'But she is going with you to Europa.' Dr Bija stayed in close contact with Dr Svarog, so she knew my general state of affairs – my job was usually only to tell her my state of mind.

Bren doesn't think it's a good idea for her to go.

'I think you should let Bren and Rose, and frankly me, worry about her. We're here to talk about you today.'

I smiled.

'For yourself, are you glad that Rose is going with you?'

More than you can possibly imagine.

'Would you like to show me?'

I touched her hand and did so. The hope and comfort the thought gave me, the excitement of the trip itself, the quiet, underlying terror of the journey which might well kill me. All of it. Dr Bija sucked in a breath and I toned my thoughts down. She was older than most of the people I touched regularly, and sometimes she found my mental exuberance a little overwhelming. It was always more intrusive to force my thoughts into the more crystallized minds of older people.

'Well. You are happy, then,' Dr Bija said.

I shrugged.

'Is there anything that is bothering you?'

I looked away, and then finally wrote it on my screen. 42's back.

'Back?' Dr Bija asked. 'You find yourself thinking of her a lot?'

No. She's back. Full force. Every snide comment, every arrogant laugh.

She waited for me to write more, but I wouldn't. 'All right. I'm surprised you haven't told me this before. How long has this been going on?'

I closed my eyes. I'm not sure, I wrote. Since this summer, I think, but I ignored her a lot. She's been getting louder slowly.

'Okay. So we're back to this. Two years ago it seemed very clear to you that this manifestation wasn't really 42. Have you reevaluated that assessment now?'

I shook my head, no.

'So do you think this voice in your head is really 42's soul?'

I shook my head again.

'So if it isn't ... if it's just a manifestation you've created of her ... why is she back now?'

I signed furiously, slapping my forehead in annoyance, *'I don't know! I don't KNOW!'*

She grabbed my wrist to keep me from injuring myself. She had been given strict instructions from Dr Svarog to keep me calm. I took a deep breath and tried to relax. Fortunately, Mina was an almost immediately relaxing personality. She let me go. 'Okay. Let's think about this.'

My personal neurosis was not something I liked to think about. It all started from thinking too much in the first place. After 42 died, I was alone and grieving. And somewhere out of my grief, 42's voice had risen out of my mind. At the time I had told myself that I had taken her spirit as she died. Rather than letting her die, I had taken her mind print into me, and I had become two people. It had been comforting. She wasn't really dead. In fact, I was never alone. She sat behind my eyes and watched everything that happened as if she were really there with me.

But after I began talking to Dr Bija, and finally admitted the existence of this 'other person' inside me, she had forced me to question it. Rather than question the existential possibilities of life after death where my telepathic powers were concerned – that was not her role as a psychologist, she said, and was more the role of a priest or a philosopher – she only asked me to question whether or not 42's presence in my mind was affecting me positively or negatively.

And I had been forced to admit that her presence had not been positive. The voice was angry and hopeless. It kept my grief fresh, and was making it difficult to form real friendships with my schoolmates – with Nabiki, for one.

Once I had come to my own conclusions that she was not helpful, I began to question whether she was really 42. I wanted it to be 42. I didn't want her to be dead. But finally, after a year of considering it, I realized that my own mind had formed through my entire childhood with the pattern of 42's mind continually in contact. 42 was gone, but the pathways she had formed in my mind were still there – and it was more likely that my own mind supplied the voice for it.

The day I realized this I'd cried in Dr Bija's office for an hour. It was as if 42 had died again – almost as if I had killed her. But after that, I felt relieved. 42's voice hadn't gone away immediately after that, but I stopped focusing on it very much. I didn't even notice when it finally faded altogether.

'When did she return?'

I swallowed. *'I really heard her properly after Rose's birthday.'*

'After your attack,' Dr Bija said. 'Why do you think this voice has manifested itself again now?'

'I don't know,' I signed again – gently, this time.

'What kinds of things does she say?'

I turned to my screen. Mostly she just laughs at me. Usually when I'm feeling sick, or someone is trying to be nice.

'Ah,' Dr Bija said.

She doesn't like Rose.

'Anything else?'

I could hear her right then, goading me. (*Go on. Tell her!*) She says I'm going to die soon.

'Do you think she's right?'

I could taste the tears in the back of my throat as I thought about this. I know she is.

'Do you think it's possible you think, somehow, that you need her to get through this troubling time?'

I shrugged. She says it's because I'm going to be like her soon, so I'm closer to her.

'Is that thought comforting, or troubling?'

I thought about this. Both, I admitted.

'Do you want to die?'

I don't have any control over that at this point. Unless you're advocating suicide.

'Never that,' Dr Bija said, only slightly humorously. 'So you don't want to die?'

I thought about this. If I am dying, and if death really is just a crossing over to some other plane, then ... I guess it's nice to think I won't be alone there.

'Do you feel alone here?'

Always.

'Even with Rose and your sisters and your friends?'

I looked down. I didn't need to write, sign or say it. It was clear my answer was yes.

'I wish I could help you, Otto,' Mina said. She usually didn't express her own feelings at all. I looked up at her, acknowledging her affection. 'Is there anything else you'd like to say?'

I took a deep breath and pulled up my screen. Finally, I wrote five simple words on it, right in the centre of everything. Five tiny, impotent words, screaming out with the voice I didn't have.

I don't want to die.

Dr Bija gently placed her hand on my wrist. *'I know you don't, Otto,'* she thought softly. 'I don't want you to, either.' Then she sighed. 'Maybe we're thinking about this the wrong way. Maybe you do only have a short time left. But you've always wanted to see Europa, haven't you? One of your lifetime goals is about to be accomplished. There are people who live their entire lives without achieving anything. It isn't the length of life – it's what you make of it.'

I know, I wrote. I can live no one's life but my own.

Dr Bija smiled, and that was the end of the session.

*

Right before I left I went to say goodbye to the simple ones. There were only six of them, and only half of them were intelligent enough to even understand I was leaving. It was always painful to visit the simple ones. Their blank faces and dull eyes did not inspire one with hope. But I managed to play a game of Go-Fish with Niney and Toseph (19 and 27) and Fifen (54) drew me a picture. Those three had an intellect about that of a four-year-old. None of the simple ones had been intelligent enough to select their own names, but their numbers had mostly degenerated into something resembling nomenclature. All of them received a farewell mindscape from me, even Three, in her large crib, who frankly didn't have much mental capacity beyond that of a newborn. I constructed a mental garden for them, something pretty with unicorns and flowers and fairies. They always loved it when I thought up pretty things for them. Fifen cried when she learned I wasn't going to be back for a long time. Toseph got angry and kicked me, but I'm used to that.

Quin and my sisters had been permitted to join me on my trip to the flight base on Luna, from which the moonliner to Europa would embark on its interplanetary journey. Luna was not as strictly regulated as the outer colonies, really only being a space-port off planet. Most earthly regulations were still in effect on Earth's moon. The journey there didn't require stasis, and only a moderate disinfection procedure, so many people travelled there on vacation, or to get a taste of colony life to see if they could endure it. Many people, they say, can't. There are all kinds of reasons why. Health concerns, gravity, nutritional deficiencies, sunlight, asthma. Human beings aren't really built to live anywhere but Earth.

I spent most of the time on Luna with a blinding headache. It had faded mostly on the morning of my ultimate departure, probably due to the huge number of drugs Dr Svarog had prescribed. I had waited, nervously, in the seated queue at the space-port, as first Xavier and then Rose had been bundled off to their final disinfection procedure. Then it was my turn. Tristan had a stranger snap a final photograph of all four of us. She and Penny had bid me a tearful farewell, and Quin carefully nodded at me, with a strange smile on his face. I stared at them, trying to memorize their faces, trembling.

I might never see them again.

Then I took a deep breath, closed my eyes, and stepped into the first disinfection chamber. Now it was over an hour later, and apparently I was finally disinfected enough to pass muster.

'Please lie on the couch for bacterial reintroduction,' the disembodied voice said sweetly.

I lay down on the cold plastic table – calling it a couch was far too charitable – and allowed mechanical arms to brush me on various parts of my body. According to the literature, they were reintroducing beneficial bacteria without which my body would be susceptible to dangerous infection. How anything that would infect me could have made it past the antiseptics and disinfectants and antibiotics and irradiation we all had to endure was beyond me, but apparently human beings – and close genetically modified cousins – could not easily function without *some* microscopic symbionts. They'd discovered this in the early days of colonization. We are not alone – we are each colonies of mites and microbes and bacteria, all functioning together to create a single entity.

So I was re-exposed to the *proper* kind of eyelash mites, the *appropriate* fingernail bacteria, and *right* sort of microscopic passengers. The disinfection protocol had been instigated during the plagues of the Dark Times, and had never been restructured.

Once I was properly reinfected, I was directed to collect my clothing and proceed through the final doors – and welcome to the moonliner *Daedalus*.

My clothing had faded and shrunk and gotten considerably more worn as it had gone through its own sterilization process, but Jamal had warned me about this. I put it back on, and it still fit well enough. I had to sit and wait for the dizziness to pass before I could go through the final doors. I'd had to do that quite a bit through this whole antiseptic odyssey. Dizzy, still a bit ill, and already missing my family so much I felt as if I'd been torn in half, I stepped through the doors and into the *Daedalus*.

'Hey,' said Quin. 'Took you long enough.'

chapter 7

I blinked in utter amazement. *'Quin!'* I signed, making the flicking sign for '5' that we signed as Quin's name.

'You recognized me. Good sign.'

'But what are you doing here?' I signed frantically.

'I'm coming with you,' Quin said, examining his fingernails. 'What, didn't I mention it?'

I glared at him. *'No.'*

He grinned broadly, his teeth showing white against his blue skin. We usually don't smile like that, so I knew he was doing it to annoy me. 'You need an interpreter,' Quin said smugly. 'Rose isn't good enough at sign, and you can't be expected to touch *everyone* on Europa.'

'But Rose …'

'Is shy, you know that,' Quin said, stopping me. 'You're not going to make her speak for you *all* the time, are you?'

I swallowed. Actually, even though Quin was an almost immediately annoying person, I was suddenly extremely glad he was going with me. *'But you didn't prepare. The antibiotics …'*

'Mr Zellwegger and I had this worked out days ago. I started the antibiotics when you did.' He shook his head. 'It was awful. It felt like something inside me died that day.'

I closed my eyes as I tried not to laugh. Laughing at Quin's jokes was one of the worst things you could do. It only encouraged him. Fortunately, I sound odd when I laugh, so

I'm quite used to suppressing it. *'Did the girls know about this?'* I asked instead.

'You're not the only one who doesn't talk,' Quin said with a wink.

'Where's Rose?'

'To your left at the passengers' dining lounge. Munching on a pre-stass special of the day.' He bowed dramatically. 'This way, my liege.'

Quin's royal sarcasm was well founded. The room in which the passengers to Europa were waiting to be taken to their designated stass chambers was opulent in the extreme. Luna base was made mostly out of radiation-shielded mudbrick, formed out of the lunar dust, and actually felt quite homey – almost tribal. It was quite utilitarian in design, and didn't add much in the way of frills or finery.

The moonliner, on the other hand, was luxurious. The light fixtures in this dining lounge appeared to be cut crystal. The ceiling held a detailed fresco depicting Daedalus with his mechanical wings soaring into the clouds away from the island of Minos. If you looked closely you could just see doomed Icarus, a tiny figure above him, flying too close to the sun. The walls were literally made of golden velvet. I touched one as I entered the lounge – my handprint stayed on the wall. I ran my fingers down it and left ploughed furrows. I was almost tempted to draw on it with my finger, but I smoothed it with the edge of my hand and the marks flowed invisibly back into the gold shine. Even going to UniPrep, I wasn't used to such luxury.

Rose laughed, and I realized she'd been watching me. I turned to look at her. I'd been too nervous this morning as we prepared to board the moonliner to really look at her carefully. I was still nervous, but now that Quin was going with me I found it somewhat easier to concentrate.

Rose was pale, and her eyes were shadowed with exhaustion. I knew that look – she hadn't slept well. She was prone to nightmares, and stress always brought them to the surface. But she was smiling. Her hair was dark, still damp from the disinfection wash, and held tightly back in a French braid. Her bronzed hair reminded me of our swim, and I found my eyes crinkling in a smile. 'I got you some fruit, and stuffed mushrooms,' Rose said. 'It's best to have a good meal in your stomach before a long stass. It makes recovery go faster.'

There were few animals and thus little meat on Luna, so the buffet mostly held vegetarian dishes. I wasn't hungry, and ate as little as Rose – who could never eat much. Quin loaded his plate with delectables and went back for seconds. I wondered how he could eat so much. *'Hey,'* he signed silently when I asked. *'If I'm going to die, I want to do it with a full stomach.'* His flippancy worried me. So Dr Svarog had illuminated the risks of stass to Quin, too.

We waited for nearly an hour while a few more passengers staggered in from the disinfection gauntlet and collapsed into dining chairs. Looking around I could see we were all universally exhausted. Something about that disinfection procedure just ate up our energy. Probably for the best, since we were about to go to sleep – sort of.

Finally we were called. 'Zellwegger, party of four?' said the steward at the end of the lounge.

The taste of iron flooded my mouth. This was it. I was about to be called into stasis … possibly into death.

'That would be us,' Xavier said quietly, and we all stood up.

My legs turned to water with fear. I'm afraid I staggered as I stood. Both Quin and Rose lunged for me, but Rose got to me first. She was terribly worried. *'I'm okay,'* I told her, but Rose was unconvinced. I couldn't hide my fear from her.

'What's wrong?'

I tried to keep Dr Svarog's fears suppressed and only said, *'Stasis. I don't know what to expect.'*

'Oh,' she said. She looked from Xavier to Quin and back to me. 'We had you scheduled to share a tube with Quin, but ...' She didn't say it, but she wondered if I'd rather travel with her.

I couldn't even find a word to express how much I would prefer that. Stay with Rose rather than spend the next forty minutes listening to Quin pontificate rudely? I was ecstatic. Rose laughed.

'I'll talk to Xavier about it,' she said, walking me towards the steward's desk.

I wondered if this meant Xavier would have to travel with Quin. 'No,' Rose told me, catching the thought. 'Xavier wouldn't let me get a double tube with him. He insisted on a single.'

I pulled my hand away quickly, but I caught something I wasn't supposed to; Xavier would not, under any circumstances, lie down in a tiny room alone with Rose. Rose, though she knew the reasons for this, was hurt.

'Are you coming?' Quin asked loudly. 'I know slime moulds who travel faster than you two!'

'Takes one to know one,' I signed at Quin, and he chuckled.

'So, we have you down for one double and two single berths,' the steward said, unconcerned with our banter. 'Your full names, please?'

'Xavier Ronald Zellwegger.'

'Rosalinda Samantha Fitzroy,' Rose said primly.

'EP Quin T. Essential and EP Octavius Sextus,' Quin said for me.

'He has to say it for himself,' the steward said without even looking up from his screen.

I clapped my hands at him and signed it for him. He stopped me before I was half done. 'Are you all right, sir?' the steward asked, horrified. 'Let me call the medical officer. Sometimes the disinfection process can cause unexpected reactions ...'

'Listen you semi-evolved simian—' Quin began.

'If you'll look on your records,' said Xavier, 'you will see that my two guests here are under special medical release. Their appearance is normal.'

The steward blinked, did a double take at Quin, flipped through pages on his screen, and finally conceded the point. I often got this kind of treatment if I travelled where people didn't expect to see me. I appeared somewhat cadaverous if you didn't realize what caused it. Quin was darker than me, so blue he was almost black, so in certain lights he could sometimes look normal. I had no such luck. 'If you two gentlemen will come this way then, please ...?' he began.

'Actually,' Rose said. 'Xavier? Would it be all right if Otto travels with me?'

Xavier looked at the two of us, and his shoulders sagged. I couldn't tell if it was disappointment or relief. 'Of course,' he said, but it sounded just as grim and formal as everything else he said.

'Meaning I get my own room?' Quin said with a raised eyebrow. 'Terrific.'

'Ahm ...' the steward looked about to protest.

'Surely there isn't any real problem?' Xavier asked.

'It's against policy ...' the steward said, and Xavier looked at him hard.

'Policy?'

One word; one cool, calm word, that was all it took. 'No,' said the steward quickly. 'No problem. Only I'd need to inform stass control and have the records shifted ... get the tubes recalibrated ...'

'Well. Do so, if you please.'

The steward hurried away, flushed, and I stared at Xavier. People feared him. People had obeyed the last leader of UniCorp, too, but the deference there was to the position. I hadn't paid too much attention to Bren's grandfather in the past, but now, due to Rose, I couldn't help but wonder over him. The respect he garnered had more to do with himself, his personality, than his role as UniCorp's CEO. I always knew he was powerful, but suddenly I came to the realization that this old man was dangerous ... in a way I wasn't sure I yet understood. I took Rose's hand again as my nerves overtook me.

It was a full ten minutes before the steward came back. 'I've arranged for the passenger transfer. If the four of you would follow Cheryl, please?' He gestured towards a powerfully attractive woman in a jacket with a great deal of braid. She stood very straight. Rose recognized that her face was bought – surgery and rejuvenants. I realized she was a higher rank than the steward. He had to have called her in. I wondered if she was the captain herself. If so, she wasn't saying.

We followed her down corridors of already closed stass tubes. We passed the glass-fronted circular doors at regular intervals, their various lights and monitors on the outside. These doors were quite large. There was an odd smell – a combination of flowers and commercial perfume, with an undertone of something acidic and chemical. It made me feel giddy. Quin sniffed. 'What is that?'

'Stass chemicals,' Rose said. 'Residuals. A more modern mix than I'm used to, though. The perfume is more subtle.' She took a deep breath. 'I approve, actually.'

'Gardenias,' Xavier said. 'I've made this run before. The *Daedalus* has been in operation for nearly twenty-five years – that's old, for a moonliner.'

Our guide stopped at an open door. 'This would be you, Miss Fitzroy. And your companion?'

'Otto,' Rose supplied for her. 'Otto Sextus.'

'Mr Sextus, if you and Miss Fitzroy would say your goodnights to the rest of your party, and take your places in the tube.'

I turned back to Quin. This was it. We might not ever wake up from this. Quin's face was impassive. 'See you in the morning, bro,' he said gruffly.

I wanted to hug him, but this was Quin. I settled for touching his shoulder, my thumb against his neck. He wasn't frightened. *'Quit cowering,'* he told me silently. *'If you die in the next half hour, you won't have to worry anymore, will you.'*

And deep in his consciousness I suddenly received a face. Quin was thinking of someone. It wasn't a face I remembered. One of us, but young, no more than five, the skin barely tinted blue. I thought Quin might have been remembering me as a child, but I wasn't sure. He pushed me out of his mind as he pushed my hand away – not ungently. 'Well, are you two finally going to sleep together or not?' Quin said, gesturing at me at Rose. 'What, you want me to watch? Move!'

I was too frightened even to blush. I signed *'goodbye'* and turned to enter the stass tube.

Rose was bright red, thanks to Quin. Xavier reached up and lightly touched the side of her face, brushing a tendril of hair off her cheek. He stared at Rose as she climbed up beside me. 'I'll be right here,' he said, taking hold of her hand.

'I swear, you're more worried about this than I am,' Rose said. 'Honestly. I'll be fine.'

Xavier couldn't shake the serious look from his face. 'I know,' he said quietly. He hugged her with one arm and lightly kissed her forehead. 'Rest well.' He smiled. 'I'll be here when you wake.'

Rose nodded and flung herself into the tube beside me.

'Right,' Quin said. He grinned lasciviously at the pretty official. 'I guess that means you get to take me to bed, now.'

An amusing mixture of emotions flashed over her face, ranging from annoyance to revulsion, with a healthy dollop of fear, all buried under the professional smile. 'Right this way, sir,' she said crisply. Quin winked at me as they left.

The door closed behind us, and we were alone, awaiting takeoff. I knew it could be anywhere from twenty minutes to near an hour. An hour of terror awaiting my possible demise ... It felt like the long walk on Death Row.

I turned to Rose. She looked right at home. Her blonde braid was drying, and she was dressed in a cream and lavender mock-Edwardian shirt she had purchased this summer. It had been fun watching her develop her own sense of style. Rather than follow the dictates of current fashion, as her mother had once done, she'd searched out possibilities and finally settled on vintage clothing and antique styles, which she mixed effortlessly with her artistic flare. She said she figured since she was vintage herself, she should put it to good use. Strangely enough, vintage fashions were beginning to become popular, and not just at UniPrep – all over the planet. From following the fashions, Rose had inadvertently gone to dictating them. Such was the power she didn't realize she held. She looked beautiful.

She crossed her arms behind her head and leaned back against the raised cushion that served as a pillow. 'Now we wait,' she said. She took a deep breath, sniffing the air. 'This really is a good mix,' she mused. 'Shame it's only for this trip.'

I frowned. *'You're actually looking forward to this, aren't you.'* I signed.

'I only caught like three words of that. Looking at what?'

I reached over and touched her wrist. *'Are you looking forward to this?'* I asked, then let her go.

Rose shrugged. 'Yes and no. I'm used to it. And Xavier and you are coming too, so it's not much of a problem.'

I raised my eyebrow. *'Bren?'* I signed.

Rose shifted subtly away from me – I wondered if she even realized she'd done it. 'I'm trying not to think about that.'

'How's that working?'

She chuckled. 'Not great. But I'm okay with it. It won't be too long, after all. It's not like it'll be decades.' She shrugged. 'Age … stopped meaning so much to me a little while ago.'

I wanted to ask her *what if something went wrong*? But I kept still.

'The stass itself isn't a problem, though. That's kind of fun. It's not scary. It's like … I can't describe it.'

'Please try,' I signed.

She looked me over. 'You're really scared,' she realized.

I nodded.

'Don't be. It's like a spa treatment or a meditation loop. It's not anything like as scary as going under anaesthesia.'

'Anaesthesia I can handle,' I signed, and I could. All of the Europa Project children had needed surgery a couple of times to correct genetic flaws in our systems. *'This is an unknown.'*

'Presuming that first sign was anaesthesia, I think I understood that. An unknown?'

I nodded. She really was getting better at sign.

'Well, that's why you have me here. Not at all an unknown to me.'

'Tell me about it?'

Rose looked up at the ceiling of the stass tube. The ceiling was a soft creamy plastic with vinework moulded into it, highlighted in gilt. The tube really was very comfortable – satin-of-silk cushions and this dizzying scent. I knew there were straps that would activate to hold us down once we were fully under, but right now it was just a gentle relaxation couch. There was even a panel on the wall where we could turn on music or a holovid while we waited for the stass to be activated. But I was far too nervous to focus on such a transparent distraction.

'Well, this is just the waiting,' she said. 'My tube at home was a little different – the music was automatic and the chemical scent was stronger. It has been nearly a century of development. Shame, though. If the residual chemicals were stronger you probably wouldn't be feeling scared right now at all.'

She'd told me about this. *'No fear,'* I signed.

'Right,' she said. 'The first few minutes are the best. It's like all your pain and fear and sadness go away. I remember you once said I used it like a drug, but there's no euphoria or high. It's just a peace of mind. A clarity. Physically, it's just relaxing. Your body will relax, your tensions melt away. You can still move, until you're completely under, so you can get comfortable. Everything seems possible.' She looked a little wistful, as if she was remembering something.

'Then come the dreams,' she said. 'They're not like ordinary dreams. At least mine aren't – I haven't done any comparative research.'

'Tell me.'

'More colourful,' she said. 'Deeper. You find corners of your own psyche you never expected to see. For me it all takes the form of landscapes and scenery. Clouds. Seas. Gardens.'

'Briar Rose.'

She smiled. She knew that sign well. 'The truth is, when you're in stasis you can heal all the hurt places. They smooth out, and you can fix them and patch them over.' She looked up at the ceiling of the tube. 'Of course, that might mean you'll let yourself be hurt more later. 'Cause after stasis it doesn't seem to hurt anymore.' Her voice became distant as she said, 'I think … I think that may be why I let them do it. My parents. They used to tell me I knew what was best, and every time it was what *they* thought was best. So even though I knew it was wrong … I didn't believe it. They thought it was best, so I thought it was best. Because the hurt didn't last. Every time they stassed me it hurt – but the very act of the stasis made me able to heal it so it didn't hurt anymore. It was like it had never happened.'

I only watched her. The sadness on her face was etched as deeply as on her Xavier's; just as ancient and just as profound. This was the old woman whose subconscious made her mind so beautiful. Just for a moment, I saw her lurking in Rose's young face. And something terrible moved in me.

I wanted her. Someone, something bigger and more real than all the superficial trivia that pervaded the minds of my peers. Even Nabiki, with all her layers of thought, was shallow compared to Rose. I wanted it. It was a sudden pang, like being struck with an arrow, and I cringed.

The movement drew her attention. 'You okay?' she asked, and she was young again, innocent again.

I nodded. For once I was glad I couldn't talk. I had the perfect excuse for being speechless.

'Okay,' Rose said. She frowned, thinking of what else to tell me. I could see the blood pulsing in the artery in her milk-pale throat. Pulse, pulse, ticking away her life. In a few minutes that pulse would cease. Good thing I'd be asleep, too, or I wouldn't be able to endure it. 'Afterwards,' she continued, 'it's a bit like getting out of a bath. I know that sounds strange, but it's as if you move from one medium into another, as if you were crawling out of water, and things – change. I'm not talking about what it's like if you've been in too long. Actual stass fatigue hurts, and you're all weak and exhausted and nothing works right.'

I almost laughed. I felt that way *now*.

'But if you haven't been in long enough to suffer fatigue it's actually really nice. You feel kind of rested and relaxed, as if you've just had a massage or something. And your mind is really clear. Oh, here's a trick I learned.' She looked excited. 'Try and remember something really sky.' She grinned at me. 'If you're thinking about something just before you go into stass, you remember it forever. It seeps into every part of your mind and you can never forget any details.' She looked over at me. Her brown eyes were very deep in the shadows of the tube. 'So, if there's anything you want to remember perfectly for the rest of your life,' Rose told me, 'now's the time.'

It was the way she put it. It was the way she put it and the threat of my demise and I think the stass chemicals were getting to me. Rose may not have thought the residue very strong, but she was desensitized to it. I could already feel it working through my brain, lessening my fears, retarding my intelligence, lowering my inhibitions.

All of these are excuses, of course. In truth, I just really wanted to.

With an urgency that surprised both of us I reached over and pulled her to me. I shifted, pressing her body down, pushing my lips down against hers in a kiss so desperate I was afraid I might shatter.

Rose was shocked. She did not try to push me off. Her mind was a torrent of emotion – surprise, horror, pity, love, even suppressed desire. I kissed her more deeply, drawing out the sensation, kissing her as she wanted to be kissed. It was marvellous, the taste of her, the feel of her smooth skin beneath my hands. Her heat seemed to pour through me to my very bones. Oh, I hadn't expected this. The sheer violence of her fire would have seared me if it hadn't felt so burned *good*.

It felt wonderful to her, too, a release, as if a dam had burst. But that very fact brought her out of it. One thought superseded her mind, and that thought was, *Xavier!* She pushed me away, gently but firmly. I lost contact with her skin, though I was still hovering half over her, her breath like a furnace against my face. Her eyes were wide with something akin to panic. I was so heated I wanted to bite her. She'd turned bright red, a Rose by any other name, and her brown eyes looked almost black with shock. 'I'm sorry,' she breathed. 'I'm sorry, I can't … I just can't.' She panted, her breath shaking in her throat. 'I love you, I do, but it's not … oh, god!' She tried to push me off her. She was trembling.

Under any other circumstances, I would have pulled back and apologized for frightening her. These weren't any other circumstances. I reached up and touched her cheek. '*Rose. Don't panic. Please, hear me out.*'

There were a thousand briar walls in her mind. Some of them tore at me, but I was getting used to Rose's thorns. The pain she could cause me didn't hurt any longer. Maybe it was the stass residue.

'I can't,' she breathed.

'I know,' I said into her mind. *'I know you still love Xavier. I know it means so much to you that he's still alive and still loves you. You think you don't want anyone right now, and I understand that. Under ordinary circumstances, I'd respect it. I'd bide my time and stay at exactly the distance you need me to be – two metres or ten kilometres. It was what I planned to do. Oh, Rose, I was so willing to wait. I'd have waited years for you – decades. But the bell is tolling, and I don't have that kind of time.'*

She slammed down on that thought, refusing to entertain it for a moment. 'Don't say that!'

'Rose, listen to me. When you open your eyes I could be dead. Within the next half hour, everything might be over.' As I told her

this I realized she'd been in denial. The words were so harsh and so shocking to her I knew she had ignored every warning Dr Svarog had given. It was one of those things she didn't want to think about, and so had pushed away. It was as if I'd taken out a gun and held it to my head in front of her.

'Don't,' she whispered to me. 'Don't say that, don't. It's not true.'

'You know I can't coiting lie!' I threw at her. This was true. In my own mind, I really couldn't. She winced at how much despair was in that thought. I closed my eyes, holding in an emotion I didn't want to be feeling. But she could feel it already, even though I wasn't trying to send it to her. Fear and hunger and desperation and just a burning, wrenching *need* for everything I knew she could do for me.

'I'm sorry,' she whispered. 'I didn't mean to do this to you.'

'*You're the most wonderful, amazing, enveloping thing I've ever experienced,'* I told her. *'The most accepting, the most loving. God, you have no idea how I envy that man. How I envy Bren. To even know that I'd even been in your thoughts for one instant ...!'*

'I don't think that way,' she told me, desperately. 'Not anymore.'

'*Oh, please, Rose, listen to me. I might never have another chance. The moment this machine turns on and strange chemicals try to make sense of my biologically tortured body, I could short out entirely. My brain is cracking. Parts of me are dying by the day. I can* feel *it. I'm scared.'*

God, was I scared. And she felt it, even though I was trying not to inundate her with it. She had a sudden image of waking up from stasis with my corpse beside her, and the pain she felt raked at me with its thorns. I was being brutal, and I knew it. Had I been planning this? Yes. I had. Every night as I lay in bed dreaming of her, every day as I watched her awkward movements attain stability and grace, every half-awake moment when I filled my overloaded mind with the visage of her, I'd been dreaming of what it would be like to feel her beneath me, feel her skin, be swallowed by her mind. Planning how I would do it. In the pool. After school. In her studio. I'd had a thousand different visions of her. And here she was, and I was so ready. *'You know how I feel,'* I told her. *'You've known it since the beginning.'*

There was an angry, unbalanced thought lurking through her head, set off by her sympathy and her genuine concern. She didn't want to have it, but it came from the part of her mind that she'd been working on cultivating since she came out of stass – the part of her that had the ability to stand up for herself. It was angry at me. Even though she didn't want to attack me, she thought, *'This isn't fair to me.'*

'*No,*' I admitted, acknowledging the thought even though she hadn't tried to give it voice. *'This isn't fair to you. I wish things were different. But it's not fair to me either. None of this is fair! But life isn't fair – and god do I know that better than anyone.'* I gazed down upon her. *'You know it, too.'*

'Don't do this,' she whispered.

'What are my choices, Rose? What other chances will I have?'

Rose's love for me bit at her, and she started to cry.

I couldn't stand that I'd made her cry. I was the one who brushed away her tears, I wasn't supposed to be the one who caused them. 'Oh, Briar Rose,' I whispered.

She gasped in surprise. She'd never heard me whisper before. 'You … I forgot.' Her voice was barely more than a whisper itself. 'You told me you could do that. I just didn't realize …'

To my own surprise, I was suddenly more human to her. It was as if her dog had suddenly started speaking to her, confessing he was a disguised prince. 'I can do … anything,' I whispered. It was true. Nabiki was destroyed because of it. *'Just let me love you, that's all I'm asking. I don't expect anything inside you to change for me. And if I survive this, I don't expect anything permanent. This isn't a betrayal of anyone. Xavier won't have to see us together, you won't have to admit that you let me do more than touch your hand. I'll take a moment of you, even if I never have anything again. It would be worth it. My whole stupid, inhuman, socially and biologically tortured life would be worth it if I could just have you for one moment.*' I took a deep breath, trying to clear my thoughts. '*I don't want to die. I don't want to hurt you. I just want you.*' I took my hand away and let her have her thoughts to herself. I moved my lips silently as she stared up at me through her tears. 'I just want you.'

Rose only gazed at me for a long time. 'Don't,' she whispered.

'I can't help it.'

'I'm not worth it. I'm broken.'

I almost laughed. I buried my face in her neck, breathing in the distinct, human scent of her – more delicate than Nabiki's, enough in itself to make my bones melt. '*I was never properly whole to start with.*'

She didn't push me away. Hesitantly, almost experimentally, I ran my lips along her skin. I gently tasted her throat, feeling the warmth, the sweet salt taste of her pale, white flesh. It felt so good to her – too good. She started and pushed me away, the thought, '*Xavier!*' flashing through her again.

'I can't,' she said. 'I want to, I do, I just … I can't. Something inside won't let me.'

I stared down at her. I had felt it too – the desperate panic as the wrong person gave her what she needed. But that was the other thing I had felt; she needed it. She missed having someone to hold her and touch her and love her the way Xavier used to do. Missed it desperately.

I knew what I could do. I'd never done it before – it breached my personal code of ethics and Tristan would have said it was a betrayal of myself and my family. It wasn't something I would ever have done otherwise. For a long moment I wrestled with myself. But then I heard 42, so quietly in the back of my mind there was no way Rose could have known she was there. *(You know what you want. Is there anyone to tell you no?)*

I shouldn't have listened to her. I should have held true to myself. But in the end the knowledge that I might have no other chance forced my hand. 42 and my own fear of an unlived life pushed me towards a decision I might not have made under any other circumstance.

'Close your eyes,' I whispered to Rose.

'Otto, I—'

'Close your eyes,' I whispered again.

With a shudder, Rose did as I asked her.

I took a deep breath, looking down at her. Did I really want to do this?

Yes. It didn't matter anymore. My life was squitch and I didn't care what was right or what wasn't any longer. I wanted this. I wanted her. And just then, I didn't care what I had to do to get it.

Gently, I took hold of Rose's face, cupping her jaw in my hand, my fingers curled behind her ear. Gently caressing her cheek with my thumb I entered her tormented, briar-filled mind. I headed straight for the most twisted and tangled corner, the deepest wounded tangle of briars, and plunged into it without any kind of mental shield.

Xavier was inside there, all her memories of him, all the pain of what she considered her own betrayal, all the horror. I skirted the fresh tangles of pain and loss that had formed when she'd come out of stasis, and went deep, deep into her ancient memories, down under that subconscious growth of more than half a century. I found her when she was still young, when she wasn't so lopsided, when even her subconscious mind wasn't much more than thirty. That was where I found Xavier and pulled him out, reading the memories, pulling them to the forefront of her mind.

Then I kissed her. I kissed her as he had kissed her, his movement, his hesitations, every nuance of his kiss. And I let her keep him; I let her mind believe it was him. Her conscious mind, her sixteen-year-old self, knew full well that it was me. But her subconscious, that huge swelling mountain of her self that had slept through most of a century believed, with every facet, that I was Xavier.

There was a groan as her body responded, a beautiful moment as every part of her cried out with relief. Finally, finally! Everything was right again. Oh, this was what I wanted. It didn't matter that it wasn't really me, I was there, and I was in her mind, and it was everything I wanted. I could feel what she felt inside her skin. She felt like lightning, ripping through her body, and it was everything she needed.

But she fought it off. With a gasp she pulled away, her eyes snapped open. Her subconscious faded beneath the awareness of her senses. 'What are you doing?'

'*What does it look like?*' I kissed her throat, dredging up another memory as I did it, ripping it from her. It was hard, fighting against her consciousness. '*What does it* feel *like?*'

'That's not you!' she breathed.

I looked down at her. We were so close, our noses touched, and we were sharing our breath. I couldn't let this end. 'If you let me, I can be whatever you want me to be,' I whispered to her. 'Even him.'

The full implication of this took a moment to sink in. Rose stared at me, her brown eyes wide with wonder and ... hunger. Then she shook her head, banishing whatever was goading her inside. 'No, Otto. That's not right. It's not fair ...'

'*To who? To you?*'

That wasn't what she was thinking. This wasn't fair to me. I deserved someone who loved me, just me, and Rose wasn't that. 'It's not right.'

'*Right.*' I was so sick of my patience and my morals and my thrice-blasted ethics! My breath came hard as I stared down at her. '*What is "right"? I don't care about right anymore, do you understand me? I want you.* Right *here,* right *now,* right *at this moment, this is as* right *as anything else. It isn't right that I was created. It isn't right that I am dying. It isn't right that I've fallen impossibly in love with the most remarkable woman in a century. It isn't right that you can't let yourself love anyone properly right now. I have the ability to make it right.* Right *now this is what I want. This is* right.' I closed my eyes, and I tried not to say what I was thinking. But she heard it, the constant drone of every cell in my body. '*Let me. Please, just let me. Please. Please let me. Let me.*' Again and again and again.

She couldn't speak, but her mind was wavering. '*I'm not sure …*'

'I'm sure!' I hissed down at her. 'I don't have the luxury of being unsure. There isn't time.'

Thoughts tangled in her brain – stasis and age and time and loss. 'The time is never right,' she whispered.

I tried to smile, but I don't think it came out very clearly. I'm sure my eyes were tragic. 'Not for any of us.'

Rose took a deep breath. She wanted to be moral and insist on everything being fair. But life wasn't fair … and she wanted this too. '*Otto … Xavier …*' she thought.

And she let me.

chapter 8

We didn't go that far, really. There wasn't time, for one. The stass tube wasn't really all that private for another, what with the glass door. And we had no equipment and had made no preparations, and I would like to think myself a gentleman. Physically, anyway. Psychically, I was being an absolute cad, but I didn't care about that at the time.

I actually didn't care about anything. Part of my mind focused on keeping her subconscious active and directed around Xavier. It was a little like reading a script, acting out a play when the words were right in front of me. But like reading a script, I was still me inside the action, and I was in heaven. My body, exhausted and aching as it had been for days, tingled under the heat of her fingertips. The constant dissatisfied ache that had been niggling at me since I first knew Rose was eased. It felt like my body had been pierced by the thorns that tangled in her mind, and the act of holding her in my arms pulled the pain away. *'Rose.'* I let her hear the name in Xavier's voice, and she clutched me tightly.

'I love you,' she breathed in my ear. 'Know it, always.'

I didn't care that she wasn't speaking to me. *I* heard the words, and *I* felt her body, and *I* was the one she held in her arms. He was only a cloak I was wearing, but I was there. I was so there. I stopped her mouth with a kiss, and she moaned softly with contentment. Or was it relief?

Rose barely heard it when a pleasant computer voice announced the incipient stages of stass – but I did. With a gasp I tensed, and Rose's eyes shot open, her dream state gone in an instant. I was still touching her. She knew what I was feeling.

'It'll be okay,' she told me quickly, catching hold of my head. 'Otto, look at me. It'll all be okay.' She stared into my eyes as I trembled. Her words meant nothing to me. This was it. These could be my last moments ...

'Otto,' she said. She touched my face gently. 'Thank you so much for this.'

That distracted me. Suddenly I could feel her again. Her body felt warm and tingling, and her heart beat in her chest loud enough that she knew she was alive. Her mind was a riot of colour. For the first time since I'd started this, I felt guilty. *'You're actually thanking me?'*

'I didn't realize how much I needed it.' She kissed me lightly on the lips, just a butterfly wing of a touch. 'Just breathe it in,' she whispered in my ear.

As the scent around us grew stronger I realized what she had done. I would have spent those final thirty seconds in a panic if Rose hadn't dragged my attention back to her. I closed my eyes as I breathed in the scent of the first wave of stass chemicals.

Rose moaned gently as the scent took her, but she shook her head, fighting it off. 'Lay back. Unh ...'

I realized as I shifted that Rose was having a very hard time keeping conscious. My fear had faded, but I wasn't near a dream state yet. *'Rose?'* I asked, and my worry carried to her.

'I'm okay,' Rose whispered sleepily. 'I'm just very used to going with it. Let it take you.' Her last words I could barely hear. 'I'll be here when you wake.'

And she was gone, her mind faded into a brightly coloured landscape almost instantly.

I had a choice, but it was a decision I had to make quickly. I could feel the stass taking hold of my limbs. I could hold her as we travelled, sharing her dreams, or I could leave her to have her own.

I hadn't shared anyone's dreams since 42 died. As my own theta state began to take over, 42 crouched in the corner of the stass tube. She was probably a dream. She studied my sleeping beauty with a critical air. (*So now are you satisfied?*) She looked over at me, annoyed. (*Somehow, I don't think you are.*)

'Don't ruin this. Please.'

(Do you intend to drag her down with you when you die?)

The thought horrified me, and I pushed Rose away. To have Rose go through what I went through – no! Even if I didn't want to die alone. That wouldn't be fair to her.

(You won't die alone,) 42 whispered. *(I'm with you.)* I could almost feel her hand in mine. *(I'm always with you.)*

'I love you,' I thought. It was my last thought, and I held it firm as the stass overtook me. *'I love you.'* I just wasn't sure which one of them I was talking to: Rose, or my sister.

My stass dreams were strange. Dark and twisted, but I didn't find them frightening. The lack of light and the strange sense of weight seemed right to me, and when I opened my eyes it was to a light prelude by Mozart. Apparently the music turned on automatically as the stass was lifted.

It took me a few moments to come back to myself. I took a deep breath, reanimating my lungs, finding all my muscles. Then I realized something. My head did not hurt.

At all.

I blinked a few times in wonder at the relief of it. My pain was gone, and my exhaustion seemed to have faded. And I wasn't dead. Stass had not short-circuited my fragile corporeal form, and I was still me. I felt strangely light – the stewards had explained to us that the rotation of the ship during this hiatus combined with an artificial grav field maintained a subtle gravity, but it wasn't as strong as what we were used to on Earth. They were trying to acclimate us to the conditions we would be exposed to on the Jovian colonies. I rubbed my face, relishing the feel of my limbs. Then I looked over, expecting to see Rose waking up as well.

Rose lay still as death. She was not breathing. I touched her, but her subconscious was so deeply buried in blackness that at first there appeared to be nothing. Finally, I saw a glimmer, but so far down I feared digging into the blackness. Digging too deep into her mind could damage her. Letting go of her mind I touched her arm instead, shaking her slightly. I wished I could speak. This was so exactly like what Rose had envisioned – her waking up from stass and finding me dead beside her. Only it was Rose who it seemed would never wake, and I was the one horrified to find her so still and pale.

I shook her more firmly, trying to drag her back to her body. There was nothing. Not a flicker of her eyelids, not a twitch of her pulse.

I batted at the handle on the glass doors, my own heart sounding loud in my ears. The doors slid open to reveal the corridor tinkling with the faint sounds of awakening passengers.

I jumped down onto the carpeted corridor, and was surprised when I bounced right back up. Pushing myself back down against the padded ceiling, I finally found my weight on my feet and moved forward, trying to find a steward.

Who I found, instead, was Xavier, who was heading down the corridor looking much more at home with the reduced gravity than I was.

In my panic I did something I'd never done before. I grabbed hold of his hand. *'It's Rose!'* I thought at him. *'Something's wrong with her, something's gone wrong! She can't wake up! I think she's dying.'*

Xavier was startled, and all his defences went up. He hurt me; unintentionally, of course, but his psyche was hard as a rock, and jagged. As always with older but healthy individuals, his mind was strong – experienced and rigid and difficult to see through. Much less flexible. It was hard to get my message across. Once he'd realized what I'd done, he smiled. I felt very strange suddenly. In the smile I could finally see the boy I had been emulating in the stass chamber. I'd never before been able to reconcile Rose's image of her teenage lover with the stolid and powerful presence of this corporate king. I was embarrassed. Particularly as Xavier's mind had gone all amused and patient. There was something else, there, beneath his indulgence. Something … sharp and violent. It disturbed me. I let go of him quickly.

'Rose told me that was odd,' he said. 'Your, ah … communication. Bren seems to take it in his stride.' Bren was so clear of mind he barely noticed. I wished Bren were there. His was the kind of mind you liked having around when you were confused. 'You're in here?' he asked. He strode up to our stass chamber and peered inside at Rose's still form. She still hadn't moved.

'*She won't wake up*,' I signed at him. I don't know if he understood sign, but he seemed to gather what I was saying. 'Wake up' is a pretty universal sign, anyway, miming the opening of eyes.

'I know,' he said with a small smile. 'She does that. It isn't dangerous unless it goes on too long.' He climbed into the tube and sat quietly beside her. He took hold of her hand and then gently kissed her forehead.

I winced. The love I saw in the chaste movements of that old man was painful. His eyes held decades of memory for a cherished lover, as well as the responsibility of a father for his child. If Rose was right, there was also the hero-worship devotion of a small boy for his big sister. There were at least three layers of love in everything he did for her. I felt very small and selfish in comparison.

'Just hold her hand,' he said to me, his eyes distant. 'She comes to find it. She only fights off anyone who tries to shake her out of it; goes deeper, holds on longer.' His thumb caressed the back of her hand. 'She'll be back in a minute.'

I stood in the door of the chamber, clutching on to the edge, my fingers white with my grip. Finally, after what seemed an eternity to me, Rose took a breath. Her hand closed around his, and her eyes flickered. 'Xavier,' she whispered.

'I'm here,' he said, his voice soft and low.

I realized I was witnessing something deeply personal to the two of them. This exchange echoed a hundred tiny deaths in her youth, tiny deaths that her Xavier had to witness again and again, and pull her back from. I wanted to turn away and give them their privacy.

And then I remembered – I had already done something far more intrusive than spy upon their awakening ritual. I had stolen Rose's memories and insinuated myself inside of them. When my death had been slowly ticking down inside that stass chamber I had felt justified. Now, standing whole and without pain in the corridor, I felt ashamed of myself.

Rose blinked and looked up at the old man, and then caught her breath. 'Otto?' she asked. Her voice sounded very weak to me.

'He's here,' Xavier said patiently. 'He was worried about you.'

Rose lifted her head and gazed at me, her eyes dark with stass chemicals. I wanted to kiss her, and I wanted to run. I felt sick. Guilt weighed on me as I looked at the two of them. My mind cast about for something, anything that would get me out of this situation. *'Quin!'* I signed, with a sudden surge of relief. *'I have to see if Quin's okay.'*

I didn't wait to hear what Rose would say to this. Instead I turned and pelted down the corridor as fast as the low gravity would let me.

By the time I made it down the next row of stass chambers the blood was roaring in my ears, but it felt good. It had been too long since I'd been able to run. My head didn't ache, and my muscles seemed to be behaving themselves. I thought stasis might actually have been good for me. I ran into Quin as he studied a map of passenger corridors. 'Otto! Told you you'd make it,' he said. 'We're both to report immediately to the medical bay, have all of our vitals checked, and then Mr Zellwegger is to erase all of the records.' He gave me a grin that seemed about as sane as a rabbit hunting for eagles. Then his eyes shadowed. 'You okay?' he asked. 'You look about to cry.'

I put my hand to my face, and clutched at my temples, trying to put myself back together. Quin jumped at me and grabbed my arm. 'Hey, bro. Settle down. How's your head?'

I pulled away, unwilling to touch him. Unwilling to touch anyone. *'I'm fine,'* I signed. *'I'm better.'*

Quin rolled his eyes. 'Don't tell me after all this trouble you've decided to go and get better on us! How dare you!' He pointed down the corridor. 'Medical bay's this way.'

The ship's doctor ran through tests on both of us, a thorough going over, confirmed us both as perfectly healthy, and then sealed the records. Quin answered her questions for me. Then she suggested that we both go to the dining lounge. I was ravenous. I followed Quin gladly down to the same opulent dining lounge we saw before we took off.

Rose was already there, trying very hard to nibble at a puff-pastry, but she looked pale. 'How's it goin', princess?' Quin said cheerfully. His loud voice caused the other passengers to glare at him, but he was oblivious. He snatched up a plate from the buffet and started shovelling spinach pasta onto it. I stopped short when I saw Rose. She smiled at me, suddenly very shy.

I lost my appetite. Rose saw me oscillating back and forth, and finally signed at me, *'Come, sit.'*

I took a deep breath and went up to her. I had no idea what I was going to say.

Rose didn't give me a chance. As soon as I came up to the table she stood up and hugged me. *'You okay?'* she asked me silently.

'I think so,' I told her. But I couldn't hide my feelings of guilt.

Rose pulled away before I could figure out what she thought of them. What I did pick up from her, however, was much more physical. *'You're feeling sick?'* I signed.

'Low G doesn't agree with me,' Rose said. 'I couldn't keep down my first plate.' She sighed. 'Six weeks in stass probably didn't help my stomach any.'

'You should pop down to the medi bay,' Quin said, plonking down his plate of delectables. 'Your century of insanity should provide them with another welcome conundrum. Right now they're busily trying to figure out whether or not *our* medical records make any sense.'

'Do they?' Rose asked.

Quin shrugged. 'How should I know? Are you going to eat that mushroom?'

Rose looked down at her plate where a mushroom stuffed with caviar twinkled up at her. 'No,' she said with a slight twitch. 'No, I'm not.'

'Oh, good,' Quin said, snatching it off her plate. He slipped it into his mouth and said with his mouth full, 'This place is lots less crowded then it was when we arrived.'

Rose looked at him with distaste. 'They don't wake everyone at once. They've split us into four sections, and we're woken up in waves. They only lay on oxygen in this part of the ship for a week, once every month and a half.'

'Right, right,' Quin said. 'Where's the communication booths? I want to send a message to someone.'

'They're to your left off the social lounges,' Rose said. She looked at me. Her lips were very red. 'You've got some messages from Bren and your sisters.'

I nodded, and made my excuses before I fled to the buffet. I had absolutely no idea what to say to Rose. I wasn't sure whether I should apologize or act like nothing had happened or, impossibly, fawn on her as if our liaison had been perfectly natural. I really hadn't planned on having to deal with the aftermath of our little tryst. And the worst of it was, I was still echoing with it. I couldn't forget the taste of her lips, the feel of her skin against mine. My skin tingled when I remembered. But hadn't I promised that it wasn't real? That we could pretend it hadn't happened? I wondered what she saw when she looked at me. Myself, blue-skinned Otto, her friend and confidant? Or the man who had raped her memories, manipulating her for his own selfish ends?

(Isn't that a little harsh?)

'No. It's true.'

(I don't see her crying into her coffee over it.)

'Rose doesn't drink coffee.'

(You know what I mean. It doesn't seem to be bothering her any.)

Rage boiled in me. *'Rose doesn't consider an assassin a poor way to say I love you! Of course she isn't bothered!'*

(So why are you letting it bother you?)

The words that entered my head were, of all things, '*Because I'm a human being!*' But of course I wasn't. I set my tray down on the edge of the buffet and looked back at Rose. She was looking at her plate, dutifully trying to choke down more of her meal. As I watched, Quin wolfed down the last of his food, kissed Rose roughly on the forehead and headed off towards the social lounges. Rose wiped the grease off her forehead with her napkin and looked around for me. I knew Quin had only kissed her to annoy me. Rose's deep brown gaze met mine, and I nearly staggered. I couldn't face her. Abandoning my plate I fled, following Quin to the social lounges.

The three large social lounges held a smattering of passengers, but Quin wasn't in any of them. I figured he was in one of the tiny communication booths on the other side of the corridor. Several of them were marked 'occupied'. Finally I stepped into a free one, sat at the screened desk, and let the retina scanner access my personal message files.

The ship had been collecting them since I'd gone into stasis. There were four messages from Penny, two from Tristan, one from Dr Bija, one from Jamal and one from Bren. I skimmed through Penny's, which were rambling discussions of her first few weeks of what she called 'real school!' since she'd only been in UniPrep's summer programme before now. Tristan's first message was from herself, telling me about getting on to the Uni track team. Her second was a video message she had made at the lab on a weekend visit to the simple ones. She had managed to get Fifen and Toseph and Niney and Thirteen to hum a song for me. It was whispery as the buzz of bees, but it was charming in its way. Fifen – who could speak – even added words about me flying to Europa. They didn't rhyme, or scan, but it was sweet of her. I sent them back a greeting with a stock video image from

Luna base, showing the *Daedalus* on her takeoff procedure, complete with a half-Earth glowing in the sky above.

Dr Bija had sent me a collection of poetry written by the Russian cosmonaut Ivan Nesytski, from around the time of the colonization of Titan. They were mostly about isolation in deep space, but I wasn't really up to contemplating them just then.

Jamal gave me a list of places I should be sure to visit on the *Minos*, and a few games I could play with the low G in the ice villages or if I ever ended up on the lower levels of the city ship. He kept telling me how much fun I was going to have.

Bren, when I finally opened his message, was more subdued. He was the first person to acknowledge that he was sending me a letter I might not ever receive.

'I really, really hope you wake up to hear this, Otto,' Bren said in his video message. He was in his own room at Unicorn, and I could see Rose's dog Dizzy behind him on his bed, gnawing on one of Bren's old tennis shoes. 'I hope you came through stasis okay, and I hope Rose's recovery hasn't regressed. Things are turning along pretty good out here. I hurt my knee again, but I still got into finals at national tennis championships.' He stopped. Bren looked depressed. 'You don't give a coit about my tennis. You want to know something scary? I don't either.' He stopped for a long time and just stared into the distance. The seconds ticked by on the message clock. 'I miss you, Otto,' he said suddenly. 'I miss Rose. I wish I could have come with you. There are some things happening down here, and … well. Never mind. It might all come to nothing, anyway. I just really wish you and Rose had been here as it all came down … but I can't even talk about it with you.' He shook his head. 'Don't know how my granddad stood it all those years. Stasis. Noid. It's like you've been dead for the last month. Take care of each other, okay?' He turned the recorder off.

I sat there, not knowing what to write him in reply. As far as I knew – and I tended to know better than most – Bren never really felt anything, good or bad. He travelled indifferently through life with an easy-going grin and a quiet acceptance. What was going on that he was so depressed now?

I pulled up a keyboard and tried to write him a response, but I didn't know what to say. As I thought, another message for me came through on my account. I opened it up, wondering if Tristan had received my note.

It wasn't Tristan.

Otto, I'm sorry. I don't know what I did wrong, but I think I can guess. I made you break your code of ethics – or you think I did. But you didn't, Otto. You didn't hurt me or do anything you need to feel ashamed about. I wanted what you did. Honest. In fact, I feel really selfish, I wanted it so much. And I'm sorry I'm so broken, and I can't love you the way you deserve. I don't know what to do about it. I just wish you'd talk to me again.

Rose.

I closed my eyes. I pulled up a reply and thought about what to write. I couldn't think of anything. Finally, I just let my fingers travel and sat back to read whatever came out.

I don't know what to do, either. I love you, you know. I love you so much it's as if I've been sliced open inside, and I can't even imagine what it would be like to lose you – really lose you. But the worst of it is, I don't need to imagine. Because I've lived through it before. I've lost people I loved, and I've done stupid things and I've hurt people and I'm sure I'm about to do it again. You may not realize it, but I've done something unforgivable. And the fact that you don't realize it is what makes it ten times worse. You are broken, and you are hurt, and I used that, and I manipulated you, and whether I'm sick or no, there's no excuse for that. I just ... Oh, gods.

There was nothing to say. I hit send quickly before I erased the whole message. A millisecond later I regretted it wholeheartedly, and wished I'd never even written it.

A few minutes later Rose sent me a reply. You haven't hurt me, Otto.

I know what I did, I sent back.

What do you want to do now?

I don't know.

You have to know.

I don't have to say! I can lie like this, so let me tell a polite lie, just for once!

There was a long pause. Please don't be angry with me.

I'd hurt her. Burn it, I was messing up all over the place! **Don't ever think this is you. This is me.**

I was there, too. I let you. That was me.

I didn't have anything to say to that.

Please tell me what you think we should do.

I really don't know that. I do know what I want. But what I want is impossible, and we both know that.

So you don't plan on it?

On what?

On doing it again.

You don't actually want me to, do you?

I don't know what I want. I wish I could just let it go and be whole again. But then I look at him, and his milky hazel eyes, and I love him so much, and I can't let it go. You can't make me better, can you?

I actually laughed. **Not without stripping you of all your memories and leaving you lobotomized. Probably not even then.**

I didn't think so.

So. What do you want to do?

I want to make you better. I want to get you to Europa and find out what's wrong with you and fix it so you'll never get sick again. I never want to lose you.

You can't let anyone go, can you.

Rose didn't answer. I sat there for a long time just waiting for her reply. Then I heard the door open, quietly, behind me. 'No,' Rose said, her voice thick. 'No, I can't let anyone go.'

I turned to look at her. She stood in the door of the booth with her feet close together, her hands clasped carefully before her. Her back was straight and her head was half bowed. She looked like a little girl, apologizing to her parents. I realized this upright, submissive pose was what she fell into when she thought she was in trouble. She looked so vulnerable, so fragile. I wanted to hold her. Well, I always wanted to hold her, but just then I wanted to protect her.

I stood up and went to her. I didn't know what to say. As I came close her gaze tilted up to examine my eyes. I'd never really realized how much taller I was than her. Whether it was the repeated stasis or her own genetics, she was quite small. She towered so in my mind that her physical form was seen as a separate entity, seen by itself, alone, with no comparisons. She barely came past my chin. And I'm not very tall, really. Tenderly I pulled her to me, cradling her head against my chest. I stroked her hair. I didn't know what to do.

'Me either,' Rose said.

I pulled away. She'd done it again – read things I hadn't actually sent to her.

'Do you think this was a mistake?'

'*I didn't care at the time,*' I signed.

'Me either,' Rose whispered. She opened her mouth to say something, then hesitated, blushing crimson. 'I didn't realize how hungry I was.'

I covered my mouth with my hand, feeling awkward. Finally I signed, *'I've made things worse, haven't I.'*

'In that sense? Yes. I can still … feel it. And the memory is so strong.'

She was feeling the same stass effects I was.

'It felt really … really nice,' she admitted, blushing. 'There's a part of me wants to kiss you, but … the thought scares me.' Rose shook her head. 'I don't know if I'm better or worse,' she said. 'I don't think I'll know until I try to sleep.' She chuckled, but it was without humour. 'See what direction my nightmares go in.'

'I'm sorry,' I signed.

'No, you usually keep my nightmares at bay,' she said. 'Or, they're worse when I don't get a chance to link up and talk with you, anyway.'

I hadn't known that.

She bit her lip. 'What do we do?'

I knew what I wanted to do. I reached for her, my fingers very gently fondling her hair. 'We could try,' I whispered.

'W-we could …'

Rose was trembling so badly her teeth were almost chattering.

'*Please,'* I sent to her, caressing her cheek.

Her mind was such a knot of panic and confusion, she had no idea whether she wanted me to kiss her or not. But I wanted to. My hand cradled her head as I pulled her mouth to mine.

If only our time in the stass tube had made this easier. It did not. Her tender pink lips were just as sweet, her scent still tea-rose soap with a delicate, feminine undercurrent, her breath still as smooth as flower petals against my skin. She lifted her face to mine and left herself open to my kiss. For one second, it was bliss. Only Rose and myself, and the universe just melted away. But it was all too brief. Suddenly she broke, her lips stretching in a tortured grimace as she sobbed. With a cry that sounded like pain she pulled away. 'I'm sorry, Otto. I can't. I still can't!'

My kiss had only brought her to tears.

'I'm sorry,' she breathed.

'*I know,*' I signed, touching my head listlessly.

'If I could ...'

'*I know.*'

'I ... I wish I could ...'

It hurt to see her standing there, trembling, hating herself. It hurt so much I lost my temper. '*Go,*' I signed, pointing her towards the door.

'I'm sorry.'

'*Just go!*' The signs were so big it looked like I was throwing something at her.

Rose went. She didn't even look at me.

I felt as if I'd been stretched too taut and broken, like a rubber band. I wanted to throw something. I wanted to break something. But there was nothing on the *Daedalus* that wasn't tied down. I kicked the wall, but it wasn't satisfying. It wouldn't break or dent or make a loud noise. All it did was hurt my foot, and I cried out a tiny, whispery grunt of frustration. I wished I was Quin. He could have started screaming. I wished I was 42. She could have just grabbed Rose and forced sense into her skull, ethics be damned. I wished I was Rose herself, who could cry and mourn and maybe go to the old man to make it all better. Most of all, I wished I was Xavier, the person she really loved. The only man she wanted.

But I couldn't scream, and I couldn't weep, and I couldn't fix this. Instead, I slid down the wall and bit my knuckle until my finger ached. When I finally released my teeth there were deep marks in my skin, and the area between them was almost white with blood loss. I watched the hard knot of tortured flesh bleed slowly back into my finger. It was numb.

I wished I was numb. But I felt everything, everybody's everything. I felt far too much.

chapter 9

The rest of that single day awake was my own version of purgatory. I forced myself back into the common area to eat, but the seemingly fine food was tasteless. Xavier said the meals were likely to get less exciting as we neared Europa. The truth was that food, not being alive, could not be stassed, so they were still reliant upon traditional methods of preserving and freezing. The caviar, he said, was likely to stay good, though – it was very well canned.

Tristan did receive my note, and she and Penny wrote up a long treatise together, telling me about what was happening at school. I sent another reply, but it was short – I had to remind them I didn't have much to say. I sent a reply to Bren, mostly saying I knew how he felt. Then I sent a letter to Dr Bija. At first I wrote up the whole situation with Rose, every voyeuristic detail, not sparing myself. Then I read through it, and felt disgusted with myself. Dr Bija had helped me to form my code of ethics. To admit to her in an impersonal letter that I had just thrown it all out the airlock was appalling. I wanted her advice, but she wouldn't be able to get back to me for over a month. Finally, I erased the whole letter and just sent her a thank you note for the poems. I read through them a few times. They were all about isolation and emptiness. They did not help.

Rose did not try to speak to me again.

Though it felt like forever, the day ticked on, and the disembodied voice over the ship's tannoy told us to resume our places in our stasis chambers and await the next leg of our journey.

Before we headed back to the stass tubes I found Quin. Rose had gotten to him first. 'You and Rose fighting?' was all he said when I saw him.

I closed my eyes and sighed. Quin surprised me by catching hold of my shoulder, lightly touching my neck. His mind exuded consolation. I shrugged him off, which he accepted without resentment. 'Apparently, I'm with you this time. Come on, dummy. Back to beddy-bye.'

Quin hopped into the double tube as if he was diving down a water-slide. I climbed in behind him a bit more sedately. As I lay back on the satin-of-silk cushions, I thought of what it had felt like to kiss Rose, and my hands clenched. I remembered it so clearly. Rose was right; stass kept things so bright and immediate in your mind. As Quin shuffled around and farted and muttered about the preserved food in the galley, I realized I'd end up remembering this terrible snapped rubber-band feeling forever, too. If anything, my mood sank even lower.

Quin finally stopped chattering and really looked at me. 'Okay, so what happened? You look better. But you're acting worse.'

I made a rude gesture at him.

He laughed. 'Honestly, Otto. Why don't you just throw her back onto a couch and snog her. What have you got to lose?'

I glanced at him. *'Who says I haven't already?'* I signed.

Quin went very still. 'And what happened?'

'Nothing good.'

'Not as hot as all that, was she?'

'Coit off.'

Quin settled down beside me and offered me his hand. Offered, didn't take.

I didn't really feel like offering the whole story. With one finger I tapped his palm, just letting him feel my frustration.

'Hm,' he said. 'You're right. Nothing good.' He considered. 'So what is the crux of the issue?'

'*The crux of the issue,*' I signed, enjoying the pattern of the words, *'is that she's in love with someone else.'*

'Bren's not here.'

I groaned and covered my face with my hands. *'Not Bren,'* I signed in frustration.

Quin grunted. 'So the rumours are true.'

I looked up. *'What?'*

'So Rose really was dating the old man, eh?'

I sat up and nearly cracked my head on the ceiling of the stass tube. *'Don't you spread that around!'*

'Everybody's guessed,' Quin said with contempt. 'We can count. Sixty-two years ago Mr Zellwegger would have been just the right age for a bit of sport.' I glared, and Quin pulled back, looking innocent. 'I've said nothing!' he said. 'I don't need to. Not everyone believes it, anyway. It shouldn't be a problem unless they're still shacking up now, right?'

I kicked Quin in the shin. Hard. The idea hurt so badly on such a number of levels, and Quin's casual quip had been like a bullet wound. I expected him to blast me back, but all he did was curl up, grabbing his leg. 'Holy coit, was that called for?' he asked, glaring up at me. He grunted. 'Nice to know you're feeling better, bro.'

'You say anything like that again ...'

'And I'm your boxing bag, yeah, I got that.' He rubbed his leg and pulled away from me. 'Noid, you and Nabiki. No wonder you were dating.' He shook his head. 'So Rose is still in love with the paramour of yesteryear, huh?'

I sagged back against the cushions and sighed.

'I really don't see the problem here,' he added.

'She's in love with someone else!'

'Some sped who's eighty years old,' Quin pointed out.

'74,' I told him. *'Quite a bit of interplanetary travel. He's lost some years in stasis.'*

'So what? It's still creepily old.'

'So's Rose.'

'Give me a break.'

I shook my head. *'Really. She's older than she looks. In many ways.'*

'So are you. You can't go through what you've been through in your life and not be older than your years.' I looked at him. Quin was almost never this serious. Or this kind.

'Old in pain, maybe, not in practice. It doesn't matter. I'm not him.'

'Well, neither is he, anymore,' Quin pointed out.

'What?'

Quin looked at me. 'She was in love with him when they were both kids, right? God, I hope that's true, unless he was defrosting her for the occasional dinner date.' I narrowed my eyes at him, but he continued. 'Look. People change. And creepioids like him grow up and let their hearts die. Maybe he was a kid like us once – maybe he was like Bren – but he can't be now. He's not the same man he was back then, anymore than you were the same when you were twelve as you are now. But Rose is still a kid. Not just from looking at her, talk to her. She acts young – sometimes younger than Penny. You're a much better choice for her at this stage than he can ever be. Anymore, anyway.'

'Since when were you in favour of this?'

'Since you had nothing left to lose,' Quin said candidly.

I thought about this. *'It doesn't matter. Rose can't let him go. Not in her heart.'*

'She'll learn to. Soon enough, she won't have a choice.'

I raised my eyebrow.

'He's a jaded corporate puppet with old man smell who has "conveniently" fallen into a position of authority, after his own boss was mysteriously killed,' Quin said. 'That's the sort of thing that happens in UniCorp. People conveniently die – including us. He's not the saint your Rose seems to make him out to be, and, eventually, she'll realize that.'

I frowned. *'What have you got against Mr Zellwegger?'*

'Nothing, all right?' Quin said. 'Nothing concrete. It's just that I can, in fact, count.'

I shook my head, not understanding.

'Yeah, it was gilded Guillory who signed off on us being created,' said Quin, looking at me as if I were stupid. 'But there were thousands of executives and dozens of board members, and not one of them stopped it.' His face twitched as he suppressed his anger. '*He* didn't stop it. That man sat back and read status reports on us as we were stolen from our species, and our DNA was mutilated, and we finally died, one by one, under their theoretically tender care. He's UniCorp. I don't like any of them.'

This was true, but I'd never heard him so burned about Mr Zellwegger before. '*Where are you getting all this?*' I asked.

'Nabiki pointed it out at your *bon voyage*,' Quin said. 'After she found out I was going too.'

I grabbed his wrist. *'Was this before, or after she broke your nose?'* I asked, teasing him. But the idea that Nabiki had beaten him didn't embarrass him. In fact, he seemed rather proud of his war wound. Nabiki was strong, strong as he was, and she …

Then I caught something I wished I hadn't. An image, much more graphic than I would have liked, of Quin and Nabiki behind the administration offices at the lab. And this wasn't imagination. This was memory. I nearly choked.

'Nabiki?'

Now Quin blushed, turning his cheeks the colour of an eggplant. But his smirk was undeniable. I had to let him go. It was just too outrageous. *'You,'* I signed. *'And Nabiki.'* I couldn't figure out if I was jealous or not.

'Would I do such a thing to my brother?' Quin asked, all innocence.

I stared at him in sheer surprise. *'How?'* I finally asked.

He grinned, more than a little embarrassed. 'She, ahm … was pretty upset at your going away party.'

'*And you comforted her,*' I signed. I could see the whole thing. Her tears, his final admittance of his feelings, her melting in his arms. Then that graphic moment – no. I was not going to think about that.

'No,' Quin said. 'I let her beat me to within an inch of my life.'

Now I was surprised. *'What?'*

'She was angry,' Quin said. 'Very, very angry.' He smirked. 'She broke my nose, I split her lip, she blacked my eye.' He touched his side and winced, remembering. 'I think she even cracked a couple of ribs. I didn't know you'd picked up someone so violent.'

I stared at him. Neither had I.

'Things, ah … got interesting about the time she had me on the ground. I mean, I probably could have stopped her, but I was starting to like it. She …'

'*Stop!*' I signed. I'd seen enough of that in his mind. I very much wished Quin hadn't told me any of this. *'So … what are you doing here, then? Why'd you leave her?'*

Quin looked annoyed. 'Falling in love is not the end-all and be-all of my existence, thank you very much. Nor should it be. Blood is thicker than other bodily fluids, and life is not about some girl I met in high school. You're my brother. I'm not going to let a couple of extremely pleasant hours with a girl change that.'

'Some brother,' I signed. I was very ambivalent about this development between Quin and Nabiki.

'Jealous, are you?'

'Shut up.'

'You didn't want her, right?' I didn't answer. 'Right?'

'It was never so simple. It's not like you care, anyway.'

'I care,' Quin said, an admittance which surprised me. 'It won't change what I do, but I care.'

'Could have fooled me.'

'Oh, let it go!' Quin rolled his eyes. 'The least you can do is forgive me for snogging your ex.' Snogging – that was putting it mildly. 'I mean, I'm giving up a year of my life and bouncing halfway across the solar system for you.'

'Who asked you?'

'No one had to. I volunteered.'

'Why? All you do is hurt people and make snide comments.'

Quin propped himself up on his elbow and looked at me. 'Look. All my life I've been jealous of you.' I blinked in surprise. 'There, I said it,' he said. 'Not just you,' he added. 'All of you. You and the others, Sven, Tristan, Una. Hell, even Penny. We've all been hacked and slashed and recombined, but you, you got powers out of it. You got the ability to enter people's minds. I never got that. All I got was a wonky heart and skin the colour of a gun barrel. Even Penny is unique. She's obviously different, in more than one way. She can't speak and she's childlike. People cut her slack. Whether they should or not is beside the point, they do. Me …' He shook his head and sighed. 'I'm just the failure.' He lay back and looked up at the ceiling. 'And I feel … I feel like it's my job to look after you all. And I hate that. I shouldn't have to do that. But I do have to. 'Cause no one else will.'

'But why?'

'Because we only have each other. I've always known that.' His eyes went distant then. 'You won't remember 49,' he said. 'No one does.'

I shook my head slightly.

'There were fifty mothers and a hundred of us,' he reminded me. 'Most of us didn't make it. Those that did were single births. 'Cept me and 49.' He looked at me then. 'You didn't remember that, did you.' I shook my head. 'He was only four when he died,' he said. 'I don't even know if his brain worked. I don't know if he was one of the simple ones or not. But he was my brother. We had shared the same blood. And his heart just stopped. I sat there with him for … I don't know how long. I couldn't tell time yet, but it felt like forever. I just sat. Watching him turn cold. I knew he was dead, and I knew how to speak … but there was no one to tell.' He looked at me. 'We're all alone out here. They built us and then abandoned us. And I knew that, when I saw him go all still. There was no one who would ever grieve for him but me. Pretty harsh thing to learn when you're four.'

We sat in stillness and silence for a moment. Finally I signed, *'What has this got to do with Rose or Nabiki?'*

'Nabiki loves you,' Quin said. 'She still loves you. I know that. That doesn't mean anything she might feel for me is less real.'

'Nabiki doesn't get panic attacks or feel guilty for loving someone else.'

'Because she knows you don't love her,' Quin said. 'Not that way, anyway. Rose is torn because that old man out there still cares for her. You can see it every time he looks at her. It probably would have been better for both of them if he'd gone away. But he didn't.' His face darkened for a moment, and he looked away from me. 'Look,' he said. 'Just don't worry about it, okay? You love Rose. She loves you. That old man is just in the way, but he's old. I don't think it's going to matter for very long.'

'I don't have very long,' I pointed out.

'You don't know that,' Quin said.

'*Since when were you the optimist?'*

Quin sighed, but he didn't answer me. He continued not answering until the stass chemicals dragged us both into unconsciousness.

chapter 10

'So you're the EP kids. I always wanted to see one of you.'

Quin turned away from the window and raised an eyebrow at the boy. 'That's funny,' he said. 'I always wanted to see an idiot. The good fairy must be in a mood for granting wishes.'

Kenji's cheeks went red and he fidgeted in his seat. 'Well, there's no need to be rude about it.'

'Oh, it's no trouble,' Quin said blithely. 'My pleasure.'

This was going to be a fun trip.

Kenji and Moriko Zellwegger were exactly the kind of people who got on Quin's nerves. They were the kind of people who got on my nerves, too, but I was considerably more tolerant than Quin about being ogled. I'd had more experience with reporters and scientists. You've never known ogling until you've been in a room with twenty neuro-medical students who all had to take notes on your active brain waves for a graduate school class.

The twins were fourteen years old, and looked alike enough to be clones, though they were only fraternal twins. I suspected it was an affectation, because they seemed to do it deliberately. Their thick black hair was cut identically short. They were dressed in matching but colour-contrasting jumpsuits, similar to the outfits Jamal wore when he wasn't in school uniform. The girl's was black and purple; the boy's was black and blue. The two had accompanied their father up to the Jove Station to retrieve the four of us. Technically, the twins were Bren's cousins, and I eyed them in the hopes of seeing some spark of the same clarity of thought that Bren possessed. No such luck. Their thoughts might have been clear, but only because their heads appeared entirely empty.

Their father seemed a pretty straight thinker. Dr Zellwegger was a middle-aged Eurasian man who wore the Europan equivalent of overalls, and a set of grim lines glowered regimentally on his forehead. Apart from the stress lines, he looked a lot like Bren's mom. I rather liked Mrs Sabah. I hoped I'd like this man, too.

Dr Zellwegger was not a bioengineer, which lifted him highly in my estimation. He wasn't a medical doctor, either, but he was working with one – a woman called Dr Shiva – who was well versed in my medical history. Dr Zellwegger was actually a scientist, with a PhD in steryochemistry, who had spent the last two years researching the natural intercellular signalling of the plankton. Not just the electro microbes, but the inter-connectivity of the plankton as a whole. He didn't talk much.

The Jovian docking station had been on a pass by Europa, so we didn't have a very long flight down to the moon. When we got into the shuttle, Moriko and Kenji had suggested we take over one of the observation bubbles. The elder Zellweggers had declined, preferring the more comfortable inner lounge. There were four observation bubbles along the sides of the ship, and while they were not as comfortable as the inner seats, I was told they would provide an excellent view.

To get to the bubble we had to climb through the floor and up to an angled dome. Once we climbed through, the gravity shifted, as the grav-mats tilted to make the side of the ship the floor. I rather liked the falling feeling as my centre shifted, but Rose cried out and stumbled, her legs going weak. She was all right after a moment, but it drew looks from the twins.

All I saw when I got into the bubble was black sky and a tiny point of light that I assumed was the sun. It seemed painfully far away. As the shuttle undocked and spun, however, I was assaulted by the sight of the largest planet in our solar system.

Describing Jupiter is something the greatest poets of our age still have trouble with. My own pitiful attempts at poetry can't even begin to encompass it. It's not just that Jupiter is a fiery, swirling mass of colour, gorgeous in its striations and awe-inspiring with its sheer beauty. It is all of that, whites and reds and oranges all layering over each other like a giant confection. That is what it looks like. But that isn't what it is.

Jupiter

is

HUGE.

There is simply no other way to describe it. I stared out of the window, and I simply couldn't fathom it. My mind couldn't stretch that far. I couldn't absorb the sight of something that large, that close. My eyes kept playing tricks on me, turning it into a tiny rubber ball not centimetres before my face, or zooming the planet out across the cosmos so there was nothing in my view except the colours, swirling and swirling, eternal storms of gas boiling in space.

Unfortunately, the twins were the jaded types who can't hold awe for more than two seconds without chittering about it on their cells and drawing the attention back to themselves. Kenji's somewhat racist icebreaker had been like a declaration of war to Quin. I could tell he had decided they were the spawn of Satan's imps, and therefore deserved a good taking down. Rose realized it too, and shifted away from the view (her artist's sensibilities probably weeping with regret) to take an active part in the conversation, and hopefully bring it to polite terms. Rose and her old-fashioned customs. Had to love 'em.

'You're Bren's cousins,' Rose said. 'He's a friend of ours.'

'I kn*ow*,' Moriko said, with a squeal in her voice I was sure I didn't like. 'We're *so* lucky to be related to him. It makes us kind of like stars by proxy.' Moriko unhooked her seat harness and hopped over to me, grinning all over her face. 'I couldn't believe it when they said you were coming!' she said. 'It's all over the moon, you know. All over the Jovian system! The EP kids! I'm so glad I get to meet you!' She grabbed at my hand as if she wanted to wring it off.

I snatched it away so fast it looked like I was trying to hit her.

She slapped both hands to her mouth in what I suspected to be mock embarrassment. 'Oh, coit, I did it, didn't I. You don't like to be touched, do you.' I didn't buy it. She had to have known this before she'd tried to touch me. After all, she hadn't come over trying to grab at Quin.

Quin wasn't buying it, either. 'No coiting kidding,' he snapped from the other side of the dome. He had his eyes fixed on the storm-torn gas giant. 'Got that from the frantic attempt to escape, did you? Brilliant.'

Moriko hunched her shoulders, a gesture halfway between obsequiousness and chagrin, and she went back to her seat near Kenji, who was lounging casually in his seat, his feet up on another one.

'What did you mean, stars by proxy?' Rose asked.

'Well ... You're celebrities up here, you knew that, right? People follow you, like holostars.'

I blinked. I hadn't known that. Neither had Quin from the look of distaste on his face. 'Follow what?'

'Oh, everything,' Moriko said. 'What your favourite bands are, how you're doing in lessons, who's dating who.'

Kenji nodded at Quin. 'You're 50, of course? So you must be ... 76?'

'Otto,' Quin said firmly, ignoring that he even got my number wrong. 'His name, even though no one actually wants to hear your nasal little whine say it, is Otto.'

'And he's Quin,' Moriko said.

'I can say my own name, thanks,' Quin said sarcastically.

'No, wait, he's 86,' Kenji said, pointing at me. 'They lost track of him, remember?'

'Yeah, he's the one that went to that school. The one with the girlfriend! Wait a minute. Are you still dating?'

'No,' Quin said, with a smirk that made me want to slap him. I shook my head, confirming the news.

'Aww!' Moriko said, her face falling. 'It was *so* romantic! That was Nabiki Sato, right? She's my mother's second cousin, once removed. I think.'

I snorted quietly, but it didn't surprise me. ComUnity was pretty small. The idea that one powerful UniCorp family had married into another powerful UniCorp family wasn't surprising in the least. Nabiki, however, was clever. These two kids, no matter how intelligent, were vacant. I didn't even need to touch them to know that.

'Nabiki was *never* romantic,' Quin added.

'How would you know?'

Quin blinked at her as if she was stupid – which wasn't a surprise, really. 'Well ...' he began. I tisked my tongue and I eyed him, daring him to spread tales about my love life – or, well, Nabiki's love life, because technically it wasn't mine anymore – to these two vapid children. Quin regarded me with a considering eye before he opened his mouth. 'Well, we're all in that school now,' he said instead.

'I *know!*' Moriko complained. 'It's been months without a legitimate update. Right now it's all bootlegs and rumours. It's driving the EP forums *mad!*'

'What?' I signed.

'Oh, I know that one, I know that one!' Moriko said with eagerness. 'That one's, ahm ... *"what"*, right? Am I right?'

'If you recognize the sign, you should realize he just asked you a question,' Quin pointed out through clenched teeth. This was a bad sign. 'Unless you haven't gotten to that level yet in basic language.'

'I just mean the followers on the EP forums,' Moriko said.

'Would you,' Quin said, 'care to elaborate on what that means for us Europan laymen?'

'The geneticists on the *Minos* have been monitoring your progress,' Kenji told us. 'They got updates once a week. The forward was eventually made public, as there were so many scientists on board. And once it was public, everyone wanted to see what was happening.'

'It's so much fun!' Moriko said. 'You want to see an episode?'

'An ... episode?' Quin said.

'Yeah! I've got some reruns on my ECell. Wanna see?' Without waiting for a reply, she jumped over to a control panel by the door of the dome and plugged her cell into the wall. The beautiful image of Jupiter was blanked out of one window by a holofeed screen. Moriko flittered through files and finally accessed one labelled, 'EP, 626'.

To the horror of both Quin and myself, a flash image of EP labs made an establishing shot. Then, with a painful juxtaposition of raucous electric music, quick cuts of me and Quin and Tristan and Penny doing various activities at the labs flittered through the holofeed. Tristan running a high jump. Me at my notescreen (my cheeks flushed as I realized I was probably updating my journal in that shot). Penny signing to her tutor. Quin in the gym at a punching bag – how many shots did they have of *that*, I wondered. Then all four of us in the common room playing a game. Various names floated in the ether below our faces, both our embryonic numbers and the names of the editors who had spliced the thing together. Then, with an artistic swirl, the words. 'The EP Kids' flashed over the screen, and settled under a group shot of all four of us.

Quin's face was purple, and I was pretty damn sure he wasn't feeling pure embarrassment, as I was. The first scene began. I realized this really was a rerun. It was from a point in my life just before I'd gotten my scholarship, and all four of us were doing research on the best topic for our essays. The cameras at the labs hadn't been equipped with sound, so the voices – or, well, Quin's voice – was dubbed with someone else's. Our sign was subtitled, and not always accurately. Quin and I sat in bemused disgust for a few more minutes. Then Quin walked through the hologram – his real body interrupting his projected one – and stabbed the programme off. He perched gingerly on the edge of a seat, his fists clenched on his knees. 'Are you telling me,' he said quietly as the image of Jupiter reappeared in the window, 'that our lives are watched up here like a holonovella?'

'Well, you were,' Kenji said glumly. 'Until last spring. Now the updates are sketchy, and don't make for as good viewing.'

That was when Rose had gotten Quin, Penny and Tristan out of the lab and into the summer school programme at UniPrep. I had always known we were being monitored, and that most of our life was public record. But there were plenty more interesting things on Earth, and it had never occurred to any of us that the recordings of our lives would be made the subject of popular social media.

'But we're starting to get some holos from the school,' Moriko said, and I stared at her in shock. The school wasn't like the lab; it wasn't riddled with cameras. Then I realized how stupid that was. Everyone had a cell, everyone had notescreens, there were even security feeds in the most public areas. Anyone with the access – and UniCorp staff had access to most of this – could easily download and search through to find enough images of us to splice together *something*. Particularly if they didn't care about narrative accuracy. 'None of the daily stuff, but we just saw 32 at the track meet, remember?'

Kenji grinned. 'Yeah, that was so sky!'

'And *you*!' Moriko gushed at Quin. 'You're such a hero! We have a copy of you pulling your brother from the pool! You should have heard the girls at school. I must have seen that feed at least a dozen times.'

'You saw …' Quin's face was dark and stiff. 'Where did they get that?'

'I don't know. It looked like a security camera.'

'You mean to say,' Quin said, his voice crisp as a new iceberg lettuce, 'that … *that* … sort of thing has been viewed as entertainment up here?'

'Only the highlights,' Moriko said. 'They edit the records before they send them out.'

This was supposed to make it better? They'd watched my seizures as if it were a scene from a holodrama, only a foil for Quin's heroic rescue. How long had this show been going? Had our Dying Times been the subject of teenage net forums and saccharine montages? With a snarl of fury 42 came back into my mind again. *(What are we, fish in a tank? It was bad enough being monkeys in a lab!)*

'Let me get this straight,' Quin said with a poisonous smile, 'because somehow I can't seem to wrap my head around it.' Moriko giggled, and I eyed Quin. She was missing the signs. Quin was about to lose it. 'You've all been watching edited selections of our lives, regularly, once a week, and chatting about it as if we were actors in some reality holoshow?'

'Well, aren't you?' Kenji asked.

I acted faster than Quin, fortunately, and I was closer to him than he was to Kenji. I stood and slammed him back into his seat, my hand on his chest. Quin's fist was clenched. Kenji had narrowly escaped a broken jaw. *'They don't understand!'* I signed at him with my left hand.

'That's because they're morons!' Quin told me roughly.

'Hey!' Moriko said, rather reasonably. 'We just watch it. We're not the ones with the cameras, and we're not the ones who put the records on Europa Net. If you've got a problem, take it up with Europa HN.'

Quin snorted, sat back, and simmered. He knew as well as I that discussing the matter with Europa HoloNetwork would be a waste of valuable oxygen. Everything on the colonies was owned by one subsidiary or another of UniCorp. There was no getting around it. We may not be treated as slaves in the sense of being made to labour in the fields, but we were owned, patented, monitored hybrids, and UniCorp could do with our records what they pleased. If that included turning our lives into a reality holoshow on Europa, we had no say in the matter.

(Ha!)

Despite 42's opinion of the subject.

'What ... *cretin* came up with this burned idea?' Quin snapped.

'I don't know. We're new to it,' Moriko said. 'We only came to Europa a year and a half ago.'

'Two years,' Kenji corrected her.

'The travel time doesn't count,' Moriko said, annoyed. 'Anyway. I think it's because they don't have celebrities up here. I mean, not home-grown ones. And there you are on Earth, and it's where everyone wants to be, but you're quintessentially Europan!'

'No,' Quin said with an evil smirk. 'Just me.'

Moriko grinned at him. 'You were always my favourite,' she said. 'I'm a follower of Quin'sQuad.'

'Excuse me?' he asked, rather politely, I thought.

'It's one of the net forums,' Kenji said. 'But I'm more into 32 and the sports.'

'Are you.' Rose said flatly.

Something about her voice made all the rest of us turn to look at her. It was the first time she'd spoken since the show started playing. There was a long pause as she stared at Moriko. 'So I'm in these shows,' Rose said finally. I blushed as I realized, if they had Quin saving me, they must have had Rose and me in the pool beforehand. Granted, what we were doing was more cerebral than physical, but it was supposed to have been personal. I knew Rose felt as violated as I did.

'Yeah! Ratings went right up when you came on ... the ... scene ...' Moriko began. She stopped, sensing something was wrong. The silence lay heavy in the dome as Rose's pale face hardened like crystal.

'Find another fandom,' she said finally. Her voice was very hard and very quiet. 'I suggest the band *Overwrought*. The EP Kids show will no longer be airing on Europa HN.'

'The updates say the first of the new episodes will be airing next month,' said Kenji, still oblivious.

Rose shifted her flinty gaze to him. 'No,' she said simply. 'It will not.'

'How do you know?'

'Because before I leave here, I intend to have a meeting with Europa HN. I very much suggest the two of you find another fandom to waste your time on.'

Kenji swallowed. Rose's personality had suddenly seemed to fill the room, and I wondered what her infamous father had been like when he got angry. He must have been formidable. I did not envy the producers at Europa HN. They'd be lucky to get out of the room with their souls.

'You tell them, Briar Rose,' I signed at her, and I grinned. Rose's eyes shot to me and she visibly shrank. It wasn't just because her anger had been spent. She blushed and looked down. I realized it was the first time I'd said anything actually *to* her since the ill-fated kiss. We'd avoided each other for the last two out-of-stasis days on the ship, and when we were in a room together, we spoke to everyone around us, not to each other.

I sighed, and shrank my signs, until they were harder to read. I doubted Moriko or Kenji knew enough sign to eavesdrop, but I didn't want to draw Quin's attention. He seemed to be watching the planet, but it was hard to be sure. '*This is stupid,'* I told Rose. '*I miss you.'*

She shook her head, and I realized she didn't know the sign for 'miss.' I spelled it out for her with one hand, and her blush went from pink to crimson. '*Me two,'* she signed, and I tried not to laugh at her mistranslation. It made me smile, though.

'Otto,' Quin said quietly, interrupting us. I turned to look at him, but he wasn't looking at me. I followed his gaze and finally saw, twisting into our view as the shuttle changed angles, the icy cracked sphere of Europa.

I'd seen pictures of her, of course, but it simply isn't the same as looking out through super-thick NeoGlass at the real thing. The giant snowball that was the moon of my origin was white and smooth, with flowing streaks of red.

'Finally!' Moriko said. 'We got another hour of this before we make it to the elevator.'

'Did you bring any crisps?' Kenji asked.

'You just ate!'

'I'm hungry again.'

They continued on like this for a while, until Quin couldn't take it anymore. 'Do me a favour,' he said. 'Do yourselves a favour. If the two of you shut up long enough, you just might be able to hear us not giving a damn.'

'You know, you're not as nice as I thought you were,' Moriko said.

I laughed. So did Rose, but she covered it quickly. Quin? Nice?

Quin glared at the twins. 'You don't even know me. I've been aggravating people since I was four. I don't actually care what those peeping toms have edited for your entertainment. It is not my job to live up to your expectations of me.'

'I thought you were clever. But you're just mean.'

'I'm violent too,' Quin said, his eyes sparking flame. 'They've diagnosed me with Belligerent Development Disorder and impulse control problems. Bet they don't show that on your weekly hits tape.' Moriko suddenly looked scared, and I didn't blame her. I knew exactly how dangerous Quin could be when he lost it. 'What else have they shown, eh? Do they edit selections of us in the bathroom for the perverts of Europa to peruse at their pleasure?'

'Quin?' Rose said.

Quin turned his ire on her. 'And what do you want, princess? My brother's attentions not enough for you? How many Eepies do you need in your bed at one time?'

Rose blushed, but she kept her back straight, and her voice was pristine. 'I just thought you might want to ask Moriko and Kenji why they came to Europa in the first place.'

'What? You mean it wasn't to follow popular net feeds?'

'No,' Kenji said evenly. 'It was because of Dad's work.'

'He's not a holoeditor, is he?' Quin asked.

'No,' Moriko said, sounding defiant. 'He's a cellular researcher.'

'Dad's working on the microbes, like the ones that made you,' Kenji said.

'What made him want to study the M9s?' Rose asked.

'Well, he studies cellular communication, and the plankton does more communication to more different types of cells than almost anything, anywhere. He says he's studying how they communicate. He's managed to keep them alive for up to fourteen days in a tank.'

That was impressive.

'There. Isn't that great, Quin?' Rose asked.

'Why?'

Rose indicated me with her eyes, and stared at him. Quin's face softened very slightly. Quin looked at the twins, and then at me and Rose. 'Just keep 'em quiet,' he said sullenly. 'My threshold for enduring idiots has narrowed yet again during the course of this interminable journey.' He glared at the twins. 'Which I had been hoping to enjoy in awestruck peace and quiet, but god forbid you do anything against your religion, like keep your burned mouths shut for ten seconds.' He turned to look back out of the window at Europa.

She approached faster than I would have thought possible, but the Jovian shuttles were built for high speed.As we zoomed in towards the surface of Europa, the gravity in the shuttle shifted as the gravity of the moon warred with the polarity of the gravity mats at our feet. Rose turned so pale she looked green. Suddenly she stood up and headed for the hatch.

'Rose?' Moriko asked, but I was already on my feet.

'I need to find the vacuum drift,' she said, pushing past me. I caught a flash of thought as she passed. Nausea. The gravity shifts were wreaking havoc on her weakened system.

About ten minutes later Rose slipped back through the hatch. I was waiting for her. I caught her arms as she dipped with the gravity shift again, and held her steady for a long moment.

'You okay?' I asked her.

She nodded. 'I don't think gravity shifts agree with me,' she said. She coughed a little, as if making sure her throat still worked. She moved all her fingers and stretched her feet out, wiggling the toes inside her shoes. Her body was still recovering from her long stint in stasis – her doctors had said she might never fully recover – and it was not used to such massive changes.

But then she looked behind me, and she stopped worrying about her body. 'Otto,' she whispered to me. 'Look.'

I turned to where she had indicated, and then gripped her hand tightly. We were low enough now to see the surface of the planet. It felt like waking from a dream. Or maybe falling into one.

The glacial ice floes surrounded the entire moon. The images of the moon from a distance made it look so smooth and spherical, like a blue billiard ball, but down here, inside the thin atmosphere, the crags and mountains became clear. They shone silver and red in the strange light. The thin atmosphere turned the sky a deep blue-black, with a pale pinprick of a sun in the middle, and several of the brighter stars still visible, even though it was the Europan equivalent of 'day'. And still, dominating the view, the crown of Jupiter himself, red and raging, taking up what seemed like half the sky. We could not see his famous 'red spot' from our position, but his heavy presence was overwhelming nevertheless. It was strange to realize that he would never move from that spot in the sky. The tidally locked Europa did not move the way Luna did around the Earth. There he was, a king on his throne, never blinking, never moving.

The surface of the moon was terrifying and beautiful. It made me feel giddy. Sudden planes of smooth red ice like lava floes had bloomed from cracks in the icy crust and made the moon seem like she was bleeding. This rusty red bled, they told me, out of the plankton. There was a rumour that evidence of 'life' had been found the moment the settlers arrived on Europa, and the information was suppressed until UniCorp could figure out how to exploit it. This didn't surprise me. If UniCorp couldn't make money, it would do nothing. If the scientists had discovered life before UniCorp had mapped and patented and made it theirs, they might have demanded ecological surveys, endangered species regulations, contamination procedures. In short, it would have damaged the bottom line.

Rose knelt on one of the seats and stared out of the window at the ice glaciers below us. I sat beside her, and also turned to watch. We did not let go of each other's hands.

The light was dim, and cast blurred shadows over the glaciers. Then, in the distance, a black hole opened into the ice. This hole grew bigger, resolving into a cavern, an open maw with myriad lights that dragged the shuttle inside and swallowed her whole.

The interior of the cavern was clearly manmade. Radiation shielded rooms dotted the corners. The lights flashed and the shuttle quietly hummed, setting itself down with a deep clunk.

'This is where we're going?' Rose asked.

'No,' said Moriko. 'This is just the elevator. This isn't even a place. No one's up here. Only a crew of twelve man the top of the elevator.'

'Because if there are only twelve of them, they don't count as "people",' Quin said scathingly. 'Now I get it.'

The view out of the NeoGlass window changed as the lights went out. Then, with a deep hum, a large square out of the landing bay began to descend, our shuttle with it. The first few metres were metal, but soon the metal walls vanished, replaced by the smooth shine of polished ice. The lights of the ship were the only illumination.

'Is this safe?' Rose asked, echoing my own fears.

'Oh, you mean the ice?' Moriko said. 'It's heavy ice, melted and refrozen to form the shaft. It's perfectly safe. Stronger than steel in this environment.'

'Yes! Heed the words of the expert,' Quin said to Moriko with a reverent bow. 'Those words, perfectly safe. The *Titanic*. GMOs. Marmots. All of them are perfectly safe.' He gave a mad grin, and Moriko cringed. I wasn't convinced either, but the ship was going slowly down and down, and I had no choice but to trust it.

The trip down, however, seemed much slower than the journey from the orbital dock. There was nothing to look at out of the window. Rose asked Kenji and Moriko about where we were headed.

'One of the old ice villages,' Moriko said. 'Mostly they're tourist destinations, now. There's six of them. We're headed to the Crystal Village. They all have different themes. There's Ice Palace, Hoarfrost Forest, the Diamond Caverns, Star Fields and Frozen Fantasy. We've only stayed at Diamond Caverns before now. They left that looking like a cave, all icicles and little tunnels.'

'It's not all tourist stuff,' Kenji said looking at Quin. He must have seen his expression. 'The villages have to keep running. They're needed to maintain the elevators and the tubes for the icebreakers. The tourist stuff just makes it so they have enough income to make it worth while.'

'When will we get there?' Rose asked.

'About another forty minutes,' Kenji said.

Quin put his cell in his ear and listened silently to some music.

Rose looked at me and sighed. She squeezed my hand. *'I'm sorry,'* she told me.

'Me too.'

And that was really all the words we needed. I chuckled at how simple it all was suddenly. *'I love it when you laugh,'* she told me. *'I wish you'd do it more often.'*

'It tends to kill all the other laughter in a room,' I told her. I expected her to try and tell me something else, but she was tired. Gently, like a child, she nuzzled my shoulder. Her thoughts were wordless, but clear. Her muscles ached. The strange gravity was making her ill, and she was worried about her nanos – tiny machines that were keeping her heart and kidneys functioning normally.

'Nanos stay active through gravitational shifts,' I told her. *'Quin loves the grav courts at school. Remember, he needs them for his heart, too.'*

That reassured her a little.She still felt ill, but it felt good to have my arms around her, to hear my heart within my chest, still beating. *'Strong heart,'* she thought.

I pressed my lips to the top of her head. *'It has to be.'*

'So how long have you two been dating?' Moriko asked suddenly.

It was an obvious assumption, and it sent both our minds reeling. We pulled away from each other. 'We're not,' Rose said quickly.

I kept very still, mostly to cover up the terrible crashing feeling that was creeping over me at her words.

'Could have fooled me,' Kenji said with contempt.

Rose's face was red, but she eyed him with cool composure. 'Well, frankly,' she said, with that polite but powerful flint in her voice again, 'such a thing really isn't anyone's business but ours.' She turned away with a look so pointed and final neither of the twins would dare to ask any more personal questions. Rose looked out of the NeoGlass window, watching the glistening ice as we descended into the darkness.

Burn them! Why did they have to get their stupid fingers into this relationship which frankly had enough problems without them? Rose was apart from me now. Not just physically, but emotionally, feeling too awkward to come back into my embrace.

I wanted to scream. The sullen silence which then descended over the observation dome continued unabated for a good twenty minutes. I rubbed my eyes as I realized my headache was coming back. Burn it all. I wished Rose would come back to me.

There was a sudden shift in the momentum of our descent. Rose went white and gripped the arm of her seat, and I shifted my attention to her. '*You okay?*' I asked, grabbing her hand.

'Yeah, I'm fine,' she said, gritting her teeth. But she gripped my hand tightly. She felt very nauseated, but there wasn't anything in her stomach. All she could do was keep her jaw tight and endure.

Soon the blackness of the ice began to turn grey, and then with great suddenness we found ourselves in another hangar. This one was smaller, no room to turn the shuttle and nowhere for it to go if one did. With a slight judder the lift settled, and we had arrived at our destination.

Moriko and Kenji grabbed their satchels and jackets and slid down the hatch, disdaining the ladder. A sign lit up, warning that outside the bubble the gravity had been reduced to Europa standard – roughly thirteen per cent of our normal body weight. The shaft was at quite an angle now. The twins knew the gravity, and jumped without hesitation. Quin scrambled down without even looking at me. Rose followed, much more subdued. I looked out of the dome at the yawning gap above us. There was no light visible from above. It was too far away. Taking a deep breath I went to the edge of the hatchway and took the plunge.

I landed as lightly as a cat, my bones hardly feeling the impact. I felt strangely free in this gravity; strong, invincible. I grinned. I rather liked Europa.

We joined Xavier and Dr Zellwegger and headed for the exit, following the small collection of passengers down the gangway. There were some people there holding sign screens, and some others waiting to greet their passengers. It looked like any ordinary flightport, save for the shuttle we were exiting and the cage of tracks that held the floor of the lift. From this end I could see the great engines on their eight tracks, ready to lift the shuttle back to the surface.

It was cold. Not deathly, alien ice-moon cold, but the cold of a deep winter. Or more like a freezer, really. Bright lights seemingly screwed directly into the ice turned the blue ice walls to white in shiny patches. We were loaded onto a decorative tram that led us through more ice tunnels, and finally into a vast chamber, like a roofed stadium. The lights on the icy ceiling were too bright to look at directly. Five tiny suns shone on – it was hard to say what it was. At first glimpse, the place was like a crystal shop, a massive, glittering diamond. When you blinked the dazzle from your eyes, you could see it was a village. A tiny paradise, with buildings formed – or at least decorated – by bricks of ice. Statues of sculpted ice graced every corner, and everything glittered and shone. It was stunningly beautiful, but something disturbed me. Everything looked false and carefully arranged.

Rose shut her eyes and grunted at the glare. I knew it was too bright for her.

'This is the Crystal Village,' Moriko told us. 'We'll only be here for a day or two, until the next icebreaker makes it up through from the *Minos*. We've got rooms in the Norway Chalet.'

The little train turned in a picturesque circle through the village, showing off all the amenities – an ice rink; a wall of recreational slides, twisting and turning where children in coats screamed joyfully; a demonstration of ice sculpting – finally stopping at a crystal clear building which was almost a fairy-tale palace. This was the 'train station' which served only as a focal point for the train to stop at. An inspector stopped each of us as we got off the tram and made us open our bags. I wished I knew what the security was worried about. What kind of things were contraband in a low-technology ice village?

By this time, Rose was shuddering with cold. She had almost no body fat, and she got cold very easily. We had not brought adequate clothing for this refrigerated paradise. Xavier took off his suit jacket and draped it round Rose's shoulders, but it wasn't going to be enough.

'We'd best get to the chalet as soon as possible,' he said as he held Rose's shivering shoulders.

'Sorry,' Moriko said. 'We should have thought about coats.'

'Or anything at all,' Quin said without a blink.

'Let's just go,' Xavier said before either of the twins could react. I could tell he was regretting bringing Quin. I couldn't blame him.

The Norway Chalet was ice-white and blue, like everything else in this village. It was formed like a Norwegian stave church, only much bigger. When we got inside, everything changed. The gravity returned to normal, the gravity pads in the floor exerting Earth force. The walls went from ice to wood, and the decor was that of a ski chalet. It was much warmer.

'We should show you around,' Moriko said. 'Meet us in the lobby in an hour and we'll go ice-skating.' She was clearly excited.

'I think I'll do something more fun,' Quin said. 'Like drive icicles into my eyes.'

'Don't mind Quin,' Rose said. 'He's always like that.'

'You know, kids,' Dr Zellwegger said to them. 'They've just had a long trip. Remember how long it took us to recover from the stass journey?'

'Yeah, but they're okay,' Kenji said.

'One of them is very sick,' said Dr Zellwegger, glancing at me. 'Rose is still fragile, and your grandfather needs to rest. Since young Mr Essential here doesn't seem interested ...'

Quin made a sound of scorn somewhere between a bark and a groan.

Dr Zellwegger's mouth twitched. I wondered if he was trying not to laugh. 'Why don't you two go out alone?' he said. 'We'll be here until tomorrow when the icebreaker gets here. Maybe you can show them around in the morning.'

'But I wanted to show them ... around ... uh, now,' Moriko said again.

'You wanted to show them off,' said Dr Zellwegger. Clearly he wasn't as oblivious as his children. 'They don't want the media attention. Go on.'

The twins headed off, looking disgruntled. 'Thanks, Ted,' said Xavier. His son only nodded at him.

We were shown into small but luxurious separate rooms, and left to our own devices. My room was beautifully decorated, with thick carpeting and plush draperies. The windows were iced over and cloudy. In fact, at closer examination, the windows were actually thick ice, which softened the harsh artificial light from the ceiling globes outside. Everything was panelled in wood and there was a subtle scent to the whole place – a kind of musty, crisp scent that seemed to soak into my pores. I went up to the roaring fire against the wall and held my cold hands to it. The heat felt wrong. I realized the fire was actually a tiny holovid, just an illusion, and the heat was coming from a small vent behind it. I supposed it wasn't safe to really burn anything here, with the oxygen levels variable. I snorted and pulled away. Did these mock memories of a distant planet really make anyone feel at home? But the chalet obviously did well for itself. Clearly, it worked.

I wasn't on my own for long. I barely had time to take a shower and wash all the residual stasis smell out of my hair before a heavy banging on my door drew me out of the bathroom. I peered through the peephole and saw Quin, fidgeting in the hallway. I let him in.

'Otto! Come on, I want to show you something.'

I shook my head and retreated back into my room. Quin followed me, agitated. 'Come on!' he repeated. 'You've always wanted to see Europa, and now you're just going to sit here in your room? What's that about?'

'*I'm sick!*' I signed, exasperated. '*If you wanted to go with the twins, you should have just said.*'

'I have no intention of following the moronic wunderkinds on a sight-seeing tour through their own bloated egos. I want to see *Europa*, not some Europa-themed tourist park.'

'*Quin,*' I signed. '*I'm not feeling well.*'

'You're standing,' Quin said.

I sighed. My head was in a painful whirl, and the idea of running around that bright, echoing cathedral of an ice palace did not appeal. '*You go on and on at me about taking care of myself,*' I told him. '*Now I am, and you're annoyed.*'

'I don't want you being stupid,' Quin said. 'But this is important.'

'*No!*' I signed, with a snap of my fingers to illustrate the point.

'What do you mean, no? How many chances like this are you going to have?' Contempt spread across his face. 'You're going to go play with your princess, aren't you,' he snarled. 'You come all this way, and you're still mooning over that ice witch!'

'*She's not an ice witch, and she's not mine,*' I signed at him.

'Well, that was your choice,' Quin said. 'And it was a coiting idiotic one.'

'*What have you got against Rose suddenly?*' I asked him.

He sighed, and I could tell he was trying not to shout at me. 'She's fine,' he said. 'But she's just a girl, and she's making you *crazy!*' He signed the word at me to illustrate *his* point.

'*You're the one with the mental diagnosis you're so proud of, Belligerent Development Disorder,*' I signed back. '*I wish you'd never come.*'

Quin stared at me, and his dark face went a shade paler. No one could have seen it but one of us. His jaw was trembling as he said, 'You know what? I wish it too.' He turned on his heel and left me alone.

I grabbed the side of my face after he was gone, pressing sense into my head. Why was I fighting with Quin? It wasn't really my nature, even though Quin was remarkably easy to fight with. Then I realized the truth. I'd lost another synapse or ten. Or a thousand. It was probably part of the personality changes I'd been told to expect when Dr Svarog told me my brain was slowly dying.

What else could that do to me? Could my code of ethics go completely out the window? What with what had happened with Rose, I wondered if it already had. A sudden terror of what kind of monster I'd be if it vanished shot a frisson up my spine.

I needed to go see Rose. She always made me feel better.

I went up to the wall in my room, where an infoscreen glowed a UniCorp logo of a charging Unicorn. Every once in a while its head would shake or legs would stomp. When I touched the screen the unicorn ran away, and I was rewarded with an information panel. Which was Rose's room? I was about to look it up when my eyes caught on the wooden walls. I looked more closely. The pattern wasn't irregular enough to be actual wood. I touched it. The material it was formed from did not feel synthetic, like plastic or metal. I scratched my nail on it, and a tiny portion came away. I sniffed it. It smelled of … I couldn't recognize it. Something musty and organic. I looked around. All the furniture was made of this mock wood, I realized. I wondered what they made it from.

I found the number of Rose's room and went up to find her. She answered the door at my knock and threw her arms around me, tightly. I was surprised. 'Hey,' I whispered in her ear. 'Everything okay?'

'I don't like this place,' Rose said, pulling away from me. 'It makes me itch, it's all cordoned off and beautiful.' She shook her head. 'It's false. Very UniCorp.' She swallowed. 'It reminds me of my mother.'

I wanted to say something, but there was nothing I could do that would have comforted her. There was something I knew which could, though. '*Where's your sketchbook?'* I signed.

Rose looked uncomfortable. 'Um … I didn't bring it.'

I blinked. Rose without her sketchbook was unfathomable.

'The weight restrictions were terrible, and paper books cost extra. Something about tariffs. They only allow up to two kilos of personal space, and I didn't want to bother Xavier with it. We were jumping through hours of red tape as it was. They said I could get paper here … though I'm not sure where.' I moved my hand, and she interpreted the sign. 'No paints, either. There are tariffs on those, too.'

'*But there's plenty of room for a sketchbook or two.'* I couldn't imagine Rose choosing to bring clothes over a sketchbook. For myself, I hadn't brought anything but some socks and underwear, and my screen, mostly because I hadn't needed anything else, though Dr Svarog had packed my medications for me.

Rose looked embarrassed. 'I … didn't use it.'

'*Why not?*'

'Well …' she swallowed. 'Your … your medicines weighed almost four kilos, and you were already over limit. I brought only light silk underclothes and managed to squeeze some more in. You had the weight for your daily stuff, but there were emergency items, IVs and things … and … there's no way we could buy them up here …'

I folded her into my arms. 'Oh, Rose,' I breathed.

'It's okay. I came here for you, not for me.'

'I'm sorry.'

'Don't be,' she said, her voice stern. 'I made the decision.' She looked me over. 'You okay?'

'*Head hurts,*' I signed. '*A little.*'

She gave me a very sad smile. 'Well. I have some pills for that, if you want.'

I chuckled, and she went and got a bottle from her bag. I didn't argue over it, I just took it. Rose lay me down on her couch and rubbed my shoulders. I barely noticed the headache with her hands on me.

We couldn't have been there more than twenty minutes. The pain had barely had time to dissipate before my rest was cut short by a terrible pop, followed by a rush of what sounded like wind. 'What was that?' Rose asked.

I shook my head, but a loud klaxon suddenly sounded outside the window. I went to look, but the window was ice beyond the insulated layer. It let the light in, but it was next to impossible to see out of. A moment later Rose's door banged open, startling us both.

Xavier stood there panting, his face grey with fright. He must have been running. It was hard to imagine the old man running, but he was only old – he wasn't dead. When he saw Rose there was a visible sagging of relief. His hands, always battling a slight tremor, were shaking badly. 'You're here,' he breathed. He glanced at me. 'Both here,' he added, but I knew he didn't give a squitch about me. 'We need to find Ted and the twins,' he said to Rose. 'I want you to stay with me.'

'Can't you cell them?'

'Try,' Xavier said.

Rose pulled her cell up from around her neck and clicked it. She clicked it again. 'There's no signal.' That was impossible. There was always a signal. 'There's nothing.'

'Stay with me,' Xavier said again to Rose. 'I don't want you out of my sight!' He took Rose's hand in his and strode out the door. I got the feeling I could have stayed stock still and Xavier would never have noticed, but Rose looked over her shoulder as he dragged her, and I knew she expected me to stay with her, too. I followed at her heels.

It was pandemonium outside the chalet. People were running and shouts echoed from the dome. That klaxon still sounded loud enough to wake the dead. The cold air was strange, misty, and a glaring orange light was coming from the centre of the village. 'Ted!' Xavier shouted. 'Ted!'

'It's hopeless,' Rose said. 'No one can hear anything in this.'

'The twins were heading to the skating rink,' Xavier said. 'We must find them.'

We darted and wove through the chaos. Xavier kept a firm grip on Rose the entire time. 'But I don't understand. What's happening?' Rose panted.

Xavier's voice was grim. 'What do you think is happening?' he asked. 'There's been a bomb.'

chapter 11

'A bomb?'

'Terrorists,' Xavier said. 'They get a lot of them up here, but the villages are usually safer than this. They usually restrict themselves to the city ships. Easier to hide in a throng of millions.'

'Then that … that light …' Rose's breath was coming in gasps. I wondered if Xavier had forgotten that Rose was still physically fragile, or if he just couldn't be chivalrous in a crisis.

'Firebomb,' Xavier said. 'Probably a hydrogen IED. They get a lot of those too. Waste gases from drawing oxygen from the water.' He pushed someone aside. 'Move! Moriko! Kenji!' he called.

We were nearly at the skating rink now. We were also near the site of the attack. I could see the impact of the firebomb on the village. One of the gorgeous ice buildings was on fire, or whatever synthetic material inside it was. The ice was half melted, leaving a skeleton of a burning building, crackling with smoke. The heat had carved a crater in the ice ceiling above us, and water was steaming around the floor of the building, so we couldn't tell if the fog in the air was mist or smoke. 'God damn it!' Xavier muttered.

'What?'

'They took out the cell tower. That's why there's no signal.'

'What?'

Xavier turned to her. 'No satellites can penetrate the ice shield. No radio waves, no cell feeds, nothing. That's why it's safe down here – the ice shield protects the colony from the radiation. Every connection from outside Europa comes down through the elevators, and is distributed through that tower. Every connection from the city ships is caught at the docks, and distributed *through that tower.* The cell tower allows our cells to link and our screens to connect. That tower,' he pointed to the simmering building, 'was what enabled us to communicate. The whole village is cut off.' He stood back up to his full height. 'Moriko!'

A terrible thought struck me. I grabbed Rose away from him. '*What about Quin?*' He'd gone out – I didn't know where. He could have gotten caught in this … thing.

Rose was a blank. This was not a crisis she felt prepared to handle. 'We'll find him,' she said. 'We'll find all of them.' She turned back to Xavier. 'Moriko! Kenji!' she cried out, her shrill, clear voice very small in the hubbub.

Xavier's wasn't much louder, aged and wavery as it was. And I couldn't shout for Quin. I didn't know what to do.

'The clinic,' Xavier said suddenly. 'If they're hurt, they'll have been brought there.' He took hold of Rose again and dragged her through the throng. I followed at her heels. We were getting farther from the site of the attack, and now there were signs beyond smoke and melting ice. Victims of the fire were being carried away, their bodies burned, their hair singed off. The moaning was terrible. I found myself in a bit of an odd position as eyes started staring at me and whispers carried up and down the rows. I'd been recognized, that was clear enough. 'Oh my god, it's 86!' a young female voice squealed, and was immediately hushed by her companions. The entire village was in chaos, and all she could think about was a passing celebrity? I tried to ignore it.

'Granddad!' The sudden cry was a relief from all the desperate shouting. Moriko and Kenji were sitting by the side of the clinic. The tiny crystal clinic wasn't large enough to accommodate all the victims, and several people were being treated on the ice outside, wrapped in warming blankets. Kenji and Moriko were well enough that they weren't on the stretchers. Moriko looked all right, but she wouldn't leave Kenji, whose leg was thrust out in front of him wrapped in a bandage. She waited for us to come to her before she grabbed Xavier in a huge hug.

Xavier knelt down beside them and touched Kenji's leg. 'What happened? Were you caught in the attack?'

'Not really,' Moriko said. And quite suddenly, and without any warning, she collapsed into tears.

Xavier let Rose go and wrapped Moriko in his arms. 'Shh, shh,' he whispered. 'It's all right, you're with us now. Tell me what happened.'

Moriko was past answering, but Kenji looked up from his seat on the ground. 'The explosion started a panic,' he said. 'Mori and I were on the rink, and people started running over the ice to get away from the fire. I got caught in the rush, and someone else's skate blade caught my leg. It's a really big gash.' He seemed almost proud of it. 'Down to the bone on my shin. Mori almost carried me here, and she answered all the questions while they numbed my leg and bandaged it.' He looked proudly up at his sister, then he scowled. 'She was great until a second ago.'

'I'm here now, she's allowed to break down,' Xavier said gently. He put Moriko gently aside and took both the twins' hands. 'Do you know where your father is?'

The twins shook their heads. Xavier frowned, and then glanced up at Rose.

Rose was almost as blue as I was, and shivering visibly. He only now realized that he had brought her out into winter temperatures without a coat. 'Stay here,' he said, and disappeared into the crowd of wounded. A moment later he returned with a single shiny warming blanket which he activated and then wrapped around Rose's thin frame. 'Hey, *I'm* cold!' Kenji said. 'They said they didn't have enough to go round.'

I had never wanted to say shut up so badly as I wanted to say it then. I glared at him, and he made a visible flinch away from me.

'I asked after Quin,' Xavier told me. 'He's not among the wounded here. Otto, could you see if anyone's still running that store?' he asked, pointing to the kind of tourist souvenir shop that dotted the whole village. 'They'll probably have coats or a sweatshirt or something.'

The store was empty, but there was a rack of coats with a 'RayonEuropa!' sign above them. I looked around for a self-serve credit point, and found one, but when I tried to run my cell over it to read my credit tick, all I got was the same 'no signal' indicator Rose had gotten earlier. The attack really had effectively frozen the entire village. I shrugged. I'd tried, and this was an emergency. Maybe we'd go back and pay later. I grabbed a woman's coat and two men's coats and carried them back out. Xavier wrapped Rose up first. I'd chosen a long white coat for her with a deep hood. It looked warm. Xavier's and mine were both blue, and he shrugged his on without a second glance. I didn't realize how cold I'd been until I zipped the coat up. I pulled up the hood, both to get warmer faster and to conceal my face.

'Come on. We have to get you back to the chalet,' Xavier said. 'Hopefully, Ted will find us there.' He handed the warming blanket to a passing man in uniform. 'Could you take that back to the clinic, please?' he said, and then turned away without waiting for a confirmation.

'Mr Zellwegger?'

Xavier turned back, looking annoyed. 'Yes?'

The uniformed man handed Xavier a small canister. 'This is for you,' he said, and turned away quickly.

Xavier frowned at the canister a moment before his eyes opened wide. 'Get back!' he shouted as he pulled back his arm to throw it far down the trail. He didn't have time. With a pop so sudden it rattled my bones the canister just disappeared. A brief flare of white flame engulfed Xavier's hand, and shrapnel flew too fast for us to see. One second Xavier was holding a cylindrical canister, and the next he wasn't; his hand was on fire and blood trickled down his face.

The force of it dropped him backwards, and a sudden spray of blood arched into the air, splashing across the ice, and across Rose's new white coat, shining luridly on her pale face. '*Xavier!*' She fell to her knees, trying to paw at the wound on his neck, which was where the spray of blood had come from, though there were injuries on his face and his hand was badly burned.

'Rose ...' Xavier flailed, and I could see that Rose was shaking too much to hold pressure on the wound. Moriko and Kenji were helpless, and everyone else was too busy running from the fresh explosion. Nothing for it, then.

I pushed Rose aside and pressed my hand to the slice. I tried to use my coat instead of direct skin-to-skin contact, but the blood seeped through so quickly that it was a fruitless defence. Xavier's pain seeped through with the blood, and his mind was a screeching storm, a blizzard in the Himalayas, frozen and painful, with ice cutting at my psyche.

A thought came through the maelstrom. *Save Rose.*

'Rose is fine!' I told him angrily. *'And she'll hate me if I let you die in front of me.'*

'She'll hate me anyway,' he thought, but the thought scattered as the blood loss fazed him. He was losing consciousness. At his age …

'No you don't!' I told him. *'She can't lose both of us, and I can't be sure I'll survive. Xavier? Xavier, you GET BACK HERE!'*

I think it was that which pulled it forward. Maybe it was the fact that I was drawing him, forcing him to come to me. Maybe it was because I called him Xavier, a name he didn't use anymore. Or maybe it was something more basic than that. Maybe he'd been looking for an escape all along. Maybe it was because half my mind was already primed by what Rose and I had done in the stass chamber. But in any case, he came back. He came back with a vengeance. But it wasn't Mr Zellwegger that fled screaming into my mind, father, grandfather, executive. It was Xavier.

Xavier, no more than nineteen, angry and frightened and lonely and hurting so deeply that I froze as he hurtled himself against my psyche and ripped holes in my sanity.

He was hate and loss and anguish. He was a twisted knot of blame and self-loathing that fed upon itself, feeling guilty for feeling guilty, which only made him angry, which made him guilty, again and again, twisting into a burning coil of torment. A soundless scream ran through my mind as the emotional personification of a young self-tormented Xavier, Rose's soul mate, railed at the old man who had failed to find Rose and had dared to keep going and live the WRONG LIFE!

I wanted to pull away, but this black knot of tortured anguish was worse than any of Rose's briars, and it held me. I hadn't realized how softened her pain was by her circumstances. The stasis itself had softened it. She did not blame herself anymore. But Xavier's pain grabbed me, squeezed me, twisted me in a maelstrom of blackness that wanted to drag down everything – himself, both young and old, Rose, then and now, her parents, the entire corporation of UniCorp, his family, everything. Xavier as a young man had been resurrected when Rose was, and he was deep inside this old executive, screaming and screaming and screaming.

The old man's natural balance was the only thing that had saved him. His very rigidity allowed him to ignore that knot of pain, lock it off behind daily needs, a schooled philosophy, the very knowledge that his life was nearing its end, and the emotional pain couldn't torture him for more than a few more decades. The monster of his younger self had been jailed behind walls of neutrality even more carefully constructed than his grandson Bren's. I realized that this man had probably been rather like Bren in his youth – clear of mind and determined of purpose. And his purpose had been to love Rose.

I don't know how long I crouched there, holding firm pressure on a potentially arterial wound, but we were close enough to the clinic that it couldn't have been more than a few moments. People were shouting all around me; some of them were probably shouting at me, but I couldn't really hear them. I was too overwhelmed by Xavier's personality. Finally, someone physically moved me, taking over the first aid, applying a wound paste bandage and checking his vitals. Rose knelt trembling beside him, her hand gripping his as if someone was trying to pull him away from her.

So I was freed to lean against a building and go quietly insane.

The echo of Xavier's beast roared at me. So much hatred, pointed mostly at himself, but twisted into everything. So much anguish. So much love, and sixty years of longing for a dead girl who wasn't dead. He'd lost Rose about the same time that the world had crumbled under the weight of the Dark Times, and his grief for her was all tangled into the chaos of the New World Order. He'd had to become a different man, and the young man he had been had simply – stopped. Xavier had become Ron Zellwegger, and 'Xavier' as Rose had known him may as well have died. When Rose came miraculously back to life, Xavier had been resurrected too. But Xavier was only a memory; he wasn't real, and that meant that the world was backwards, and he was trapped in the mind and behind the body of Ron, an old man, who wouldn't, couldn't, let him out.

I know now it wasn't actually Xavier that was inside me. I know it was only the strength of his troubles which had affected my mind. I wasn't possessed by any real spirit, there was no transfer of a soul. The trapped Xavier beast was no more real inside me than 42. But he was there as surely as she was, and I was oppressed by him. More so than I'd ever been by 42. 42 had been a companion beside me. This beast was hungrier than that. He didn't want to just talk to me. He wanted freedom.

I sank my head down onto my knees and gave myself over to someone else's tears.

I'd never cried like this. It wasn't in my nature. When 42 died I went still and tragic, and when I cried the tears were few, and they came silently, privately, usually late at night. These weren't tears of only grief, though they were that. They were tears of rage and powerlessness, of helpless guilt, of bitter longing. I hugged myself, moaning, half screaming in my awkward, childlike non-voice, and I couldn't care that someone might hear me. But there was too much chaos out there in the street for anyone to care what was happening to me.

When I think back on it, I know things would have happened differently if I'd been on Earth. I'd have gone to see Dr Bija immediately, and her trained psychology would have brought me back out of it. She would have pointed out my vulnerable mental state: half drugged, half weightless, tens of thousands of kilometres from home, having suffered weeks of pain and exhaustion, paralyzing fear, the threat of death, the distance from my sisters, not to mention the shock of having made any headway with Rose, and the personal compromise I had made to get it. My psyche might as well have been cut open and laid bare. And because of that, I allowed myself to succumb to a form of psychic madness.

When I had kissed Rose, I'd allowed myself to play a part. It was a script written by a memory – a strong, stass-reinforced memory, but a memory nonetheless – of someone else. It was Rose's impression of Xavier, and I had put it on like a suit of clothes. Now I had been battered by a psyche-induced persona of an old man's tortured youth. Because I was already primed by my submission to Rose's memory, it invaded me, occupied me, overlay all my own impulses – and I was emotionally weak enough to simply let it take over.

I became Xavier.

chapter 12

Going mad is difficult to describe. I'd like to say that my own persona split off and sat back, watching everything that the Xavier persona did with detached interest. It would make everything I relayed after that very simple. But it wasn't like that. I was still me. I was simply Xavier. I know – but it made sense at the time.

I wept in impotent fury for I don't know how long. Then I realized my head was in my hands, and that I had hands to hold my head in. My sobbing eased off. I wiped my eyes and looked down at my hands. They were bluish. They weren't supposed to be blue, but of course they were blue, they'd always been blue. It was a detail that was unimportant. I dismissed it. That I had hands was the important thing. I wasn't trapped anymore. The old man no longer held me.

I clasped my hands on my lap, my index fingers in a steeple. It was Xavier's gesture – one Rose remembered and the old man still did. I didn't make any decisions about which parts of me were me and which parts were Xavier, or have any sudden realization that something had changed. Everything that didn't make sense didn't matter, so I didn't pay attention to it. I stood up and did what Xavier would do – I went to find Rose.

She was nowhere to be found. In the further chaos of the street, we'd become separated. My memory had faded as if into greyscale behind my madness, and though I remembered that I had been in a hotel of some sort, I could not recall where it was.

A sudden blow nearly knocked me over, then, as a cowled figure grabbed me roughly and hugged me tight enough that I couldn't breathe. I tried to fight him off, and he released me. 'What the hell are you doing out here?' the figure shouted.

I pulled away and stared at him. Who ...? Blue-grey skin, arrogant yellow eyes, quite a lot of strength if the way he grabbed me was any indication. Right, his name was Quin, and he was an annoyance. In the same way that a mosquito might be an annoyance. 'What the coit, you're just sitting here? I thought you were dead! Everyone's in a panic. Noid, you're covered in blood.' He lunged for me, as if he was to grab me again, and I shied away. I did not want him to touch me – I hadn't yet remembered why. I opened my mouth to say that I was fine. It was only the old man's blood, and I hoped he died from it, the thieving old screw. The only sound that came out was a whispery croak, and I shut my mouth hastily.

Clearly, I had to figure out how this body worked. I opened and closed my fists to assess strength. Stronger than the old man, but weaker than I had been when I was still wholly myself. And blue. And I couldn't talk.

'Otto? What's going on?'

Otto. That was the name of the body I was in. Right. And this Quin considered himself Otto's brother, and I'd best say something to him or he was going to touch me, and ...

Right. That was how I got here in the first place.

'*I'm fine.*' I dredged the sign up from greyscale memories, and then moved my hands to see if I remembered any more. Cool. I still remembered the language. '*I have to find Rose.*'

Quin glowered. 'Rose. You're drenched in blood, abandoned in the middle of a riot at the site of an explosion, I risk life and limb to find you, and you want to find the girl who left you here.'

'*She didn't know who I was,*' I signed. '*It's fine. Where is she?*'

Quin frowned. 'You're looking a little weird, bro, what's going on?'

'*Nothing. Where is the hotel?*'

Quin tilted his head away as if he was looking at something decidedly creepy. 'Back that way,' he said warily. 'But half the streets are cordoned off. Come on. We gotta get you back to the docs.'

'*I do not need a doctor,*' I signed patiently. '*I simply need to find Rose.*'

'She's probably with the doctor,' Quin said. 'Come on.'

Quin grabbed me roughly by the sleeve of my coat and yanked me through the milling crowd. He kept throwing me odd looks as he manoeuvred his way through the Crystal Village. The old me would have recognized the signs of barely contained fury, but at that moment, I didn't care. When we finally arrived at the Norway Chalet, it was clear that things had changed a great deal since our easy, incognito arrival.

The chalet was sealed off, and small troop of uniformed guards were standing at the main entrance. I half expected them to shout, 'Halt! Who goes there!' as we approached, but all they did was lower their squat, compact weapons and glare. 'State your business.'

Quin lowered his new cowl and promptly yanked my bloodstained blue hood off my head. 'Let us in.'

The guns were put up, and one of the guards unlocked the door and ushered us through.

The general pandemonium outside was echoed as we entered the lobby, as nurses and uniformed security and several harried-looking hotel employees tried to placate a shouting young woman in the middle of the room. 'What do you mean you can't find him!' Rose barked. 'How hard can it be? It's not as if he doesn't stand out in a crowd. What do we pay you for, to sit on your thumbs and eat bonbons? Where is the security on this hell hole?'

'If you'll just calm down,' said a nurse.

Rose rounded on him. 'And you! You drag us all away without even checking to see if all our party is still with us? What kind of system do you run up here? Otto is sick, he could be dying. He could have been kidnapped, for all you can tell me!'

One of the security guards said, 'Now, then,' but Rose cut him off. 'And what are you still doing here? I told you to go out and *find* him, and all you do is tell me it's being handled? It is *not* being handled, or you'd be out there yourselves. I am not one of your pretty city-ship aristocrats to be distracted and placated; I'm the Fitzroy, and I expect results, and I expect them *immediately*, or there *will* be consequences, mark my words.' She rounded on another nurse, 'And don't you dare approach me with that damned needle, sir! I will *not* be drugged into submission.'

I was almost laughing. I had never seen Rose so strong, not in either set of memories, and the idea that she was this angry over me was delightful. I pushed through the crowd and threw my arms around her for what felt like the first time in decades. There she was, whole and perfect and mine, and I kissed her and kissed her and kissed her, right in front of everyone, until she pushed me away with a gasp. Her mind was a white noise of shock, but I wasn't really paying attention to what she thought right then. I stood back and grinned at her.

'Where … you finally found him?' Rose glared at the chief security guard in the group.

'Actually, *I* found him,' Quin said loudly from the middle of the room, and everyone turned to look at him. 'Your pet security hadn't actually *looked,* princess, and neither had you. He was right where you left him.'

'You were still by the clinic?' she asked me.

Quin laughed. 'Of course he was, princess. Your little blue puppy dog here wouldn't *dream* of straying long from his only source of passionate romantic melodrama.'

'Get out, all of you,' Rose said imperiously. 'And you'd best hope I never learn your names.' The contempt was strong in her voice.

They *scurried*. She was so wonderful I couldn't help it. I kissed her again.

'Otto!' Rose pushed me away again, and I let her, with the realization that I probably had to take this a little more slowly than I wanted to. 'Oh, you're cold as ice. He was still near the clinic?'

'Yeah,' Quin said, 'and you'd best call back one of your docs to take a look at him, 'cause he's acting weird.'

'*I am not*,' I signed.

'You let me be the judge of that,' Quin said.

'*No*,' I signed. '*I'm no child that you need to coddle.*'

'I saved your life, Mister Sit-in-the-cold-till-everyone-thinks-I'm-dead. Twice now.'

'*That doesn't give you power over me.*'

'Oh, bull, that's why I'm here in the first place.'

'What? To pretend to be the hero?'

'Pretend? You're forcing me into it! You're the one who went out onto a bomb site and let yourself get lost. I never should have left you alone.'

'I don't believe for one moment you actually care about me.'

'You go to hell!' Quin snapped, his patience broken. He grabbed me by the arm and shook me. 'I'm here for you, or I wouldn't be here at all!'

He was furious – furious in a way that both startled and angered me. I was Xavier. Half of me thought, very strongly, that I barely knew this jerk, and he had no jurisdiction over me. *'Get the hell off me!'* I sent at him.

He threw me against the wall. It hurt. 'I thought you were dead! I wish I'd been right!'

With an instinctive movement I shot my leg out and hooked it around Quin's ankle. As he toppled I pulled him down, kneed him in the stomach, and then knocked him sideways with my elbow. It was over in a few seconds, and Rose stared at me, mouth agape.

Quin looked up at me from the floor. His voice was hoarse and very soft. 'Who the coit *are* you?'

I looked down at Quin, Quin, 50, my brother, and for a moment was fully and wholly myself. I looked at my hands. I had no idea where I had gotten those skills. Then 42 whispered in my mind. (*They're his. Xavier's. He learned them during the Dark Times.)* I bent my head, trying to find myself.

Quin climbed shakily to his feet, staring at me. 'You okay?' Rose asked, reaching down for him.

Quin yanked his arm away. 'You get the coit away from me! This is all your fault, anyway.'

'What is?'

'Him! Can't you see it? He's going insane, and it's a pretty short trip, really.'

Rose rolled her eyes. 'Fine. I'm just going to assume you're brothers and let you deal with it.'

'Good plan,' I signed.

'Yeah, we can deal with it,' Quin said, came up to me and feinted a punch at my face. If he'd actually hit me, it would have knocked me against the wall. As it was I pulled back and blinked. Whatever instinct Xavier had induced in me before, it was gone now. 'If you weren't sick!' Quin hissed at me.

'Well, the fact is, he is, Quin!' Rose cried. 'So get over it!'

Quin turned and blinked at her. 'Get *over* it?' he asked incredulously. 'Get over what, princess? My mutilated biology or my institutional upbringing?'

Rose visibly shrank. 'I just meant him disappearing. He didn't mean to worry us.'

Quin glared at her, but his anger was fading. He snorted at me. 'Hope you were getting some ice-village tail, ladies' man, put *her* in her place.' He turned to leave while Rose blushed bright red.

Rose came up and hugged me. I pulled my head away to keep from touching her. I was shaking, and it wasn't only the cold. I didn't know what was happening. 'Are you okay? Really?' Rose asked.

I closed my fists as Xavier took over again.

'Why did you leave me?' I whispered in Rose's ear.

'I didn't mean to,' Rose said, pulling away, 'it all happened so fast. The clinic was full up, thanks to the explosion, so the EMTs arranged to bring Xavier here. He's okay. Just stunned, and they gave him a transfusion because of his age. They thought he might have lost too much blood. There are nurses here to monitor him, but there shouldn't be any lasting damage. Oh, Otto. You saved him, do you realize that?'

I kept myself from saying I didn't care what happened to the old man. I nodded yes. Then I reached for her, pulling her into a fierce embrace. 'I missed you,' I whispered.

'You've only been gone a few hours.'

I stared at her. 'It felt like a lifetime.'

Rose smiled, and then pulled away as someone came into the lobby. It was Dr Zellwegger. 'Quin tells me you're not feeling well?'

I rolled my eyes. *'I'm fine!'* I signed, exasperated.

Dr Zellwegger turned to Rose for the translation. 'Well, Quin seems fairly certain that something is wrong with you, Otto. That you're acting erratic. I think we'd better give you a work-up.'

I sagged. There was nothing wrong with me that an hour in Rose's arms wouldn't cure. '*No!*' I signed. '*Can't it wait until the morning? Isn't everyone busy?*' That was it. '*Worry about Xavier,*' I signed.

'He says we should worry about your father, not him,' Rose said. 'Look, I'll stay with him. Arrange for a work-up in the morning, all right?'

'You'll stay with him?' Dr Zellwegger asked. 'All right. If he has an episode, or another seizure ...'

'I know what to do.'

Dr Zellwegger nodded his goodbyes and left.

'Otto, you are acting weird,' Rose said.

I smiled at her.

'Like that,' Rose said. 'Since when do you smile?'

'Come,' I signed, grabbed her by the sleeve, and dragged her up the stairs to her suite. She was panting by the time we got up and opened the door.

'Otto!' she said. 'You know I can't run like you can!'

I wasn't listening to her. Almost violently, I pressed her against the back of the door and kissed her, running my fingers down her arms like I knew she loved. She was wildly confused, turning her face away. 'Otto!'

'Don't call me that,' I whispered.

'What? *What?*'

'Rose, can't you see me? It's me. I'm here, I'm free.'

'Otto, what are you talking about?'

'I'm free, I escaped. I've been right here, all the time, trapped in that old man's body. If I could have killed him to get to you, I would have. Rose, let me touch you. I've missed you so much.' Whispering was hell – I wished I could shout, I was so glad I could touch her.

'Otto!' I reached to kiss her, but she turned her face again. 'Stop it!'

I stopped, but I was frantic. 'It's me,' I whispered, getting desperate now. I hadn't escaped just to have her deny me. 'Come on, you have to see me. You have to recognize me. I'm me. Xavier. The old man was dying, and your friend reached for that life and he found me, and I took his hand and I held on! I held on, and I escaped, and I can have you now.' I touched her soft, pale cheek. '*Finally, I can have you.*' This thought communication thing was going to be a blast. She could hear my voice, now, inside her head. *My* voice, Xavier's young, hungry voice.

'What have you done?' she whispered, terrified. She had finally understood what I'd been clumsily trying to say. She rejected the thought the moment the implications struck her, and she pushed me away, pacing up and down in agitation. 'No. No, this – I've got to be misunderstanding something.'

I shook my head, silently pleading with her to believe me.

'Otto, look at me. Are you trying to tell me that suddenly you're Xavier?'

'*Can't you see me?*' I said, reaching for her hand.

She snatched her hand away paced into the centre of the floor, holding her head in dismay. 'Oh, this is insane. What have I done to you?'

'*Nothing,*' I signed. '*It's just me.*'

'Then where's Otto, suddenly?' she demanded. I reached for her. 'No! What's going on? I need to talk to Otto. Otto!'

I grabbed her hand anyway. Signing was far too slow, and whispering wasn't intense enough. '*He's fine. I'm fine, we're fine. But now you don't have to worry,*' I told her. '*I'm here for you.*' I reached for her neck, her shoulders, all the places I knew she wanted to be touched. '*Just kiss me,*' I begged. '*Kiss me, and you'll see me. You know you will.*'

'Oh, god, I gotta get you to a doctor,' she groaned. She headed back for the door.

I – or, Xavier, really – slammed her against the wall. I was not going to let her run away from me again, not now. She was always running away. I'd made that mistake before. I wasn't letting her go again. '*Don't. Please, what's a doctor going to do? Pump me full of drugs? I feel* great. *I feel better than I've ever felt in my life.*'

'And who's telling me this? You, or Xavier?'

'*There's no difference,*' I insisted. '*You loved me, you loved him. And I'm here! Whoever I am, it's me. Rose.*' I had to make her understand. '*I know you're broken. You're torn apart from what those vampires have done to you, and I watch it every day, and I* need *to help you. And I can't. I couldn't. You have no idea what it's like, wanting to touch you every single second of every single day. But now I can. I'm here! Please!*' Xavier's broken heart screamed out, and I sobbed. '*Please don't leave me again.*'

Rose was tortured. The expressions on my face were Xavier's, not Otto's. There were times she'd dreamed about what it would be like if a young Xavier could come back to her. But it was a fantasy, not something she'd actually wanted in any real sense. She would never have wanted to trade Otto's life for it. She reached up to touch my cheek. 'But Otto. Otto, you gentle soul. It's not real. It was one thing when you knew it wasn't, but this is madness.'

'I don't care,' I whispered. 'Not real, not right, not going to last. I don't care about any of it anymore. I love you.'

'Otto, it's another symptom. It's got to be. You could be dying ...'

'Good!' I hissed. '*Let* me die! I'd rather die like this with you beside me than live another god damned wrong life!'

Rose's eyes went wide. 'Oh, god, it is you, isn't it.' she said, suddenly horrified. She remembered something Xavier had said to her, the first time he'd finally spoken to her properly after she came out of stasis. *I split in two inside,* he had said.

Like I'd failed to take the life I was meant to have, and someone else's life came and stole all those years. There was me, father, grandfather, businessman. And then this angry, wounded teenage boy surged up from out of nowhere. She sagged against the wall, overwhelmed, and I held her up, like I used to do when we were young. She was always so weak, so damaged. 'I don't know what to do.'

I let my head droop, cheek to cheek. 'Just hold me, Rose,' I whispered into her ear. 'I don't care who you think I am. I just don't want to be all alone anymore.'

'Oh, god, don't do this to me.' Rose said, both tortured and annoyed. I was tempting her beyond all sense. I laughed, and it sounded strange. It was strange to her, too. My expressions were Xavier's, but my laugh was Otto's. She shrugged me off and made me look at her. 'You're not well,' she said firmly.

'This body is dying, I know that,' I whispered. 'It's okay.'

'That's not what I meant,' she said.

I didn't have a reply. I stared at her, pleading silently, and Rose's eyes slowly softened. 'Okay, sit down,' she said, and pulled me to the bed. She sat down beside me and put her hand carefully in mine. 'How much of you is still Otto? Can you show me what happened?'

It was a difficult memory to find. Most of my Xavier memories were carefully reinforced by Rose's own, but my Otto memories were all my own, and sort of buried under my new persona. I found it, though, and gave it all to her quickly. How Rose couldn't save him, and the blood soaked through so quickly, dropping me into the old man's pain. How he wanted to die, and I dragged him back, and got more than I bargained for. Rose probed for more, but I took my hand away. 'That's it,' I whispered.

'That's not it,' Rose said.

'Yes it is,' I said firmly.

'So, what, you just took Otto over?'

'He invited me,' I whispered. I reached up to touch her cheek. 'Otto loves you, too. I couldn't have you in that old man's body, and your friend couldn't have you without me. Don't send me away again,' I begged. 'I've missed you so much.'

Rose bowed her head. She wouldn't let herself say it, but her thoughts were clear enough. *'I've missed you, too.'*

'*So stop thinking about right and wrong and real. Just kiss me.'*

'But Otto ...'

'Kiss me,' I whispered. 'You can take me to the doctor tomorrow, and we'll worry about this perishable form then. Kiss me.' She was very worried. 'Rose, please. All I want to do is hold you. Just hold you. I've been aching to hold you,' I breathed. 'No one knows you better than I do. No one ever will. Just close your eyes, and it'll be me. Completely me.'

She hesitated.

'Know that I love you, always,' I whispered.

That did it. I'd known it would. She winced as if I'd twisted a knife. I reached down to kiss her, and she didn't even have a moment when she thought to turn away. I clung to her like I'd been missing her for a lifetime. Always. That was Rose and Xavier all over. Love you. All ways.

chapter 13

She curled up beside me as if we'd never been apart, exhausted from the day's exertions. We'd been in stasis just that morning. Very quickly, she was asleep. I knew it by the way her mind suddenly grew around me, roaring silently with colour. Oh, yes, god, give me this. Give me this every night of my life. I almost didn't care how short that life might be.

(Pretty short at the rate you're going.)

'*Don't ruin this,*' I told 42, told myself. '*I haven't shared anyone's dreams since you died.*'

(I miss those sometimes.)

I actually wasn't sure which part of my head had said that, if it was 'her' or 'me'. Whoever it was, 42's mocking voice stopped, and I was left with nothing but Rose. It didn't take long before my eyes closed and mind was caught up, whisked away, drowned in the ocean of her subconscious. I hadn't realized how tired I was. It felt like the day had lasted over seventy years. Whatever my dreams would have been, they were completely subsumed by her. I spent half the night immersed in her, wild bursts of colour and strange insights. It gave me solace. But sometime during the night, we rolled away from each other. My subconscious seized on the moment of solitude.

I was in a garden. Rose's garden, from UniCorp estates, but Rose's internal briars tangled over everything. I knew I was in a dangerous place.

'It's not fair that you're dying.'

It was Xavier. He was standing in the middle of a clearing on the path where Rose used to meet him. He was young – not more than eighteen. I barely recognized his face compared to the old man. But I'd seen enough of Rose's portraits. I knew full well who it was.

'You didn't ask,' I told him. *'You were screaming a little too loud to have heard me even if you had.'*

He sighed. 'It wouldn't have mattered. You think the old man isn't dying?'

'He's got years ahead of him. I may not have more than a month … even a week.'

'Suppose I'll have to make the best of the time I've got.'

I felt bad about it, though. *'Rose is confused.'*

'I'm confused,' he admitted.

'Are you regretting your choice? Is this body not to your liking?'

'It's not to yours,' he told me pointedly. I sat down heavily on a bench. The briar roses twisted in the breeze, creeping closer to me. Their scent was the musty scent of the plankton. 'Do you regret it?'

I thought about this. Everything I'd thought I was had fallen away, like rotting apples off a neglected tree. My ethics, my sense of self, my serenity, my acceptance. I'd worked so hard for so long to own who I was, to accept my life as mine. Now I'd abandoned it to wear the life of someone who had essentially died half a century ago. I'd put on Xavier like Mr Zellwegger's old castoffs.

But I had Rose. And she wanted me. And strangely, even Xavier's personality running around in my head felt comforting. Like with 42.

I wasn't alone.

As if thinking of her had summoned her, she was sitting on my other side. *(He's not helping, 86,)* she told me.

'I'm giving him what he wants,' Xavier told her. 'The chance to be who he wants to be.'

42 ignored him. *(How much room do you have in this brain?)* she asked me. (*How many of us can you keep alive? Me, him. You'll be keeping Rose too, at this rate. What's going to happen to you?)*

'Maybe I'll go away. Maybe that's how I'll die. I'll let my body keep walking around, but I won't be in it.'

(You don't think it'll be so easy. You don't really think you can avoid death by leaving before you have to face it?)

'*I've already faced it once!*' I stared at her. Her face held no guilt. *'Why should I have to do it again? Tell me why!'*

42 cocked her head at me. She looked so young to me, suddenly. Thirteen. She never would grow up. (*You facing death was never my idea.)*

And as happens in dreams, the entire memory came unbidden in a millisecond in my mind.

42 had been screaming down in the driveway. I had wrestled out of bed and to my window at the lab. 42 was down there, wrestling with two UniCorp security. I pelted down the stairs in a flurry of panic. '*I'll take her!*' I signed furiously. '*Let her go!*'

The security didn't understand me, of course, but the two lab techs and the nurse who had come out to deal with the fuss glanced at me. 'We'll handle this, 86,' the nurse told me. 'Go back to bed.'

I backed off a bit. That was a direct order, and we were really supposed to obey the nurses and lab techs. I was only thirteen, and none of us had really learned to fight yet. Apart from 42.

'Get your burning hands off me, you over-zealous, trumped-up ratbag! You dare! You *dare!*' She was screaming blue murder, and lights were going on all over the lab as the rest of the EPs peered out in bewilderment.

'We found her at the u*Night*ed,' one of the UniCorp security was saying to the nurse. 'Don't know how she snuck in. When last call came at two, she jumped up onto the stage and turned the music back on. All the other patrons started cheering. She nearly started a riot.'

I could barely hear them over 42's shouts. 'Let me go! Get *off!*' 42 twisted and managed to get her hand on the security guard who was holding her. He'd been holding her by her shirt wrists, clearly to avoid exactly this. He grunted with pain the moment she touched him, and looked tempted to hit her. He pushed her over his knee instead, shoving her bodily to the ground, and began wrestling with half of a pair of handcuffs which had already been put on one wrist. She'd fought so hard they hadn't managed to get the other one on. They couldn't touch her skin.

'She's been gone three days,' said the nurse. 'Is this the first disturbance she's caused?'

'God, no!' said the one who was wrestling with her. 'Shut up, bitch!'

42 was screaming. I couldn't take it anymore. 'Stop!' I squawked.

The sound was strange enough that everyone turned to stare at me, apart from 42, who kept struggling, but at least stopped screaming. 'What the coit?' said the security guard.

'*I'll take her,*' I signed to the nurse.

'86, I told you to go back to your room—'

I touched the back of her hand. '*I said I'll take her!*' I told her with as much compulsion as I could muster. She swayed, more stunned by my action than influenced by it. I'd probably overdone it; I didn't have as much control in those days. I knelt down and touched 42's cheek. '*Just shut up for ten minutes and I'll get you out of this.*'

'*Don't,*' she was thinking. '*Not you.*' But she didn't fight.

I very calmly pushed the security guard off her and pulled her up beside me. Then I held my hand out for the key. 'Now wait just a damn minute,' said the other guard.

But the one who had been fighting 42 tried to bat my hand away, as I'd known he would. The moment he did, he found himself reaching for the key. I don't know if I'd influenced him enough to actually give it to me, but I snatched it from his hand before he'd had time to shake me off. I unlocked the cuff and pushed 42 towards the lab. '*Go!*' I handed the cuff back to the guard politely. '*Thank you,*' I signed, then I ran after 42 before the lab techs had time to drag her back to her room.

I pushed past them and grabbed 42's arm. '*I've got this,*' I signed, and ran.

42 ran with me, but she stopped at the entry to my room. She was pale and sweating, and there were deep bruise-like shadows under her eyes. 'No,' she said. 'I should go to my room.'

I took hold of her wrists and led her in with me, all the while telling her, '*Don't. You've been gone for days, I worried about you. 11's started getting sick, and 50's getting dangerous and 99 is in hysterics. I'm all alone, here.*' I'd never been all alone before. 42 and I were best friends, peas in a pod, inseparable. The only two who could both send and receive without limits, without draining our energies, without going mad. We were the same mind in two bodies; she the voice, the strength, the shield; I the soul, the peace, the poet. But she'd been distancing herself since she started getting sick. First she'd pulled away from me, for weeks. Then she'd disappeared completely, and I'd been going crazy.

She'd just needed to get away.

I didn't want her to go.

We were both scared.

We'd fallen back into our dual equilibrium immediately, the perfectly shared mind. She realized it and tried to pull away again, but I wouldn't let her. There were grass stains on her clothes and she stank of nicohol from the dance club, but I didn't care. It was such a relief to have my voice back. And she was in pain.

Nothing. It was nothing, she just needed to sleep.

She meant for me to let her go to her room, but I wouldn't let her. I pulled her to my bed again – we often shared a bed. Contact was important for us, because it was the way we communicated, and there was nothing sexual about it. We were kids, for one. For another, there were cameras everywhere. Privacy was not a luxury we were afforded at EP laboratories. 42 and I been sleeping beside and against each other since we were old enough to crawl. I was suddenly desperately afraid to be alone.

She didn't want me to be afraid, but I couldn't help it. So many of us had died. We had lost half a dozen of the simple ones. 17, 78 and 39 had already failed, too. It seemed as if it was the ones with our gift who died fastest.

'*It's because we're the least human,*' she told me.

'*But we aren't different physically. They've checked. We're just susceptible to allergies and, well, blue.*'

She had a different take on it. Human or not, whatever they called us. The UniCorp scientists had tried to play god, and we were the unholy result.

'*You don't really believe in god.*'

'*God is an invention, the same way we are. God is bound to be flawed. Human beings can make nothing that isn't flawed. It was nature who made man – and it took nature millennia. Human beings make some kind of biological sense. We are made from unholy alliances, the scientific mating of man and alien beast, an abomination that nature could never have created without several billion years of evolution, and probably not even then.*'

'*You've been listening to the evangelists.*'

No, she hadn't. She'd found her own religion in the last few days. A religion of broken things. For the last three days she'd been breaking things all around ComUnity to prove it – hoverskiff windows and parking meters, credit machines, and even people's faces when they tried to stop her. Everything was broken. It was human nature that was flawed, and we were the result of it. Of course we were deteriorating. '*Whatever made them think they knew better than nature? We were bound to die from the moment they'd spliced us together. We have to pay for the sins of our "fathers".*'

I told her not to think that way, but she wasn't listening. She felt very hot against me.

Without knowing how, I knew she was dying. She pulled away. 'I'm not!' she said with finality. Then she winced and folded in on herself, as if in pain. 'Get the nurse!' she whispered to me. 'Please, just get the nurse!'

I ran to the door to find the nurse on duty, but she was still outside placating the UniCorp security. I stabbed the emergency button – which was silent apart from the tiny beep in the cells of all the nurses within call distance – and ran back to 42.

My real self told me to wake up. I didn't want to see this part again. But all my skills at lucid dreaming were clearly part of the bits of my brain which had already gone down the vacuum drift. I was trapped experiencing it all again as I ran down the corridor, too slow already to stop what was happening.

42 was lying on the floor, blood streaming from her eyes and ears. I knew the moment I saw it that she'd only told me to call the nurse to get me out of the room. She'd hoped to be gone by the time I came back. But she wasn't so lucky. Death didn't come as quickly as she'd hoped.

I couldn't make myself wake up, but I couldn't live it again. I tore away from my dream self, and watched instead. Watched helplessly as the two figures on the floor twitched, and the young boy became drenched in the blood of his best friend. At least I wasn't experiencing it again. The electrical cascade as the oxygen left her brain, flashing her life before her, before me, pouring her, entire, into my brain. And then the darkness. The death. But I remembered. I wished I could forget.

'*Don't make me do this again!*'

I was in blackness now. Cold, glittering blackness, like the false night sky above the Crystal Village. 42 was behind me, her warm hand on my shoulder. *(You shouldn't have done it the first time.)*

'*What did you want me to do? Let you die alone?*'

(Yes.)

I whirled, knocking her hand away. '*Not fair!*'

42 cocked her head at me. So young. *(You suddenly think life should be fair? What's fair about us? What's fair about this?)*

'*I died once. I shouldn't have to do it again! Not so soon!*'

(That's hardly my fault.)

I reached for her, hoping to hit her or hug her, I wasn't sure which. It didn't matter. She was out of my reach.

(But you couldn't let me go.)

'*You ran away,*' I accused her. '*You were going to leave without me. You left me* alone!'

(What choice did I have? I didn't ask to die.) She fell to the ground again before me, blood pouring from her ears, seizing violently. Just like last time. My arms went out, but I couldn't reach her. Instead, briar roses burst from her flesh, piercing me. The briars swirled around me, gripping us, pulling us. Pain stabbed me, a harsh lance of terror as the briars dragged me into the same icy death I had known once before. But this time I fought it, desperate not to leave, to hold on to what I had – Rose and life and everything.

And Xavier was there, anger on his face. 'No! He's mine now! You have to give him back!' He tried to pull the briars away, but they engulfed him, too, and we were tangled together. He screamed out, vanishing into the thorns, and I was alone again.

I knew I was next.

'I don't want to die! I don't want to die!'

I was dragged down and down, back into the hollowness of death.

'I don't want to die! I don't want to die!'

And Rose was suddenly there, in my mind and before my open eyes, staring down into my face. It was real, I was awake, for whatever that was worth. I saw myself as Rose saw me, pale blue and sweating, and I was Rose, and Xavier, and 42, I was anyone but me. That blue, mad, wreck of a body before Rose's eyes couldn't possibly be *me*. I hated it.

I don't know if my own subconscious had recognized the imminent failure in my sleep, or if it was one of those unpredictable coincidences that can happen in severe illness, but when I woke up, it was not to the control of my own body. Everything shook and shuddered, I felt stiff, and I was utterly and completely incapable of controlling anything. It was as if some unseen force had taken over, as if I was hooked into some kind of control collar, and the person or computer who ran it was running through an earthquake.

'Otto? Otto!' Rose's face was ruddy in the holofirelight, but I could tell she was pale. I wished I could tell her not to panic. I wished I could do anything at all. But I couldn't even force my eyes to look at her properly as every part of me shook in an uncontrollable seizure.

After a moment of initial shock, Rose placed her hands on either side of my head and held me tightly, staring into my eyes. 'I'm here,' she whispered. She was handling this remarkably well. I realized that if Dr Svarog was using her as the courier for my medication, he'd probably have warned her what to do if I went into another seizure. I blessed him with every atom for telling her what to do in advance. But if I couldn't control my own body, I certainly couldn't control hers, and I could tell her nothing. I no longer felt anything from her. I couldn't control myself enough to read her. I felt locked away – horribly locked away. Was this how everyone felt? The seizure aside, the complete isolation was horrifying to me.

I was utterly alone in here.

But then, I wasn't. Xavier was with me, and 42, but they couldn't do anything either.

Rose's hands trembled, but this was only her own concern, not anything passing through from me. I was glad this was better than last time, when I couldn't *stop* sending everything, and she'd had to fight to control her own body in the water. Rose glanced up – she was looking at the clock on the bedside. 'Hang on, Otto. It's only been a minute. Under five minutes, and you should recover on your own.' She sounded so steeled and steadfast she almost sounded like the flinty heiress who could not be gainsaid. I wished I could do something to help her, but I was in the crumbling prison of my own body, and I couldn't even call out to her.

It went on forever. I wished I could see the clock, but my vision was shaking as my eyes rolled, and couldn't focus on anything. Then, as suddenly as it had started, it stopped. I felt as if I'd been switched off. The first thing I did was open my mind. '*Rose.*'

Rose sighed with pained relief and released my head. 'Oh, Otto.' She sagged with weariness.

I didn't want her out of my mind. I groped for her, with hands that seemed weak as a baby's, and finally found contact with her again. '*Don't let go!*' I told her.

'I'm here,' she said.

I reached for her, pulling her back to me. '*I'm sorry. I'm so sorry to put you through this.*'

'It's not your fault.' She trembled. 'One minute, forty-seven seconds, give or take a few. You should be okay.'

'No,' I whispered. I wasn't.

'What's wrong?'

I couldn't hold it back. I wished I could. But this was Rose. '*I'm scared!*' The words were a soundless scream of rage and fear that I couldn't control. And I *was* scared. I felt like a child after a nightmare, a victim of an attack. I wanted to be strong. I wanted to stand tall and say I was ready for anything. But I knew what death was – or I thought I did – and I did not want to go there again!

Rose reached for me, wrapping herself around me like a cloak. 'Oh, Otto.'

'I don't want to die,' I whispered to her. I felt like a fool to be confessing this to her, but I couldn't stop it. I felt naked and helpless. 'I don't, I don't. Rose. Help me!'

She smoothed my hair from my face, leaned forward and kissed me. It was sweet, and so heartfelt. Her mouth tasted of salt. I realized she was crying for me. Tenderly, gently, she lay me back on the bed and kissed me, my throat, my jaw, her breath hot and moist against my skin. Oh, yes. Yes, *please.*

The fear died under her touch. There was nothing but her. For a few blissful moments, it was perfect. Then the old familiar guilt began to creep through her. She ignored it, at first. As it grew stronger she rejected it, kissing me fiercely until it almost caused her physical pain. There was an ache in her chest, a brutal, intense guilt, and it was gnawing at her. Until she couldn't take it any longer. With a cry of frustration she pulled away from me again, panting with escaping tears. 'God *damn* it!'

I reached for her, pulling her hand back to me. '*It's okay. Just hold me.*'

'It is not okay!' she told me fiercely. 'Do you hear me? This is *not* okay!'

'*Rose, it's just you. You and me and him, and none of it is fair, and I know that. Just come back to me.*' I closed my eyes, feeling vulnerable in the darkness. '*I don't want to be alone.*'

Rose stared at me in the dim light. The images I had just sent her – herself, myself and him, all at once. With a sudden pounce she threw herself on me, staring deep into my eyes. 'Take it,' she said.

I didn't want to know what she meant.

'Just take it!' she said. 'Do whatever it takes, take all of it. I don't care!' And she started pouring images into my head – herself as a little girl, no more than nine, reading stories to him. Playing board games in her huge closet, her stasis tube looming, a malignant refrigerator behind him. Illicitly picking flowers together in the garden at Unicorn Estates. How he fell in love with her, a slow, gradual blossoming, as his own childish devotion developed harder edges of lust. And the final break, as they fell into each other, tender evenings with her maid quietly pretending not to be in the next room. Heated moments in the grass in the garden. Every hot, passionate moment she could think of, bestowing them on me like kisses, as if she could throw them away to make room for me.

I wouldn't do that to her. I wasn't that cruel. Instead, Xavier came back, wormed his way inside the memories and folded her into my arms.

She had no idea who I really was as I pressed her gently against the bed. She wasn't really trying to pretend that I was him, but she had half forgotten I was me. All she cared about was just doing what it took to ignore the sharp-toothed briars of pain, guilt and confusion. Every single concept of identity had melted, and I was quite content to let it do so. I had no desire to be me. I did not *want* to feel so frightened. I did *not* want to be dying. The only thing I knew for sure was that I wanted *her*. Beneath the salt taste of her translucent skin, the soft heat of her body, and the rainbows of her mind, we let absolutely everything fade quietly away.

chapter 14

None of us had slept well, and we were all bleary eyed and monosyllabic at the Norway Chalet's gourmet breakfast. Breakfast on Europa consisted of a good portion of processed plankton. The differences lay only in the levels of processing and the quality of the flavour additives. The villagers Quin and I had seen the day before would have been eating theirs plain and only slightly processed, mixed with water as a gruel or soup, or with a little salt and baked into cakes atop their heating units. The plankton cakes that were served alongside the powdered eggs Benedict at the Norway Chalet had been processed down to nothing but a powder, heavily mixed with wheat and butter flavouring, and dusted with actual sugar. The morning coffee was flavoured plankton as well, as was the hot cocoa.

Rose could hardly swallow it. She said it all tasted false and syrupy. My initial impulse was that it tasted fine to me, though not particularly impressive. Rose was right – it did taste false – but then, so did most commercial soft drinks and candies. Then I remembered; Rose rarely ate anything that wasn't completely organic. Her stomach was sensitive enough without trying to make it digest chemicals and preservatives. She must have eaten less than half a cup of food that morning. Had she eaten anything the day before? I knew she'd been sick. I hadn't seen her eating. I hoped she'd had a good dinner while I was out, but, knowing Rose, I somewhat doubted it. '*You should eat,*' I signed to her.

'It's making me sick,' Rose said.

I wasn't up to arguing with her. My head was throbbing with pain. I didn't know if it was just the illness' natural progression, or if it was a reaction from the seizure, or, perhaps, from the mental and physical overstimulation which had followed. Rose had told them I'd had a seizure, but that it had seemed to be within the safety range that Dr Svarog had spelled out. The general consensus was that they needed to get me to the *Minos* as soon as possible.

'Unfortunately, that's not going to be possible,' Xavier said when he came in to breakfast. 'The village has been closed off. No one is allowed out until they find the perpetrators of the attack.' He was pale and slow, and a clean white bandage graced his throat. Looking at him made me feel even sicker.

'But what about Otto?' Quin demanded. 'He needs to start treatment. He's been getting worse by the hour.'

'He is not,' said Rose.

'Settle down!' Xavier said sternly.

'But what if they don't figure out who did it?' Quin asked. 'Is the slaughter of a bunch of freedom fighters worth watching my brother die?'

'Freedom fighters?' Rose asked. 'More like murderers. Look what they did to Xavier!'

'If I was in their position, he'd look like a viable target to me.'

Rose went white. 'Shut up!'

I leaned my head on my hand, covering my eyes, and let them fight it out above me. It always seemed as if someone else made my decisions for me. *(I thought that was how you liked it,)* 42 whispered.

'You were never someone else,' I told her. *'You were always just another part of me.'*

'All right, stop it,' Dr Zellwegger said over everyone. 'No one is talking about mothballing Otto's treatment, Quin. This is a delay, but not a severe one. They'll find who did this – they always do – and then we'll be on our way. In the meantime, Otto has a work-up scheduled for this morning, and a courier has arrived from the *Minos*. They sent an emergency communicator down to make contact. We still won't have cell reception anywhere but in the hydrobay, but I've made contact with my team on the city ship, and they'll be ready when we get there. Captain Jagan and his family have arrived to get the formal reception underway, so when we get to the *Minos*, we won't have to waste time there.'

'What's the point of this stupid reception, anyway?' Quin asked.

'There has to be a formal reception of a visiting head of state,' Rose told him. 'If there wasn't, it could spark a war.'

'Not even UniCorp would start a war because their grand princess wasn't greeted by some jag-off and his cronies.'

'You'd be surprised,' Xavier said darkly. 'Besides, Captain Jagan can't know that. He has to show all hospitality to Rose and myself. His entire authority here supposedly resides only in his affiliation with us. He could declare himself independent of UniCorp, but it would have difficult economic consequences, as would any of our attempts to shake him from his seat. Politics, even corporate politics, is an intricate dance of polite interactions and tacit approval. Communication is key. The terrorists seek to disrupt that balance, which is why they destroyed the cell tower.'

'For all the good it did them,' Dr Zellwegger muttered. 'I wish they'd do more to educate them up here. The only thing these terrorists are doing is inconveniencing people, and making themselves seem like animals. They didn't even manage to kill anyone, and if they had, that wouldn't have helped them, either. What are they expecting with their bombs?'

'I think they're just trying to get attention,' said Xavier.

'Well, they've got it!' said Dr Zellwegger. 'They should clean those tunnels out. You know that's where the terrorists hide.'

'It's also where they hide the children,' Quin said loudly. 'You're right. Let's just send cyanide gas through the whole warren. Solve everyone's problem.'

'Quin!' Rose said.

'Can you not recognize sarcasm when you hear it, Fitzroy?' Quin snapped.

Rose's cheeks were red. 'I'm sure Ted didn't mean that.'

'Why not?' Quin asked. 'That's how UniCorp thinks, right? Something's not working out?' His look passed to Xavier. 'Cut your losses and move on.'

Xavier actually smiled condescendingly.

'Anyway,' Quin went on. 'If I was a terrorist, I'd consider having you two and the Jagans all in one place a perfect opportunity. They've got you exactly where they want you.'

'Which is why we've increased security,' Xavier said. 'Captain Jagan is insistent on meeting with us, as scheduled, this afternoon. His own circumstances depend on it. If he were not to take on an authoritative role over us while we visited the moon, one of the other city-ship captains might take on the mantle, and that would shake his position. Captain Jagan will be bringing his own security force with him, I understand, and I have no doubt that they will be most effective.' He glanced nervously at Rose at that point, but I was the only one who noticed it. 'Captain Jagan's icebreaker will be here this evening, just at sundown.'

'You mean lights out,' Quin quipped.

'Yes,' Xavier said. 'We will meet him formally in the hydrobay, and return here to change, and then proceed to a formal reception and ball in the train station. Security forces will be patrolling the streets and completely surround this hotel, the hydrobay, and the train station. In any case, they will likely have found the terrorists by then. This is a small community.'

'They'll have found *someone* by then,' Quin muttered. 'Who says it'll be the right ones?'

I was too tired to play referee. I went to my medical work-up – I did not ask what it said, and they did not volunteer information. Then I went out to the lobby and fell asleep on the couch. My head was splitting. *(You've got too many people in here,)* 42 said, but I brushed her off. As Xavier, I didn't want anything to do with her.

It was Rose who woke me to take me to the dock after 'nightfall'. A security guard stood behind her, but otherwise we were alone. 'The others have already left,' she said kneeling by the sofa. 'I wanted to let you sleep. You don't look so good.'

'*I feel fine,*' I told her, stroking her cheek. It was a lie – my head still hurt – but it wasn't as bad as it had been that morning. *'Just stay with me.'*

She touched the side of my throat, concern seeping through her. 'I have a handful of your meds, here. Then we have to go.'

I swallowed pills and dragged myself up and out into the evening of the Crystal Village.

The place really was scintillating at night. Lights glimmered and glistened through a thousand facets of ice. The over-bright day lamps in the ceiling had been dimmed to a bluish shimmer, and false ice-sculpted trees sparkled like it was Christmas in downtown ComUnity.

Rose looked stunning, with her white coat and her blonde hair, leading me through the sparkling fairy lights. There was a gentle music coming from a corner café. It was a shame, really. If this place hadn't been built on a lie, it might have been rather nice. '*Stop,*' I sent, squeezing her hand. '*There's no need to rush it. We've got time.*'

The terror she felt as I said that was palpable. I pulled her to me. 'Hey,' I whispered. 'What is it?'

Time, time, always time. Time was Rose's enemy. It was always rushing off without her, ticking away until she felt she could never catch up. I sighed and kissed her throat, trying to calm her mind as I did. My head was still aching, so it was a trick to do. 'I know,' I breathed into her ear. 'That's why I'm trying to enjoy what I've got.' I twirled her away from me to the music and then pulled her close, until we were dancing under the lights. A sudden gust of sparkle made us gasp, and we looked up. An ice machine had just gone off, sending a cascade of tiny ice crystals through the air. I'd noticed these machines on the way through the village before. They had seemed a silly, unrealistic reference to the snows of Earth. Now seen in the glittering night lights, it was clear this was how they were meant to be enjoyed. I pulled Rose to me again, and now our dance was under the gently falling frozen fires of ice. I kissed her tenderly and then stood back to gaze at her, holding her thin, chill hands. Oh, yes. This was how I wanted to remember her. Backlit and glorious and surrounded by sparkles.

With a sudden gasp, Rose snatched her hands out of my grip. I turned to see what had distracted her, but I'd already guessed. The frisson of horrified guilt I'd felt just before she let go had been a pretty good indicator.

Xavier stood in the light pooling from the café. He stared at us, his face completely unreadable. For a long moment, time was as frozen as the ice beneath our feet. Him and her, and me between them. Finally, Xavier blinked, breaking the spell. 'We'd better hurry. We'll be late.'

His voice was very quiet.

He turned his back to us and headed towards the docks without another word. Rose stared after him for a moment, trembling, her face white. She opened her mouth as if to say something to me, shaking her head slightly. But she couldn't find the words. She broke then, running after him like an abandoned puppy.

My head sank. By the time I looked up again, she was walking beside him. Neither of them was speaking. I looked away to try and compose myself, only to find myself looking at a knot of teenaged Europan kids – wealthy from the colours of their garb – staring at me from the door of the café. 'Is that really him?' 'Go talk to him!'

I wanted every one of them to melt into the ice. Instead, I raised my hand to them in what could have been interpreted as a friendly greeting and followed after Xavier and Rose.

I didn't catch up to them until we were at the hydrobay. The hydrobay was a large hollowed cavern, lower than the rest of the Crystal Village by a good two hundred metres. There were treacherous-looking stairs down to it carved into the ice, but an open lift had been made ready for us, rather like the elevator down to the village proper. It was lit by its own central sun-light, dimmed to an eerie blue by the supposed 'night'. It was an awesome sight seen from the top of the lift. Half the bay was open water, kept free of ice by a rim of machines that agitated the water at all times. The rest of the bay was a chasm of icicles of all sizes, as the ionized water dripped and froze from the ceiling and walls. It echoed worse than the village had.

In the centre of the bay floated Captain Jagan's icebreaker. The icebreakers were strange, drill-shaped submarines, equipped to break through the occasional surprise patches of ice that sometimes formed in the lower ocean. It looked vaguely like a narwhal. I wondered how intentional that was – the oceanic equivalent of the UniCorp unicorn.

A rather sizeable crowd had gathered at the side of the hydrobay, and they cheered as Rose and I exited the lift. Rose glanced at them nervously, and Xavier gestured to them with his chin. 'They've all been vetted and searched,' he told her. 'And as you can see, we're not lacking in security.' The security guard which had been standing behind us had joined a contingent of at least thirty, who ringed a perimeter with lethal-looking charge guns, stumble sticks at their hips in case those failed. Something looked odd about some of these security guards. Most of them stood in braces of two, backing each other up, occasionally making eye-contact with each other, us, or a member of the crowd. But a half a dozen each stood alone, weapons at the ready, with cold, dead eyes in neutral faces.

When I realized what they were, I hoped Rose wouldn't notice them.

Quin and Dr Zellwegger were already waiting. As we approached them, a middle-aged man in ceremonial uniform came up to us. 'Mr Zellwegger, Dr Zellwegger. Miss Fitzroy,' he said, with a deep bow. '*Nameste.*'

'*Nameste,*' Rose replied, though I could see she was blushing.

'And you,' he said, gazing at Quin and myself. He gave us no greeting, and Quin offered none. He took a deep breath and shook himself, turning back to Xavier. 'The captain and his family will disembark shortly to greet you. If you'll wait on the carpet we have indicated, you can receive them there.'

'That should be sufficient,' Xavier said.

'There is a full contingent of security,' he added. 'And a turma of Plastines have been reassigned to personnel protection. I trust that's in order?'

'As Captain Jagan sees fit,' Xavier said.

Rose went white. 'Plastines?'

Xavier took her hand. 'Colony laws,' he said. 'Plastines are common here. Can you do this?'

Rose looked over to me, and then back to Xavier. 'Yes,' she said, but she held his hand tightly.

We took our positions where the man I couldn't help but think of as the Master of Ceremonies had indicated, and the hatch in the icebreaker opened.

A vast roar echoed as the crowd at the edges realized the captain was approaching. Quin and I found each other's hands in silence as we both realized we'd just walked unwillingly into a state reception. For once, Quin's mind wasn't jarring. We both felt exactly the same.

The platform was carpeted in a muted brownish red – probably another product made out of RayonEuropa – and a banner had been hung above our heads, with the UniCorp unicorn rampant shining garishly under a bright light. There were cameras on the stage, too – hovering spherical holovid cameras, blasting our images in 3D to Europa HN. Rose hated cameras, but Xavier's hand on her back held her steady.

'Just smile,' Xavier said, *sotto voce*, to all three of us.

Rose was shaking, and I wasn't surprised.

Captain Jagan exited the hatch and made a gesture for the crowd. Beside him stood his wife, and a girl about twelve, who I took to be Jamal's sister, Nila. He'd mentioned her, in passing. She'd be going to UniPrep in a few more years. Beside them stood three things which definitely wouldn't have been seen on Earth. The first two were Plastine bodyguards. Their shiny, surreal-looking faces stared blankly ahead, and they each carried stumble sticks on their hips, and cruel-looking rifles in their arms. My arm ached with an unpleasant memory. I didn't know how they could bear to have them so close. The other paced peacefully beside the girl, nearly as tall as she was, fur sleek and muscles liquid strength. It was a black panther.

Captain Jagan strode forward to meet Xavier, who took his arm warmly. 'Captain Jagan. So pleased to see you again. I would like to introduce you to my ward, Miss Rose Fitzroy.'

'You can't believe how pleased I am to finally meet you, Miss Fitzroy,' Captain Jagan said. 'I've been anxious to hear about you from the moment the news reports reached us.'

'And of course these are Mr Otto Sextus and Quin Essential, whose arrival I'm sure you have been anxiously anticipating.'

'It is truly an honour,' said Captain Jagan, nodding his head respectfully in my direction as he held out his hand.

I stepped back. No. Absolutely not him. His son was one thing, but Jamal was young. His mind was still malleable, and I didn't even like everything I saw there. Quin kindly covered my blunder by taking the hand himself. 'The honour is entirely yours,' Quin said bluntly. Nila's huge smile faltered.

Xavier interposed himself between them before Captain Jagan caught that. 'Please, introduce me to your lovely daughter. You had not yet been blessed with her when I last saw you.'

The girl came forward and politely introduced herself to Xavier and Rose. 'My name is Nila Jagan. And this is Bagheera,' she added, proudly.

Xavier smiled at the big cat. 'Charming. Named for Kipling?'

'Who?' the girl asked.

'Bagheera. The panther in Kipling's *Jungle Book*,' Xavier said.

'Never read it,' the girl said. 'He came with the name.'

Yep. That was Jamal's sister. I could tell.

Quin eyed the beast with suspicion. 'Is he, ah … declawed?'

'What? Oh, no, he's just a Geemo.'

'A what?'

'Genetically modified organism,' the girl said. 'Are you stupid?' Her mother tried to hush her.

Quin blinked at her, incredulous. 'Don't try to match wits with me, hon. I know goldfish who can insult me better than that.' Well, Quin was getting on wonderfully. 'What's Geemo about your kitty cat?'

She glared at him. 'Bagheera is Geemo nonaggressive. If he even wanted to hurt something he'd fall over in a faint.' She tousled the fur on the big cat's head. 'Daddy got him for me as a cub last year. I wanted a griffin, but Daddy says the design isn't finished yet, and they're not safe. Baggy'll be dead in a year or so, and then we'll see. Right, Daddy?'

Captain Jagan chuckled and said, 'We'll see, darling.'

I blinked. Were they saying what I thought they were saying?

They were. 'There are few regulations on genetically modified organisms up here,' Mr Zellwegger explained to us at Rose's look. 'The Ganymede colony was recently refounded about fifteen years ago, to provide a safe environment for genetic experimentation. This panther would have come out of those programmes.'

My eyes widened in horror. This cat had been genetically modified, like I had. And it had been designed with a limited life span ... planned obsolescence on a living being, so customers would have to purchase newer models of pet. How many other animals and plants were being spliced together in some lab, here or on Ganymede? For each successful organism, how many were mutated, unviable or dangerous? I suddenly felt nauseated.

And the old man just took it in his stride. My hatred for him spiked.

Rose jumped forward and took hold of my arm. *'Hang on,'* she thought to me. *'Just hang on.'* She was appalled, too. Quin was looking at the cat as if it were a bloody corpse. I gripped Rose's hand tightly.

And Captain Jagan just chatted on, oblivious. 'I am so glad to see you are recovering nicely from yesterday's unpleasantness. It is a pity that something so upsetting had to mar your visit to our fair moon, but rest assured, such a thing is easily dealt with. I have arranged for a ball this evening in honour of your visit. It really is almost fortunate that this happened. The Crystal Village is ideal for a fairy-tale evening. A fairy-tale evening for our Sleeping Beauty, yes?' He beamed at Rose. 'And I understand you've been going to Unity Preparatory? My son goes there, I understand you know him? I cannot wait to converse more this evening.'

'You know something?' Quin said suddenly. Rose blanched, and debated trying to put her hand over his mouth. She ultimately decided she couldn't afford to replace the fingers, but it was a tough call. 'We just travelled six hundred and thirty million kilometres over the last five months because my brother is dying. Not so you could play tea party with the UniCorp execs. If you please, I would much prefer you and your barbarous family could quit with your semi-diplomatic chats and get us to your ever so beneficent lab, so that I can get out of your benighted company as soon as humanly, or inhumanly, possible.'

'Quin!' Rose cried.

'*It was the panther,*' I told her. '*He'd have held his tongue but for that.*'

Jamal's family looked shocked. Quin could be pretty shocking to people who didn't know him. 'You'll have to excuse Mr Essential,' Xavier said calmly. 'He's been in a constant state of worry for some time now.'

'No call to be rude,' Nila muttered.

'I'm not being rude. You're just insignificant.'

She blushed. She was the daughter of the captain of the *Minos*. I don't think anyone had ever dared to call her something like that before.

'And contemptible,' he added, and Nila's eyes shone with tears of embarrassment.

'Could you at least *try* to be polite?' Rose asked.

Quin looked at her, eyebrow raised. 'I could try. I would fail.'

'Yes,' said Captain Jagan. 'Well. I am sure that we can solve any difficulties at the reception.'

'Yeah. When you receive my fist in your face, maybe,' Quin muttered.

Xavier took up the conversation as if Quin hadn't spoken. 'I'm looking forward to seeing more of Europa's hospitality,' Xavier said. 'Shall we, then?' He turned to the people and took Rose's hand. 'Bow,' he said to her, Quin and myself. He stepped forward with Rose and made a respectful greeting, to the cheer of the crowds.

It looked wrong, the old man beside her fresh, young face. Neither I nor Quin bothered to bow. We followed Dr Zellwegger back to the lift. When Rose caught up to me and took my arm, I sighed with relief.

chapter 15

'That was a very reckless public display, Quin,' said Dr Zellwegger as we all piled into the lobby.

'I don't like them.'

'So you couldn't keep your mouth shut for ten minutes? The cameras have all of that, you know. It'll be all around the colonies in half an hour.'

'Not if the cell tower is still out of commission.'

'We have a message link in the bay,' Dr Zellwegger said. 'That meeting was being broadcast live back to the *Minos*, and there are other feeds from each of the villages. What were you thinking!'

'What were they thinking?' Quin shouted. 'Parading that panther around, bragging about how it's about to die. Do they talk like that about us, too?'

'I'm not here to get into GMO politics with you, Quin. My job is to try and save your brother.'

'And a great job you're doing of it, too, poncing about this tourist trap like it's heaven on Europa. Why don't you get on with it?'

'I'm trying!' Dr Zellwegger said. 'We'd be on the *Minos* already, prepping Otto for the procedure as we speak, if those terrorists hadn't mucked everything up.'

'They did exactly what everyone expected them to do,' Quin said. 'They did what they're *designed* to do! It's not the so-called terrorists keeping us in limbo, here, it's your wretched security!'

'It's not my security,' Dr Zellwegger said. 'I'm just a scientist.'

'It's mine,' Xavier said evenly. 'And it isn't safe for us to leave yet, Quin.'

'But it's safe for Captain Jag-off to parade around like the second coming?'

'That was his call. My first priority is to keep you, all of you, alive. Otto will not be saved if he's killed on the way.'

'You don't care what happens to us,' Quin snapped. 'You're just worried about your precious underage princess, you sicko.'

'That's where you're wrong,' Xavier said. 'I care very much what happens to you and Otto. You're more valuable than you realize.'

I saw Quin stiffen when the word 'value' was applied. He didn't like thinking of us as commodities. 'Right. Am I to take it you actually gave a rodent's posterior before your pretty trophy child began whimpering at your heels for her favourite toy?'

'Please do not speak of Rose that way. I have done everything in my power for you, Mr Essential,' Xavier said quietly. I was worried. I knew this old man very well – I felt I was him, in a strange, mad, way. And in the same way I knew how dangerous Quin could be, I was certain that the old man could be even more deadly. 'If I am to continue with this dangerous venture on behalf of your brother, whom you purport to care about, I expect a certain level of respect from you towards myself and the officials of this moon. You do not have to like them. You do not even have to speak to them. But I would appreciate it if you could curb your tongue until the cameras are turned off. Is that understood?'

'I don't care what you'd *appreciate*,' Quin said.

'Then you are banned from tonight's festivities, until I feel I can trust you in public.'

'Oh!' Quin cringed as if he'd been shot, staggering back several steps. 'My heart is breaking! In case that wasn't clear, that was sarcasm,' he added. 'I hadn't planned on going to your kennel club show in the first place. And since we are neither prisoners nor pets, I suggest you take that answer at whatever *value* you think it's worth.'

'You appear to value yourself at a considerably lower rate than anyone else in the system,' Xavier said to him coolly. 'You appear to believe yourself expendable. I have tended to disagree in the past, but perhaps I'm mistaken. The billions spent in your daily upkeep was perhaps a wasted investment, but to your good fortune I have never been one inclined to cut his losses and move on. Unlike many other executives of my acquaintance.'

'And what's that supposed to mean, old man?' Quin snarled.

'It means you are both alive only at my discretion, and you are only here because there is someone who has a vested interest in keeping you that way,' he said. 'I suggest you treat her with some measure of respect.'

'Is that a threat?' Quin asked.

'It doesn't need to be,' Xavier said evenly. 'And you know that as well as I do.'

'Xavier,' said Rose. 'Let it go. It's just Quin. He's always like this.'

'Yes,' Xavier said, without taking his eyes from Quin's. 'He is.' To my surprise, it was Quin who looked away first.

Xavier turned to Rose. 'I've arranged for clothing for all of you. You can find something to do with Quin's suit, I'm sure. Toilet paper is in short supply on this moon, I understand.'

Rose chuckled.

He turned to Quin, who was sulking. 'You,' he said to Quin, 'should guard yourself and your tongue with more care.'

'Remind me to pretend to give a squitch,' Quin muttered.

Xavier only gazed at him for a long moment and then shook his head. He left without another word.

Rose rounded on Quin. 'And what's up your butt?' she snapped.

I laughed. Rose's prim little antiquated accent sounded so pristine in contrast to her words.

'Seriously!' she said to both of us, leading us back to her suite. 'Don't tick Xavier off, you have no *idea* how hard it was to get you two up here!' She shook her head in disbelief and rubbed her face.

'He doesn't care,' Quin said.

'Yes, he does. He was already angry when you snuck off this morning.'

'*What?*' I signed.

'Yeah, he vanished while you were asleep,' Rose told me. We followed Rose into her room as she unlocked it. 'Caused quite the buzz when he dodged security.'

'*What were you doing?*' I signed.

'I was seeing Europa. You know. The reason we came here.'

'The reason we came here was to cure Otto,' Rose snapped. 'You disappeared just after a bombing!'

'They happen all the time,' Quin said. He flung himself down casually on Rose's couch. 'No one's happy in this village. They're all starving or freezing to death, or both.'

'How do you know?'

'Who do you think I was talking with?' Quin asked.

Both Rose and I turned to him. '*What?*'

'How did you find them?'

'They found me,' Quin said. 'I thought at first they were going to kidnap me or something, but they told me they don't do that. Not unless someone deserves it.'

'As if Xavier deserved to be attacked,' Rose said with scorn.

'You'd be surprised, princess,' Quin said.

'Stop it,' Rose said. 'I know Xavier. He's the kindest, loyalist, most generous person you could imagine.'

'*Thank you,*' I signed automatically.

She ignored me. 'If those criminals you were playing with think he deserves to die just because he's head of UniCorp, they're wrong. *You're* wrong!'

'The poor aren't criminals, they're just stuck,' Quin said. 'Just because they agree with the *Harvestaras* mission doesn't mean they all agree with their methods.'

'Wait,' Rose said. 'Wait, that means you know where they are! You need to tell Xavier. We'll catch them, and then we can get down to the *Minos*, and Otto will be—'

'I can't tell them anything,' Quin said. 'I didn't see their faces, and I don't know where they base. They have tunnels, all through the walls around here, did you know? I'd get lost before the second turning. It's a labyrinth in there. What you see of this village is just, well, the tip of the ice-burg.' He laughed at his own joke.

'*Wait a minute,*' I signed. '*Slow down. Quin, where have you been?*'

'I was hoping you'd ask, bro,' Quin said. He jumped up and grabbed my head.

His thoughts were spiked with anger. He had never felt so strongly about anything in his life, and it was like being hit by a jackhammer. Some of the memories were actually from yesterday, before the bombing. *Bang!* He'd been wandering the tourist trap in disgust until he found the hole in the wall. *Bang!* Disappearing into dark tunnels like worm holes. Lost, alone, frightened and cold, until he was found, *Bang!* by a knot of people on their way through the tunnels, who recognized him immediately. Some of them even spoke English, and *Bang!* he was taken under their wing, shown the poverty of the village. People, hundreds of people, thin and pale and ragged, infesting the walls like maggots. *Bang!* Tiny warm rooms where a dozen people lived almost atop each other for warmth. *Bang!* Hungry children eating hard dry cakes of unprocessed plankton. *Bang!* Jerry-rigged stabilizers and oxygen filters, failing NeoFusion batteries, flickering dying lights, dim corridors. *Bang!* A room of metal cylinders, *Bang!* a religious ceremony in a darkened room, open to the ocean. *Bang!* Hungry faces of abandoned children.

'Stop it!' Rose grabbed at Quin's arms, yanking him off me in terror. Each of Quin's disconnected images had jolted through me like electric shocks, and I'd been flinching at each one, as if in pain. Rose pushed him away and took hold of my face, gently staring into my eyes. She was horrified.

'*I'm not hurt,*' I told her. '*Quin just has a very powerful mind. I don't touch him often.*'

Rose sighed, but looked daggers at Quin. 'Your brother is sick! He doesn't need you mentally shouting at him.'

'I was just telling him about the village,' Quin said. 'Or the villagers. You should come with me.' He stared at her. 'They're starving, and they're uneducated, and they're freezing to death, and no one gives a squitch. Princess.'

'Of course they are,' Rose said.

Quin and I both blinked at her. Rose, eternally compassionate Rose, was so matter-of-fact about Quin's revelation that we were both taken aback. She looked back and forth between us and shrugged. 'Well, what did you expect to find?' she asked. 'It's a colony.'

'You think that's *right?*' Quin asked.

Rose shrugged again. 'I don't know.'

'*You knew,*' I signed. Then a dark, world weary fatigue gripped me, and I sank onto the sofa. Of course she knew. I already knew she'd known. Or part of me did.

Quin laughed cruelly. 'You're surprised?' he asked me. 'Of course she knew.' He stared at her. 'She's one of them. Give her another two years, she'll be just like them.'

'Just like who?' Rose snapped at him. 'Like you? Like Otto? You both knew too. It's not as if Jamal is quiet about what it's like up here, and there's stuff about Europa on the net. I've never heard you moaning about the injustices of the universe before.'

'But you knew how bad this was?' Quin demanded.

'Not exactly,' Rose said, yawning. 'It just doesn't surprise me, is all.'

Quin's rage boiled behind his eyes. The yawn was misplaced – it made Rose seem bored, rather than exhausted with the stress of the afternoon and the Europan gravity compounded with her stass fatigue. I held my hand out at Quin, as if I were holding him in his chair, though I didn't even touch him. *'Rose. Tell Quin what you mean,'* I signed.

She blinked in confusion for a moment and then sighed in sudden understanding. 'I told you this place reminded me of my mom,' she told me. 'It's not just her, this whole place reminds me of … back then. The opinions of the people, the structure of the village itself. It's all to make money for the corporation. This is pre Dark Time mentality. This is just …' She held her hand up helplessly. 'What it was like.'

'That's disgusting,' Quin said.

Rose shrugged. 'Well, yes, but what do you expect? It's a problem they don't really care about, so their solutions are callous, and they don't work very well. They think if you put the poor out of sight, they stop existing. That's what those tunnels are. If you beat and starve and work the lower classes into submission, they won't interrupt your holiday. But then the under-served get angry and riot or go rogue. So you need to suppress them more to make them pay. One of those vicious cycles. This was my childhood. Beautiful and decadent on one hand, and slimy and hopeless on the other.'

'And you're okay with this, *princess?*' Quin growled.

'I didn't do it.'

'This colony was founded by your father.'

Rose looked down. 'I know.'

The guilt was heavy on her face. I glared at Quin, and he glared right back. This wasn't Rose's fault, but all her life she had been reared to take the blame onto herself for her parents' wrongdoings. Finally, very gently, I touched her hand. Her thoughts had turned to her parents, and they were dark and conflicted.

'Yeah, but you're like gods out here,' Quin went on. 'You're telling me there's nothing you can do?'

'Xavier's trying,' Rose said, pulling away. 'He doesn't feel he has a lot of power out here.'

'Yeah, right. You can do everything else. Do you know how hard it is to get a passport to the colonies? I'm not talking Luna. Out here, do you know what it takes to get permission to enter the Jovian system? It takes a year-long application process. We got up here in a *week*.'

'And you're complaining about this?' Rose asked. 'That's red tape, this is economics!'

'And that makes it okay?' Quin was infuriated.

'No, it makes it complicated,' Rose said. 'And I don't have the training yet to know how to fix it. And neither do you!'

'I know we have to do *something*. You seem content to just let it go on.'

'I have no choice! Xavier explained it to me before we left. The colony was set up and then kind of left to go on its own momentum. Remember, the Dark Times didn't happen up here. There were no plagues, no wars. All that happened was that each of the colonies grew more isolated, more cut off from Earth, and less reliant on Earth's orders and policies. Europa is the bread-basket of the outer colonies. There's enough water to provide Callisto and Ganymede with ample supplies, and a lot of its produce even gets shipped all the way to Titan – and not just the plankton, the hydroponics produce, too, grown in the cities. These villages are only way stations. The tourist sections were actually a concession by the ruling families, an attempt to make these transportation blocks less distasteful to those who had to travel through them. They do supply the villages with an economy, of a kind.'

'And they love it so much,' Quin said. 'That's why they're bombing it.'

'I didn't say they loved it,' Rose said. 'I said it was someone's attempt, feeble though it may have been, to solve a problem that had been going on since the colony was founded.' She swallowed. 'Actually, I think it was my mother's. This looks like her version of charity. Very glittery.'

'I'm not in the least surprised, *Fitzroy*,' Quin said.

Rose went white. 'Are you blaming me for this?'

'Should I be?'

For a moment, Rose's mouth hung open in bewilderment. 'I was stuck on Earth in a thrice-burned stasis chamber when all this was thought up!' she shouted, her voice more tortured than I'd ever heard it.

'Waiting for the next diamond necklace,' Quin said. 'Well, this is it, princess, a glittering diamond jewel, crowning your greatest achievement – a warren of hunger and blood.'

'So what do you want me to do?' she cried. 'Tell me something sensible, and I'll see it's done!'

'Quit acting like it's all just part of the *status quo*!'

'It *is* the *status quo*!' Rose shouted back.

I grabbed Quin's arm. Rose was red with indignation. '*Give her a break, Quin. How is she supposed to fix it? She's rich, she's not a fairy godmother. She can't just wave a magic wand and fix a flawed society. It took her six months to quit vomiting every time she ate. What do you want? She's only seventeen.'*

'And you said she's older than she looks,' Quin snapped. 'Let her explain.'

'I can't just fix it, Quin,' Rose said, trying to sound reasonable. 'Xavier can't either. He's tried before. He says it blew up in his face. The colony isn't run by us, not really.'

'Right,' Quin said. 'With the UniCorp logo on everything including the ice-cubes.'

'That's a very old conceit they just keep up for appearances. The colony is really run by the ruling families of the submarine cities – people like Jamal's family. It's like a tributary. All hail the king, but the real ruler is the governor. Right now, the city captains hold a nominal loyalty to UniCorp and therefore to me and Xavier. But if we start pushing them too hard in the wrong direction, they'll break that tie.'

And they could do it, too. Europa wasn't like the other colonies. Because of the ocean and the plankton, their resources were a thousand times beyond the other colonies.

'And if Europa breaks its tie with UniCorp,' Rose went on, 'you know what would happen next. Callisto and Ganymede and Titan would be cut off, or at the complete mercy of their monopoly. Right now there have to be some concessions between the colonies, or the trade would suffer, as the shipments are controlled by the corporation. But without that, the ships would be controlled by the richest moon – and that's Europa. They'd have ultimate power over everything. People – would – *die*, Quin. Once you control the supply of food, you control everyone.' She looked down. 'My father taught them that, too.'

She looked ashamed. She'd been just as dominated by her father as the poor here in this colony. And it was

UniCorp's policies with the Global Food Initiative that had poisoned the grain and caused the wide spread sterility that had been the final blow of the Dark Times. Control the food. Control everything.

'And I should accept the word of some last-gen corporate apologist?' he asked.

'That's not fair,' I signed to Quin.

'Look, I'll talk with Xavier,' Rose said. 'You're right, Quin. Okay? Happy? You're right! It's just a slow process – it took a disaster to change things on Earth, and a third of the population died. We'd rather avoid that here. But you're right. We weren't looking at the villages; they were so pretty and efficient. My mother was good at that. Designing things that drew the eye. Distracting people. Painting things over.' She gave a rueful laugh. 'I got my artistic impulses from *somewhere*, anyway.' She'd gone white again. 'And you're wrong, Quin. This isn't a diamond necklace, it's just ice. I hate it here.' And she started to cry.

I folded her into my arms and kissed her temple. The poor girl was wondering how many years she spent in stasis while her mother designed places like this to cover up the inequities caused by her father's callous business practices. There was one four-year stint when she was seven. Before that, she had no idea.

'I don't buy it,' Quin said. 'And I can't believe you're on her side, Otto!'

'Whose side should I be on?' I signed back.

'What do you mean? Your own! Have you looked around? These aren't just the poor. These are our people.'

I shook my head. These were not our people. Apart from ourselves, we had no people. I signed something to that effect.

'You can't see anymore,' Quin said, and he sounded contemptuous. 'Look at yourself. Just look at yourself. Not your skin, not what the scientists did to us. Just look.'

'What do you mean?' I signed.

'He means you,' Rose said quietly. 'I've been noticing it since we got here. Whatever embryo they adapted came from here. You're of the same race. If you weren't an EP raised on Earth, you'd look just like them.'

I considered this. There was something about the shape of their eyes, their build, their bone structure. Certainly the hair was the same. But I felt no close connection. Clearly nothing like what Quin was feeling.

'And you don't see it,' Quin said. 'Really. Oh, burn it, what has she turned you into?'

Rose went red. 'It wasn't me,' she said hotly.

Quin glared at her. 'You're poisoning him. Nabiki knew it,' he said. 'She could see it happening even before she broke it off.'

'*Who?'* I signed.

'Nabiki,' Quin said.

I stared at him in blankly.

'Nabiki?' he said. 'Your ex?'

I had no idea who he was talking about.

'Nabiki Sato. Seventeen, Asian, fights like a tiger in the sack?'

I was totally bewildered. My own memories had faded under the sea of Xavier's.

'You know. Bad tempered, beautiful, contradictory? You used to describe her as having layers of thought?' I barely remembered Nabiki. It took a moment before my own memory surfaced. The memory was distant, when it came, and couldn't touch me.

But Quin was on me, now. 'You don't remember, do you. Do you remember anything? Una. Una Prime, they numbered her 11. Took five days to die. Spent the last day moaning as if she could feel each cell dying one by one? 18? Went into convulsions? 63, just didn't wake up? Penny, Tristan? Your sisters, waiting for us on Earth? Anything?' His eyes were bright as he advanced on me. '71, just screamed for an hour, and they had to tie him down, because the drugs did nothing? 42? Tell me you remember 42!'

(*Leave him alone, 50!*) She shouted at him, but of course he couldn't hear her.

'42? Bled out from a brain haemorrhage in front of you and nearly took you with her! And those of us left fought like hell to keep you alive, because the scans showed you were brain dead. It took us three days to wake you, and I spent the whole bloody time feeling useless while Tristan and Una and all the ones with your stupid bloody gift tried to call you back from nothing, and all I could do was stand like a sentry in your doorway keeping the vultures from pecking at your corpse. And you don't remember any of this, do you!' He grabbed me by the head and shouted at me both mentally and physically. *'DO YOU!'*

I was bewildered, swaying with shock, and Quin's desperation raked at me. Rose lunged forward and grabbed at him. 'Leave him alone!'

'What have you done to him, you whore?' Quin shouted, backhanding her in the face.

My shock evaporated in an instant as Rose fell backward. She looked up. A thin line of blood trickled from her nose, glaring like a crack on her upper lip, starkly beautiful against her pale skin.

Now I had memories of Quin – Quin shouting and rampaging, destroying the common room in a fit of passion. Quin, bullying freshmen students this last summer at UniPrep. Quin, twelve years old and terrifying, raging at me, until I'd knocked him down and he kicked my leg out from under me, snapping my tibia and dislocating my knee. Quin's face, harsh and heartless, so deeply, painfully angry. So angry it spilled out into everything he touched, every emotion he ever had. I'd never understood that anger before. Even 42's anger was never violent like Quin's.

But there were other memories which invaded me, or which I had embraced. Xavier was in me somewhere, and Xavier understood it. And he knew – though he didn't want to – where it could lead. I grabbed at him. '*You leave her alone!*'

Quin shook his head. '*Nabiki saw this,*' Quin said silently, his thoughts as violent as his nature. '*She saw it months ago. From the moment you touched that whore. And now you're even worse. I can't believe I encouraged you.*' He didn't say it, or even think it in words, but it was there. He wanted her dead. He wanted Rose dead and Mr Zellwegger dead and Jamal's entire family. There was no thought of mercy. No thought of justice. Only boiling hatred and rage. Quin's deep, passionate devotion to me and Tristan and Penny, to the simple ones, to all of us, had been twisted, expanded, and had suddenly encompassed this whole village, probably the entire moon. They were *his people*, and he had been ripped from them, kept from them, while he was genetically mutilated and they were economically tortured. And he blamed Rose, and Mr Zellwegger most of all.

But Mr Zellwegger was Xavier. And Xavier was me. There was a part of me that saw Quin's hatred as hatred of me. Xavier knew how to hate as surely and violently as Quin did. With a roar of fury – a roar that came out whispery and dolphinish – my arm went up and bashed Quin in the jaw.

As always when I hurt someone with my fist I felt the blow as strongly as if it had happened to me. As unpleasant as that was, it was only mental and not physical damage, so what tended to happen was a surge of adrenaline that slowed everything down and made it hard to catch me. The more I hurt my opponent the better I fought – and the longer it took me to recover afterward. I'd become something of a pacifist from the age of twelve, after that terrible fight with Quin when he had broken my leg, and my pain returned to him had nearly stopped his weak heart. I had realized there was really nothing that could justify my fighting someone. In hurting them, I only hurt myself.

Quin reeled, flying backwards in the low gravity, until he crashed into the wall. He made a dull thud against the mock wood, and when he looked up, his eyes were lit with a fanatic joy. He snarled as he leaped at me. Rose screamed. The two of us grappled. Despite my headache, the roaring in my ears, and my own somewhat quiet nature, my madness was on me in full. I was Xavier, and I knew what it was to suffer loss, and this zealot had just called my Rose a whore, and he wanted her dead. I wanted him broken. Broken beyond repair.

I rolled him over and started hitting him, hard as I could, again and again and again, pounding so hard into his face I heard the bones click in my hand. Quin's nose had broken again, and blood streamed down his face. I was winning. The pain swirled through me, both mine and Quin's, and I was nothing but rage and pain. But without warning Quin twisted, bringing his knees up into my stomach, and kicked me off.

On Earth, I would have fallen onto my back a few inches from him, scrabbled back into the fray, and we would have been at it again within seconds. In Europan gravity, the moment I left the influence of the Norway Chalet's grav mats I was launched several feet into the air, hit the ceiling, and then crashed into the wall. The breath was knocked out of me, and I couldn't focus.

'Both of you! Someone, help!' Rose was screaming down the corridor, and had been for some time. It was only then that help arrived, in a form none of us had expected.

A shiny, dead-eyed Plastine pushed past Rose and grabbed Quin before he had a chance to go at me again. Rose screamed as her nightmare descended. I was woozy from the blow, and I could barely understand what was going on. Quin was purple with rage, and he did not stop shouting. 'What did you do?!' he roared at Rose. 'What did you do to my brother?!'

'It wasn't me,' Rose kept saying. 'It wasn't me.'

I tried to find my feet, but my body said no. No, we're just going to rest here for a while.

'Get your pet monster off me!' Quin shouted.

The Plastine said something in its cold, machine voice, but it wasn't in English, and none of us paid attention. I stopped paying attention to anything for a while as I tried to put myself back together, both mentally and physically. Neither of my personalities seemed up to the challenge just then, and it was actually 42 who started issuing orders, like a command sergeant. (*Get up. Use your legs, then your stomach muscles. Support with your arms. Come on, we need to move.)*

When I found my way to my feet, the chaos had increased. Xavier – the real Xavier – had come into the room, alongside another Plastine and two uniformed guards. Quin was still shouting unintelligible curses. Rose was crying, trying to explain between shouting back at Quin. Her face was a mass of red, flushed and bloody. She hadn't bothered to wipe her lip, but the blood had smeared over her cheek, and was still trickling a little. Ultimately Xavier said something to the Plastine holding Quin, and it set him down automatically. Quin made a lunge as if he was about to hit Xavier, but the other Plastine moved, and Quin thought better of it. With a curse, he backed off through the door, throwing a rude gesture for good measure, and then ran. I could hear his feet for only a few seconds on the rayon-carpeted floor.

Rose came to me then, holding the side of my throat and caressing my cheek with her thumb. 'You okay? Otto, look at me, are you okay?'

I wasn't okay. Physically, I was bruised and woozy, but uninjured. But Quin's rage had shattered me, and I wasn't sure who I was. I didn't seem to have any memories at all. I knew I loved Rose, but that seemed to be it. I sobbed without tears and let my head sink onto her shoulder.

chapter 16

The terrible thing about personal trauma, is it has no effect whatsoever on the normal course of the world. Not for anybody else. Despite Quin's explosion and my own confusion – or insanity – there was still a ball to attend and politicians to mollify.

Rose tried to reassure me as she straightened my new, insulated Europan dress shirt. It was warm as a coat, and made to look impressive in the frigid ice-box of the Crystal Village. It was a lovely thing, heavily hand-embroidered, but with few colours. Time and hands they had to spare on Europa. Dyes were harder to come by.

Quin was missing. He hadn't gone back to his room, and the security at the door said he'd gone out. After that, the security cameras had lost him in the village, as his new brown coat looked just like half the other coats of the village.

'They're doing everything they can to find him,' Rose said. 'We don't know if he's in any danger. They'll let us know the moment we hear anything.'

'*So why can't I wait here in my room?*'

'Because Captain Jagan wants you there,' Rose hissed at me. 'And if he's not happy with you, he might not sign off on Ted's experiment. He's already furious with Quin for breaking protocol and making his daughter cry. On planetary holovision!'

'*Are you telling me that he's not worried about Quin just because Quin was being an ass, the same as usual?*'

'Otto, I don't even know if *you're* worried about Quin, really. I think you think you should be.'

She was right. By the time Rose had explained the circumstance and the Plastines had been told to stand down, I had found a personality again. My memories were still sketchy and I wasn't sure which ones were mine, and which ones were *mine*, but so long as I held on to Rose, it didn't seem to matter. Quin was a more difficult person to hold in my head. Half of me loved him, but was afraid of him, and half of me hated him, but was afraid *for* him, and I wasn't sure which was which, or why. I didn't know why Xavier would have any opinion about Quin at all. Rose, I loved no matter who I was.

'I don't want to go.'

'We have to. I know, you shouldn't have to, but you do. This is how this *works*. I've done this. My mother used to take me to these expensive dinners and fine charity galas. I had to be on my best behaviour, look my best, be perfect. I was …' She sighed. 'I was an accessory,' she said suddenly. 'Like a handbag or a Chihuahua.'

That was one of the harshest things I'd ever heard her say directly about her mother.

'I know how these supposed leaders think. To them, people are what they mean, not who they are. My parents needed a daughter. It made them family people, it humanized them to the masses. If I didn't play that role – well. You know what they did. You, you are a rarity, more impressive than diamonds. Xavier and I are royalty, enough to raise Jagan's status among the captains of Europa – among the leaders of the entire Jovian colonies. That's what Jagan wants to do now, with you, with me, with Xavier. Show us off. If we take that away from him, we cut his authority. If his authority is threatened, he'll have to do something else to assure it. That could be anything

– impressing extra tariffs on Callisto's trade goods or banning stop-overs from Titan-bound vessels. He could even declare your treatment too experimental or expensive.' She touched my face, her eyes twisted in worry. 'We can't afford it.'

I swallowed. '*I didn't know it was this dangerous out here,*' I told her.

'Frontier law,' Rose said. 'This is like Queen Victoria visiting the Wild West.'

'*And Quin is out in it.*'

'What do you think he's going to do?'

I shook my head. '*He'll do whatever he thinks is in my best interest. I'm sick. I don't think he'd jeopardize my treatment.*'

'I hope not. But those terrorists ... they're killing people. Innocent people. Quin wouldn't do that, would he?'

I didn't answer. I knew what Quin thought, and I didn't want to. Quin's belief was that there *are* no innocent people.

'We'll find him tomorrow,' Rose reassured me. 'Let's just get through tonight.'

My head tilted to catch her lips in a kiss, but she pulled away from me. I wasn't sure if it was intentional or not, but it bothered me anyway.

Xavier met us as we came down the stairs. He too was dressed in an insulated dress shirt. Rose had been given a full insulated dress, darted with glass beads so that she looked half made of ice, and frosted with a thick white cloak that sparkled so it looked like new fallen snow. She'd pulled up her hair into an intricate crown, studded with sparkling pins. With her pale skin and white-blonde hair, she looked like the Snow Queen. She always made everyone think of fairy tales. 'Are you feeling better, Otto?' Xavier asked as we arrived.

I nodded, but I wasn't sure I was telling the truth.

'You selected this for me, didn't you?' Rose said, gesturing to her dress as she took his arm with a white gloved hand.

'I added the cloak, too. I wasn't sure you'd be warm enough.'

'Thank you.' She reached up to kiss his cheek. He let her, but then he pulled away. I didn't know why, considering I'd had more than mere pecks in the last few days, but I burned with jealousy. I took Rose away from him, and they both let me. I had to hold her arm hard in order to feel as if she wasn't about to be stolen from me.

The glittering ice palace of the train station shone in the centre of the darkened village. All the scintillating fairy lights of the cafés and street stores were either shut down or simply dimmed in comparison by the thousands of tiny lights that twinkled in the train station. It was as if we were travelling into a nebula, a birth place of stars. It was so beautiful, I could almost ignore the two Plastines trailing behind us like a pair of grim chess pieces.

Rose was more leery of them, but Xavier seemed to take them in his stride. I had a dim memory of having my arm broken by a Plastine once, and they made me nervous, but not as much as they did Rose.

We arrived at the ball, but were not announced as I'd half been afraid. Captain Jagan darted up to greet us, and spoke mostly to Xavier, while Rose and I slid unobtrusively into the crowd. Instead of a rich classical quintet, as would have been on display on Earth, a man who was some kind of classical DJ carefully monitored a musical display. Instruments were probably too difficult to transport and maintain on Europa. There wasn't much dancing. Little circles of people clustered nonchalantly around strategically placed heaters – some looking like roaring fires, some decorative fire flowers, one a crystalline dragon sculpture that smouldered and occasionally belched real flame. Richly dressed Europan élites sipped champagne out of ice glasses and admired one another. The conversation encompassed trade deals and new technology, complaints about declining harvests and corrosive elements in the ocean, deteriorating infrastructure and rebel elements in the lower levels. In short, money, money, and money.

Our inconspicuous entrance did not help us long. Very soon we were surrounded by people asking questions, begging to let them take snapshots, and admiring Rose's dress. Xavier seemed in his element, schmoozing and shaking hands. He had been here before over a decade ago, back when he was a relatively younger executive. At that time he had made a lot of friends – or at least ingratiated himself to a lot of people. Rose was at first overcome with a terrible fit of shyness. Then I saw her visibly square her shoulders and put graciousness on like a cloak. From then on she passed light small talk, laughed politely, and smiled agreeably at everyone. She even danced with some of the younger, less offensive élites. I was astonished. I had never seen Rose put on exactly this persona before.

She also barely looked at me. I thought at first that she was just playing the society girl for the aristocracy, but then I noticed how Xavier rarely took his eyes off her. She kept throwing him surreptitious glances, as if afraid to be caught out in a *faux pas*.

Actually, no one bothered much with me. I couldn't schmooze, and I was too confused to make any non-verbal social efforts. I was too sick to feel like dancing. Mostly I just wanted a chair, but what seats they had were occupied, or clustered around the heaters, and there were far too many people in those areas. Several people did come up to admire me, as one would admire a sculpture, or Captain Jagan's pathetic panther. Mostly I stared at them with my yellow, accusatory eyes, and they quietly hurried away. I began to develop a headache.

The food was well enough, but I couldn't eat. For one, the company disturbed me. For another, a display had been set up in the centre of the ice palace. An almost spherical fish tank with bioluminescent fish that swam in unison. At first I thought they might have been Europa natives – the largest members of the plankton, I'd been told, were tiny, delicate fish-like creatures – but closer examination revealed that they were genetically engineered tetras and other Earthly fish. I turned away, disturbed, and watched the people. It didn't help. At least three of the women had hairstyles that actually incorporated live Geemo birds. None of them tried to move or flit like an ordinary bird would, and one of them actually chirped a popular song when it was tapped. They all made me feel sick. Finally, I couldn't take it any longer. I slipped out an unwatched door, and found myself in a gently sloping ice tunnel.

This must have been one of the service tunnels, like the ones Quin had visited. This one, I realized, led to restrooms. It was a stark contrast to the glittering ice-diamond of the train station, and the village as a whole. It was bare, undecorated, almost feral, like a bear cave. Harsh utility lights studded a power cord planted in the ceiling, and that was the only indication that the tunnel wasn't simply a natural hollow in the ice. It was actually soothing, after all the sparkling expense out there. I went into the men's room and washed my eyes, splashing steaming warm water on my face, then wiping it quickly with a scratchy paper napkin provided, so the cold wouldn't freeze it to me. The toilet seats were heated, but the room was still made of ice. The paper towel smelled of the plankton. Everything was made from the plankton, from half the food I ate at the buffet, to the rayon dress shirt I wore, to the pressed-and-formed furniture of the village. If Rose ever managed to get a sketchbook, I knew it would be made from the plankton, too.

I felt lost and unfocused without Rose in the room, so I decided to go back to the party, no matter how disturbing.

I went back into the tunnel, and stopped. A soft rumble indicated that I was not alone there. With a jolt I realized that Nila's black panther was lurking by the entrance, as if it were a discarded handbag. It was so passive that I had walked past it on my way in without even noticing. It was all alone, and looked a little lost. I went up to it and let it smell my fingers. Instantly, stupidly, it began to purr. I scratched its ears, and then pulled away, feeling ill.

The poor thing was in agony. Its brain was worse than the simple ones'. Not merely animal, but empty. It had been modified to be wildly infantile, and there were ramifications to this. It could barely see, all its bones ached, and it couldn't think about anything that wasn't immediately in front of it. If it wasn't led to food and had it placed before its nose, this thing would waste away without even being aware of it. It was freezing, and no one cared, nor would it try to find heat to save itself. It was already dying. Less than a year old and born only to die young.

Someone had made this? Someone had deliberately tortured this animal at a cellular level, for profit. The cruelty of it was more than I could bear. I wished I had a knife so I could slit the poor creature's throat, and put the unnatural thing out of its misery.

Then I realized there were probably people who felt the same way about me. I felt sick, so sick I couldn't fight it down. I retched in a corner, ridding myself of what little I'd managed to choke down at the banquet. The sour taste of acids was better than the bitter taste left in my mind from the dying beast.

Soft hands on my hair and neck stroked me, smoothing away the sweat of horror. It was Rose. Her mind was full of sympathy and fear. 'Oh, Otto,' she breathed.

I spat and wiped my mouth on my embroidered sleeve. 'They don't care about us,' I whispered. 'None of us. We're all just strings of DNA, building blocks, tinker toys, to play with as they will and throw away.' I turned to her, grabbing her head to stare into her eyes. *'Tell me they didn't plan this,'* I begged. '*Tell me they didn't build my entire family only to die when they were done studying us.*'

Rose was white with pity. 'I don't know,' she said.

I groaned and turned away.

'What's wrong with him?' Quin asked. He'd come through the door behind Rose.

'It's the cat,' Rose said.

'Ah, yes. The perfect personification of their callous brutality.'

'You're one to talk!' Rose snapped. She looked back to me. 'That's why I came to get you. Quin's back.'

Quin looked awful. His nose was bruised and his hair was mussed. He was still wearing the brown Europan coat. It looked very slummish compared to Rose's crystal dress. '*What are you doing here?*' I signed. '*I thought you were banned from this party.*'

'Security didn't know that,' Quin said. He came up to me and took my shoulder. 'Look, I'm not angry anymore. But I need to talk to you. It's important.'

His finger grazed my neck. His thoughts were a slimy turmoil of emotions, and I shrugged him off quickly. '*What do you care?*' I signed.

'Look, I came back,' he said. 'I didn't mean ... These people here are ...' He paused. His voice sank low so that Rose couldn't hear. 'Look. I'm in trouble. Or ... or I will be. They've been *waiting* for us! The answers were here, no secrets, no lies. It was here, all along.'

I shook my head, I don't understand.

'How about I show you?' Quin asked. 'You have to see for yourself.' He pushed me ahead of him past the pitiful panther and down the hall.

'What are you doing?' Rose asked behind us.

'Just going to show Otto some of the great stuff I found earlier today,' Quin said. 'They're wonderful people here, you know that? And they all love us. It's not just that stupid show, we've taken on legendary status up here.' He never stopped pushing me along. I didn't like it.

'*Let go!*' I told him, pushing his hand off me.

'Otto, I need you to come with me,' Quin said.

'He's needed here,' Rose said.

'No, he's not,' Quin muttered. 'What he needs is to come with me.' He pointed down the tunnel. 'If we go down this way, there's a crawl space that'll lead to the rest of the tunnels. I really want to show this to you.'

'Why?' Rose asked. 'What's so bloody important that can't wait until tomorrow?'

'Will you just come on?' Quin snapped, somewhat desperately. 'You can come too if you must, princess.'

Rose stopped. 'I've got a party to attend.'

Quin actually laughed.

'And so does Otto,' she added, grabbing my arm away from Quin.

Quin's eyes narrowed. 'You let my brother go, little girl. Right now.'

'Why? Because you're being a selfish sped like always?'

'Because I'm sick of him mooning about, licking the tails of murderers!' He turned me and stared into my eyes. 'Otto, listen to me. It's important. I've been finding things out. The people here, they've told me things, and you need to hear it from them, or you won't believe it. Hell, I didn't believe it. I need you to come with me.'

'He needs to come back with me, or they'll start wondering where we are,' Rose said.

'So?'

Rose was incredulous. 'I'm trying to save Otto's life. Or have you forgotten why we're here?'

'No!' Quin shouted the word loud enough to echo down the hallway. His face was twisted in rage, and there were almost tears in his eyes. 'No, I haven't.' He turned back to me. 'Please. Just come with me. Now. There's no more time!'

'Time for what?' Rose demanded. 'What are you . . . ?' Then her face went white as she stared at us. A flash of panic flickered through her eyes as she intuited what Quin's behaviour meant. 'Xavier,' she breathed. 'No!' She whirled, running haphazardly down the hallway in her pretty white boots.

I started after her. Quin wouldn't let go of my shirt. 'Otto,' Quin said, his voice deep. 'Don't do this.'

I stared at him for a long moment, shaking my head. Then I touched his hand, thinking of the most painful thing I could imagine. The funny thing was, it was one of Xavier's memories – I didn't focus on which one.

Quin flinched, just enough to release me, and I took off after Rose.

'Otto, let her go! Get back here!' There was a rough groan of despair. 'You're supposed to leave with me!'

I didn't wait for him. I was at Rose's heels by the time she made it back. Rose was trembling as she turned the corner back into the party.

'Xavier, everyone, get out! There's a bomb!'

There was a moment of silence amidst the tinkling crystal. Then, with practised efficiency, the party filed rather neatly out the three main doors, complaining. I was impressed. Apparently, this happened frequently enough that no one even questioned it.

Xavier and Captain Jagan joined us in the hallway. 'Where?' Xavier asked.

'I don't know. I'm just sure there is one. Let's go!' She pushed Xavier ahead of her down the direction Quin had tried to drag me.

'I don't know about you, young lady,' Captain Jagan said, clutching the hand of his wife, who was holding tightly onto Nila. 'But I happen to have excellent security and an extensive network of informants, and I've heard nothing about an attack planned for this evening.'

'Did you hear about one yesterday?' Rose asked pointedly.

'There were rumours,' Jagan said. 'But nothing that caused me undue concern.'

'Xavier nearly died!' Rose snapped. 'And you didn't think to *warn* us?' I'd never heard her so angry. 'Believe me. Something nasty is about to go down in that room.'

'Nothing is going to happen! I had the entire place swept before the party, the security is top notch.'

'Rose, how do you know—' Xavier began, but he never got the chance to finish. With a poisonous hissing, a flare of deadly heat blasted us from behind as the firebomb went off in the room behind us. We found out later, it was in the base for the fish tank. At the time, it seemed to come from everywhere. We all went flat. Rose's hand gripped mine, and her terror raked at me. We were splattered in shattered ice and melted water that burst through the open doorway and cracked the icy walls, but we heard none of it. Our ears were muffled in cotton from the sound of the blast.

I crawled out from under the coating of crushed ice, pulling Rose with me. I had hold of her wrist. She was unhurt. That was all that mattered to me.

'Rose!' I recognized the panic in the muffled voice. It was the same panic I would have had, if I'd thought I might have lost her. Xavier picked his way through the icy rubble towards us, blood trickling from a cut on his forehead. It wasn't until he had taken Rose's hands and picked her out of the debris that the terror left his eyes.

I had a bit more trouble finding my feet. I'd thrown myself between Rose and danger, again, and I had received my usual reward. Everything hurt.

Frightened, hurt, and wary, we all picked ourselves up and stared dismally back at the flames flickering from the open gap to the icy ballroom. Everything that could burn was on fire – the banquet table, the plastic musical display, the decorative heating elements. Everything else was crushed, melting and dripping, or stained with black soot. The ceiling of the ice palace had collapsed – that was what had blasted through the doors after us. The glass fish tank had been flattened, its glass unrecognizable amidst the shattered ice, the fish already dead, a few still shining like stars beneath the ice. There did not appear to be any human bodies, but it would have been hard to tell beneath some of the piles of ice. The lights that had illuminated the train station were out, and apart from the bioluminescent fish, the only light out there was from the night-dimmed ceiling suns.

Then someone sobbed. We looked. It was Nila, crouching by her black panther, who hadn't survived the blast. She lifted his massive furry head onto her lap, and caressed the coal black fur between his ears. It was the picture of misery, and I had to look away. I didn't want to be the one to tell her that he'd already been half dead from the cold two minutes before. She was careless with her toys, that one.

'This is madness.' Captain Jagan turned on Rose. She cringed as his eyes met hers, and stepped back, closer to Xavier. 'What exactly do you know, young lady? Who told you there was a bomb?'

Rose visibly shrank, and her gaze darted around the corridor in vain. Quin was already long gone.

chapter 17

'I will ask you one last time, young lady: what made you think there was a bomb?'

Rose kept looking at her shoes. We were trapped in her hotel room. Rose had withstood Captain Jagan's interrogation at first, deflecting questions and giving half answers. After about five minutes it had worn her down, though, and she'd devolved into staring at the floor with her hands clasped like a little girl. I'd been told to stay with her, but Xavier had been redirected to have his cut treated. I found myself furious at him. He knew Rose couldn't take this level of direct conflict from an authority figure, particularly a male – I knew it, and mostly from his memories. But I couldn't step in, because I had no words, and I wasn't going to touch Captain Jagan unless a life depended on it.

'Did you see who planted it?' Jagan asked for what must have been the fourth time. 'Did you hear something? Where was the bomb situated?'

'Can't your forensics team figure that out?' Rose asked – for the second time – but Jagan wasn't having that.

'I'm asking you,' he said. 'Did someone warn you? Who?'

Rose glanced at me, but said nothing.

The confusion after the blast had lasted an hour at least. The first step was to make sure that everyone was accounted for. There were several injuries, but no deaths, this time. No one seemed to realize Quin had been there, and the cameras that would have shown him were destroyed in the blast.

'If you do not tell me where you received your information, I'll be forced to consider you a suspect,' Captain Jagan said finally. 'Do you understand that? Under Europan law, I can have you detained indefinitely. Even you, Miss Fitzroy. Who are you protecting? Is it your blue friend, here?'

'You leave Otto alone!' Rose barked.

'I have no intention of harming your friend, Miss Fitzroy. But you must understand, unless you can explain yourself, your actions can lead to only one conclusion. That somehow, in some way, you were involved in this attack.'

'No!' I tried to say. An awkward, impotent squawk.

'Otto, it's okay!' Rose said. 'I was not involved. I just knew.'

'You'll pardon me for saying, that seems unlikely, Miss Fitzroy.'

The frustrating thing was, that was exactly what had happened. Quin's actions were suspicious, but he hadn't warned us that anything was about to go down. If Rose hadn't been as intuitive and right-brained as she'd always been, we'd probably have been halfway down that corridor when the bomb blew, and Captain Jagan and Xavier would be buried under a half ton of crushed ice. I hit the side of my chair in annoyance.

'Is there something you would like to say, Mr Sextus?'

I stood up, ready to find some way to tell him where he could go with his questions, when we were rescued by the door opening. Xavier came in, yet another bandage gracing his aged face, took in my defensive stance and Rose's downcast head, and jumped to the proper conclusion. 'Rose is still a minor, Captain Jagan,' he said. 'I know you wouldn't risk jeopardizing your investigation by questioning her without a guardian present?'

'Such regulations do not exist on this moon, Mr Zellwegger,' Captain Jagan said in his pristine accent. 'If she is over the age of ten, she is considered an adult.'

'I believe we fall under diplomatic immunity. There could be very serious consequences if Rose suffered undue psychological harm. But this is unnecessary. If you have questions, feel free to ask, now that I'm here.'

'Miss Fitzroy does not seem to have the answers I seek,' Jagan said. 'Mr Sextus, there, however, seemed to have something he wanted to say?'

I glared at Xavier and gestured to Rose, incredulous. Seriously? Look at her!

'I believe Rose's friend was merely attempting to convey that Rose has endured enough questions, for now,' Xavier said. 'At least from you.'

Jagan scoffed. 'If you think you can get more out of her, my friend, I suggest you do so quickly. Else, we have more experienced interrogators who can make her tell us what we need to know.'

'Do not threaten me,' Xavier said darkly. 'You do not want me as your enemy. Remember, your son is on Earth, in a UniCorp run school.'

There was a moment of silence as the tension flickered between them like heat-lighting. 'How did she know about the bomb?' Jagan asked carefully.

'I suspect the initial report from your forensics team can be more helpful to you in this regard,' Xavier said. 'Why don't you go and see what they have to tell you? We'll be right here,' he added, 'if you have any questions after that. We shan't go anywhere. It's a small moon, Captain Jagan, and you have more power – *here* – than I do.'

Captain Jagan regarded Xavier for a long moment before he turned back to Rose. 'I still have questions, young lady. I suggest you try to find some answers before I have them asked.' He turned and left, closing the door behind them. I couldn't help but notice the guard posted outside.

The moment the door closed Rose ran up to Xavier and wrapped her arms around him. He did not return the embrace at all, even stepping back as if she made him uncomfortable. With one hand he awkwardly stroked her hair and then put her away from him. 'Rose,' he said earnestly, his voice very different from the corporate king he had been a second ago. 'What are you doing?'

'Nothing. I didn't do anything.'

'No?' He pulled a cell out from his pocket and plugged it in to the wall screen. The video that played was occasionally blurry with pixellation, but it was clear enough. A security video of Quin entering the service tunnel and speaking to us urgently, pulling us down the corridor. It did look as if we'd been warned. 'We haven't run lip reading software – don't even know if it'll work. The file is damaged somewhat. Jagan's probably getting this now. What did Quin tell you?'

'Nothing, really,' Rose said, and then added what she hadn't said to Captain Jagan. 'Sometimes I know things, just little things, usually. Mostly they show up in dreams, but sometimes I just know them. It's happened ever since I woke up from stass. Otto?'

I nodded, it's true.

'I don't know why. Otto thinks it's something to do with my brain,' Rose went on. 'As if I spent too much time dreaming, and I'm … lopsided or something. I just sort of know things.'

'Right-brain intuitive thinking,' Xavier said. 'I suppose that makes sense. But what was it that you were … reading?'

'Well, look,' Rose said, gesturing to the video. 'I know Quin looks suspicious, he sounded suspicious, too. I didn't want to say anything – I don't know if he was involved, or if he actually knew anything, or if he was just being his usual sped self. Not for sure. I just knew there had to be a bomb. And I couldn't let you—'

'Rose.' Xavier stopped her. He hesitated, anxious. 'So you were only trying to protect Quin? Otto was not involved in this? You have to tell me. I'll try to protect him, but I need to know now.'

Rose took a step back. 'Of course Otto wasn't involved. He's so sick he can hardly stand up half the time!'

'So he has little to lose,' Xavier said, looking over at me. 'And more to avenge.'

Rose stepped completely away from him and grabbed hold of my arm. 'Otto wouldn't. Never. He has no reason to!'

I felt sick.

'And Quin? Do you think he was involved?' Xavier asked.

'He doesn't have any reason, either!' Rose said hotly. 'I don't know why he was acting that way, it just worried me, okay?'

'Rose,' Xavier said. 'It's very important that you tell me everything. You don't understand. This is not a game.'

'I'm not playing a game!'

'You can't just put this one aside, Rose, and think about it tomorrow. This is very serious, very real. I may not be able to help. Jagan has torture squads to deal with this kind of thing. If Quin is involved, and if he is caught, you have no idea what they will do to him.'

'Then he wasn't involved,' Rose said. 'Obviously.'

'Don't protect him, just tell me the truth.'

'I am!'

I couldn't watch any more. I disengaged myself from Rose with a meaningful look and went into the bathroom. My head ached. I could hear them talking through the door, but I had other things to think about. Quin. Of course Quin was involved. He was my brother, and he already felt as if he'd lost me.

My brother … I could barely remember him beyond this journey. His childhood was all but lost to me. All I knew was that he was violent, and angry. But I was angry, too. I looked up at the mirror and stared at my reflection.

I did not look like myself. I knew who I was, and I was not this voiceless blue-skinned alien hybrid with the drawn face and the mouth with no natural smile. I was human, I was whole, I was Rose's beloved friend Xavier, and I was never going to let her go again. I reached for the wall and placed my hands on either side of the mirror, staring into my own yellow eyes as if I could drag the proper reflection out of them. (*Don't do this to yourself,*) 42 whispered.

'I can't,' I whispered back.

(*You know you have to tell her.*)

'I can't. It wasn't my sin, I don't have to know.'

(*Then you have to make* him *tell her. Because you do know. You don't want to, but you do.*)

Tears leaked from my eyes. 'Why'd it have to be him?' I asked. 'Why this? Why couldn't I have found myself in someone else? Anyone else? Why did I have to escape to *this* body, burning all around me?'

(*Because you set it on fire,*) 42 told me. (*And you made the only door. If you were going to escape, it had to be here.*)

I closed my eyes. *'I can't remember Otto's life anymore,'* I confessed. *'Just how unhappy it was.'*

(*I'm still here,*) 42 said. (*He was my brother. I'll hold it for him. You do what you have to do.*)

I grunted in frustration as unwanted knowledge burned in the corner of my brain. I shouldn't have to know this stuff. It was the old man's sin, not mine. I was eighteen and innocent and ready to find Rose and live happily-ever-after. No Dark Times, no corporatocracy, no mistakes. Why couldn't I just be innocent again? For the first time, I wished I was still just Otto.

I went back into the room. The old Xavier was sitting as if exhausted in one of the chairs, pinching the bridge of his nose, as Rose stood before him in her glittering party dress, the personification of every mistake he'd made in the last sixty-two years. 'I can't help you if you're not honest with me.'

'I am honest with you. Why would Otto hate you? I can't speak for Quin, he seems to hate everybody, but I don't know if Quin was involved, or even why he would be. He's sympathetic to these *harvestaras*, but I don't think he would have planted an actual bomb. There's no reason for it.'

I took hold of Rose's arm. *'Rose. I need you to ask him a question. And you'd better sit down.'*

Rose looked at me. 'Okay,' she said curiously. She perched on the edge of her bed, and moved her cloak onto the floor so that I'd have space to sit beside her. My eyes flickered to the old man's drawn, pensive face. He knew so much more than he was saying. So much more than he ever said.

'Xavier?' she asked. 'Otto wants me to ask you a question.'

The old man looked tired.

Rose knew the look on his face. She had seen it before – not sixty years ago, but no more than a few months (not counting stass time). *'What has he done?'* she wondered. *'Why does he feel guilty, still?'*

I told her to ask a question, and her eyes widened. She stared at me. *'Ask,'* I told her.

She took a rather shaky breath. 'Otto thinks you know what made Quin so angry,' she said. 'Do you?'

Xavier shook his head, but the guilt was very clear in his eyes. 'Of course not,' he said. 'How could I know what's in his head? That's your purview, Otto, not mine.'

Of course he wouldn't answer. Not with Rose so fond of me. I told her to ask a more direct question.

'No!' Rose said, snatching her hand out of mine. 'I'm not asking that. That's insane!'

'Please,' I signed. *'Ask.'*

Rose rolled her eyes, and reluctantly, almost dismissively turned back to Xavier. 'Otto wants me to ask if it was you who commissioned the EP project eighteen years ago.'

She'd already decided the answer was no. She wasn't wrong.

'No,' he said evenly.

For no reason that I could see, Rose's face paled, and she froze. 'Xavier,' she said. 'Tell me you had nothing to do with it.'

'It was never my idea,' he said, looking right into her eyes.

'I know when you're lying,' she said, and her voice shook. 'I've known you too long.'

He sighed. 'I'm not lying,' he said. 'I didn't commission anything.'

She stared at him, and a wordless communication which was easily as intimate as anything I could do passed between them. I recognized it, but I couldn't read it, even with all I'd absorbed and become. He sighed and broke her gaze, looking down at the ground. 'But I was sent to implement it,' he admitted.

There was a heavy weight of silence as Rose took that information in. 'They died,' she whispered. 'You sentenced them to death from the moment of their birth. How could you?'

'You couldn't understand.'

She looked up, angry now. 'Try me!'

'It's not as simple as you make it sound,' Xavier said.

'Isn't it?' Rose said. 'It was amoral, it was evil, it—'

'I know what it was. I know better than anyone.' Then he looked at me. Stared at me. I could see his throat move as he swallowed. 'It all turned out worse than I had hoped.'

'You thought they'd all live?' Rose asked.

'No,' Xavier said. He didn't take his eyes off my face. 'I prayed every day that every one of you would die.'

Rose stood up from the bed. Red spots shone high on her cheeks, and her hands clenched by her thighs. Her eyes were shining with accusation. 'What. Happened,' she asked, each word stark and precise.

For a long time the old man looked at her. Just looked at her. Finally, he opened his mouth. 'Life,' he said pointedly. 'Brutal, unfair, complicated, and sordid. I have lived for over seventy years. Many of them through wars and plagues and deaths you cannot imagine – and I'm glad of that. If there is one thing I am glad of it is that you were spared those times. Unfortunately, as I slogged my way through it alone, I learned a few unpleasant truths. Like sometimes, it is impossible to keep your hands clean.'

The words were accusatory, and I knew why. I knew how angry Xavier really was at Rose for leaving him in the first place. I felt that anger, too – been fighting it ever since I'd touched him. He loved her, loved her desperately, but anger doesn't negate love.

'Tell me what happened,' Rose said again. She was not going to let it go.

The old man took a deep breath. 'Twenty years ago,' he said quietly, 'I was sent to oversee the development of the Europa Project. When it was instigated, it was not intended as an attempt to develop human beings with the traits of the microbes. At least that's what I was told. My understanding of the project was to coordinate scientists in the hopes of discovering a way of keeping the EM microbes alive long enough to bring them to Earth, and study them there. That's all it was. A research project on a single-celled organism. All attempts at this, as you know, failed. In twenty years of research, only Ted has gotten as far as he has, and even he can't keep them alive for more than a few weeks. Finally, the demand was too great. I received a message from Reginald Guillory, who was on track to be appointed as CEO of UniCorp, to deliver an ultimatum to the scientists. These included, unfortunately, bio-engineers as well as geneticists and exobiologists. Get the DNA to Earth alive. It didn't matter how.'

'That's insane,' Rose said. 'That has nothing to do with creating human hybrids!'

'You wouldn't have thought so, would you?' Xavier asked. 'And you'd be right. But Guillory had his own ideas. He had arranged for all GMO restrictions to be lifted for the Europa Project. Here in the colonies the only genetic laws involve the development of human-like organisms – anything more than three per cent human is prohibited. On Earth, genetically modified organisms are all but completely abolished. Reggie and people he had worked with had been lobbying extensively for eases in the restrictions ever since the EM microbes had been discovered. The Europa project waiver gave the scientists free reign to do anything they wanted.'

'But not from you,' Rose said. 'Why didn't you protest, or—'

'I did,' he said. 'But there was a limit to what I could do. Guillory had pulled this as a political ploy. He had only narrowly been promoted over me, and that was only because I didn't want the position. I had no desire to climb to CEO. But Guillory never believed that.' He shook his head. 'He set me up.'

'How?'

He sighed, rolling his eyes. 'At the time the Europa Project was instigated the colonies were in a state of upheaval. Like right now, only worse. This place erupts into rebellion every couple of months, it seems. At least once or twice a decade. It was set up to do so. Fitzroy set it up that way. Any culture in a constant state of upheaval is ripe for exploitation. My job here had been two-fold. I was to both oversee the Europa Project, and to act as a secretary of state. My role had been to negotiate with the workers in the hopes of stopping riots – riots and terrorists which were much more bloody and brutal than what is going on right now.'

'Hundreds have already died,' Rose said. 'How can you say that?'

'Because thousands were being slaughtered,' Xavier said. 'Sabotage was rampant. Some of the workers had decided to poison the food supplies, particularly of exports. Oxygen deprivation was used as a weapon, by both sides – either officially or through sabotage. Hydrogen explosions were happening everywhere. You've seen what happens with those. The burns and deaths were terrible to see. People were starving. The cities were over populated, and some thought that mass killings, or just letting the rabble kill each other, was the solution. I did not. My goal, at the time, was simply to stop the terrorism. I didn't care about anything else.'

'Terrorism?' Rose asked. 'You call starving people fighting for freedom terrorism?'

He blinked at her. 'Rose.' He looked at the ceiling, and then rubbed his eyes under his glasses. 'You're still so naïve,' he whispered to himself. The thought pained him, you could see it. 'There's no such thing as freedom,' he said, speaking for her to hear again. 'Not the way you mean, with everyone dancing happily in the streets, all righteousness and charity. I have seen … too many resource wars, too many riots, too much death. I know one thing. It doesn't *work*. I have seen too many attempts at revolution go spiralling down into degeneration and self-destruction.' He gestured around him. 'Take these people. Not here on Europa, but back on Earth, before they were emigrated. India was united under a brutal, exploitative British imperialism. Nehru and Ghandhi and the freedom fighters of the time shook off the yoke of oppression … only to fall into a civil war between Muslim and Hindu that cost the lives of millions. Entire trainloads of innocent people, slaughtered in violent sectarian attacks. Freedom, but at what cost? The country split, and India and Pakistan remained in a state of perpetual war for centuries!

'Then the genetics wars came about, and the countries were forcibly united again under the auspices of the South Asian Union. The union was brutal and totalitarian, too. People fought. Entire rebel villages were slaughtered. How do you think UniCorp was able to recruit so many willing volunteers to come to a barren and inhospitable ice moon six hundred and thirty million kilometres from their home? Millions came. Because millions more were dying, under the banner of the freedom fighter.' He was angry. Oh, he was angry. His eyes glared. 'And that was even before the Dark Times struck, and half the population sank under disease and war. You should know all this! You were there with me; you saw it, or at least what you weren't sleeping through.'

Rose's face went red again, but her lips were pale and tight.

He stopped, realizing what he'd said. 'I'm sorry.' His head sank onto his hand and the persistent tremor which was always with him was very pronounced. 'I'm sorry, I ... It wasn't your fault. We were children,' he said. 'And selfish. I know that. Neither of us was paying much attention at the time.'

'We had our own problems,' Rose said quietly.

Xavier looked at her. 'We did.'

'Tell Otto what happened,' Rose demanded. Her voice was gentle, almost soothing, but it was a demand nevertheless. I didn't need to know – I knew it already. Xavier had known it, so I did, too. But shifting the question on to me was easing her pain, and I wasn't about to stop her.

'Where was I?'

'Freedom fighters,' Rose said. 'Terrorists.'

'Right,' Xavier said. He looked immensely tired. 'It had to be stopped. I'm not proud of what it took, either. The oxygen taxes were my idea. I devised a series of sanctions which, I'm afraid, ultimately solidified the power of the captains of the three city ships. This was Captain Jagan's father, and he seized on the powers and enforced them to the fullest extent. The people had to pay for their oxygen … but the fighting stopped. Rather than killing them, I saw to it they were beaten economically.'

Rose was not mollified. 'And how many have died from starvation or overwork, trying to pay off those oxygen fees?'

'The bloodshed stopped,' he said, with the finality of an axe blow. 'You don't even know what you're accusing me of. The children stopped being murdered. That was all I wanted to do.' He rested his head in his hands and shook his head. 'That's all I had the power to do. I couldn't devise a democratic structure that gave everyone what they deserved. The captains wouldn't have stood for it, and the rest of the colonies would have suffered from their split from UniCorp.' He looked at me, and then to Rose. 'I had four colonies to think of, not just one.' He looked away, into the distance of nothingness. 'Blame me. I don't even mind. Not even from you. I'll gladly take the blame for those deaths by overwork. One man's conscience is a small price to pay for what I stopped.'

Rose's face was white and stern. 'None of this explains Otto and the others.'

'I was *busy*,' the old man said, with a voice so raw and pained even I felt sorry for him. 'I couldn't find the time to oversee the scientists. I could barely find the time to *sleep*. The floors of the lower levels of the city ships were running with blood – literally running red with it, it was contaminating the air supply! – and I handed over Guillory's waiver and left them to it and gladly. By the time I finished with the political nightmare of the revolution I came back and found myself in the middle of a Frankensteinian horror show.'

His voice was coming quickly now. 'The last I'd heard of the project they had planned to implant the M9 DNA into living tissue – just muscle or skin tissue, not a functional being. Apparently, the cells died almost immediately when the sequence was inserted. By the time I got back the scientists had abandoned this and implanted the sequence into embryonic stem cells, which they claimed were the only things which didn't self-destruct. This meant each of them – each of you, Otto – had the potential to become living beings, and the only way to transport you to Earth was in stasis, implanted in a surrogate mother as a viable embryo.'

'You must have known what would happen,' Rose said. 'Why didn't you stop it there?'

'I wanted to go home,' he said, without sparing himself. 'It was selfish of me, and I know it. I should have said no. I should have put my foot down and ended it there, but it would have meant my career. Not to mention four, five, ten months to dismantle the project, and god knows, Guillory could have just sent someone else to restart it as soon as I was done. I'd been on this ice rock for four, blood-soaked months, and I'd lost half a year in the travel. I missed my wife. I was going to miss the birth of my oldest grandson. I was missing it!' His eyes searched Rose's face. 'You know what that's like. I *needed* to get back.'

He turned away from Rose and looked to me. 'I never meant for this to happen,' he told me. 'Guillory assured me, when I expressed my … distaste for the direction this project had taken, that the embryos were to be aborted, frozen and studied on Earth. They would never be developed into sentient creatures. I made myself believe him.' He shook his head. 'I did it. I finished the project. Tied up all the loose ends. Fifty women were hired and assigned two embryos each. Mostly they were scientific assistants, or maintenance workers, middle-class, educated, for here. Upper level. I insisted on this. I would not allow helpless women to be exploited without their full understanding. I was rigid in my demand for their qualifications. I tried …' He closed his eyes, and his voice was soft. 'I tried so hard to make it all right. They were cells. Just a few cells. It shouldn't have been anything.'

He shook his head. 'I was a fool,' he said. 'Guillory had been planning for this. When I returned to Earth with the women, I found their contracts had been subtly manipulated. The contracts were extended, not for as long as the trip to Earth, but for as long as the embryos were established within their bodies. I had been assured this meant the cells would be aborted, and the women would be free. But UniCorp owned the rights to their bodies for as long as the embryos were implanted, and that included the right to an abortion. They were … enslaved. For as long the pregnancy lasted, they did not own themselves. So long as those cells were in their bodies, they were owned and controlled by UniCorp.'

I blinked. To my surprise, my own memories surfaced briefly. I had never realized that my mother – my surrogate mother, not related by our genes, but nurtured by her shared blood – had been as enslaved as I was. I had always resented her. Her name was in my records, but she had never been one of the few mothers who had banded together and insisted on human rights for us. I'd always been rather scornful of Penny's surrogate, who sent her birthday cards and a single Christmas present once a year. That didn't seem like enough of a mother to me – and why carry a child if you didn't want to be a mother? I had thought my surrogate was callous, more inhuman than I ever was, who viewed the pregnancy as a rental, sold her body as surely as a prostitute, for a moonliner ticket and a few credits. But to be forced to carry a child to term when it wasn't your own choosing …?

'The women were established in a dorm situation in a laboratory – your lab, Otto,' Xavier continued. 'The development of the foetuses was monitored and recorded meticulously. But frankly, my attention was not on the developing cells, but the indentured women. I blamed myself, and I was desperate to do something to help them. I had had no idea I was being used to traffic human slaves.' He looked at me. Square into my eyes. 'I campaigned for abortions – particularly as many of the foetuses died. Many of the surrogates were horrified at the thought of these … inhuman … creatures developing in their wombs. A few went mad. Two of them committed suicide. They had not signed up to be mothers for monsters – they had signed up to earn free passage to a new and better life on Earth.

'There was a major international debate on the ethics of the EP children.' He scoffed. 'Children. Even the title is suggestive. The news community, no doubt at the prompting of UniCorp, which owned most of the news agencies, instantly called the embryos "children", thus framing the debate in religious terms. DNA splicing was banned on Earth, but these "children" came from Europa. The religious communities were split between the sanctity of life, and the sanctity of human life. Many of the hardest core, staunch fundamentalists suddenly found themselves in favour of abortion. Many called the children abominations.' I cringed. I'd heard that. I'd had it thrown into my face. I knew there were people who would gladly kill me because of it. Fortunately, none of them could easily get into the controlled UniCorp ComUnity, and for the most part I'd been kept safe from them.

I glanced at the old man. Who had made sure of that?

'While the debate raged, the embryos developed into foetuses. Several of them miscarried, as you know, leaving their mothers free. I established these women carefully in rehabilitation homes, shielding their identities from the press. This gave most of the other surrogates hope. All they had to do was wait it out.

'UniCorp was at the centre of a major controversy. And of course, which shouldn't have been a surprise, I found that Guillory had passed the buck to me. He officially placed the entire development of the EP children on my supervision.' He shook his head. 'Guillory had what he wanted. I was politically ruined. It effectively removed all possibility of my ever being made CEO. I actually welcomed this development – you know I never wanted everyone's eyes on me,' he said to Rose. 'But this wasn't how I would have wanted it to happen.

'Soon, the babies were born …' He looked at me. 'And they were human. Painfully human. They looked human. They acted human. They cooed and cried and reached for their mothers. It was … terrifying to know what had been done to them. Many of the women wanted to keep these children they had been forced to carry.' He sighed. 'I did what I could. I got them lawyers and enabled them to campaign, but it failed. At this point I was called a flip-flopper by the press – suddenly they were human, and I was scorned and utterly derided. None of them understood; I was worried about the women. I was *their* advocate; what *they* wanted was what I strove for. For all the good it did them. Technically, the children were not human, and the surrogate mothers had no genetic claim, as the embryos had come from other women entirely. I managed to establish you with human rights – at least I did that much. Rights against abuse, unlawful imprisonment, campaigned for free access. I'm afraid it isn't much more than the rights endowed upon gorillas and chimpanzees a century ago. But the surrogate mothers had free visitation rights, and UniCorp had to treat you as children, not laboratory subjects. This gave you the right to an education,' he told me. 'If I hadn't fought for that, you'd still be in that lab, mute and unable to read. You'd be an animal. But, as a parent has rights over a child, UniCorp held the rights over the EPs, and they were held under UniCorp guardianship.'

The old man took a deep breath and looked at both of us. 'I didn't know this when I started ... but the scientists had been hoping for you, Otto. They were actually *looking* for communication with a sentient being on a cellular level. I don't know why they thought it would succeed. I don't even know why they wanted it. But they did think so, and it did succeed. They got what they wanted out of you all. The cost, I felt, was astronomical. I ... I hated all of it. I set up an endowment to support the children and I walked away, trying to close my eyes to it. When some of the children died at an early age ... I hoped none of you would make it beyond three.' He straightened his back and took a deep breath. 'I am sorry, Otto.'

Rose took a deep breath. 'You were sent to do this. Didn't you know what it meant?'

'Yes. When it became clear to me, I was disgusted, but it was still narrowly within the realm of my moral compass, such as it is.' He scratched a spot on the back of his hand and lifted up a small flake of dry skin. 'Three cells are not a human being, any more than this is.' He flicked it away. 'It was only when those three mutilated cells were essentially forced into human consciousness, and their mothers denied the rights to their own bodies, I found myself embroiled in the most sordid and amoral crime that UniCorp has ever committed. Rose, you know, better than anyone, how much of a fool I can be. Do you think this – any of this – was what I wanted?'

Rose looked down.

He looked at me. 'I did what I could for you – all of you. I paid for your lawyers, Otto, when Guillory wanted to deny you the right to accept your scholarship to UniPrep. I signed and allowed for your name changes. I changed your doctors when I thought your medical conditions were being exploited, and you were being held prisoner that way. I kept the lab open, permitted outside scientific study, kept you in the public view, so UniCorp could not hide you away and do whatever they wanted to you.'

'Like what?' Rose asked.

The old man shrugged wildly. 'Kill you, clone you – charge admission. They could have done anything; it was all within their patent.'

Rose's face had turned white again as she stared at him. 'And you never told me this?' she said quietly. 'You've lived with me all these months, while Otto was my friend – Bren's friend! – and you never said?'

The old man gazed at her steadily. 'I told you, when you first asked to live with me, that I couldn't. There was more than one reason.'

He had bought respect from his family with his silence. The price for that silence was to be the lives of innocents on this barren hailstone of a moon. She stood up and walked across the room, her back very straight. She paused at the edge of the wall screen. 'I suppose you're too old for me to scold you any longer,' she said still turned away.

'Please do,' Xavier said. 'If anyone can, it's you. But for some things, I know there is no atonement.' He looked back at me. 'Many things.'

She wouldn't look at him. She'd closed off, the briars strong and impenetrable in her face, ready to pierce him to the heart if he dared to touch her. He knew it. The green in his eyes, that she remembered as new leaves, had cooled over the years to the dying grey of winter. He was no more touchable than she. 'I am sorry,' he said again. 'I do not pretend it to be anything other than my own fault. I'm responsible.' He paused. 'I am responsible,' he said again. 'For all of it.' He glanced over at her stiff back, her clenched, trembling hands. 'Take care of her,' he whispered to me, too softly for her to hear. And he left.

Rose seemed to deflate after he had gone, and she turned to me, her face stark and pale as she crumbled inside. 'Otto,' she whimpered, her voice as small and helpless as a child's. 'I'm so sorry.'

I held my arms open to her, and she lay down beside me, burying her head in my chest. Rose felt betrayed, abandoned, terrified and guilty all at once. She longed for stasis. She wasn't used to processing betrayal and abandonment without the chemicals of a stass tube. Her subconscious was roaring and roiling, thorny briars of intuition and emotion raking her consciousness until it bled. I was sick, probably dying, but I still knew how to help her. Quietly, unobtrusively, I entered her mind and tried to still the writhing thorns until I could reach her consciousness. Then, very gently, I sent it away, folding it into my hand, and drawing Rose into sleep. Her dreams overtook her, and I mentally stepped back, watching them – twisted, confused things as immense as the sky. She needed the time to assimilate all she had just learned.

Frankly, I did, too. I closed my eyes, and 42 stared at me from my own subconscious. *(Quin is lost to his hatred, now,)* she told me. *(And your emotionally fragile Briar Rose has reached the edges of her strength. You're not even yourself anymore. You don't have the power to solve this, not even with all your gifts. Feel in over your head yet?)*

'Shut up,' I told her, but she already knew what I was thinking. Things were starting to look easier on 42's side of death.

chapter 18

We were shocked awake by a strong hand shaking the bed. 'Get up! Move. We have to get out of here.'

Rose blinked sleepily, overheated in her glamorous insulated dress. 'What's wrong?'

Dr Zellwegger stood over us, his face flushed. 'Your friend's unspeakable brother, that's what,' he said. He dragged Rose off the bed and pushed her towards Moriko and Kenji, who huddled behind him, frightened.

'What's Quin done now?'

'He's joined the rebels,' Dr Zellwegger said. 'And they're destroying the village.'

'That's absurd!' Rose snapped.

'Absurd or not, we're leaving,' Dr Zellwegger said. 'Captain Jagan has his icebreaker ready at the hydrobay. We're going now.'

'Where's Xavier?' Rose asked.

'I don't know,' Dr Zellwegger said. 'Move.'

Rose stopped short. 'I'm not leaving without Xavier.'

'I don't know where he is,' Dr Zellwgger said. 'He's not in the hotel. He's probably already on the ship.'

'No,' Rose said. 'He'd never leave without me.'

'We have to go!' Dr Zellwegger said firmly. 'Listen.' A rough bang vibrated beneath our feet. 'Do you hear that? The rebels have declared the ice village a decadence for the wealthy, and they're blowing up each of the buildings one by one.'

'Why doesn't Captain Jagan stop them?'

'He's trying,' Dr Zellwegger said, 'which is why people are dying. The rebels are actually allowing people to leave the buildings, but those Plastines don't care what they're doing. They're going through, picking up anyone they think might be a rebel, and detaining or killing them, no probable cause required. Basically being outside without an escort right now is tantamount to an admission of guilt.'

'But Xavier's out there!' I grabbed Rose's hand. 'And Quin,' she added.

'They won't hurt my father,' Dr Zellwegger said. 'It's not as if he looks like a rebel.'

He didn't mention Quin.

'Jagan assigned us this unit. He'll take us to the ice-breaker,' Dr Zellwegger added, gesturing towards a dead-eyed plastic escort who waited in the hallway, beside two more conventional guards. The guards were armed with antique, wicked-looking guns, but the Plastine was terrifying just by dint of existing.

Rose balked, swallowed, and then snatched up her cloak. 'Let's go.' She took my hand and walked calmly down the corridor. Her straight back belied her fear. She was just as frightened of the Plastines as she was of the bombers, but she wasn't going to cower and whimper in a corner, as part of her wished it could. We stepped outside, where things were even worse. The terrifying pops and bangs of the hydrogen IEDs were compounded by shattering ice and burning gear. People screamed, the sound echoing in the vaulted ceiling of the village chamber. Plastines ran past carrying struggling, soot-stained rebels – at least one looked like he wasn't alive. Rose gripped my hand tightly.

'You can do it, love,' I told her silently. *'You'd be shocked at the things I've managed to do.'* I was thinking of the Dark Times,

and all the other riots I – as Xavier – had survived. Then, as if compounding my madness, I began arguing with myself. *But I didn't do those things. The old man did those things, and I'm not him. I'm Rose's Xavier, and I'm as innocent as she is.*

'Otto, it's okay,' Rose whispered. 'We just have to hold on a little while longer.'

'*What are you talking about, it's okay?*' I asked her. '*It's a war out there!*'

'Just breathe. We'll make it to the ship, and then I'll get you some more—' She cut herself off. 'Otto's medicines!' She snatched her hand out of mine and turned back to Dr Zellwegger. 'I have to get Otto's medicines!'

'We'll have to do without them,' Dr Zellwegger said. 'We can't go back.'

'Like hell we can't!' Rose snapped. She started back towards the hotel.

The Plastine approached and said something in its Europan Hindi style language. It placed one hand on Rose and pushed her back towards Dr Zellwegger. Dr Zellwegger barked at it in the same language, and it froze, but it didn't back down. 'We're not going back, Rose,' Dr Zellwegger said. 'The Plastine isn't mine, I don't have the power to change its orders. It won't turn.'

'I'm going back,' Rose said.

'We have medicines on the *Minos*.'

'That's squitch, I know you don't have what Otto needs, or I wouldn't have had to bring it,' Rose snapped.

'I can't turn back,' Dr Zellwegger said, and there was a touch of panic in his voice. 'We can't leave without an escort. I have to get Moriko and Kenji to safety.'

Rose stopped struggling and gazed at Xavier's grandchildren. 'Okay,' she said. 'You three go on. Take Otto with you, I'll be right back.'

I grabbed her and pulled her to me. I didn't even have to tell her, '*No way, I'm coming with you.*' It was pretty obvious in my face.

'You can't go back without an escort!' Dr Zellwegger said. 'You'd be taken by the rebels, and your friend there isn't … well …' He trailed off. It was clear that I was not on the list of non-combatants, as far as Captain Jagan was concerned.

'I will take them,' one of the human guards said, then. I turned to look at him. He was slight, and rather young, no more than twenty or so. 'We will get the gear and meet up at the port.'

'I don't think I can make this Plastine wait that long, and it's not safe out here.'

'Go on without us,' Rose said. 'We'll catch up. Hold the ship. I'm not leaving if Xavier's not there, anyway.'

'Rose!'

'Go, Ted!' Rose said. 'Your dad'll never forgive me if I let you and the twins get hurt.' To my surprise, she jumped up and hugged him. Then she grabbed my hand and, gesturing to the guard, headed briskly back towards the hotel.

The guard repositioned his weapon and followed right at our heels, more alert and responsible than he'd been a second ago with the Plastine dogging his tail. Rose gripped my hand, and I realized why she'd hugged Dr Zellwegger. In a different life, he could have been her son. '*No,*' I thought to her. '*It's my life. It's this one.*'

'Otto,' Rose said carefully. 'Let's just get you your medicines. We can take care of the rest later.'

'*My name's not Otto,*' I almost growled into her mind.

She stopped and stared at me. 'Love,' she said, not arguing the point. 'We have to hurry.'

I searched her face. She'd let go of me, so I couldn't read her, and I felt terribly unsettled. I wasn't Otto, and I wasn't

Xavier, but I was both of them and neither of them and my brow furrowed in confusion. She caught my head in her hands and kissed me firmly. It relaxed me considerably. (*Oh, stop it, you're just making things worse.)*

Rose stepped back and stared at me. 'Shut up!' I muttered to 42. Another explosion shook the ground as a building a block away went up in a fireball of shattering ice. Rose started, then looked back to me. The fear was stark on her white face.

'Excuse me, but we must move, yes?' the guard said quietly.

'Right,' Rose said, and she ran off, dragging me with her. 'What's your name?' she asked the guard.

'Rahul,' the guard said. 'Pleased to meet you.'

'Mutual,' Rose panted. 'Thanks for offering to help us.'

'It is no problem,' Rahul said. 'I would rather protect you. I do not enjoy working with the dead ones.'

'Not surprised,' Rose said, picking up her pace. 'One tried to kill me, once.'

We made it back to the Norway Chalet. That corner of the village was completely deserted, and our feet echoed strangely on the grooved and pitted walkway ice. My head ached. 'Otto, you wait here,' Rose said. She took Rahul up to her room while I was left, my mind whirling, in the lobby.

The wall screen in the lobby had been left on, but the volume was low. I was able to tune out the language that I did not understand, but then something in English caught my ear.

'I'm telling you to stop this.'

I turned and looked. There was the old man, bruised, bound, on display, and presented to a news camera. One of the rebels – I thought I recognized his face from previous news stories – was facing him with a weapon in his hand. I turned the volume up.

There were clearly others in the icy room with the two of them – rustled movement and the occasional arm, leg, or top of a head was captured by the edge of the camera. The rebel that spoke back to Xavier was wearing the same type of brown coat that Quin had been wearing, earlier. In one hand he held a long, serrated blade. One of my memories recognized it as an ice-saw.

'I will not stop,' said the rebel. 'We have here Ron Zellwegger, leader of UniCorp itself! The architect of the oxygen tax, favoured emperor of the city ships. He is ours! He is our captive!' There was a rough cheer from whoever else filled the icy room.

'I've come here willingly,' Xavier said. 'I've come here to negotiate, unaccompanied, unarmed. You have your cameras, now let us talk.'

'No!' the rebel said. 'I did not bring you here to spread more of your lies.'

'If you brought me here to publicly execute me, you're wasting a valuable opportunity,' Xavier said.

'I am not going to execute you,' said the rebel. 'Though we have every reason to. Your people have abandoned us, imprisoned us, starved us, enslaved us, and taxed us for the privilege.'

'I don't deny that your circumstances are dire,' Xavier said. 'But for the sake of sanity, let us talk! Nothing can change if you persist in this violence.'

'Talk has changed nothing before.'

'Talk is the only thing that ever changes anything,' Xavier said. 'There is no war that did not end, except with people talking. There is no enslavement that was not abolished, except by people talking. There is no injustice, no barbarity, no insurrection that did not ultimately end, except with—'

'This is not your planet!' the rebel interrupted. 'This is not your court to make your speeches!'

'Your violence will only postpone the speeches and the laws that must be made to change. Nothing evil ever ends until people talk. Even if it is only the last ones left.'

'Quiet!' the rebel yelled. 'You have taken our food. You have robbed us of our freedom. You have impoverished us for the air we breathe. But we are only your slaves. Now among us is one you have wronged far worse. You have robbed him of his life, of his humanity. I will not execute you. It is not my place.' He handed the ice-blade to someone on his right.

The camera swung, and there, standing unharmed and unbound, was Quin. His eyes were bloodshot from lack of sleep, and his nose was still bruised from our fight. 'You are one of us, now,' the rebel said. 'His life is yours.'

'No.'

The anguished whisper came from behind me, and I knew Rose had come back. We watched in horror as Quin lifted the blade and looked at it, then looked down at Xavier, bound and kneeling before him.

'No!' Rose ran to the wall screen, hitting the wall with impotent fury. 'Quin, no!'

Quin stared at the blade for a long time. Neither Rose nor I had any doubt that Quin had it in him to kill. It was what he was built for, what his life had conditioned him for, what his every moment and every move had been leading towards. Then Quin glanced up. He seemed to look right at me, and his face hardened. He had recognized the camera. 'I've had my entire life recorded for others to watch,' Quin said quietly. 'Turn that burned thing off.'

The camera tilted, wavered crazily, and then cut out. 'No!' Rose yelled, but an anchorwoman had already taken the place of the transmission, and it was clear they were going to spend the next four hours talking about what 'all this' could mean with Europan pundits that I had no interesting in hearing pontificate.

Rose beat the wall beside the screen, and I grabbed her and tried to calm her. '*It's okay, it's over. Don't you see, this solves it!*'

'Get off me! Nothing is *solved*.'

'*He's not dead!*' I said. '*He's not dead, he just escaped, that's all. He just left that part behind.*' And without bothering to try and make it logical with words, I forced her to know how I was thinking, or how my sheer madness was making sense of it all. Rose couldn't be with Otto, and Xavier couldn't be with Rose, so Xavier had escaped into Otto, leaving behind all the ugly pieces of himself – his age, his guilt, his crimes. He'd come into Otto and cleared out all the ugliness there – Otto's own troubles, his moral dilemmas, his violent brother. Then the two leftover pieces had cancelled each other out. Otto's family and his past had just eliminated the old man, the useless, guilty, leftover old Xavier, so that Otto could reject it and abandon it. Now there was only me – whoever I was – a young guiltless Xavier; a sane, unreserved Otto; the best, refined version of both of them, Rose's lover, perfect, whole.

Rose stepped back and slapped me, hard. 'I hate you!' She was crying. She moved and grabbed Rahul's arm. She hoisted her bag of medicines higher on her shoulder and shoved him towards the door. 'Get us out of here,' she said. She looked back at me. 'Come on!'

It was an order, such as her father would have given.

I stood stunned, bewildered, no idea what was happening. (*Move it. Now.*) I couldn't even listen to 42, so she stepped out of my head and grabbed me by the arm, dragging me after Rose with all her slight, sickly, thirteen years of dying weight.

By the time I caught up to Rose, 42 was gone, (or had never existed in the first place) and Rose's tears had dried. I tried to reach for her hand, but she slapped me away – all I caught from her mind was frustration – and pulled on her white gloves.

Another explosion rocketed behind us, and Rahul suddenly turned, holding his gun at the ready.

'What is it?' Rose asked.

'Otto!'

The voice came from above and behind us. Rose turned, and there was Quin, standing on the roof of one of the buildings, surrounded by rebels in brown coats. Rose's cheeks flushed, and she gripped her hands tightly. 'I will see you dead, 50,' she shouted back, her voice even and clear. 'You will not escape me.'

'Shut the coit up, princess, I wasn't talking to you,' Quin said. 'Otto! Just wait there, I'm coming down.'

'No, you're not,' Rose said. 'Turn yourself in now, 50, and I won't see you hanged.'

'Like you have any power here, witch,' Quin scoffed.

Rose swallowed, opened her satchel, and pulled out what looked like a cell. 'Fugitive five-zero Quin sighted at signal location,' she announced into it. 'All Plastines, converge and detain. Lethal force authorized. Authorization, RS Fitzroy, authorization number two-two-one, Beta.' She looked back up at Quin as every Plastine we could see – and there were half a dozen in just that block – stopped what they were doing and turned to converge on Quin's building. 'Die,' she said coldly, turned around, and headed towards the port.

What the hell ...?

I followed and snatched the device from her hand, the question clear in my eyes. 'I got it from Xavier's room,' she said dully. 'It's a priority one channel. Xavier gave me clearance because the Plastines made me nervous. Only Xavier, myself, or the three city captains can rescind that order, now. Captain Jagan is on the ship. The other captains don't care what is happening here. And Xavier ... won't.' She wouldn't admit he was dead – because he had to be dead. Assuming that Quin would turn away from violence would have been as mad as I was. She also didn't mention the last option. She wasn't going to rescind that order, either. Unless Quin surrendered – and we both knew Quin could never surrender – it was over.

Quin was as good as dead.

Rose's voice was so calm and her eyes were so cold. I realized I recognized it. At least one set of my memories had seen it before, repeatedly, and hated it. I had no idea how it could have happened. She was so accepting, so passive, so kind. Generous, thoughtful, artistic, submissive Rose had gone and done the unthinkable.

Rose had become her father.

chapter 19

We made our way to the elevator to the hydrobay, chaos in our wake. We were passed by at least twenty Plastines, all converging on the area where we had last seen Quin. Unfortunately, that meant the Plastines had all abandoned their previous tasks, which was to search out the bombers and stop them. The number of explosions doubled, and people who had been hiding in neighbourhoods they thought were safe were suddenly rousted from their bolt holes, and shuttled to and fro. No one seemed to know what was best to do. Many people were heading towards the hydrobay, but there weren't enough icebreakers to take them all to the city ships – they had to know that.

Rahul pushed ahead of us, shouting at most to move aside, actively threatening others as they tried to get in the way. Rose stood as if it was all just proper, which I suppose to her it was. I felt strange. My head ached, and things jumped in the edges of my vision. There was enough chaos that people actually were jumping at the edges of my vision, but 42 kept telling me it was okay, this was normal. She didn't mean the chaos. She meant what was happening to me.

I didn't like to think what she meant.

Rahul managed to get us to the elevator, which had been shut down in the chaos. Rose needed to use her clearance number to reactivate it. Rahul kept the refugees from pouring in on us. The treacherous staircase cut into the ice was frozen in a traffic jam of desperate people.

Captain Jagan's icebreaker was sitting by itself in the centre of the bay, too far from the gangway to risk the now-homeless refugees swarming aboard. But the door to the hatch was open, and Dr Zellwegger and the twins were standing, waiting for us. Dr Zellwegger waved hugely when he saw us, making sure we'd seen him, and shouted behind him, probably ordering the icebreaker to come back to the gangway for us to board. Rose leaned against the metal bars of the lift as it descended, as if she carried a hugely heavy weight on her shoulders. I wanted to hold her, but she'd been so angry…

'Rose Fitzroy!'

The three of us looked up. Leaning over the edge of upper level was Quin – impossibly, Quin – surrounded by more of those brown-coated rebels.

'I'm trying to talk!' Quin shouted down at her.

'Shoot him,' Rose said quietly.

Rahul looked at her askance. 'Are you sure of this? I think …'

'Shoot him,' she said again.

Rahul looked to me, but I was in too many levels of shock. I had nothing to say. Rahul aimed his gun and shouted a warning. 'Step away from the lift, or I will be forced to shoot!'

'I need to talk to that stuck-up princess!' Quin shouted back. 'Otto, talk some sense into her, will you?'

Rose grabbed Rahul by the shoulder. 'I said, shoot—'

She was cut off as the gun went off, probably accidentally. It was not properly aimed. There were screams from both above and below from the shipless refugees and the rebels on the upper level. The sound hurt my ears more than it should have. I'd gone hypersensitive, and 42 told me again, this is normal. I had to hold my ears to muffle the sounds, but I kept my eyes fixed on Quin.

Quin had been shot. It was plain to see. He was clutching the side of his waist with both hands, and his face was twisted in a grimace. Then suddenly he turned as some one of the rebels came past him with a large metal canister. The rebel threw the canister over the edge, and Quin abandoned his wound, turning on the perpetrator with his hand in a fist. I saw them both go down, wrestling on the edge of the ledge, in a fight exactly like all the others Quin always got himself into.

That was all I had a chance to see before the canister struck the edge of the open elevator, bounced off, fell, and exploded beneath us.

We'd almost been to the ground level, and the elevator itself was torn from the icy walls. The metal of the platform was stronger than the ice of the floor, and the ice broke before we did. The entire icy floor of the port level cracked, and the three of us were thrown through the air, and struck one of the huge fragments of floor. My system was shocked, and it wasn't surprising to find that much of the next ten seconds was thrown out of my head.

I opened my eyes to find us bobbing up and down, on a chunk of broken ice slowly floating out into the centre of the bay. Rahul lay beside me, a twisted chunk of metal from the elevator slicing through his chest. His blood stained the white ice crimson. I didn't even have to touch him to know he was already dead.

'Rose!' '*Rose!*' (*Rose!*) Every single part of me was suddenly terrified, and I scrabbled to my knees, searching the impromptu iceberg.

'Help!' Rose whimpered, and I whirled. Rose was floundering in the freezing water at the edge of the iceberg, trying to flop herself back onto the ice in her thick, insulated dress, heavy with water. I scrambled to her on my stomach, and tried to reach for her. But the moment I touched her, I seemed to short out, as if my entire brain was tuned to static. I couldn't hold onto myself through it, and my hands let go automatically.

What had happened? She was wet, I realized. It was the waters of Europa, all the millions of tons of plankton, influencing itself in the icy ocean. I reached for her again, and another wave of pure static hissed through me, turning off my own signal. A third time, and this time I nearly fell into the water.

'I can't touch you!' I hissed, and looked around, desperate for anything that might prove capable of dragging her out. The only tool available was the bloody corpse of Rahul. On the one hand, it was horrible. But on the other, he was a guard – it was his task to protect and save her, even if he couldn't do it himself. A part of me didn't hesitate – the part that had done this sort of thing before. Xavier knew that fastidiousness and moral dilemmas meant nothing when lives were at stake. I grabbed the still warm bleeding corpse – nothing inside, empty like a piece of meat – and dragged it out towards Rose, holding on to his boots. His head and torso dangled into the water. Rose made a noise of despair, but she climbed him like a ladder, and then without a word helped me drag him back up onto the ice with us. Use him in this instance, we might, but we wouldn't discard him like so much garbage.

Rose knelt by his wet head and brushed the hair from his staring eyes. 'Poor, brave Rahul. Thank you,' she whispered.

I staggered and sat down, unable to stand any longer. The chunk of ice tilted dangerously as my weight shifted. My ears were still roaring from the static I'd experienced, and I gripped the sides of my head in the hopes that it would calm it all down.

'Otto, don't,' Rose said, coming back to me. I was afraid to touch her, and tried to pull away, but she grabbed my hands. The static I'd felt when I touched her before was gone, and I gasped with relief. She was cold as ice, but she didn't even care. 'I'm sorry.'

My body ached, and I wished I could scream. I told her I hurt.

'I know. I'm sorry. I lost my satchel in the water. Your medicines … I can't fix this, Otto.'

'I'm not Otto,' I half-heartedly tried to tell her, but she grabbed me and kissed my face, rocking me back and forth.

'Yes, you are!' she whispered. 'God damn it. I wish I could have you back. I didn't know how much I'd loved you until I'd lost you.' She kissed my forehead and held me to her, her heart beating so fast I worried for her nanos. 'I know you're still in there, somewhere. Underneath all the holes in your mind and the delusions and the personalities you've absorbed, I have to believe you're still in there. Do you know what you've meant to me? I couldn't have made it this far without you. I'd have paid a thousand fortunes to find another stass tube and disappeared into it for another hundred years.' She kissed me again. 'I love you. I love *you*. I loved Xavier, but you're not Xavier, and you're not you, and I hate this weird crazy thing you've become. I miss you so much. I wish you'd come back to me.'

I closed my eyes, and let Rose hold me, and 42 sat on my other side and brushed the tears from my face, and Xavier – my strange, desperate, mad, previously unknown friend – quietly disengaged himself from my mind. '*Don't go,*' I whispered to him. '*You made it easier.*'

'You don't need me,' he told me. He blew Rose a little kiss, that she couldn't see. 'She doesn't either. Not anymore. She's outgrown me.'

'But I don't want to die alone.'

42 stepped away from me and took Xavier's hand. (*He can stay with me, if you'd like. We'll wait for you.*) She looked up at Xavier with a strange smile on her face. (*You okay with that?*)

'Neither of us is real,' he pointed out.

She shrugged. (*Then we'd be perfect together.*)

I think I laughed. Even my insanity didn't want anyone to be alone.

Then they were gone. Just like that.

'Otto?'

I looked up at Rose, completely alone in my thoughts for the first time in I couldn't remember how long. It was very peaceful.

'What just happened?'

'I think I'm sane again,' I told her. I hadn't been sending her any of what just happened, so all she'd seen was whatever leaked out that her subconscious was able to read without me. It was confused and misty and mostly emotion, as far as she was concerned, and mostly my thoughts had just become … quieter. That was all she saw. I swallowed. *'And I think I'm dying.'*

Rose closed her eyes. She'd already known it, but she denied it anyway. 'No,' she said. 'No, we'll … we'll get you … get you down to the *Minos*, and …' She looked around. The icebreaker was still there, but it was twenty metres away, and the gangplank was long gone. A sob fought in her chest, but she forced it down. 'No,' she whimpered.

'Yes,' I whispered for her. 'You should. You should go for the icebreaker.'

'You'll come with me,' Rose said, determined.

'I can't,' I whispered. 'I can't touch the water. It was shorting me out, I can't swim.'

'Then I'll take you there!'

'Rose, look at me.'

Rose looked down. I sat up, and it was difficult. I was dizzy. I did know this feeling. 42 knew this feeling. My arms and legs were numb, and it wasn't from the cold. My blood was concentrating on my brain and heart, as I didn't have enough to keep the rest of me functioning. That was probably why I was sane again; my body had abandoned trying to keep the rest of me alive, so my mind was clear for the first time in months. 'You're going to have to let me go.'

'I can't.'

I kissed her. '*You know you can,*' I told her. '*You've done it before. You're strong. People see you as passive and weak, but we know the truth. You're a briar rose. You're a survivor. Your body is frail, but you fight until you find your strength, until you force your way through solid stone. You bend, passive, with the wind, but you do not break. You snap back and whip those that force you in the face. And when you're uprooted and abandoned, you absorb the sun and the rain and form new roots and grow again.*' I kissed her eyelids. *'I'm sorry I have to abandon you. But I need you to survive. I need you to grow again, to be the briar hedge, to grow strong, to protect, to tear apart those who would force their way through you. Will you promise me that?'*

Rose shuddered, but she stared at me. 'Yes,' she said. 'But I'm not abandoning you here. I'll go to the icebreaker, but I'm taking you with me, do you hear me? You may be dying – you'd know better than I would – but you're not dying of exposure all alone out here on this ice cube.'

'Rose, it's safer for you—' I whispered.

'Don't fight me on this, Otto,' Rose said firmly. 'You belong to me, remember.' She took my head, and her thumb caressed my cheek. 'We're family.'

I closed my eyes. I loved her so much. 'Okay,' I whispered.

'Okay?'

'Okay. But if you think you can't make it, you leave me, you hear? Promise me.'

Her eyes grew hard. 'I'll make it,' she said.

She kissed me briefly and then turned to the icebreaker. They were still watching from the portal, and they waved at her, shouting something that could not be discerned over the noise and the distance.

Using her hands to communicate while she shouted, she announced her intentions slowly to those waiting on the icebreaker, telling them to prepare warming blankets and get ready for us. We couldn't quite hear them over the noise, but they seemed to understand, and someone went off to fetch the equipment they'd need.

I took Rose's hand. '*Rose? Given what happened when I tried to touch you in the water, you know I might not survive this.*'

'I know,' Rose said evenly. She turned around. 'Unzip me. I can't swim in this sea anchor.' I unzipped her gently. She was already almost as blue as I was, and her shivering became more pronounced as I stripped her down to her light silk shift. I took off my heavy dress shirt, and then held her to my bare chest, trying to will all the warmth I could into her thin, shivering frame. 'W-we don't have much t-time,' she shivered, and kissed me fiercely. 'I love you, Otto,' she whispered.

'I love you,' I whispered back.

We dove into the freezing water.

According to witnesses, and the footage from Moriko's cell camera, I went rigid the moment I touched the surface of Europa's half-frozen sea. Rose dragged me in a life-saving grab, swimming one armed until she made it to the icebreaker, where they hauled us up and wrapped us both immediately into warming blankets, and forced warm liquid into Rose. She went severely hypothermic in the cold. She actually passed out for a second once, and nearly dropped me twice, but she forced herself to keep going until they could drag her inside. It was a heroic swim, a life-affirming video, and was shown and copied all over Europa. If Rose hadn't already been famous, she would have been made a hero overnight from that video alone. It solidified her power base, and no one in the colonies, and almost no one on earth, would ever dare to dismiss her again.

And believe it or not, it was even more interesting from my point of view.

chapter 20

The first moment when I touched the water was static, it shorted me out completely. I was gone. There was cold, weighty emptiness. Then, with an awareness as startling as a meteor in the dark, there was a deep, throbbing *concept* in my mind. There were no words. There had never been any need for words. But the concept by itself was so shocking and so radical to that consciousness, that it created something akin to a word almost by itself. And that word, that concept, was,

You!

It remembered creatures like me. It had touched them before, but they were hollow, empty, unconnected parasites. But this was different. This was change. Until I had touched it, there had never been anything else. There was only the one, the self, the ***I***. I had touched it and it had become aware of me, but I was not part of it. I was not of the ***I***. I was something else. And that something else was ***You***.

The idea that there could even be a 'you' was beyond the very concept of existence for the ***I***. The ***I*** was ancient, ageless, blind, yet completely aware. The ***I*** was a lifeform. The ***I*** was of the water. The ***I*** was existence itself. And the ***I*** was terrified. Because the ***I*** was dying.

What was the ***I***? Europa, whole and entire, a world itself alive with awareness on a level that I myself, with my five pitiful human senses, could barely begin to contemplate.

The ***I*,** as I encountered it then, was like an infant. Unaware of anything beyond itself. Unaware even that itself was something other than what had always been. Compared to the ***I***, I was puny, insignificant, limited. I was so painfully weak, and terribly mortal. And yet I was so much more aware – of everything. I had been raised with the concept of *you*. And with *you* came, *us* and *them*, *mine* and *theirs*, *there* and *here*, *then* and *now*. With the concept of the *other* there came a reason for names, and with names came words, and with words came reason, and with reason came knowledge, and I *knew*. And because I *knew*, the ***I*** could know.

The ***I*** wanted *everything*. Everything I was, everything I had ever been, everything I had ever known. It nearly killed me with a desperate grab for everything I was, but it was ancient, and it had been trying to understand what *humans* were, for ... well, for the ***I*** it was a blip of time, but for a human it was more than sixty years. Ever since the first human probe had breached the ice skin and dropped its researchers and its submarines and its icebreakers and eventually its city ships.

And because the ***I*** wanted to understand me, it gave me what it could of what it knew.

The ***I*** was a single entity, distributed across the whole ocean of Europa, following the veins of the geothermal fissures, making ice-sculptures and farming parts of itself to feed other parts, always changing, always the same, always eternal. The ***I*** was the plankton. The whole of the plankton. It was made up of dozens if not hundreds of different types of creatures, but all of them were moved together and manipulated by the ***I***. The M9 microbes that had been used to create the Europa Project children were what, if the ***I*** was a being as we understood it, would be termed as brain cells. The rest of the creatures of the plankton were maintained and moved by these cells. These cells communicated with each other the way the cells in a brain interacted, and the brain in turn interacted with the body.

And then the parasite had come. There had been no word to describe it, because it was not of the ***I***. At first, the ***I*** had not been bothered, or even noticed, when the scientists, and later the city ships, had begun harvesting. Portions of the ***I*** die all the time, disconnected, lost in the ice. When portions of the ***I*** were lost in the current, they died, the way that cells cut from our bodies die. Eventually these dead cells would drift back into the veins of the living, and their bodies were eaten and absorbed, but the ***I*** was never bothered by this – any more than a human being is bothered by the dead cells that form their hair.

But the parasite had begun to capture vast sections of the ***I***. Entire heat-veins were all but eviscerated. And when the cells that had not been harvested were left behind, there were not enough of them to remerge with the ***I***. They had died. The three massive harvesting ships travelled slowly about the planet, lobotomizing, cannibalizing, slowly killing the being that was the ***I***.

There was no way to stop it. The ***I*** did not have arms and legs to remove the worm from its watery flesh. It did not have weaponry or the equivalent to antibodies to kill the ships where they stood. While it could heal itself, and did, the surviving cells dividing and reproducing, the ships did not give it ample time. Before a heat-vein was properly repopulated, another ship would bear down, scooping up the nascent cells, wounding it all over again. The ***I*** was already losing memory. It had forgotten the pattern of the ocean floor, lost the memory of how to carve certain ice-sculptures. If something was not done to stop it, the ***I*** would not survive.

The concept of *death*, a final death of consciousness, had never before occurred to the ***I***. It was a concept as world shattering as the idea of an *other.* It began to look for ways to escape the destruction. But there was no place to go – there was no other place but *beneath the ice.* It could not escape, any more than a human could escape its own skin.

This was a feeling I knew. I too was dying, and I too was terrified. But the ***I*** wanted nothing more than to destroy the disease that was killing it. Every single microscopic portion of the ***I*** had been directed to one goal – destroy.

But there was no way to do this. It would take several hundred years of evolution before the many cells of the ***I*** evolved enough to attack the alien newcomers who had invaded its waters.

But there was something odd about the parasite. Something inside it similar to the ***I***. It felt similar – tiny fingers of something that was almost, but not quite, *thought*, as the ***I*** thought of it. It would reach out, trying to enter that thought, become part of it, make it part of itself in the hopes that, if nothing else, the ***I*** might survive in some form. But until the ***I*** had encountered myself, a human being with the skill to both share and receive information the same way the ***I*** did within itself, it had not occurred to it that this *danger*, this parasite, was another creature. A separate creature. A whole colony of creatures, with individuality and language and *otherness.*

And the ***I*** wanted more of this – desperately. It wanted to *understand*.

I took all of this in, and I had to interpret it. The ***I*** was so loud and so overwhelming that it was hard to find my own thoughts inside it. But it realized this, and quieted its thoughts, and shrank its being as small as it could in the hopes that I could encompass it. I couldn't – I hadn't a prayer. I could have stayed inside that vast alien consciousness for a thousand years and only barely begun to understand it. But eventually it was quiet enough that I could at least hear myself think.

The plankton was a being – a single, diffuse being – and the Europan city ships were systematically slaughtering it. The harvesters – those different and odd people who had become a caste within themselves, who had become rebels, who were trying to destroy the other humans on this planet – had been in lifelong contact with the living plankton. And some of this plankton, separated from itself, had tried to bond with the living thing that held it – and that was the harvesters. And the one thing that it had been able to do was send a message. A very distinct message: destroy.

Yes, human society on Europa was flawed by its very make-up. But the *I* had been feeding the dissonance at every step. That was why the violence had never abated. That was why neither side was ever willing to negotiate. It had no concept of compromise, because it had no concept of other. And every human being that had been in contact – mostly the harvesters who captured and processed the plankton, but every human being that had ever touched the water, was being shouted at by the goddess of the planet as a whole – destroy.

I knew I could control people. Not very effectively, not very well. But I had convinced the bouncer at the club to let me, an underage madman, into the u*Night*ed. I had convinced Penny to calm herself. I helped Rose find herself. The ***I*** was doing the same. It was influencing everyone on the planet, the wealthy and the workers alike, to destroy each other.

And there was something else I knew. I knew it the same way the plankton knew it. I could not survive without the ***I***.

We had died, 42, my siblings, all of them had died because we were disconnected. All disconnected plankton might as well have been dead. Just as any cell cut from our human flesh might as well be dead already. Each and every cell had their own self-destruct, a saving grace from being thoughtless, only a fraction of itself. Before puberty our EP cells had been in development, not fully mature. But the adult hormones had acted like an igniter, and the self-destruct inherent in our DNA was activated.

And I had been saved. I had been saved only because 42 had died for me. She had self-destructed, and dragged me down with her, and my cells had thought it was over. They had performed their duty, and did not need to activate their own self-destruct. It was not until I fell truly in love with Rose, and my hormones had changed – or maybe it was the contact with her highly-developed mind, I would never know – that my cells had realized again that they were disconnected, and had begun, slowly, to destruct. Nabiki had been right. Rose was killing me. But it was likely that it would have happened eventually anyway. 42's death would not have fooled my DNA forever.

That was why stasis had made me feel better. The tiny death I had undergone had stayed the self-destruct for a few days, as well. But eventually, even that reprieve would have failed.

I needed the ***I***. And the ***I*** needed me. It needed me to speak for it. If there was a ***you***, and a ***them*** and *words,* then it had to be possible to – '*become **one***' was the way the ***I*** thought of it, but I personally thought of it as 'communicate'. The ***I*** was still a little shaky on the concept of the *other.* It kept trying to make me think in terms of *oneness*, while I was trying to get it to think in terms of *cooperation.* Humans functioned as a whole as a society. The ***I*** functioned as a whole as a single being. It was going to be a trick playing ambassador.

And then I was taken from the water. I had no sense of time when in contact with the ***I***, but Rose told me later that the entire exchange – the intellectual birth of an entirely new form of consciousness – had taken less than seven minutes. That was how long it took Rose to drag me through the icy water.

It took another forty minutes before Quin had the chance to tell her that Xavier wasn't dead.

I sensed his mind before I really regained consciousness. I opened my eyes to find Quin sitting by my bedside, my hand held in a steady grip. His left hand was heavily bandaged, probably from a burn, and there was a deep cut on his cheek. The red against the blue looked like the red striations across Europa's icy surface. He held himself stiffly – the wound in his side itched more than ached, they had him so drugged up. 'Otto?' Quin said when he saw me looking at him. His voice was very gentle. Surprisingly so.

So was his mind, come to think of it. 'Otto? Is that you?'

I couldn't find my way to answer him. My thoughts were still twisted and weighted down by the overwhelming communication of the ***I***. I gazed at his face.

'Have you come out of it yet?' His voice was shaking. 'Give me a sign. Anything. Send me something.' I understood, but I couldn't find a word to send him. Any words. They were gone. Buried. Lost in the torrent that had been the ***I***. 'This is the third time you've opened your eyes,' Quin told me. 'You've been sending the weirdest things. I can't read them. Rose can't, either. It's not human ...' He sighed. 'At least you're not screaming this time.'

I blinked at him. Screaming? It took me a while to remember what the word meant.

Quin stared at me for a long time, and then, to my surprise, his face crumpled. His hand clenched mine and he started to cry. There was no anger at all in his mind. Nothing but grief. He thought I was gone. He had finally lost me, and he wasn't going to be able to pull me back, because he didn't have my power. My brain waves had spent the last twenty-four hours displaying nothing but static, and everyone thought I – my personality – had been erased. It was the last straw.

So much sorrow. Was this even Quin? Yes. Yes, it was. A tested, tried and tired Quin, who had been through hell and back in just a few days. Very, very, hesitantly I went searching for a word. At first, I'm afraid all I could find was, *'You?'*

Quin's head snapped up and he looked at me. 'Otto?'

Otto. Quin. *You*, in this instance was, *'Quin?'*

'Yes!' Quin hissed. 'Oh, god! Oh, thank god.' His relief was palpable.

Words were coming back now. I remembered. I needed them. Words were very, very important. Things were falling back into place now that I was fully conscious. *'What happened? The riots?'*

Quin shook his head, dismissing it. 'They're done for now. Everyone's safe for the moment.'

'Rose?'

Quin almost smiled. 'Mr Zellwegger made her go lie down. She's been sitting here for the last twenty hours. I said I'd spell her.'

'What happened?'

'You passed out when you touched the water, Rose says. I'm not surprised.' He swallowed. 'I … I've been with the *harvestaras*. You have no idea … Otto, they knew. They had to have known. You, me, they're why they made us. The *harvestaras* are like us!'

I shook my head. *'No, they're not,'* I told him. *'They're more like … like Nabiki. She was changed by being with me. They're people who have been in perpetual close contact with …'* And the memory of the ***I*** superseded all other thought again. Quin grunted as I hit him with even a portion of it, and tried to let go of my hand. I snapped it shut, like closing a door. It was easy. I had more control over my mind than I ever had before. I took a deep breath before I told him, *'It's been affecting their minds for generations now, thinking, feeling, trying so hard to be understood. But it had no words. This moon is alive, Quin. A single being. A person!'*

Quin nodded. To my surprise, he was not wholly shocked. 'The *harvestaras* said much the same,' he told me. 'But with them, it's like a religion. They don't know, they just believe it.' He hung his head. 'I thought I'd killed you.'

That last seemed disconnected, but really it wasn't. It was the thought that had been pounding repeatedly in his head for the past two days. He didn't ask for forgiveness. He didn't have to. The need for it was burning in every corner of his mind.

'Quin,' I sent to him. *'I'm your brother.'*

There was really nothing else that needed to be said.

'You are?' Quin asked. 'You really are? The doctors say your brain waves don't look remotely human anymore. I didn't think you were going to come back. Not this time.'

I didn't know what my brain waves were doing, but I was beginning to feel more like me. Properly me, even. Not dying and not insane. But there was something different. Something … clear … *'What's happened to my brain?'*

Quin shook his head. 'The doctors are still trying to work that out. Dr Zellwegger says your cellular structure has stabilized, and Dr Shiva – she says your mind … your brain waves don't make any sense anymore. They say what they're reading is more like what happens in the open ocean out there.'

That made sense. '*But the rest of me is fine?*'

'Blood pressure,' heart rate, organ function, all normal as far as they can see. Rose was a little weird for a bit, but she's normal now, too. She said you were ... I don't know. Screaming at her as she dragged you through the water. Like, rock concert level screaming at her. Mr Zellwegger had her checked out, but she seems to have gone back to normal – or as normal as she ever is.'

'*So he's alive, too?*'

Quin looked down. 'Yeah.'

'*We thought you'd killed him.*'

Quin stared at me evenly. 'I thought I was going to.' He shrugged. 'It was what I'd set off to do.' He looked down. 'I met these *harvestaras*, and they were ... so happy to see me. They've been waiting for us – for you, really, but they honour me, too. They didn't tell me everything when I first met them, but they made it clear they wanted to meet you. While you were sleeping, I went and told them that Captain Jagan was coming, and that there was going to be this grand ball at the train station. I didn't realize ...' He stopped. 'Maybe I did. I didn't want some stupid party – I wanted them to call it off. Maybe a security breach would make them grow up. And then after I met those rich goblins, it was so much worse. I knew Jamal was a sped, I didn't realize his entire family were parasites. And you were so sick. When I realized how far gone you were, I ... I think I went a little crazy myself. I went off again and I told the rebels, and they panicked. They told me they'd set up a bomb at the party. I told them I couldn't let them kill you, and they let me go. They said I could go save you, if I wanted.' He sighed. 'Maybe I should have just told Captain Jagan, but I hated them all so much. I just knew I had to go get you. I screwed up.' He stood up, angry again. 'And then I totally lost it.

They lied to me! Jagan told the news service that you'd been killed in the blast.'

'*He thought I was involved,*' I signed to him. '*Maybe he thought it would flush you out of hiding.*'

'Yeah, well, it didn't,' Quin muttered. 'Then that old man just walks out into the lions' den, telling them he's looking for me.' Quin shook his head. 'For *me!* Since when does he give squitch about me? What has he got, a death wish?'

'*Yes,*' I told him honestly. '*He hates himself a thousand times more than you ever could. But that's a secret.*'

Quin looked at me. I'd never told him anything I'd ever read in anyone's mind before – and I probably never would again – but it changed Quin's face. It softened. 'I guess I can see that. He said it was just that he'd ... remembered he was responsible for me. I took it the wrong way, I think. I told them he deserved to die. Then they did this ... press conference, and they told *me* to kill him!'

'*I know,*' I signed. '*You turned off the camera.*'

'I needed time to think,' Quin said. 'I thought about 49, and you, and Una and all the other dead ones. And the simple ones, and poor Penny with her emotional damage, and Tristan never allowed at the Olympics, no matter how good she gets. I *wanted* him dead. I wanted someone to pay for all that. And I told him that, and then he told me you weren't dead.' Quin shook his head. 'I had thought I already had blood on my hands. I thought I'd killed you – or at least let you die. When he said I didn't, I just ... I realized I didn't have to do it. I mean, I'm angry, I'm always going to be angry. I know what I am,' he said, looking at me. 'You know what I am,' he added. 'I'm never going to be able to stop ... this.' He closed his hand into a fist, then he bit his knuckle. 'But I don't have to be a killer, do I.' He took a deep breath. 'So I told them to talk to him.'

'*Told them?*' I asked.

'Okay, I talked them into it,' Quin said. 'I guess I never realized before what kind of power I *did* have. I mean, with all of you with all this magicky mind-reading stuff, I'd forgotten that most people control others' minds just with words.' He shrugged. 'I have words.'

'*I know,*' I signed. '*I've always been jealous of you, because of it.*'

Quin paused, and then made a gesture, something between a salute, and the signs for *you're welcome* and *I know.*

'I talked to them,' he said. 'I know how it feels to be angry, and they're angry. Oh, they are so angry. But I persuaded them that if I was willing to abandon my anger for a bit, they could, too. Mr Zellwegger wasn't Captain Jagan. Maybe he was right. Maybe they just needed to talk.'

I looked at Quin's hand, and his cut, and how he held his head. Quin had changed. Quin was a soldier now. A soldier for his people. A leader. He didn't really know it yet, but I knew it. As surely as I knew who I was, and who Rose was, and who everyone had to be. The ***I***, I realized, had done things to my perception.

Quin went on. Negotiating the harvesters' demands had been more difficult for the old man than placating Quin. He and the rebels had gone off to talk, and Quin had gone off to try and find me. 'Your passive little princess is a lot stronger than she looks!' Quin said. 'If Mr Zellwegger hadn't been there to call those Plastines off, they would have killed me. What was she thinking?'

'*You got her angry,*' I told Quin with a bit of a smile. '*Don't get Rose angry. She melted a Plastine once, all on her own.*'

'Yeah, well, she got me shot.'

'*Yes,*' I signed simply.

Quin glared at me. 'She nearly started a war, and got you all killed. When that rebel threw the bomb after you, I broke my hand on his jaw, I was so angry.'

'That's not her fault. To be fair, you weren't being very clear in your communication. You should have started the negotiations off with, "I didn't kill him".'

Quin rolled his eyes. 'How was I supposed to know she was suddenly interested in the news? She never has been before.'

'Don't dismiss her.'

'Don't worry,' he said with a grin. 'No one's ever going to make that mistake again. Not after her heroic swim. You know she sinks like a stone, she's got so little body weight? I mean … how?' He gestured to me, and how much bigger I was than her. How had she managed to drag me through below-freezing temperatures while I was mentally screaming at her?

'She's determined.'

'Clearly. I watched the whole thing. I was sure you were dead. By the time I came down, you were totally out. We were both so worried, we just … didn't talk about any of it. It was like none of it had ever happened.'

They had sat by my bedside, hoping I'd come out of it. Neither of them had been sure I would. They'd talked, Quin said, but he wouldn't say about what. They seemed to have come to a full truce. I was more important, anyway. They took turns holding my hand, trying to call me back. They weren't sure if they could. My brain waves had changed. My entire mental structure had shifted subtly to better match that of the conditions in the Europan ocean. In short, I was like the ***I*** now. A true child of the ***I***. And I would never think as a human being again.

Once I could sit up, I called a meeting between myself and Quin, Mr Zellwegger, Dr Zellwegger, Rose, the *harvestara* leader that Mr Zellwegger had negotiated with, and all three city captains. I'd written up what needed to be said, and gave it to Quin. I arranged to have the meeting in the icebreaker bay of Diamond Caverns – the Crystal Village being too damaged among the ice villages to host a summit. Then I told him to set up a camera, and I put it on a live feed.

'My brother called this meeting to act as ambassador,' Quin told them. 'The moon of Europa is calling for a truce.'

'What?' Captain Jagan was annoyed.

'The moon is alive,' Quin said. 'Otto has communicated with it. And moreover,' he looked Dr Zellwegger square in the face, 'you must have known he would have.'

Dr Zellwegger looked confused. 'Why me? What are you looking at me for?'

'The EPs were created as human beings capable of communication with another being on a cellular level,' Quin explained. 'There's only one reason why anyone would need to create such a thing. There was something you needed to communicate with, on a cellular level. Which meant you knew – or someone knew – that this planet was alive, and was trying to communicate.'

'That's one crackpot theory out of a dozen, yes,' Dr Zellwegger admitted. 'The plankton comprise a complex ecosystem, it was possible that there was something more than mere instinct in play. But there are ten other theories equally as plausible, and as a scientist, that one seems unlikely. What makes you look at me like I knew something?'

'Well, you don't look shocked, for one,' Quin said. 'For another, neither does my rebel friend, there. In fact, all the *harvestaras* have believed that Europa was alive for decades, now.'

Captain Jagan dismissed it. 'That's just the religious absurdity of a radical fringe.'

'Which someone believed so whole-heartedly that they invested tens of billions of credits, and condemned a hundred lives to inhuman cellular vivisection,' Quin said acidly. 'Doesn't sound like a radical fringe to me.' He looked around. 'And the fact that none of you are saying that it's nonsense leads me to think that you believe Otto. Which means part of you already believed it before we said it.'

Jagan just looked disgusted. 'I am simply listening to what you children have to say,' he said. 'Though why the UniCorp executive is so willing to be led by children's mysticism is beyond me.' He looked daggers at Xavier.

'And I don't know any such thing,' Dr Zellwegger added. 'I'm a scientist. I'd need more proof before I'd believe something so extreme.'

'But you do believe it,' Rose said. 'You helped implement this whole thing.'

'What are you accusing me of?' Ted said. 'I was still in gradschool when this … project was instigated.'

I looked over at Rose and she sighed. I'd explained the whole tangled problem to her as I'd explained it to Quin. It made her sad to think that Xavier's son might have been just as corrupt as his father. Xavier had complicated reasons for the mistakes he'd made. She didn't want to think about what Ted might have done, and why. 'There was never any treatment,' Rose said. 'Was there. You brought Otto up here only because he was dying, and it was the last chance to see if the experiment would work.'

'That's not fair,' Dr Zellwegger said. 'I did have theories of cellular maintenance. I told you it was a long shot when I invited you. I didn't lie.'

'You didn't tell the whole truth, either,' Quin said. 'Who told you to invite us up here?'

Ted looked confused. 'I don't know. Everyone. No one. It was just … general scientific consensus. Anyone who had ever worked with anyone who'd worked with the EPs said to bring you here. The entire team down on the *Minos* …' He stopped, pondering. 'It's a protocol,' he realized. He stood up in a flurry and went to a wall screen by the lift of the hydrobay.

'What are you …'

'Shh!' Ted said, and he started drawing open files, dismissing them, and then drawing others. Then he grunted. 'Dad, do you still know the old passkeys?'

'They might have changed,' Xavier said, and he stood up to go to the screen. Between the two of them, the next five minutes were hushed and expectant on our side of the bay, and hurried and confused on theirs. 'There!' Xavier said suddenly. He stood back and pointed. 'There it is.'

'We found it,' Ted said. 'Down in the original code for stage seven of the Europa Project. That's you,' he added to Quin and I. 'It would have permeated the conversation, how every discussion was framed, from the very beginning. By the time I joined this project, it would have just been consensus, no reason or source even needed. I must have picked it up unconsciously. But here it is. Ultimate goal is reunification upon the moon proper. But in the same protocol, it specifically says you are to be raised on Earth.'

I nodded, and told Quin what to say. 'Because an ambassador has to know both cultures. Somebody, somewhere, knew something.'

Dr Zellwegger shrugged, looking lost. 'I'd say that I'm sorry, but I don't know why I should be. Maybe I did just swallow a conversational undercurrent, but I wasn't lying. I did think my cellular maintenance might help.'

'It might have,' Rose said. 'Otto is better now because of something similar.'

'That's all right, Ted,' Quin said with jocular familiarity. 'No one's going to blame you for jumping on a bandwagon, or being an idiot.'

'God help the moon if you're her ambassador, Quin,' Ted said.

'He's not. Otto is,' Rose said firmly. 'Otto?'

I looked down, feeling shy, then pointed the proper paragraph out to Quin on his screen.

'Right,' Quin said, and he stood up. 'The moon of Europa formally requests the cessation of hostilities, and the end of the genocide.'

'This is ridiculous,' Captain Jagan snapped. 'These children are claiming to talk to amoebae!'

'Billions of amoebae,' Quin said. 'Or rather, a single being. Otto was very clear about this. It exists. It's real.'

'I refuse to listen to this absurdity.'

I sighed. I'd known it would come to this. I'd already tried it with Quin and with Rose. It had made Rose cry. It made Quin kneel with his hand in the water as if trying to reach his own mother, until I feared he'd get frostbite in his hand. I took hold of Captain Jagan's hand with a small smile of reassurance. I no longer feared touching him, or anyone. Everyone was very small now that I knew the ***I***. Jagan was very small indeed. He was very like his son – nothing seemed to really matter, and everything belonged to him. I led him to the water, and reached down to introduce them.

HELLO!!!!!!

That had become the ***I***'s favourite word, a grasping, searching call for attention, which hit Captain Jagan as if he'd just been shot. He snatched his hand out of mine as if I'd electrocuted him – which in a way I had.

'*She's still learning not to shout,*' I signed for Quin to translate. '*If anyone else wants proof?*' I offered myself to them, each and every one of them, as ambassador and translator and avatar for the goddess.

It was a long meeting.

I wasn't the same anymore. It was very clear to everyone. I

didn't notice much difference, personally. The change was too subtle for my consciousness to be affected. My subconscious, however ... that had changed dramatically.

I was more like Rose now. But rather than a hundred years of dreams, I had touched a million years of another consciousness. I kept having insights into how things worked, and what people were thinking – whether I was touching them or not. It wasn't prophecy or clairvoyance. It was just a million years of deep, strange, thought, revolving around *oneness*. I saw people not as individuals, now, but as part of a whole, a moving cell inside the single being of a society. People were, on the whole, interchangeable. It didn't make them any less precious, but it did blur them together in my mind. They were all just people. This made everyone very predictable.

I needed Quin. He was the voice to the people – and I was the voice of the ***I***. Xavier instantly called for a moratorium on all harvesting. The captains were in an uproar – the entire economy of Europa and much of the colonies was based on the harvesting of the Europan plankton. Colonial economics shut down overnight, and for three tense days, everyone wondered if the colonies would slowly starve.

It was true, the ***I*** was being over-harvested, and dying. But there was no need to stop all harvesting forever. I made sure that was communicated clearly. The ***I*** needed time to heal – a year, I thought, should do it, but I would monitor its progress. After that, harvesting could resume, slowly, presuming we paid for and replenished what we took. After all, we, as human beings, would not be opposed to selling cuttings of our hair if someone needed it, and the ***I*** felt much the same about its surplus cell base. And we could pay for it – because what the plankton needed to thrive was something we could supply.

The plankton could not survive without heat. This was

why it followed the veins of geothermal fissures in the ocean floor. Our ability to create heat through NeoFusion and hydrogen made us, in essence, a plankton farm. If we were to supply extra heat, and thus allow the ***I*** to breed faster, there would be ample plankton for our needs, as well as the ***I***'s. Between Quin and myself, we managed to negotiate this truce. This pleased the harvesters – though there were more problems on the social structure of the moon than could be solved by fixing this ecological crisis.

Mr Zellwegger was put to work there, and he was busy. I didn't even understand most of it. Quin gave up after two days and handed negotiations over to the headmen. He retreated to Crystal Village and helped organize the people and the Plastines into repairs. Sometimes he was called on to explain a compromise to the people. He also translated for me – and there was a lot I had to relay for him to translate. Everyone wanted to understand the ***I***, and I couldn't sacrifice myself twenty-four hours a day for all of them. The ***I*** was a goddess, and I was the ambassador to a goddess, and Quin was the voice for everyone, myself and the people of Europa and the people of Earth. He made a charismatic and devoted figurehead. Like 42 used to do, he stood for me, and before me. His anger had faded to a mild roar. His sarcasm, much to everyone's chagrin, had not.

He went with Rose and I to Rahul's funeral. The less said about that the better.

Which left only me and Rose to sort out.

Rose seemed different to me after I first woke up from my understanding of the ***I***. I loved her just as much, but she had grown small, human. There were things in my mind that she could never understand … and frankly, they hurt her.

No one else would – could – sense it. If I touched someone

they noticed no difference in my communication. Maybe it was a little more clear to some people – like Quin, and the harvesters – but it was basically the same as it had always been.

To Rose, however, I had expanded. She had grown used to sensing just about everything I thought, her intuition and subconscious more powerful than anything I had ever experienced. Now, she was young, and small, and limited. She was sweet and charming and talented and I adored her. But there was a part of me that was now beyond her … and she found it as frightening as I had at first found the vast, echoing, thorny gardens of her mind.

We couldn't share our dreams anymore. She would wake up screaming from a sense of falling, or drowning, and there was nothing I could do to prevent it. I could keep secrets from her now. There were places in my mind she couldn't reach and couldn't see, no matter how much she wanted to. There was one secret I kept hidden from her for as long as I could, until a message from Earth finally forced my hand.

We were in her room after dinner. Rose was smiling as she turned the message on. We'd been too busy to really check our messages from Earth, and this was the first time she'd gotten a chance in nearly two weeks on Europa. I'd been waiting for messages from my sisters – I was hoping Tristan, at least, would be interested in coming to Europa. I was a little afraid that one day she'd need the ***I*** as much as I did, and frankly I could have used the help, if she could have learned how. It was hard being the only messenger. But this message was from Bren, and Rose opened it first. It was addressed to both of us.

'I just got your message this morning,' Bren said on the screen 'You can't believe how glad I am to hear Otto's going to be okay. It really takes a load off my mind. Which is good, because we have plenty else to deal with down here. Rose?

I need to tell you something that I haven't been telling you for the last three months. I hope you're sitting down, Rose. They think we've found your sister Sarah.'

Rose's face went white and she gripped the edge of the desk.

'I didn't want to say anything, because they weren't sure at first, and … well. Frankly, she's not well. They told Dad because you and Granddad were in stasis, and he's been overseeing the revival. It took them weeks to get her out of stasis. They weren't sure if there was anything left of her. At first she was just a vegetable, and Dad decided not to tell you. Now they think her brain might be okay, or at least … well, there's something there. But she has a hard time staying conscious. It's not a coma, it's like … she just goes back into stasis by herself sometimes. Without the tube. She speaks a little, but she doesn't make much sense, and of course she doesn't know anyone. But Rose, she's mentioned you. Her little sister, she says. They think seeing you, knowing you, would help her stay connected to the world.

'There's other things, too. Her revival is messing up UniCorp. Technically, Rose, she's older than you, so … she owns the company. They're trying to take it away from you. We're ending up with factions, it's brewing into a showdown. The ones who back Sarah mostly want her because she's helpless. If they win, she'll be trapped. Mom and Dad are trying to protect her, but they don't actually have any legal claim. You do. We need your help.

'In other words, we need you back here, quick. I didn't want to tell you until we were sure Otto would be okay. But we need you back as soon as possible.

'Before you ask, we didn't find any sign of your brother. There was another stass tube beneath the townhouse where we found your sister, but it was empty. It was emptied decades ago. We don't know what happened there.

'Come back quick, Rose. Sarah needs you, and ... well, I actually miss you, which is weird. Mom misses you. And Dizzy – come here, boy!' Bren patted his lap and Rose's fluffy Afghan dog poked his nose into view on the screen, licking Bren's face. Bren pushed him away again, ruffling his ears. 'Let us know. Dad sent a message to Granddad this morning, but I asked to be the one to tell you. We all miss you both. Hope to see you as soon as we can.' Bren opened his mouth to say something else, and then stopped. 'Take care,' he said, but I could tell it wasn't what he'd meant to say.

The message flicked out.

Rose was white and still. But there was nothing odd in that. She had been growing more habitually still for the last two weeks. She found it hard to coordinate her muscles in the uncertain gravity. Though her rooms had grav-mats, they were never exact, and her body was sensitive enough to feel it.

I sighed. I hadn't wanted to do this yet. I wanted to draw it out, work on Rose's mind, make it less of a shock. But maybe a clean break was better, anyway. It would certainly be easier on Rose – physically, at least.

I put my hand on the back of her neck. *'You should go.'*

Rose started, suddenly becoming animated again. 'No,' she said. 'It's not important.'

She was lying, and we both knew it. *'She's your sister.'*

'So? Annie will take care of her, Bren's mom is good at that. I can send her messages, I can ...' Tears were starting in her eyes. 'It's not like she'd know me, anyway. I was only six the last time she saw me.'

I folded her into my arms and kissed her eyes, kissing away the tears. *'Rose, you have to go. It wouldn't have mattered, anyway. This has only hastened the inevitable.'*

'What are you talking about?' Rose said. She did not want

to admit it.

I held her warmly for a moment before I turned her around. With my arms still embracing her I directed her attention to the full-length mirror on the wall. 'Look at yourself, my Briar Rose,' I whispered into her ear. 'What do you see?'

'You,' she said. 'And me. Together. Like it should be.'

'Look again,' I whispered.

She didn't want to see it, but I quietly directed her attention. She was very, very good at not thinking about things she didn't want to think about. She had been avoiding this since the first day she landed on Europa.

Rose looked terrible. I had grown healthier since my introduction to the ***I***, and with repeated exposure, daily contact, there were no more symptoms. I had found the cure – or at least continual treatment – for the 'there shouldn't be anything wrong' that had been killing me. Apart from beginning to develop chilblains in my hands from the ice-water – and Dr Zellwegger was working on a heated tank to prevent that – Europa had made me better.

Rose, on the other hand, looked like a cancer victim. Her clothes hung on her. She had lost almost all of the weight she had put on in the last year. Her skin was pale and sallow. Her hair had gone lank and brittle. Her eyes held deep shadows, as if she were bruised. I knew her skin was hypersensitive to touch and she could hardly hold down a meal. She was developing a wheeze from the recycled air. Rose was dying. She could have hung on, wasting away, for a year, maybe more. But she would never thrive on the colonies. Even if she had wanted to, she could not stay.

Mr Zellwegger and I had already talked about it. Rose's passage was already booked on a transport coming in from Titan in six months. But there was no reason she couldn't go back to Earth on the *Daedalus*. It had had its month-long maintenance check, waiting for another launch window, and now it was ready to take passengers back to Earth.

Tears filled her brown eyes, and she trembled in my arms. 'No,' she whispered. 'No.'

'*You can't change who you are,*' I told her. '*You've hated this place from the moment you set foot on it.*'

She turned around. 'No! I didn't come all this way to lose you now.'

My thumb caressed her lips. 'I'm not going to let you die, Rose,' I whispered. 'You need to go home. You need the sun and the air and the earth beneath your feet.' I filled her mind with pictures, memories of that beautiful paradise planet on which I had been born. I had never been so glad I had studied poetry. She needed words to show her the truth. Words had more power than anything else in the universe. 'You need to breathe in the scent of flowers in the springtime, and new mown grass in the summer, the decaying leaves of autumn and the spicy tang of the winter wind. You need to paint dreamscapes by natural sunlight. You need to hear birds singing in the morning and crickets chirping in the evening. You need to rejoin your own time, to be with Annie and Mina and Bren. You need to cuddle up to your dog at night, and listen to cello music as you fall into your studio for hours. You need the chance to be yourself, to live your life, as you have always wanted. You need to go home, Rose.' I kissed her cheek and whispered into her ear. 'I need you to go home. I need to know you're okay, somewhere.' I kissed the tender skin near her hairline. 'And we both know, I'm not really me anymore.'

'Yes, you are!' Rose whimpered. She grabbed my face with both hands and stared defiantly into my eyes. 'You've changed, but it's still you.'

I shook my head. '*I don't belong to you anymore. I belong to Europa. She's swallowed me, and I don't even think the same way. Look at you, so young, so wounded. All I do is hurt you.*'

'That's not true. You're Otto, and I love you.'

I looked at her. *'Then go,'* I told her.

'No,' she said determinedly. 'You've been telling me that I'm strong and I can make my own decisions. Well, this is one. I'm staying with you.'

Decide to waste away? To die? I knew I couldn't let her. She knew it too, but she didn't want to admit it. For a long time I let her mind remain still. Then, out of the stillness, I made an offer. I meant it … but I knew what her answer would be.

'Then I'll come back to Earth with you.'

For a painful eternity of seconds Rose's mind absorbed everything I had just offered. 'NO!' she cried. She wrapped herself around me so tightly I thought she would bruise herself. 'No! I can't let you!'

'Then you know what has to be done,' I told her gently. We were in exactly the same position. She couldn't live here. I couldn't live there. Neither of us could let the other destroy ourselves. With a feeling like cracking ice, Rose knew I meant it. Her mental briars fell, dull and lifeless with defeat. For the first time ever, she couldn't fight. She couldn't fight this *at all.* I wished there was some other way. We both knew there wasn't.

Rose looked up at me through her tears. 'You had this all planned.'

I couldn't answer, not in words. It wasn't that I had planned it. I simply knew what had to be. Like the ***I***, who had had no concept of any being outside of itself, I knew there was only one path, and that was the one you were on. Even if you changed direction, even if you turned away from where you expected to go, you were still only and ever living one life.

Your own.

Our paths had to be different. There was no other choice. There was no other life.

'This totally burns,' Rose muttered.

I chuckled. She was right. For a long time we stood in each other's arms, trying hard to let go.

'No,' Rose said at last.

I closed my eyes, ready to go through the whole thing again. But she stopped me.

'We still have three days,' she said. Her voice was very small.

I blinked at her. Her forest pool eyes were red and shining with tears, and her hands were shaking. Then I kissed her, deeply. She was right, again.

Three days can be a very long time.

epilogue

Three days later, Mr Zellwegger and I stood on the observation deck of Jove Station, watching the *Daedalus* as she disconnected from the space dock and began the long journey back to Earth. Rose had gone through the final gate two hours earlier, but neither of us had wanted to leave until we knew she was gone.

Mr Zellwegger had offered to abandon his plans of negotiation and travel with her, but Rose had said no. He was needed here. She'd made her goodbyes to each of us separately. It was easier on her that way.

She'd kissed me as deeply as she could right before she entered the *Daedalus*. I knew she meant to keep that kiss in her mind as the stass overcame her. That kiss was intended to last forever.

Deep space travel is a slow ballet, and it was some minutes before the *Daedalus* was fully disconnected and far enough away from the space station that it felt like she was really gone. Mr Zellwegger and I had spent the entire time in silence. Neither of us had had anything to say. After being with the ***I***, I no longer felt as though I couldn't talk. Much of the time, I no longer felt any need to.

Finally. I turned away from the slowly dwindling image of the moonliner and turned towards the Europa shuttle port. I had to go back today – I had to get back to the ***I*** within forty-eight hours or I began to get ill again.

'Thank you, Otto,' Xavier said behind me, and I turned back. He was still looking out of the window. It was possible he could see me in the reflection, but he wouldn't meet my eyes. 'I'm … not very good at saying the truth about how I feel, particularly where Rose is concerned. It's very confused. But I've been very afraid that Rose would never move on without me. I've always thought of you as a mistake, one of my life's greatest regrets. And in many ways, Rose is, too. But I think it could only have been someone as … extraordinary as you to help Rose through this last year. So maybe … maybe my two mistakes cancelled each other out. I've never believed in fate, but …' He shrugged. 'Maybe you two were meant for each other. At least for this short amount of time.' He sighed. 'Rose and time, are …' He trailed off. 'Thank you for helping her,' he said instead.

The heartbroken, tormented young man lurked in his face. He still loved Rose. Yes, like a brother, and yes, like a father, but that young man that he kept chained inside him loved her with a hunger that would never be appeased. And it would have been so easy to let him loose. Rose was wounded enough that she would have allowed anything, and it was only his own strong sense of ethics that had kept him from allowing their relationship to turn pure poison. And it tortured him every day.

'What about you?' I whispered.

He looked at me then, surprised to hear my whisper. He shrugged. 'I was meant for her, once, too,' he said quietly, recognizing the honour of hearing my tiny voice. 'Rose's whole life has only been little bites of time. I didn't have the power to change it when I was young. I don't have the power to heal it, now. I can only keep it from getting worse.' He looked into my eyes. 'I think you've helped her to heal, in a way I never could.'

'I wasn't talking about her,' I whispered. 'I know how you feel.'

He shook his head, an amused, condescending smile touching the corners of his mouth. He thought it was a platitude, that I imagined something that my own seventeen-year-old mind could never really understand. I reached for his hand. '*I know,*' I showed him.

He made a sound, as if someone had punched him in the stomach, as I showed him what had happened. How the screaming, tortured young man he'd been shackling had fled into my burning mind during the attack. He was still there, young Xavier, loving, missing, wanting Rose as his lover, railing against his bonds. Xavier pulled his hand away, backing off, his face pale as if he'd seen a monster. He looked uncertain for a moment, and then finally buried his face in his hands. I'd never seen such a perfect image of despair.

I came up and took a hand from him, holding it before us as I stared into his eyes. '*You do not need to feel ashamed. Your behaviour has been exemplary. No one would expect you to feel otherwise. It is not your doing, that your childhood sweetheart was dropped into your lap at the wrong time of your life.*'

'It was the wrong life!' both parts of him shouted at me, deep in his mind.

'There is no wrong life,' I told him. '*This was the life you had.*'

But it was still the wrong life. He still couldn't sleep, fighting the longing for her. It *wasn't fair!* And it wasn't right – it so wasn't right.

'*You've been a paragon, compared with me,'* I told him. '*And I have the power to make it right. I robbed you, stole your life, first just her memories, and then your own. And what I did with it was unconscionable. So now, my unwitting friend, I return it.*' I opened my mind and gave him every moment that I had spent with Rose as him. It was only a few days, a few precious, deeply confused hours. But they were his, and he had earned them with his patient reserve. I hadn't.

I didn't give him every moment with Rose. The times with only her and me were private. But every kiss, every touch, every caress that I had felt as him I gave back to him, as the proper owner. He groaned, swaying, as the screaming young man in his subconscious sighed with relief. If I hadn't been in contact with the ***I***, I wouldn't have been able to do it. I wouldn't have had the clarity, the surgical precision to cut those memories out and give them so completely. But I did, and he deserved it.

I let go his hand, and he opened his eyes. 'Why?' he whispered.

I shrugged.

'You should hate me.'

I smiled for him. My own limited expressions were back, but I think I'd kept his smile. It was easy. I shook my head. 'When I think on it,' I whispered, 'you're probably the closest thing I'm ever going to have to a father.' I tilted my head at the irony. I tapped my head. 'You're always going to be in here. It's only fair.'

He reached for me, and hugged me, as I'd seen him do with Bren. 'I'd be honoured,' he said softly. Then he turned away, his eyes shining, to watch the tiny moving dot that was the *Daedalus*, and Rose.

I headed back to the Europan shuttle alone. Xavier was scheduled to head down to Ganymede, to oversee what the conditions were there. He suspected trouble. I did not envy him his diplomatic role.

I had a hard enough time playing ambassador to the ***I***.

The flight back to Europa was uneventful. I was the only passenger, though apparently there were some Geemos in the cargo hold on their way from Ganymede. We really had to do something about that colony. I sat in one of the observation bubbles, watching my pearly blue moon turn to a red-streaked glacier landscape. I thought about what I would write to Rose, to greet her as she woke up from stasis en-route to Earth. The thought pleased me. She had to live apart from me, but she lived. And so did I.

As we approached the elevator housing I turned my gaze from the fierce boiling presence of Jupiter, and turned to look up at the Sun. It was too far away to damage my retinas. I couldn't see Earth from here, not without a telescope, but I knew she was somewhere in that direction. I felt a tinge of regret. I'd never really appreciated her beauty before. I'd spent all my life dreaming of Europa, gazing up at the sky, thinking of some other place as my home. Why had I done that? I'd missed so much.

Earth. The blue skies and the feel of the wind. Her rolling oceans and the sound of the trees. Birds and beasts and the natural rhythm of life. My Rose. The birthplace of humanity. The paradise planet. Where most of my DNA had originated. The planet of my origin.

I'd never see her again. I touched the glass, as if I could reach her. But it was impossible.

I closed my eyes. I had Europa now. I *was* Europa. I had to let her go.

I had no life but this one.

acknowledgments

The many years it has taken me to drag this particular book up out of a very tumultuous time in my life have of course been punctuated by a lot of people who have been invaluable in its research. Dr Joanne Holland helped with all the cellular research which almost instantly ended up on the editing floor because it didn't forward the plot, but at least I personally know what's actually happening with Otto on a medical/cellular level, so that's got to have resonated in the text somehow, yes? Samantha Lawler of CalTech, introduced to me by my wonderful mathematician cousin Claire, told me everything I know (and much that is pure theoretical speculation) about Europa, and anything that is now inaccurate is entirely my own fault. Jordan Bouray suffered through more versions of this absurdity than anyone apart from my editors, and his unfailing faith has been baffling. I can't acknowledge my wonderful partner Tom enough, for insisting that I was right the first time, and that Otto really needed to go properly insane. And all those wonderful people in life and on the internet – writers and clever clogs and everyone else – who filled Quin with quips and sarcasm which I could never have thought up on my own. I don't know which bits of what Quin said originated with me, and which bits with others (I think Quin quotes Greg House at least twice, but I don't remember where) but I do not claim to take credit for all of Quin's cruel cleverness. Thank you everyone.